Tom:

This book is not to be chewed and digested — merely tasted. You will get a "Chuckle" or two —

E. McCuaden.

May 9. 1961.

MR. TUTT AT HIS BEST

MR. TUTT
AT HIS BEST

By Arthur Train

A COLLECTION OF HIS MOST FAMOUS CASES
SELECTED, AND WITH AN INTRODUCTION, BY

Judge Harold R. Medina

New York

CHARLES SCRIBNER'S SONS

Contents

Introduction

Shortly after I left the law office of Davies, Auerbach & Cornell, where for six years I had been a clerk, and opened a little office of my own in the old Mutual Life Building at 34 Nassau Street in downtown Manhattan, Arthur Train's Mr. Tutt stories began to come out in the *Saturday Evening Post*. That was in 1919. And, as the long succession of books of Mr. Tutt stories were published by Charles Scribner's Sons, I read them over and over. They fascinated me, as they did thousands of other young lawyers eager to believe that justice was not necessarily at the mercy of prosecutors who wanted convictions, sometimes from motives that were none too pure, or of the large number of unscrupulous persons in various categories connected or not connected with the law, who seemed so often in real life to prevail over the righteous and the just. And I am glad to say that I am personally acquainted with at least one person who was so enthralled by the prospect of fighting for justice against heavy odds, as reflected in these stories, that he changed other plans for the future and became a lawyer. Mr. Tutt was my hero. And so I agreed with some enthusiasm to make the selection of the stories to be included in this volume and to write the Introduction.

First, a word about background. The American Bar has developed many great advocates, and not a few of them were defense counsel in some of our most celebrated criminal trials. But by and large the great bulk of the Bar have little or nothing to do with criminal cases. Every lawyer should know that his function in society cannot be fully or properly performed unless he has sympathy for those in trouble and distress and puts his sympathy into action by representing in or out of court those who need the services of a lawyer, even if particular situations are sordid and unpleasant, even if those who need his services are not possessed of much in the way of worldly goods and money in the bank, and even if these particular situations involve some of the "big boys" hovering in the background and the man fighting for justice is likely to get hurt in the melee. But by reason partly of their social contacts and the friends they make in

vii

college and law school, and the very natural desire to support their families and make their way in the profession, many of the lawyers shy away from matrimonial controversies, negligence cases and above all the criminal law. This is all wrong, but it is one of the facts of life. So at least until the law schools devote more time and effort to giving the students a better idea of what is and must be the function of lawyers in society, we should not be surprised to find bright boys and girls in the law schools looking forward to the time when they will be specialists in Tax Law, or legal representatives of the captains of industry, the corporations and the banks, and others who are able to pay substantial fees.

There is thus a whole world that is a closed book to a very large segment of the legal profession. The police courts are filled with humanity day and night. The minor and major criminal courts grind out convictions, and occasional acquittals, in numbers that sound absolutely fantastic. Most of those involved in one way or another, as complainants, or witnesses or defendants, in the shootings, stabbings and miscellaneous assaults, robberies and grand and petty larcenies in New York City are working people, many of them scrambling for bare existence or on relief. While there has been considerable improvement in the intervening years, in Arthur Train's day the court-rooms were dirty, smelly and always overcrowded; and the whole atmosphere was far from attractive to persons of fastidious tastes, especially if they knew and wanted to know little about the great mass of those whose living conditions were unspeakably bad, who had little or no education beyond a few years in elementary grammar school, and to whom involvement in a criminal case was nothing short of disaster. Of course, all those caught in the meshes of the criminal law were not poor. Moreover, those indirectly concerned came from every walk of life. But more than once have I heard a lawyer, whose record in Martindale-Hubbell's Lawyers Directory was respectable, say that he had never been in a criminal court in his life, as though this was something he was proud of.

It is in this world of fifty years ago, literally a *terra incognita* to many if not to most lawyers, that a sort of jungle struggle went on. This is where the effect of the tie-up between politics and the courts was most manifest. District Attorneys and their assistants knew where to look for promotion. At least some of them hoped to be judges some day. Many an indictment was quietly pigeonholed and never heard of again. Old grudges might be paid off in one way or another, and the assignment of a lawyer to defend an indigent person charged with murder might be anything but a gesture of good will. There were always hangers-on who knew how to squeeze the last penny from the family of the accused, but who gave in return little or nothing by way of effective legal defense.

Those were the good old days of the breach of promise of marriage and the alienation of affection cases that have since been outlawed in New York because they were the happy hunting ground of blackmailers. In those times the criminal bar knew such great personalities as John B. Stanchfield, Max D. Steuer, Martin Conboy, and DeLancey Nicoll in New York, and Stephen C. Baldwin and Henry Uterhart in Brooklyn and Nassau County. Those were also the good old days of Howe & Hummel, the wickedest and most feared of all the lawyers in their day, and of Big Bill Fallon to whom subornation of perjury and jury fixing were mere child's play until, as happened to diamond-studded William F. Howe and little Abe Hummel, he was finally caught in the grip of the law he so often flouted and subverted. And those were the good old days when the Wall Street lawyers wore silk hats and striped trousers and Prince Alberts or cutaways.

An Assistant District Attorney of New York County under a Tammany regime and also under William Travers Jerome at the time he was pursuing Howe & Hummel, Arthur Train knew what he was writing about when he laid the scene of many of Mr. Tutt's extraordinary performances in the little world of the police courts and the old Criminal Courts Building and the Tombs in New York City.

By way of contrast, Arthur Train summoned up in his mind's eye Pottsville, a peaceful, quiet little hamlet in the Mohawk Valley in up-state New York where the fishing was good and the judge who occasionally held court there was always a Republican. The people were different, so was the scenery; but good old human nature turned out to be just about the same as in the big city.

And so one of the truly interesting characters of legal fiction was born in the person of Ephraim Tutt. He is a tall, inscrutable, "ramshackly, old fellow with a whimsical, deeply wrinkled face, dressed in a funny old frock coat and black string tie." His hair grows long behind his ears, and he wears a pretty well battered old stovepipe hat and congress shoes. He always carries a mahogany, ivory-headed cane. His curious, rat-tailed stogies cost $2.85 per thousand; and at times he takes a sip of "Malt Extract" in the office or opens a bottle of "foaming Burgundy" at his home, where he sits by his sea-coal fire in a sway-backed horsehair-covered rocker. The original illustrations by Arthur William Brown hit Mr. Tutt off to perfection, and they contributed in no small way to his fame and his popularity.

The shabby suite of the law offices of Tutt & Tutt suggests the habitat of a secondhand furniture dealer. But the old boy has a host of influential friends and he often plays poker with some of them at the Colophon Club as they attend the weekly "Bible Class." Some of those who meet him on the firing line in court call him a shyster, but I know he isn't. Just the same, when he has pulled a particularly fast one, he is apt to dance a jig and recite his favorite jingle:

> I run the old mill way down by Reubenville;
> My name is Joshu-ay Ebenezer Fry.
> I know a thing or two!—You bet your life I do!
> Can't catch me, for I'm too darn sly!

The office force is, to say the least, a remarkable aggregation of various and miscellaneous talents. The "rubicund and wayward Samuel" is the other Tutt of the firm of Tutt & Tutt. Miss Minerva Wiggins is the "omniscient chief clerk." She keeps the firm respectable and it is sometimes hinted that but for her Tutt & Tutt really would be shysters. Bonnie Doon is a most extraordinary character. As he is always a snappy dresser and very good looking, he performs the most incredible feats serving summonses and subpoenas. And the way he ferrets out badly needed information on short notice would qualify him for a good position in any first-class detective agency. Freckle-faced, gum-chewing, ubiquitous Willie Toothaker is the office boy, "the aureate-haired lady stenog" is Miss Sondheim, and old Scraggs, "the alcoholic scrivener," sits in a wire cage where he keeps the books.

When the scene shifts to Pottsville we find as Mr. Tutt's chief antagonist "Stinker" Hezekiah Mason, generally referred to as Squire Mason. He is the one who, in Train's novel about Mr. Tutt, prosecuted James Hawkins, known as Skinny the Tramp for the murder of Wilbur Drake, the Hermit of Turkey Hollow, and he was caught red-handed suppressing the evidence that finally got Skinny off. He is the meanest man in Pottsville, and makes a specialty of skulduggery connected with mortgages and wills. But a dishonest penny is always attractive and no legal technicality is beneath his notice. Mr. Tutt gives the Squire many a good trimming. The center of activities is the Phoenix House, a rickety old country tavern without electric light or running water in the bedrooms, and this haven of rest is presided over by "Ma" Best. In later years when improvements came fat Deputy Sheriff Sam Bellows sometimes acted as headwaiter. But most of the work is done by "Ma" Best's daughter Betty and a Negro boy named Ulysses or Joe. Sheriff Moses Higgins is the Grand Supreme Exalted Patriarch and Ruler of an organization known as the Sacred Camels of King Menelek. "Toggery Bill" Gookin, proprietor of the Pottsville Dry Goods Emporium is the Grand Supreme Keeper of the Wampum, and Cy Pennypacker of the Art-Foto Saloon is the Grand Supreme Scribe, one of whose functions is to "enumerate the mystic marbles" on the various occasions when "Stinker" Mason and other unpopular personalities are blackballed. Mr. Tutt of course is one of the Sacred Camels and so is Judge Ebenezer Tompkins of Rochester, who frequently is assigned to hold court in Pottsville.

The reader may be surprised at some of the seemingly strange procedures followed in some of Mr. Tutt's famous trials and especially by the occasional comments and questions by the jurors. It is well to remember, however, that practically anything can happen in real life and in real courtrooms and these unorthodox happenings more often than not actually do smooth the road to justice, even in this day and age.

The melody running through these stories is summed up in a question addressed one day to Mr. Tutt by Miss Wiggins:

"I wonder, Mr. Tutt, if you would be willing to take a criminal case where there wouldn't be any prospect of a fee, simply to prevent a miscarriage of justice."

For that was what Mr. Tutt was doing all the time. His motto was, "Never turn down a case;" and doubtless he earned and received many a good fee. But a miscarriage of justice was something he just could not stomach. And when this sagacious, astute, wily and resourceful old lawyer girded his loins, he was hard to beat. The human heart was an open book to him and when the jurors looked to Mr. Tutt to find a way to give the wretched prisoner at the bar another chance they never looked in vain. He was Robin Hood and Don Quixote and Sir Galahad all rolled into one; and he did not give a continental who his adversary was or how much money or influence might be used against him. He meets the most desperate situations with a smile and with amazing wit and good humor.

Every lawyer, good, bad and indifferent, at some time in his life dreams of himself as a knight in shining armor fighting for right and justice, protecting the poor and the helpless, humbling the rich and the powerful, and making the world a better place to live in. But somehow or other the dream seldom or never comes true. We picture ourselves in imaginary court battles where the blue chips are down and the stakes are high and we are worsting an unscrupulous and resourceful adversary by pulling a few fast ones ourselves and fighting fire with fire in the interest of justice. But in real life we don't do these things, because we are afraid the influencial members of the bar will call us shysters—and that is precisely what they will do whenever their fingers are burned and they lose a case they thought was in the bag.

One of the most interesting and alluring features of the career of an author is that by good luck or perseverance or somehow or other he may actually create a new character whom the public will take to its bosom and cherish. Hundreds of new puppets are moved across the stage of literature every year. Many of them seem quite real, too, for a time. But in the end they do not measure up and they dissolve into thin air and disappear. Why does Ephraim Tutt survive, after all these years?

I think the reason is that he touches our hearts so closely and because he represents the ideal of what lawyers and those who are not lawyers think lawyers ought to do. Above all he has a sense of humor, and with it a tenderness and a kindliness that go well with his profound knowledge of the law and his wily ways and strategems.

In the course of time and as a tour de force Arthur Train published in 1943 his "Yankee Lawyer: The Autobiography of Ephraim Tutt." It was a glorious hoax. The learned law reviews speculated on the subject of whether or not Mr. Tutt was a shyster, as though the world might so forget the substance of things as to disbar a lawyer whose guiding star from first to last was to bring succor to the unfortunate and those buffeted by fate and to prevent miscarriages of justice.

Best of all came the day when the Yale Law Journal published a book review of "Yankee Lawyer: The Autobiography of Ephraim Tutt" written and signed by Arthur Train himself, praising the book to the skies. What a blessing to find a lawyer or a judge with a sense of humor! Imagine the creator of Mr. Tutt having the gall to publish a book review of his own book and lay on the praise and adulation as thick as the icing of a luscious lemon meringue pie, or thicker! I have always thought the Yalies had their full share of wit and humor. I honor them for it. It is to the everlasting credit of the scholarly and hardly-ever-stuffy Yale Law Journal that it published the review. If this is whimsicality, by all means let us have more of it—especially in the domain of legal literature.

By way of anti-climax, Arthur Train boasted of the fact that his publishers intervened just in time to prevent the publication of a biography of Ephraim Tutt, also by Arthur Train, in *Who's Who in America*.

HAROLD R. MEDINA

UNITED STATES COURTHOUSE
NEW YORK CITY

MR. TUTT AT HIS BEST

THE HUMAN ELEMENT

"Although men flatter themselves with their great actions, they are not so often the result of great design as of chance." —LA ROCHEFOUCAULD

"He says he killed him, and that's all there is about it!" said Tutt to Mr. Tutt. "What are you going to do with a fellow like that?"

The junior partner of the celebrated firm of Tutt & Tutt, attorneys and counselors at law, thrust his hands deep into the pockets of his yellow checked trousers and, balancing himself upon the heels of his patent-leather shoes, gazed in a distressed, respectfully inquiring manner at his distinguished associate.

"Yes," he repeated plaintively. "He don't make any bones about it at all. 'Sure, I killed him!' says he. 'And I'd kill him again, the ——!' I prefer not to quote his exact language. I've just come from the Tombs and had quite a talk with the defendant in the counsel room, with a gum-chewing keeper sitting in the corner watching me for fear I'd slip his prisoner a saw file or a shotgun or a barrel of poison. I'm all in! These murder cases drive me to drink, Mr. Tutt. I don't mind grand larceny, forgery, assault or even mayhem—but murder gets my goat! And when you have a crazy Italian for a client who says he's glad he did it and would like to do it again—please excuse me! It isn't law, it's suicide!"

He drew out a particolored silk handkerchief and wiped his forehead despairingly.

"Oh, indeed!" remarked Mr. Tutt with entire good nature. "He's glad he did it and he's quite willing to be hanged!"

"That's it in a nutshell!" replied Tutt.

"What is our client's name?"

"Angelo Serafino."

" 'Not Angles but Angels'!" mused Mr. Tutt.

The senior partner ran his bony fingers through the lank gray locks over his left temple and tilted ceilingward the stogy between his thin lips. Then he leaned back in his antique swivel chair, locked his hands behind his head, elevated his long legs luxuriously, and

1

crossed his feet upon the fourth volume of the American and English Encyclopedia of Law, which lay open upon the desk at "Champerty and Maintenance." Even in this inelegant and relaxed posture he somehow managed to maintain the air of picturesque dignity which always made his tall, ungainly figure noticeable in any courtroom. Indubitably Mr. Ephraim Tutt suggested a past generation, the suggestion being accentuated by a slight pedantry of diction somewhat out of character with the rushing age in which he saw fit to practise his time-honored profession. "Cheer up, Tutt," said he, pushing a box of stogies toward his partner with the toe of his congress shoe. "Have a weed?"

Since in the office of Tutt & Tutt such an invitation, like that of royalty, was equivalent to a command, Tutt acquiesced.

"Thank you, Mr. Tutt," said Tutt, looking about vaguely for a match.

"That conscienceless brat of a Willie steals 'em all," growled Mr. Tutt. "Ring the bell."

Tutt obeyed. He was a short, brisk little man with a pronounced abdominal convexity, and he maintained toward his superior, though but a few years his junior, a mingled attitude of awe, admiration and affection such as a dickey bird might adopt toward a distinguished owl.

This attitude was shared by the entire office force. Inside the ground glass of the outer door Ephraim Tutt was king. To Tutt the opinion of Mr. Tutt upon any subject whatsoever was law, even if the courts might have held to the contrary. To Tutt he was the eternal fount of wisdom, culture and morality. Yet until Mr. Tutt had finally elucidated his views Tutt did not hesitate to hold conditional, if temporary, opinions of his own. Briefly their relations were symbolized by the circumstance that while Tutt always addressed his senior partner as "Mr. Tutt," the latter accosted him simply as "Tutt." In a word there was only one Mr. Tutt in the firm of Tutt & Tutt.

But so far as that went, there was only one Tutt. On the theory that a lily cannot be painted, the estate of the one, seemingly, was as good as that of the other. At any rate there never was and never had been any confusion or ambiguity arising out of the matter since the day, so long ago, when Tutt had visited Mr. Tutt's law office in search of employment. Mr. Tutt was just rising into fame as a police-court lawyer. Tutt had only recently been admitted to the bar, having abandoned his native city of Bangor, Maine, for the metropolis.

"And may I ask why you should come to me?" Mr. Tutt had demanded severely from behind the stogy, which even at that early date had been as much a part of his facial anatomy as his long ruminative nose. "Why the devil should you come to me? I am nobody, sir, —nobody! In this great city there are certainly thousands more qualified than I to further your professional and financial advancement."

"Because," answered the inspired Tutt with modesty, "I feel that with you I should be associated with a good name."

That had settled the matter. They bore no relationship to one another, but they were the only Tutts in the city and there seemed to be a certain propriety in their hanging together. Neither had regretted it for a moment, and as the years passed they became indispensable to each other. They were the necessary component parts of a harmonious legal whole. Mr. Tutt was the brains and the voice, while Tutt was the eyes and legs of a combination that at intervals made the law tremble, sometimes in fear and more often with joy.

At first, speaking figuratively, Tutt merely carried Mr. Tutt's bag, —rode on his coat tails, as it were; but as time went on his activity, ingenuity and industry made him indispensable and led to a junior partnership. Tutt prepared the cases for Mr. Tutt to try. Both were well versed in the law if they were not profound lawyers, but as the origin of the firm was humble, their practice was of a miscellaneous character.

"Never turn down a case," was Tutt's motto.

"Our duty as sworn officers of the judicial branch of the Government renders it incumbent upon us to perform whatever services our clients' exigencies demand," was Mr. Tutt's way of putting it.

In the end it amounted to exactly the same thing. As a result, in addition to their own clientele, other members of the bar, who found themselves encumbered with matters which for one reason or another they preferred not to handle, formed the habit of turning them over to Tutt & Tutt. A never-ending stream of peculiar cases flowed through the office, each leaving behind it some residuum of golden dust, however small. The stately or,—as an unkind observer might have put it,—the ramshackly form of the senior partner was a constant figure in all the courts, from that of the coroner on the one hand to the appellate tribunals upon the other. It was immaterial to him what the case was about,—whether it dealt with the "next eventual estate" or the damages for a dog bite,—so long as he was paid and Tutt prepared it. Hence Tutt & Tutt prospered. And as the law, like any other profession, requires jacks-of-all-trades, the firm acquired a certain peculiar professional standing of its own, and enjoyed the good will of the bar as a whole.

They had the reputation of being sound lawyers if not over-afflicted with a sense of professional dignity, whose word was better than their bond, yet who, faithful to their clients' interests, knew no mercy and gave no quarter. They took and pressed cases which other lawyers dared not touch lest they should be defiled,—and nobody seemed to think any the less of them for so doing. They raised points that made the refinements of the ancient schoolmen seem blunt in comparison. No respecters of persons, they harried the rich and taunted the powerful, and would have as soon jailed a bishop or a judge as a pickpocket, if he deserved it. Between them they knew more kinds of law than most of their professional brethren, and, as Mr. Tutt was a bookworm and a seeker after legal and other lore, their dusty old library was full of hidden treasures, which on frequent occasions were unearthed to entertain the jury or delight the bench. They were loyal friends, fearsome enemies, high chargers and maintained their unique position in spite of the fact that at one time or another they had run close to the shadowy line which divides the ethical from that which is not. Yet Mr. Tutt had brought disbarment proceedings against many lawyers in his time and—what is more—had them disbarred.

"Leave old Tutt alone," was held sage advice, and when other lawyers desired to entertain the judiciary they were apt to invite Mr. Tutt to be of the party. And Tutt gloried in the glories of Mr. Tutt.

"That's it!" repeated Tutt as he lit his stogy, the cub of a Willie having foraged successfully in the outer office for a match. "He's willing to be hanged or damned or anything else just for the pleasure of having put a bullet through the other fellow!"

"What was the name of the unfortunate deceased?"

"Tomasso Crocedoro—a barber."

"That is almost a defense in itself," mused Mr. Tutt. "Anyhow, if I've got to defend Angelo for shooting Tomasso, you might as well give me a short scenario of the melodrama. By the way, are we retained or assigned by the court?"

"Assigned," chirped Tutt. "And—if he's convicted, as of course he will be,—we stand a good chance of losing our reputation as successful trial counsel. Why not beg off?"

"Let me hear the story first," answered Mr. Tutt. "Angelo sounds like a good sport. I have a mild affection for him already."

He reached into a lower compartment of his desk and removed a tumbler and a bottle of malt extract, which he placed at his elbow. Then he leaned back again expectantly.

"It is a simple story," began Tutt, seating himself in the chair reserved for paying clients—that is to say, one which did not have the two front legs sawed off an inch or so in order to make lingering uncomfortable—"a plain, unvarnished tale. Our client is one who makes an honest living by blacking shoes near the entrance to the Brooklyn Bridge. He formed an attachment for a certain young lady who had previously had some sort of love affair with Crocedoro, as a result of which her social standing had become slightly impaired. In a word, Tomasso jilted her. Angelo saw, pitied and loved her, took her for better or for worse, and married her."

"For which," interjected Mr. Tutt, "he is entitled to everyone's respect."

"Quite so!" agreed Tutt. "Now Tomasso, though not willing to marry the girl himself, seemed to have resented the idea of anyone else doing so, and accordingly seized every opportunity which presented itself to twit Angelo about the matter."

"Dog in the manger, so to speak," nodded Mr. Tutt.

"He not only jeered at Angelo for marrying Rosalina, but he began to hang about his discarded mistress again and scoff at her choice of a husband. But Rosalina gave him the cold shoulder, with the result that he became more and more insulting to Angelo. Finally one day our client made up his mind not to stand it any longer, secured a revolver, sought out Tomasso in his barber shop and put a bullet through his head. Now however much you may sympathize with Angelo as a man and a husband, there isn't the slightest doubt that he killed Tomasso with every kind of deliberation and premeditation."

"If the case is as you say," replied Mr. Tutt, pouring out a tumbler of malt extract and flicking a stogy ash from his waistcoat, "the honorable justice who handed it to us is no friend of ours."

"He isn't," assented his partner. "It was Babson, and he hates Italians. Moreover, he stated in open court that he proposed to try the case himself next Monday and that we must be ready without fail."

"So Babson did that to us!" growled Mr. Tutt. "Just like him. He'll pack the jury and charge our innocent Angelo into the middle of hades."

"And 'Bloodhound O'Brien' is the assistant district attorney in charge of the prosecution," mildly added Tutt. "But what can we do? We're assigned, we've got a guilty client, and we've got to defend him. Bonnie Doon says it's the toughest case he ever had to handle in which to find any witnesses for the defense. There aren't any. Besides, the girl bought the gun and gave it to Angelo the same day."

"How do you know that?" demanded Mr. Tutt, frowning.

"Because she told me so herself," said Tutt. "She's outside if you want to see her."

Tutt retired and presently returned half leading, half pushing a shabbily dressed young Italian woman. She wore no hat and her hands and finger nails were far from clean, but from the folds of her black shawl her neck rose like a column of slightly discolored Carrara marble, upon which her head with its coils of heavy hair was poised with the grace of a Roman empress.

"Come in, my child, and sit down," said Mr. Tutt kindly. "No, not in that one; in *that* one." He indicated the chair previously occupied by his junior. "You can leave us, Tutt. I want to talk to this young lady alone."

The girl sat sullenly, with averted face, showing in her attitude her instinctive feeling that all officers of the law, no matter upon which side they were supposed to be, were one and all engaged in a mysterious conspiracy of which she and her unfortunate Angelo were the victims. A few words from the old lawyer and she began to feel more confidence, however. No one, in fact, could fail to realize at first glance Mr. Tutt's warmth of heart. The lines of his sunken cheeks, if left to themselves, automatically tended to draw together into a whimsical smile, and it required a positive act of will upon his part to adopt the stern and relentless look with which he was wont to glower down upon some unfortunate witness in cross-examination.

Inside, Mr. Tutt was a benign and rather mellow old fellow, with a dry sense of humor and a very keen knowledge of his fellow men. He made a good deal of money, but not having any wife or child upon which to lavish it, he spent it all either on books or on surreptitious quixotic gifts to friends or strangers, whom he secretly admired or whom he believed to be in need of money. There were vague traditions in the office of presents of bizarre and quite impossible clothes made to office boys and stenographers; of ex-convicts re-outfitted and sent rejoicing to foreign parts; of tramps gorged to repletion and then pumped dry of their adventures in Mr. Tutt's comfortable, dingy old library; of a fur coat suddenly clapped upon the rounded shoulders of old Scraggs, the antiquated scrivener in the accountant's cage in the outer office, whose alcoholic career, his employer alleged, was marked by a trail of empty rum kegs, each one flying the white flag of surrender.

And yet old Ephraim Tutt could on occasion be cold as chiselled steel, and as hard. Any appeal from a child, a woman or an outcast always met with his ready response. He would burn the midnight oil with equal zest to block a crooked deal on the part of a wealthy corporation or to devise a means to extricate some no less crooked rascal from the clutches of the law, provided that the rascal seemed the victim of hard luck, inheritance or environment. His weather-beaten conscience was as elastic as his heart. He had, indeed, when under the expansive influence of a sufficient quantity of malt extract or ancient brandy from the cellaret on his library desk, been heard to enunciate the theory that there was very little difference between those in jail and those who were not.

He would work for weeks, without compensation, to argue the case of some guilty rogue before the Court of Appeals, in order, as he said, to "settle the law," when his only real object was to get the miserable fellow out of jail and send him back to his wife and children. He went through life with a twinkling eye and a quizzical smile, and when he did wrong he did it—if such a thing be possible—in a way to make people better. He was a dangerous adversary and judges were afraid of him, not because he ever tricked or deceived them, but because of the audacity and novelty of his arguments, which left them floundering. He had the assurance that usually comes with age and with a lifelong knowledge of human nature, yet apparently he had always been possessed of it.

Now as he gazed at the tear-stained cheeks of the girl-wife whose husband had committed murder in defense of her good repute, he vowed that so far as he was able he would fight to save him. The more desperate the case the more desperate her need of him,—the greater the duty and the greater his honor if successful.

"Believe that I am your friend, my dear!" he assured her. "You and I must work together to set Angelo free."

"It's no use," she returned less defiantly. "He done it. He won't deny it."

"But he is entitled to his defense," urged Mr. Tutt.

"He won't make no defense."

"We must make one for him."

"There ain't none. He just went and killed him."

Mr. Tutt shrugged his shoulders.

"There is always a defense," he answered. "Anyhow, we can't let him be convicted without making an effort. Will they be able to prove where he got the pistol?"

"He didn't get the pistol," retorted the girl with a glint in her black eyes. "I got it. I'd ha' shot him myself if Angelo hadn't. I said I was goin' to, but he wouldn't let me."

"Dear, dear!" sighed Mr. Tutt. "What a case! Both of you trying to see which can get hanged first!"

The inevitable day of Angelo's trial came. Upon the bench the Honorable Mr. Justice Babson glowered down upon the defendant flanked by his distinguished counsel, Tutt & Tutt, and upon the two hundred good and true talesmen who, "all other business laid aside," had been dragged from the comfort of their homes and the important affairs of their various livelihoods to pass upon the merits of the issue duly joined between The People of the State of New York and Angelo Serafino, charged with murder.

Each of them, as his name was called, took his seat in the witness chair and perjured himself like a gentleman in order to escape from service, shyly confessing to an ineradicable prejudice against the entire Italian race and this defendant in particular, and to such an antipathy against capital punishment as, he unhesitatingly averred, would render him utterly incapable of satisfactorily performing the functions of a juryman. Hardly one, however, but was routed by the Machiavellian Babson. Hardly one, however ingenious his excuse, —whether about to be married or immediately to become a father, whether in the last stages of illness or obliged to be present at the bedside of a dying wife—but was browbeaten and ordered back to his place amidst the waiting throng of citizens so disinclined to facilitate that system of trial by jury, the failure of which they so loudly at other times condemned.

This trifling preliminary having been concluded, the few jurymen who had managed to wriggle through the judicial sieve were allowed to withdraw, the balance of the calendar was adjourned, those spectators who were standing up were ordered to sit down and those already sitting down were ordered to sit somewhere else, the prisoners in the rear of the room were sent back to the Tombs to await their fate upon a later day, the reporters gathered rapaciously about the table just behind the defendant, a corpulent Ganymede, in the person of an aged court officer, bore trembling an opaque glass of yellow drinking water to the bench, O'Brien, the prosecutor, blew his nose like a fish horn, Mr. Tutt smiled an ingratiating smile which seemed to clasp the whole world to his bosom,—and the real battle commenced, a game in which every card in the pack had been stacked against the prisoner by an unscrupulous pair of officials whose only aim was to maintain their record of convictions of "murder in the first" and who laid their plans with ingenuity and carried them out with skill and enthusiasm to habitual success.

They were a grand little pair of convictors, were Babson and O'Brien, and woe unto that man who was brought before them. It was even alleged by the impious that, when Babson was in doubt what to do or what O'Brien wanted him to do, the latter communicated the information to his conspirator upon the bench by a system of preconcerted signals. But no such system was necessary, for the judge's part in the drama was merely to sustain his colleague's objections and overrule those of his opponent, after which he himself delivered the *coup de grâce* with unerring insight and accuracy. When Babson got through charging a jury the latter had always in fact been instructed in brutal and sneering tones to convict the defendant or forever after to regard themselves as disloyal citizens, oath violators and outcasts; although the stenographic record of his remarks would have led the reader thereof to suppose that this same judge was a conscientious, tender-hearted, merciful lover of humanity, whose sensitive soul quivered at the mere thought of a prison cell, and who sought to surround the defendant with every protection the law could interpose against the imputation of guilt. He was, as Tutt put it, "a dangerous old cuss."

O'Brien was even worse. He was a bull-necked, bullet-headed, young ruffian with beery eyes, who had an insatiable ambition and a still greater conceit, but who had devised a blundering way of conducting himself before a jury that deceived them into believing that his inexperience required their help and his disinterestedness their loyal support. Both of them were apparently fair-minded, honest public servants; both in reality were subtly disingenuous to a degree beyond ordinary comprehension. In a word, they were a precious pair of crooks, who for their own petty and selfish ends played fast and loose with liberty, life and death.

Both of them hated Mr. Tutt, who had more than once made

them ridiculous before the jury and shown them up before the Court of Appeals, and the old lawyer recognized the fact that these two legal wolves were, in revenge, planning to tear him and his helpless client to pieces, having first deliberately selected him as a victim and assigned him to officiate at a ceremony which, however just so far as its consummation might be concerned, was nothing less in its conduct than judicial murder. Now they were laughing at him in their sleeves, for Mr. Tutt enjoyed the reputation of never having had a client convicted of murder, and that spotless reputation was about to be annihilated forever.

He well knew that although the defense had thirty peremptory challenges, Babson would sustain the prosecution's objections for bias, until the jury box would contain the twelve automata personally selected by O'Brien in advance from what Tutt called "the standing army of the gibbet." Yet the old war-horse outwardly maintained a calm and genial exterior, betraying none of the apprehension which in fact existed beneath his mask of professional composure. The court officer rapped sharply for silence.

"Are you quite ready to proceed with the case?" inquired the judge with a courtesy in which was ill-concealed a leer of triumph.

"Yes, Your Honor," responded Mr. Tutt in velvet tones.

"Call the first talesman!"

The fight was on, the professional duel had begun between traditional enemies, in which the stake—a human life—was in truth the thing of least concern. Yet no casual observer would have suspected the actual significance of what was going on or the part that envy, malice, selfishness and ambition were playing in it. He would have seen merely a partially filled courtroom flooded with sunshine from high windows, an attentive and dignified judge in a black silk robe sitting upon a dais, below which a white-haired clerk drew little slips of paper from a wheel and summoned talesmen to a service which outwardly bore no suggestion of a tragedy.

He would have seen a somewhat unprepossessing assistant district attorney lounging in front of the jury box, taking apparently no great interest in the proceedings, and a worried-looking young Italian sitting at the prisoner's table between a rubicund little man and a tall, grave, longish-haired lawyer with a frame not unlike that of Abraham Lincoln, over whose wrinkled face from time to time played the suggestion of a smile. Behind a balustrade were the reporters, scribbling on rough sheets of yellow paper. Then came the rows of benches, upon the first of which, as near the jury box as possible, sat Rosalina in a new bombazine dress and wearing a large imitation gold cross furnished for the occasion out of the legal property room of Tutt & Tutt. Occasionally she sobbed softly. The bulk of the spectators consisted of rejected talesmen, witnesses, law clerks, professional court loafers and women seeking emotional sensations which they had not the courage or the means to satisfy otherwise. The courtroom was comparatively quiet, the silence broken only by the droning voice of the clerk and the lazy interplay of question and answer between talesman and lawyer.

Yet, beneath the casual, almost indifferent manner in which the proceedings seemed to be conducted, each side was watching every move made by the other with the tension of a tiger ready to spring upon its prey. Babson and O'Brien on the one hand were engaged in forcing upon the defense a jury composed entirely of case-hardened convictors, while upon the other Tutt & Tutt were fighting desperately to secure one so heterogeneous in character that they could hope for a disagreement.

By recess thirty-seven talesmen had been examined without a foreman having been selected, and Mr. Tutt had exhausted twenty-nine of his thirty challenges, as against the prosecution's three. The court reconvened and a new talesman was called, resembling in appearance a professional hangman with a predilection for the execution of Italians. Mr. Tutt examined him for bias and every known form of incompetency, but in vain;—then challenged peremptorily. Thirty challenges! He looked on Tutt with slightly raised eyebrows.

"Patrick Henry Walsh—to the witness chair, please!—Mr. Walsh!" called the clerk, as he drew another slip from the box.

Mr. Walsh arose and came forward heavily, while Tutt & Tutt trembled. He was the man they were most afraid of,—an old-timer celebrated as a bulwark of the prosecution, who could always be safely counted upon to uphold the arms of the law, who regarded with reverence all officials connected with the administration of justice, and from whose composition apparently all human emotions had been carefully excluded by the Creator. He was a square-jawed, severe, heavily built person, with a long relentless upper lip, cheeks ruddy from the open air; and he had a brogue that would have charmed a mavis off a tree. Mr. Tutt gazed hopelessly at Tutt.

Babson and O'Brien had won.

Once more Mr. Tutt struggled against his fate. Was Mr. Walsh sure he had no prejudice against Italians or foreigners generally? Quite. Did he know anybody connected with the case? No. Had he any objection to the infliction of capital punishment? None whatever. The defense had exhausted all its challenges. Mr. Tutt turned to the prospective foreman with an endearing smile.

"Mr. Walsh," said he in caressing tones, "you are precisely the type of man in whom I feel the utmost confidence in submitting the fate of my client. I believe that you will make an ideal foreman. I hardly need to ask you whether you will accord the defendant the benefit of every reasonable doubt, and if you have such a doubt will acquit him?"

Mr. Walsh regarded Mr. Tutt suspiciously.

"Sure," he dryly responded. "Oi'll give him the benefit o' the doubt, but if Oi think he's guilty Oi'll convict him."

Mr. Tutt shivered.

"Of course! Of course! That would be your duty! You are entirely satisfactory, Mr. Walsh!"

"Mr. Walsh is more than satisfactory to the prosecution!" intoned O'Brien.

"Be sworn, Mr. Walsh," directed the clerk; and the filling of the jury box in the memorable case of People versus Serafino was begun.

"That chap doesn't like us," whispered Mr. Tutt to Tutt. "I laid it on a bit too thick."

In fact, Mr. Walsh had already entered upon friendly relations with Mr. O'Brien, and as the latter helped him arrange a place for his hat and coat the foreman cast a look tinged with malevolence at the defendant and his counsel, as if to say: "You can't fool me. I know the kind of tricks you fellows are all up to."

O'Brien could not repress a grin. The clerk drew forth another name.

"Mr. Tompkins—will you take the chair?"

Swiftly the jury was impanelled. O'Brien challenged everybody who did not suit his fancy, while Tutt & Tutt sat helpless.

Ten minutes, and the clerk called the roll, beginning with Mr. Walsh, they were solemnly sworn a true verdict to find, and settled themselves to the task.

The mills of the gods had begun to grind, and Angelo was being dragged to his fate as inexorably and as surely, with about as much chance of escape, as a log that is being drawn slowly toward a buzz-saw.

"You may open the case, Mr. O'Brien," announced Judge Babson, leaning back and wiping his glasses.

Then as his fellow conspirator undertook to tell the jury what it was all about, he surreptitiously began to read his mail. One by one the witnesses were called,—the coroner's physician, the policeman who had arrested Angelo with the smoking pistol in his hand outside the barber shop, the assistant barber who had seen the shooting, the customer who was being shaved. Each drove a spike into poor Angelo's legal coffin. Mr. Tutt could not shake them. The evidence was plain. He had come into the shop, accused Crocedoro of making his wife's life unbearable, and—shot him.

Yet Mr. Tutt did not lose any of his equanimity. With the tips of his long fingers held lightly together in front of him, he smiled benignly down upon the customer and the barber's assistant as if these witnesses were merely unfortunate in not being able to disclose to the jury all the facts. His manner indicated that a mysterious and untold tragedy lay behind what they had heard, a tragedy pregnant with primordial passions, involving the most sacred of human relationships, which when known would rouse the spirit of chivalry of the entire panel.

On cross-examination the barber testified that Angelo had said: "You maka small of my wife long enough!"

"Ah!" murmured Mr. Tutt, waving an arm in the direction of Rosalina. Did the witness recognize the defendant's young wife? The jury showed interest and examined the sobbing Rosalina with approval. Yes, the witness recognized her. Did the witness know to what incident or incidents the defendant had referred by his remark —what the deceased Crocedoro had done to Rosalina—if anything? No, the witness did not. Mr. Tutt looked significantly at the row of faces in the jury box.

Then, leaning forward, he asked: "Did you see Crocedoro threaten the defendant with his razor?"

"I object!" shouted O'Brien, springing to his feet. "The question is improper. There is no suggestion that Crocedoro did anything. The defendant can testify to that if he wants to!"

"Oh, let him answer!" drawled the judge.

"No—" began the witness.

"Ah!" cried Mr. Tutt. "You did not see Crocedoro threaten the defendant with his razor! That will do!"

But, forewarned by this trifling experience, Mr. O'Brien induced the customer, the next witness, to swear that Crocedoro had not in fact made any move whatever with his razor toward Angelo, who had deliberately raised his pistol and shot him.

Mr. Tutt rose to the cross-examination with the same urbanity as before. Where was the witness standing? The witness said he wasn't standing. Well, where was he sitting, then? In the chair.

"Ah!" exclaimed Mr. Tutt triumphantly. "Then you had your back to the shooting!"

In a moment O'Brien had the witness partially rescued by the explanation that he had seen the whole thing in the glass in front of him. The firm of Tutt & Tutt uttered in chorus a groan of outraged incredulity. Several jurymen were seen to wrinkle their foreheads in meditation. Mr. Tutt had sown a tiny—infinitesimally tiny—seed of doubt, not as to the killing, but as to the complete veracity of the witness.

And then O'Brien made his coup.

"Rosalina Serafino—take the witness stand!" he ordered.

He would get from her own lips the admission that she had bought the pistol and given it to Angelo! But, with an outburst of indignation that would have done credit to the elder Booth, Mr. Tutt was immediately on his feet protesting against the outrage, the barbarity, the heartlessness, the illegality of making a wife testify against her husband! His eyes flashed, his disordered locks waved in picturesque synchronization with his impassioned gestures. Rosalina, her beautiful golden cross rising and falling hysterically upon her bosom, took her seat in the witness chair like a frightened, furtive creature of the woods, for one brief instant gazed, with those great black eyes of her, upon the twelve men in the jury box, and then with burning cheeks buried her face in her handkerchief.

"I protest against this piece of cruelty!" cried Mr. Tutt in a voice vibrating with indignation. "This is worthy of the Inquisition. Will not even the cross upon her breast protect her from being compelled to reveal those secrets that are sacred to wife and motherhood? Can the law thus indirectly tear the seal of confidence from the Confessional? Mr. O'Brien, you go too far! There are some things that even you—brilliant as you are—may not trifle with."

A juryman nodded. The eleven others, being more intelligent, failed to understand what he was talking about.

"Mr. Tutt's objection is sound—if he wishes to press it," remarked the judge. "You may step down, madam. The law will not compel a wife to testify against her husband. Have you any more witnesses, Mister District Attorney?"

"The People rest," said Mr. O'Brien. "The case is with the defense."

Mr. Tutt rose with solemnity.

"The court will, I suppose, grant me a moment or two to confer with my client?" he inquired. Babson bowed and the jury saw the lawyer engage his partner in what seemed to be a weighty discussion.

"I killa him! I say so!" muttered Angelo feebly to Mr. Tutt.

"Shut up, you fool!" hissed Tutt, grabbing him by the leg. "Keep still or I'll wring your neck."

"If I could reach that old crook up on the bench, I would twist his nose," remarked Mr. Tutt to Tutt with an air of consulting him about the Year Books. "And as for that criminal O'Brien; I'll get him yet!"

With great dignity Mr. Tutt then rose and again addressed the court:

"We have decided upon all the circumstances of this most extraordinary case, Your Honor, not to put in any defense. I shall not call the defendant——"

"I killa him——" began Angelo, breaking loose from Tutt and struggling to his feet. It was a horrible movement. But Tutt clapped his hand over Angelo's mouth and forced him back into his seat.

"The defense rests," said Mr. Tutt, ignoring the interruption. "So far as we are concerned the case is closed."

"Both sides rest!" snapped Babson. "How long do you want to sum up?"

Mr. Tutt looked at the clock, which pointed to three. The regular hour of adjournment was at four. Delay was everything in a case like this. A juryman might die suddenly overnight or fall grievously ill; or some legal accident might occur which would necessitate declaring a mistrial. There is always hope in a criminal case, so long as the verdict has not actually been returned and the jury polled and discharged. If possible he must drag his summing up over until the following day. Something might happen.

"I shall need about two hours, Your Honor," he replied.

The jury stirred impatiently. It was clear that they regarded a two-hour speech from him under the circumstances as an imposition. But Babson wished to preserve the fiction of impartiality.

"Very well," said he. "You may sum up until four-thirty, and have half an hour more to-morrow morning. See that the doors are closed, Captain Phelan. We do not want any interruption while the summations are going on."

"All out that's goin' out! Everybody out that's got no business with the court!" bellowed Captain Phelan.

Mr. Tutt with an ominous heightening of the pulse realized that the real ordeal was at last at hand, for the closing of the case had wrought in the old lawyer an instant metamorphosis. With the words "The defense rests" every suggestion of the mountebank, the actor or the shyster had vanished. The awful responsibility under which he labored; the overwhelming and damning evidence against his client; the terrible consequences of the least mistake that he might make; the fact that only the sword of his ability, and his alone, stood between Angelo and a hideous death by fire in the electric chair—sobered and chastened him.

For his client was foredoomed,—foredoomed, not only by justice, but also by trickery and guile,—and was being driven slowly but surely toward the judicial shambles. For what had he succeeded in adducing in his behalf? Nothing save the unsupported speculation that the dead barber might have threatened Angelo with his razor and that the witnesses might possibly have drawn somewhat upon their imaginations in giving the details of their testimony. A sorry defense! Indeed, no defense at all. All the sorrier in that he had not even been able to get before the jury the purely sentimental excuses for the homicide, for he could only do this by calling Rosalina to the stand, which would have enabled the prosecution to cross-examine her in regard to the purchase of the pistol and the delivery of it to her husband—the strongest evidence of premeditation. Yet he must find some argument, some plea, some thread of reason upon which the jury might hang a disagreement or a verdict in a lesser degree.

With a shuffling of feet the last of the crowd pushed through the big oak doors which were closed and locked. An officer brought a corroded tumbler of brackish water and placed it in front of Mr. Tutt. The judge leaned forward with malicious courtesy. The jury settled themselves and turned toward the lawyer with a defiant attention, hardening their hearts already against his expected appeals to sentiment. O'Brien, ostentatiously producing a cigarette, lounged out through the side door leading to the jury room and prison cells. The clerk began copying his records. The clock ticked loudly.

And Mr. Tutt rose and began going through the empty formality of attempting to discuss the evidence in such a way as to excuse or palliate Angelo's crime. For Angelo's guilt of murder in the first degree was so plain that it had never for one moment been in the slightest doubt. Whatever might be said for his act from the point of view of human emotion only made his motive and his responsibility under the statutes all the clearer. There was not even "the unwritten law" to appeal to. Yet there was a genuine defense, a defense that could not be urged even by innuendo: the defense that no accused ought to be convicted upon any evidence whatever, no matter how conclusive, when his trial has been conducted with essential unfairness.

Such was the case of Angelo. No one could demonstrate it, no one could with safety even hint at it; any charge that the court was anything but impartial would prove a boomerang to the defense; and yet the fact remained that the whole proceeding from start to finish had been conducted with illegality, that the jury had been duped and deceived, and that the pretense that the guilty Angelo had been given an impartial trial was a farce. Every word of the court had been an accusation, a sneer, an acceptance of the defendant's guilt as a matter of course, an abuse far more subversive of the administration of justice than the mere acquittal of a single criminal, for it struck at the very foundations of liberty,—the guarantees of the presumption of innocence and "due process of law."

Unmistakably the proceedings had been conducted throughout upon the theory that the defendant must prove his innocence and that presumably he was a guilty man; and this, as well as his own impression that the evidence was conclusive, the judge had subtly conveyed to the jury in his tone of speaking, his ironical manner and his facial expression. Guilty or not, Angelo was being railroaded. That was the real defense—a defense that could never be established even in any higher court.

And so Mr. Tutt, boiling with suppressed indignation, weighed down with the sense of his responsibility, fully realizing his inability to say anything in behalf of his client based on the evidence, rose with a genial smile upon his puckered old face and with a careless air, which however seemed to indicate the utmost confidence and determination, and with a graceful compliment to his arch enemy upon the bench and the yellow dog who hunted with him, assured the jury that the defendant had had the fairest of fair trials and that he, Mr. Tutt, would now proceed to demonstrate to their satisfaction his client's entire innocence; nay, would indeed show them that he was a man, not only guiltless of any wrong-doing, but worthy of their hearty commendation.

With anecdotes not too unseemly for the occasion he overcame their preliminary distrust and put them in a good humor. He gave a historical dissertation upon the law governing homicide, on the constitutional rights of American citizens, on the laws of naturalization, marriage, and the domestic relations; waxed eloquent over Italy and the Italian character, mentioned Cavour, Garibaldi and Mazzini in a way to imply that Angelo was their lineal descendant; lauded Mussolini; and quoted from D'Annunzio back to Horace, Cicero and Plautus.

"Bunk! Nothing but bunk!" muttered Tutt, studying the twelve faces before him. "And they all know it!"

But Mr. Tutt was nothing if not interesting. These prosaic citizens of New York County, these saloon and hotel keepers, these contractors, insurance agents and salesmen were learning something of history, of philosophy, of art and beauty. They liked it. They felt they were hearing something worth while, as indeed they were, and they forgot all about Angelo and the unfortunate Crocedoro in their admiration for Mr. Tutt, who had lifted them out of the dingy sordid courtroom into the sunlight of the Golden Age. And as he led them through Greek and Roman literature, through the early English poets, through Shakespeare and the King James version, down to John Galsworthy and Rupert Brooke, he brought something that was noble, fine and sweet into their grubby materialistic lives.

"Bang!" went Babson's gavel just as Mr. Tutt was leading Mr. Walsh, Mr. Tompkins and the others through the winding paths of the Argonne forests, with tin helmets on their heads, in the struggle to make the world safe for democracy.

"You may conclude your address in the morning, Mr. Tutt," said the judge with supreme unction. "Adjourn court!"

Gray depression enveloped Mr. Tutt's soul as he trudged homeward. He had made a good speech, but it had had absolutely nothing to do with the case, a fact which the jury would perceive as soon as they thought it over. It was a confession of defeat. Angelo would be convicted of murder in the first degree and electrocuted, Rosalina would be a widow, and he would be in a measure responsible for it. The tragedy of human life appalled him. He felt very old, as old as the dead-and-gone authors from whom he had quoted with such remarkable facility. He belonged with them; he was too old to practise his profession.

"Law, Mis' Tutt," expostulated Miranda, his ancient negro handmaiden, as he pushed away the chop and mashed potato, and even the glass of claret, untasted, in his old-fashioned dining-room on West Twenty-third Street, "you ain't got no appetite at all! You's got a misery, Mis' Tutt."

"No, no, Miranda!" he replied weakly. "I'm just getting old."

"You's mighty spry for an old man, yit," she protested. "You kin make dem lawyer men hop mighty high when you tries. Heh, heh! I reckon dey ain't got nuffin' on ma Mistah Tutt!"

Upstairs in his library, Mr. Tutt strode up and down before the empty grate, smoking stogy after stogy, trying to collect his thoughts and devise something to say upon the morrow, but all his ideas had flown. There wasn't anything to say. Yet he swore Angelo should not be offered up as a victim upon the altar of unscrupulous ambition. The hours passed and the old banjo clock above the mantel wheezed eleven, twelve; then one, and two. Still he paced up and down, up and down, in a sort of trance. The air of the library, blue with the smoke of countless stogies, stifled and suffocated him. Moreover he discovered that he was hungry. He descended to the pantry and salvaged a piece of pie, then unchained the front door and stepped forth into the soft October night.

A full moon hung over the deserted streets of the sleeping city. In divers places, widely scattered, the twelve good and true men were snug in their beds. To-morrow they would send Angelo to his death without a quiver. He shuddered, striding on, he knew not whither, into the night. His brain no longer worked. He had become a peripatetic automaton self-dedicated to nocturnal perambulation.

With his pocket bulging with stogies, and with one glowing like a headlight in advance of him, he wandered in a sort of coma up Tenth Avenue, crossed to the Riverside Drive, mounted Morningside Heights, descended again through the rustling alleys of Central Park, and found himself at Fifth Avenue and Fifty-ninth Street just as the dawn was paling the electric lamps to a sickly yellow and the trees were casting strange unwonted shadows. He was utterly exhausted. He looked eagerly for some place to sit down, but the doors of the hotels were dark and tightly closed, and it was too cold to remain in the open air without moving.

Down Fifth Avenue he trudged, intending to go home and snatch a few hours' sleep before court should open, but each block seemed miles in length. Presently he approached the Cathedral, whose twin spires were tinted with reddish gold. The sky had become a bright blue. Suddenly all the street lamps went out. He told himself that he had never realized before the beauty of those two towers reaching up toward eternity.

He remembered having heard that a cathedral was never closed, and looking toward the door he perceived that it was open. Wearily he climbed the steps and entered its dark shadows. A faint light came through the tops of the stained-glass windows. Down below, a candle burned on either side of the altar and a flickering gleam shone from the red cup in the sanctuary lamp. Worn out, drugged for lack of sleep, faint for want of food, old Mr. Tutt sank down upon one of the rear seats by the door, and resting his head upon his arms on the back of the bench in front of him, fell fast asleep.

He dreamed of a legal heaven, of a great wooden throne upon which sat Babson in a black robe and below him twelve red-faced angels in a double row with harps in their hands, chanting: "Guilty! Guilty! Guilty!" An organ was playing somewhere, and there was a great noise of footsteps. Then a bell tinkled and he raised his head and saw that the chancel was full of lights and white-surpliced priests. It was broad daylight. Horrified he looked at his watch, to find that it was ten minutes after ten. His joints creaked as he pulled himself to his feet, and his eyes were half-closed as he staggered down the steps and hailed a taxi.

"Criminal Courts Building—side door. And drive like hell!" he ordered the driver.

He reached it just as Judge Babson and his attendant were coming into the courtroom and the crowd were making obeisance. Everybody else was in his proper place.

"You may proceed, Mr. Tutt," said the judge after the roll of the jury had been called.

But Mr. Tutt was in a daze, in no condition to think or speak. There was a curious rustling in his ears and his sight was blurred. The atmosphere of the courtroom seemed to him cold and hostile; the jury sat with averted faces. He rose feebly and cleared his throat.

"Gentlemen of the jury," he began, "I—I think I covered everything I had to say yesterday afternoon. I can only beseech you to realize the full extent of your great responsibility and remind you that, if you entertain a reasonable doubt upon the evidence, you are sworn to give the benefit of it to the defendant."

He sank back in his chair and covered his eyes with his hands, while a murmur ran along the benches of the courtroom. The old man had collapsed! The defendant was cooked! Swiftly O'Brien leaped to his feet and began his summation. There had been no defense, he shouted. The case was a plain as a pikestaff. There was only one thing for the jury to do,—return a verdict of murder in the first. It would not be pleasant, but that made no difference! He read them the statute, applied it to the facts, and shook his fist in their faces. They must convict—and convict of only one thing— nothing else—murder in the first degree. They gazed at him like silly sheep, nodding their heads, doing everything but bleat.

Then Babson, rising in dignity, expounded the law to the sheep in a rich mellow voice, in which he impressed upon them the necessity of preserving the integrity of the jury system and the sanctity of human life. He pronounced an obituary of great beauty upon the deceased barber,—who could not, as he pointed out, speak for himself, owing to the fact that he was in his grave. He venomously excoriated the defendant, who had deliberately planned to kill an unarmed man peacefully conducting himself in his place of business, and expressed the utmost confidence that he could rely upon the jury, whose character he well knew, to perform their full duty no matter how disagreeable that duty might be. The sheep nodded.

"You may retire, gentlemen."

Babson looked down at Mr. Tutt with a significant gleam in his eye. He had driven in the knife to the hilt and twisted it round and round. Mr. Tutt did not look at the jury as they went out. They would not be long, and he could hardly face the thought of their return. Never in his long experience had he found himself in such a desperate situation. Heretofore there had always been some argument, some construction of the facts upon which he could base an appeal, however fallacious or illogical.

He leaned back and closed his eyes. The judge was chatting with O'Brien, the court officers were betting with the reporters as to the length of time it would take the twelve to agree upon a verdict of murder in the first. The funeral rites were all concluded except for the final commitment of the corpse to mother earth.

And then without warning Angelo suddenly rose and addressed the court in a defiant shriek.

"I killa that man!" he cried wildly. "He maka small of my wife! He no good! He bad egg! I killa him once—I killa him again!"

"So!" exclaimed Babson with biting sarcasm. "You want to make a confession? You hope for mercy, do you? Well, Mr. Tutt, what do you wish to do under the circumstances? Shall I recall the jury and reopen the case by consent?"

Mr. Tutt rose trembling to his feet.

"The case is closed, Your Honor," he replied. "I will consent to a mistrial and offer a plea of guilty of manslaughter. I cannot agree to reopen the case. I cannot let the defendant go upon the stand."

The spectators and reporters were pressing forward to the bar, anxious lest they should lose a single word of the colloquy. Angelo remained standing, looking eagerly at O'Brien, who returned his gaze with a grin like that of a hyena.

"I killa him!" Angelo repeated. "You killa me if you want."

"Sit down!" thundered the judge. "Enough of this! The law does not permit me to accept a plea to murder in the first degree, and my conscience and my sense of duty to the public will permit me to accept no other. I will go to my chambers to await the verdict of the jury. Take the prisoner downstairs to the prison pen."

He swept from the bench in his silken robes. Angelo was led away. The crowd in the courtroom slowly dispersed. Mr. Tutt, escorted by Tutt, went out in the corridor to smoke.

"Ye got a raw deal, counselor," remarked Captain Phelan, amiably accepting a stogy. "Nothing but an act of Providence c'd save that Eyetalian from the chair! An' him guilty at that!"

An hour passed; then another. At half-after four a rumor flew along the corridors that the jury in the Serafino case had reached a verdict and were coming in. A messenger scurried to the judge's chambers. Phelan descended the iron stairs to bring up the prisoner, while Tutt to prevent a scene invented an excuse by which he lured Rosalina to the first floor of the building. The crowd suddenly reassembled out of nowhere and poured into the courtroom. The reporters gathered expectantly round their table. The judge entered, his robes gathered in one hand.

"Bring in the jury," he said sharply. "Arraign the prisoner at the bar."

Mr. Tutt took his place beside his client at the railing, while the jury, carrying their coats and hats, filed slowly in. Their faces were set and relentless. They looked neither to the right nor to the left. O'Brien sauntered over and seated himself nonchalantly with his back to the court, studying their faces. Yes, he told himself, they were a regular set of hangmen—he couldn't have picked a tougher bunch if he'd had his choice of the whole panel.

The clerk called the roll, and Messrs. Walsh, Tompkins, *et al.*, stated that they were all present.

"Gentlemen of the jury, have you agreed upon a verdict?" inquired the clerk.

"We have!" replied Mr. Walsh sternly.

"How say you? Do you find the defendant guilty or not guilty?"

Mr. Tutt gripped the balustrade in front of him with one hand

and put his other arm round Angelo. He felt that now in truth murder was being done.

"We find the defendant not guilty," said Mr. Walsh defiantly.

There was a momentary silence of incredulity. Then Babson and O'Brien shouted simultaneously: "What!"

"We find the defendant not guilty," repeated Mr. Walsh stubbornly.

"I demand that the jury be polled!" cried the crestfallen O'Brien, his face crimson.

And then the twelve reiterated severally that that was their verdict and that they hearkened unto it as it stood recorded and that they were entirely satisfied with it.

"You are discharged!" said Babson in icy tones. "Strike the names of these men from the list of jurors—as incompetent. Haven't you any other charge on which you can try this defendant?"

"No, Your Honor," answered O'Brien grimly. "He didn't take the stand, so we can't try him for perjury; and there isn't any other indictment against him."

Judge Babson turned ferociously upon Mr. Tutt:

"This acquittal is a blot upon the administration of criminal justice; a disgrace to the city! It is an unconscionable verdict; a reflection upon the intelligence of the jury! The defendant is discharged. This court is adjourned."

The crowd surged round Angelo and bore him away, bewildered. The judge and prosecutor hurried from the room. Alone, Mr. Tutt stood at the bar, trying to grasp the full meaning of what had occurred.

He no longer felt tired; he experienced an exultation such as he had never known before. Some miracle had happened! What was it?

Unexpectedly the lawyer felt a rough warm hand clasped over his own upon the rail and heard the voice of Mr. Walsh with its rich brogue saying: "At first we couldn't see that there was much to be said for your side of the case, Mr. Tutt; but when Oi stepped into St. Patrick's on me way down to court this morning and spied you prayin' there for guidance, I knew you wouldn't be defendin' him unless he was innocent, and so we decided to give him the benefit of the doubt."

THE SHYSTER

Shyster, n. [Origin obscure.] *One who does business trickily; a person without professional honor: used chiefly of lawyers; as, pettifoggers and shysters.*
—CENTURY DICTIONARY

When Terry McGurk hove the brick through the window of Froelich's butcher shop he did it casually, on general principles, and without any idea of starting anything. He had strolled unexpectedly round the corner from his dad's saloon, had seen the row going on between Froelich and the gang of boys who after school hours used the street in front of the shop as a ball ground, and had merely seized the opportunity to vindicate his reputation as a desperado and put one over on the Dutchman. The fact that he had on a red sweater was the barest coincidence. Having observed the brick to be accurately pursuing its proper trajectory he had ducked back round the corner again and continued upon his way rejoicing. He had not even noticed Tony Mathusek, who, having accidentally found himself in the midst of the mêlée, had started to beat a retreat the instant of the crash, and had run plump into the arms of Officer Delany of the Second. Unfortunately Tony too was wearing a red sweater.

"I've got you, you young devil!" exulted Delany. "Here's one of 'em, Froelich!"

"Dot's him! It was a feller mit a red sweater! Dot's the vun who done it!" shouted the butcher. "I vill make a gomblaint against him!"

"Come along, you! Quit yer kickin'!" ordered the cop, twisting Tony's thin arm until he writhed. "You'll identify him, Froelich?"

"Sure! Didn't I see him mit my eyes? He's vun of dem rascals vot drives all mine gustomers avay, mit deir yelling and screaming. You fix it for me, Bill."

"That's all right," the officer assured him. "I'll fix him good, I will! It's the reformatory for him. Or, say, you can make a complaint for malicious mischief."

"Sure! Dot's it! Malicious mischief!" assented the not over-intelligent tradesman. "Ve'll get rid of him for good, eh?"

"Sure," assented Delany. "Come along, you!"

Tony Mathusek lifted a white face, drawn with agony, from his tortured arm.

"Say, mister, you got the wrong feller! I didn't break the window. I was just comin' from the house——"

"Aw, shut up!" sneered Delany. "Tell that to the judge!"

"Y' ain't goin' to take me to jail?" wailed Tony. "I wasn't with them boys. I don't belong to that gang."

"Oh, so you belong to a gang, do ye? Well, we don't want no gangsters round here!" cried the officer with adroit if unscrupulous sophistry. "Come along now, and keep quiet or it'll be the worse for ye."

"Can't I tell my mother? She'll be lookin' for me. She's an old lady."

"Tell nuthin'. You come along!"

Tony saw all hope fade. He hadn't a chance—even to go to a decent jail! He had heard all about the horrors of the reformatory. They wouldn't even let your people visit you on Sundays! And his mother would think he was run over or murdered. She would go crazy with worry. He didn't mind on his own account, but his mother— It was too much. With a sudden twist, he tore out of his coat and dashed blindly down the street. As well might a rabbit hope to escape the claws of a wildcat. In three bounds Delany had him again, choking him until the world turned black.

But this is not a story about police brutality, for most cops are not brutal. Delany was an old-timer who believed in rough methods. He belonged, happily, to a fast-vanishing system more in harmony with the Middle Ages than with our present enlightened form of municipal government. He remained what he was for the reason that farther up in the official hierarchy there were others who looked to him, when it was desirable, to deliver the goods—not necessarily cash—but to stand with the bunch. These in turn were obligated on occasion, through self-interest or mistaken loyalty to friend or party, to overlook trifling irregularities, to use various sorts of pressure, or to forget what they were asked to forget. There was a far-reaching web of complicated relationships—official, political, matrimonial, commercial and otherwise—which had a very practical effect upon the performance of theoretical duty.

Delany was neither an idealist nor a philosopher. He was an empiricist, with a touch of pragmatism—though he did not know it. He was "a practical man." Even reform administrations have been known to advocate a "liberal enforcement" of the laws. Can one blame Delany for being practical when others, so much greater than he, have prided themselves upon the same attribute of practicality? There were of course a lot of things he simply had to do or get out of the force; at any rate, had he not done them his life would have been intolerable. These consisted, in part, of being deaf, dumb and blind when he was told to be so,—a comparatively easy matter. But there were other things that he had to do, as a matter of fact, to show that he was all right, which were not only more difficult, but expensive, and at times dangerous.

For example he had never been called upon to swear away an innocent man's liberty, but more than once he had had to stand for a frame-up against a guilty one. According to his cop-psychology, if his side partner saw something it was practically the same as if he had seen it himself. That phantasmagorical scintilla of evidence, needed to bolster up a weak or doubtful case, could always be counted on if Delany was the officer who had made the arrest. None of his cases were ever thrown out of court for lack of evidence, but then, quite naturally, Delany never arrested anybody who wasn't guilty!

Of course he had to "give up" at intervals, depending on what administration was in power, who his immediate superior was, and what precinct he was attached to, but he was not a regular grafter by any means. He was an occasional one merely; when he had to be. He did not consider that he was being grafted on when expected to contribute to chowders, picnics, benevolent associations, defense funds or wedding presents for high police officials. Neither did he think that he was taking graft because he amicably permitted Froelich to leave a fourteen-pound rib roast every Saturday night at his brother-in-law's flat. In the same way he regarded the bills slipped him by Grabinsky, the bondsman, as well-earned commissions, and saw no reason why the civilian clothes he ordered at the store shouldn't be paid for by some mysterious friendly person—identity unknown,—but shrewdly suspected to be Mr. Joseph Simpkins, Mr. Hogan's runner. Weren't there to be any cakes and ale in New York simply because a highbrow happened to be mayor? Were human kindness, good nature and generosity all dead? Would he have taken a ten-dollar bill—or even a hundred-dollar one—from Simpkins when he was going to be a witness in one of Hogan's cases? Not on your life! He wasn't no crook, he wasn't! He didn't have to be. He was just a cog in an immense wheel of crookedness. And when the wheel came down on his cog he automatically did his bit.

I perceive that the police are engaging too much of our attention. But it is necessary to explain why Delany was so ready to arrest Tony Mathusek, and why, as he dragged him into the station-house, he beckoned to Mr. Joey Simpkins, who was loitering outside the deputy sheriff's office, and whispered behind his hand, "All right. I've got one for you!"

Then the machine automatically began to work. Tony was arraigned at the bar, and, having given his age as sixteen years and five days, was charged with the "malicious destruction of property, to wit, a plate-glass window of one Karl Froelich, of the value of one hundred and fifty dollars." Mr. Joey Simpkins had shouldered his way through the smelly push and taken his stand beside the bewildered and half-fainting boy.

"It's all right, kid. Leave it to me," he said, encircling him with a protecting arm. Then to the clerk: "Pleads not guilty."

The magistrate glanced over the complaint, in which Delany, to save Froelich trouble, had sworn that he had seen Tony throw the brick. Hadn't the butcher said he'd seen him? Besides, if he took personal responsibility, it let the Dutchman out of a possible suit for false arrest. Then the magistrate looked down at the cop himself.

"Do you know this boy?" he asked sharply.

"Sure, Yerroner. He's a gangster. Admitted it to me on the way over."

"Are you really over sixteen?" suddenly demanded the judge, who knew and distrusted Delany, having repeatedly stated in open court that he wouldn't hang a yellow dog on his testimony. The underfed, undersized boy did not look more than fourteen.

"Yes, sir," said Tony. "I was sixteen last week."

"Got anybody to defend you?"

Tony looked at Simpkins inquiringly. He seemed a very kind gentleman.

"Mr. Hogan's case, judge," answered Joey. "Please make the bail as low as you can."

Now this judge was a political accident, having been pitch-forked into office by the providence that sometimes watches over sailors, drunks and third parties. Moreover, in spite of being a reformer he was nobody's fool, and when the other reformers, who were fools, got promptly fired out of office he had been reappointed by a supposedly crooked boss simply because, as the boss said, he had made a hell of a good judge and they needed somebody with brains here and there to throw a front. Incidentally, he had a swell cousin on Fifth Avenue who had invited the boss and his wife to dinner, wherefore the soreheads, who lost out, went round asking what kind of a note it was when a silk-stocking crook could buy a nine-thousand-dollar job for a fifty-dollar meal. Anyhow, he was clean and clean-looking, kindly, humorous and wise above his years—which were thirty-one. And Tony looked to him like a poor runt, Simpkins and Delany were both rascals, Froelich wasn't in court, and he sensed a nigger somewhere. Had he had any excuse he would have turned Tony out on the run. He hadn't, but he tried.

"Would you like an immediate hearing?" he asked Tony in an encouraging tone.

"Mr. Hogan can't be here until to-morrow morning," interposed Simpkins. "Besides, we shall want to produce witnesses. Make it to-morrow afternoon, judge."

Judge Harrison leaned forward.

"Are you sure you wouldn't prefer to have the hearing now?" he inquired with a smile at the trembling boy.

"Well, I want to get Froelich here,—if you're going to proceed now," spoke up Delany. "And I'd like to look up this defendant's record at headquarters."

Tony quailed. He feared and distrusted everybody, except the kind Mr. Simpkins. He suspected that smooth judge of trying to railroad him.

"No! No!" he whispered to the lawyer. "I want my mother should be here; and the janitor, he knows I was in my house. The rabbi, he will give me a good character."

The judge heard and shrugged his bombazine-covered shoulders. It was no use. The children of darkness were wiser in their generation than the children of light.

"Five hundred dollars bail," he remarked shortly. "Officer, have your witnesses ready to proceed to-morrow afternoon at two o'clock."

"Mr. Tutt," said Tutt in a depressing manner, as he watched Willie remove the screen and drag out the old gate-leg table for the firm's daily five o'clock tea and conference in the senior partner's office, "if a man called you a shyster what would you do about it?"

The elder lawyer sucked meditatively on the fag end of his stogy before replying.

"Why not sue him?" Mr. Tutt inquired.

"But suppose he didn't have any money?" replied Tutt disgustedly.

"Then why not have him arrested?" continued Mr. Tutt. "It's libelous *per se* to call a lawyer a shyster."

"Even if he is one," supplemented Miss Minerva Wiggin ironically, as she removed her paper cuffs preparatory to lighting the alcohol lamp under the tea-kettle. "The greater the truth the greater the libel, you know!"

"And what do you mean by that?" sharply rejoined Tutt. "You don't——"

"No," replied the managing clerk of Tutt & Tutt. "I don't! Of course not! And frankly, I don't know what a shyster is."

"Neither do I," admitted Tutt. "But it sounds opprobrious. Still, that is a rather dangerous test. You remember that colored client of ours who wanted us to bring an action against somebody for calling him an Ethiopian!"

"There's nothing dishonorable in being an Ethiopian," asserted Miss Wiggin.

"A shyster," said Mr. Tutt, reading from the Century Dictionary, "is defined as 'one who does business trickily; a person without professional honor; used chiefly of lawyers.'"

"Well?" snapped Tutt.

"Well?" echoed Miss Wiggin.

"H'm! Well!" concluded Mr. Tutt.

"I nominate for the first pedestal in our Hall of Legal Ill-Fame— Raphael B. Hogan," announced Tutt, complacently disregarding all innuendoes.

"But he's a very elegant and gentlemanly person," objected Miss Wiggin as she warmed the cups. "My idea of a shyster is a down-at-the-heels, unshaved and generally disreputable-looking police-court lawyer—preferably one with a red nose,—who murders the English language—and who makes his living by preying upon the ignorant and helpless."

"Like Finklestein?" suggested Tutt.

"Exactly!" agreed Miss Wiggin. "Like Finklestein."

"He's one of the most honorable men I know!" protested Mr.

Tutt. "My dear Minerva, you are making the great mistake—common, I confess, to a large number of people—of associating dirt and crime. Now dirt may breed crime, but crime doesn't necessarily breed dirt."

"You don't have to be shabby to prey upon the ignorant and helpless," argued Tutt. "Some of our most prosperous brethren are the worst sharks out of Sing Sing."

"That is true!" she admitted, "but tell it not in Gath!"

"A shyster," began Mr. Tutt, unsuccessfully applying a forced draft to his stogy and then throwing it away, "bears about the same relation to an honest lawyer as a cad does to a gentleman. The fact that he's well dressed, belongs to a good club and has his name in the Social Register doesn't affect the situation. Clothes don't make men; they only make opportunities."

"But why is it," persisted Miss Wiggin, "that we invariably associate the idea of crime with that of 'poverty, hunger and dirt'?"

"That is easy to explain," asserted Mr. Tutt. "The criminal law originally dealt only with crimes of violence—such as murder, rape and assault. In the old days people didn't have any property in the modern sense—except their land, their cattle or their weapons. They had no bonds or stock or bank accounts. Now it is, of course, true that rough, ignorant people are much more prone to violence of speech and action than those of gentle breeding, and hence most of our crimes of violence are committed by those whose lives are those of squalor. But"—and here Mr. Tutt's voice rose indignantly—"our greatest mistake is to assume that crimes of violence are the most dangerous to the state, for they are not. They cause greater disturbance and perhaps more momentary inconvenience, but they do not usually evince much moral turpitude. After all, it does no great harm if one man punches another in the head, or even in a fit of anger sticks a dagger into him. The police can easily handle all that. The real danger to the community lies in the crimes of duplicity— the cheats, frauds, false pretenses, tricks and devices, flimflams— practised most successfully by well-dressed, gentlemanly crooks of polished manners."

By this time the kettle was boiling cheerfully, quite as if no such thing as criminal law existed at all, and Miss Wiggin began to make the tea.

"All the same," she ruminated, "people—particularly very poor people—are often driven to crime by necessity."

"It's Nature's first law," contributed Tutt brightly.

Mr. Tutt uttered a snort of disgust.

"It may be Nature's first law, but it's about the weakest defense a guilty man can offer. 'I couldn't help myself' has always been the excuse for helping oneself!"

"Rather good—that!" approved Miss Wiggin. "Can you do it again?"

"The victim of circumstances is inevitably one who has made a victim of someone else," blandly went on Mr. Tutt without hesitation.

"Ting-a-ling! Right on the bell!" she laughed.

"It's true!" he assured her seriously. "There are two defenses that are played out—necessity and instigation. They've never been any good since the Almighty overruled Adam's plea in confession and avoidance that a certain female co-defendant took advantage of his hungry innocence and put him up to it."

"No one could respect a man who tried to hide behind a woman's skirts!" commented Tutt.

"Are you referring to Adam?" inquired his partner. "Anyhow, come to think of it, the maxim is not that 'Necessity is the first law of Nature,' but that 'Necessity knows no law.'"

"I'll bet you don't know——" began Tutt.

"If I recall correctly," ruminated Mr. Tutt, "Shakespeare says in 'Julius Cæsar' that 'Nature must obey necessity'; while Rabelais says 'Necessity has no law'; but the quotation we familiarly use is 'Necessity knows no law except to conquer,' which is from Pubilius Syrus."

"From who?" cried Tutt in ungrammatical surprise.

"Never mind!" soothed Miss Wiggin. "Anyway, it wasn't Raphael B. Hogan."

"Who certainly completely satisfies your definition so far as preying upon the ignorant and helpless is concerned," said Mr. Tutt. "That man is a human hyena—worse than a highwayman."

"Yet he's a swell dresser," interjected Tutt. "Owns his house and lives in amity with his wife."

"Doubtless he's a loyal husband and a devoted father," agreed Mr. Tutt. "But so, very likely, is the hyena. Certainly Hogan hasn't got the excuse of necessity for doing what he does."

"Don't you suppose he has to give up good and plenty to somebody?" demanded Tutt. "Cops and prison-keepers and bondsmen and under-sheriffs, and all kinds of crooked petty officials. I should worry!"

> *"Great fleas have little fleas upon their backs to bite 'em,*
> *And little fleas have lesser fleas, and so ad infinitum,"*

quoted Miss Wiggin reminiscently.

"A flea has to be a flea," continued Tutt. "He, or it, can't be anything else, but Hogan doesn't have to be a lawyer. He could be an
honest man if he chose."

"He? Not on your life! He couldn't be honest if he tried!" answered Mr. Tutt. "He's just a carnivorous animal! They talk about
scratching a Russian and finding a Tartar; I'd hate to scratch some
of our legal brethren."

"So would I!" assented Tutt. "I guess you're right, Mr. Tutt.
Christianity and the Golden Rule are all right in the upper social
circles, but off Fifth Avenue there's the same sort of struggle for
existence that goes on in the animal world. A man may be all sweetness and light to his wife and children and go to church on Sundays;
he may even play pretty fair with his own gang; but, outside of his
home and social circle, be a ravening wolf; at least Raphael B.
Hogan is!"

The subject of the foregoing entirely accidental conversation was
at that moment standing contemplatively in his office window smoking an excellent cigar preparatory to return to the bosom of his
family. Raphael B. Hogan believed in taking life easily. He was
accustomed to say that outside office hours his time belonged to his
wife and children; and several times a week he made it his habit,
on the way home to supper, to stop at the florist's or the toy-shop
and bear away with him inexpensive tokens of his love and affection.
On the desk behind him, over which in the course of each month
passed a great deal of very tainted money, stood a large photograph
of Mrs. Hogan, and another of the three little Hogans, in ornamental
silver frames, and his face would soften tenderly at the sight of their
self-conscious faces, even at a moment when he might be relieving a
widowed seamstress of her entire savings-bank account.

He was fat, jolly and sympathetic, and his smile was the smile of
a warm-hearted humanitarian. The milk of human kindness oozed
palpably from his every pore. In fact, he was always grumbling
about the amount of work he had to do for nothing. He was a genial,
generous host; unostentatiously conspicuous in the local religious
life of his denomination; in court a model of obsequious urbanity,

deferential to the judges before whom he appeared and courteous to all with whom he was thrown in contact. A good-natured, easy-going, simple-minded fat man; deliberate, slow of speech, well-meaning, with honesty sticking out all over him, you would have said; one in whom the widow and the orphan would have found a staunch protector and an unselfish friend. And now, having thus subtly connoted the character of our villain, let us proceed with our narrative.

The telephone buzzed on the wall set beside him.

"That you, chief?" came the voice of Simpkins.

"Yep."

"Got one off Delany."

"What is it?"

"Kid smashed a window—malicious mischief. Held for examination to-morrow at two. Five hundred bail."

"Any sugar?"

"Don't know. Says his father's dead and mother earns seventeen a week in a sweatshop and sends him to school. Got some insurance. I'm going right round there now."

"Well," replied Hogan, "don't scare her by taking too much off her at first. I suppose there's evidence to hold him?"

"Sure. Delany says he saw it."

"All right. But go easy!"

"Leave that to me, chief!" assured Simpkins. "See you to-morrow."

It will be observed that in this professional interchange nothing at all was said regarding the possibility of establishing Tony's innocence, but that on the contrary, Mr. Simpkins' mind was concentrated upon the widow's ability to pay. This was the only really important consideration to either of them. But Hogan did not worry, since he knew that Simpkins would skilfully entangle Mrs. Mathusek in such a web of apprehension that, rather than face her fears, she would if necessary go out and steal the money. So Mr. Hogan hung up the receiver and, with his heart full of gentle sympathy for all mankind, walked slowly home, pausing on the way to buy some roses for Mrs. Hogan.

Now, just at the moment that his employer was purchasing the roses, Mr. Simpkins entered the apartment of Mrs. Mathusek and informed her of Tony's arrest and incarceration. He was very sympathetic about it, very gentle, this dapper little man with the pale gray eyes and inquisitive, tapirlike nose; and after the first moment of shock Mrs. Mathusek took courage and begged the gentleman to sit down.

There are always two vultures hanging over the poor—death and the law; but of the two the law is the lesser evil. The former is a calamity; the latter is a misfortune. The one is final, hopeless, irretrievable; from the other there may perhaps be an escape. She knew Tony was a good boy; was sure his arrest was a mistake, and that when the judge heard the evidence he would let Tony go. Life had dealt hardly with her and made her an old woman at thirty-four, really old, not only in body but in spirit, just as in the Middle Ages the rigor of existence made even kings old at thirty-five.

Mrs. Mathusek distrusted the law and lawyers in the abstract, but Mr. Simpkins' appearance was so reassuring that he almost counteracted in her mind the distress of Tony's misfortune. He was clearly a gentleman, and she had a reverential regard for the gentry. What gentlefolk said was to be accepted as true. In addition, this particular gentleman was learned in the law and skilled in getting unfortunate people out of trouble. Now, though Mr. Simpkins possessed undoubtedly this latter qualification, it was also true that he was equally skilled in getting people into it. If he ultimately doubled their joys and halved their sorrows he inevitably first doubled their sorrows and halved their savings. Like the witch in Macbeth: "Double, double, toil and trouble." His aims were childishly simple: First, to find out how much money his victim had, and then to get it.

His methods were no more complicated than his aims and had weathered the test of generations of experience. So:

"Of course Tony must be bailed out," he said gently. "You don't want him to spend the night in jail."

"Jail! Oh, no! How much is the bail?" cried Tony's mother.

"Only five hundred dollars." His pale gray eyes were watching her for the slightest sign of suspicion.

"Five hundred dollars! Eoi! Eoi! It is a fortune! Where can I get five hundred dollars?" She burst into tears. "I have saved only one hundred and sixty!"

Mr. Simpkins pursed his lips. Then there was nothing for it! He reached for his hat. Mrs. Mathusek wrung her hands. Couldn't the gentleman go bail for Tony? He was such a dear, kind, good gentleman! She searched his face hungrily. Mr. Simpkins falteringly admitted that he did not possess five hundred dollars.

"But—" he hesitated.

"But—" she echoed, seizing his sleeve and dragging him back.

Mr. Simpkins thought that they could hire somebody to go bail; no, in that case there would be no money to pay the great lawyer whom they must at once engage to defend her son,—Mr. Hogan, the one who had the pull and called all the judges by their first names. He would not usually go into court for less than five hundred dollars, but Mr. Simpkins said he would explain the circumstances to him and could almost promise Mrs. Mathesek that he would persuade him to do it this once for one hundred and fifty. So well did he act his part that Tony's mother had to force him to take the money, which she unsewed from inside the ticking of her mattress. Then he conducted her to the station-house to show her how comfortable Tony really was and how much better it was to let him stay in jail one night, and make sure of his being turned out the next afternoon by giving the money to Mr. Hogan, than to use it for getting bail for him and leave him lawyerless and at the mercy of his accusers. When Mrs. Mathusek saw the cell Tony was in she became even more frightened than she had been at first. But by that time she had already given the money to Simpkins.

Second thoughts are ofttimes best. Most crooks are eventually caught through their having, from long immunity, grown careless and yielded to impulse. Once he had signed the complaint in which he swore that he had seen Tony throw the brick, Delany had undergone a change of heart. Being an experienced policeman he was sensitive to official atmosphere, and he had developed a hunch that Judge Harrison was leery of the case. The more he thought of it the less he liked the way the son-of-a-gun had acted, in especial the way he'd tried to get Mathusek to ask for an immediate hearing. Why had he ever been such a fool as to sign the complaint himself? It had been ridiculous,—just because he was mad at the boy for trying to get away and wanted to make things easy for Froelich. If he went on the stand the next afternoon he'd have to make up all sorts of fancy details, and Hogan would have his skin neatly tacked to the barn doors for keeps. Thereafter, no matter what happened, he'd never be able to change his testimony. After all, it would be easy enough to abandon the charge at the present point. It was a genuine case of cold feet. He scented trouble. He wanted to renege while the reneging was good. What in hell had Froelich ever done for him, anyhow? A few measly pieces of roast!

When Hogan returned home that evening, with the little Hogans, from the movies, he found the cop waiting for him outside his door.

"Look here," Delany whispered, "I'm going to can this here Mathusek window case. I'm going to fall down flat on my identification and give you a walkout. So go easy on me—and sort of help me along, see?"

"The hell you are!" said Hogan indignantly. "Then where do I come in, eh? Why don't you come through?"

"But I've got him wrong!" pleaded Delany. "You don't want me to put my neck in a sling, do you, so as you can make a few dollars? Look at all the money I've sent your way. Have a heart, Rafe!"

"Bull!" sneered the Honorable Rafe. "A man's got to live! You saw him do it! You've sworn to it, haven't you?"

"I made a mistake."

"How'll that sound to the commissioner? An' to Judge Harrison? No, no! Nothin' doin'! If you start anything like that I'll roast the life out of you!"

Delany spat as near Hogan's foot as he elegantly could.

"You're a hell of a feller, you are!" he growled, and turned his back on him as upon Satan.

The brick that Terry McGurk hurled as a matter of principle through Froelich's window produced almost as momentous consequences as the want of the horse-shoe nail did in Franklin's famous maxim. It is the unknown element in every transaction that makes for danger.

The morning after the catastrophe Mr. Froelich promptly made application to the casualty company with which he had insured his window, for reimbursement for his damage. Just as promptly the company's lawyer appeared at the butcher-shop and ascertained that the miscreant who had done the foul deed had been arrested and was to be brought into court that afternoon. This lawyer, whose salary depended indirectly upon the success which attended his efforts to secure the conviction and punishment of those who had cost his company money, immediately camped upon the trails of both Froelich and Delany. It was up to them, he said, to have the doer of wanton mischief sent away. If they didn't cooperate he would most certainly ascertain why. Now insurance companies are powerful corporations. They can do favors, and contrariwise they can make trouble, and Lawyer Asche was hot under the collar about that window.

This, for Delany, put an entirely new aspect upon the affair. It was one thing to ditch a case and another to run up against Nathan

Asche. He had sworn to the complaint and, if he didn't make good on the witness stand, Asche would get his hide. Then he bethought him that, if only Froelich was sufficiently emphatic in his testimony, a little uncertainty on his own part might be excused.

In the meantime, however, two things had happened to curdle Froelich's enthusiasm. First, his claim against the Tornado Casualty Company had been approved, and second, he had been informed on credible authority that they had got the wrong boy. Now he had sincerely thought that he had seen Tony throw the brick—he had certainly seen a boy in a red sweater do something,—but he realized also that he had been excited and more or less bewildered at the time; and his informant—Mrs. Sussman, the wife of the cigar dealer —alleged positively that it had been thrown by a strange kid who appeared suddenly from round the corner and as suddenly ran away in the direction whence he had come.

Froelich perceived that he had probably been mistaken, and being relatively honest—and being also about to get his money—and not wishing to bear false witness, particularly if he might later be sued for false imprisonment, he decided to pass the buck to Delany, who was definitely committed. He was shrewd enough, however, not to give his real reason to the policeman, but to put it on the ground of being so confused that he couldn't remember. This left Delany responsible for everything.

"But you said that that was the feller!" argued the cop, who had gone to urge Froelich to assume the onus of the charge. "And now you want to leave me holdin' the bag!"

"Vell, you said yourself you seen him, didn't you?" replied the German. "An' you svore to it. I didn't svear to noddings."

"Aw, you!" roared the enraged cop, and hastened to interview Mr. Asche.

Aping a broad humanitarianism, he suggested to Asche that, if Mrs. Mathusek would pay for the window, they could afford to let up on the boy. He did it so ingeniously that he got Asche to go round there, only to find that she had no money, it all having been given to Simpkins. Gee, what a mix-up!

It is quite possible that, even under these circumstances, Delany might still have availed himself of what in law is called a *locus pœnitentiœ*, had it not been that the mix-up was rendered still more mixed by the surreptitious appearance in the case of Mr. Michael McGurk, the father of the actual brick-artist, who had learned that the cop was getting wabbly and was entertaining the preposterous possibility of withdrawing the charge against the innocent Mathusek, to the imminent danger of his own offspring. In no uncertain terms the saloon-keeper intimated to the now embarrassed guardian of the public peace that, if he pulled anything like that, he would have him thrown off the force, to say nothing of other and darker possibilities connected with the morgue. All of which gave Delany decided pause.

Hogan, for his own reasons, had meanwhile reached an independent conclusion as to how he could circumvent Delany's contemplated treachery. If, he decided, the cop should go back on his identification of the criminal, he foresaw Tony's discharge in the magistrate's court, and no more money. The only sure way, therefore, to prevent Tony's escape would be by not giving Delany the chance to change his testimony; by waiving examination before the magistrate and consenting voluntarily to having his client held for the action of the grand jury, in which event Tony would be sent to the Tombs and there would be plenty of time for Simpkins to get an assignment of Mrs. Mathusek's insurance money before the grand jury kicked out the case. This also had the additional advantage of preventing any funny business on the part of Judge Harrison.

Delany was still undecided what he was going to do, when the case was called at two o'clock. It is conceivable that he might still have tried to rectify his error by telling something near the truth, in spite of Hogan, Asche and McGurk, but the opportunity was denied him.

At two o'clock Tony, a mere chip tossed aimlessly hither and yon by eddies and cross-currents, the only person in this melodrama of motive whose interests were not being considered by anybody, was arraigned at the bar and, without being consulted in the matter, heard Mr. Hogan, the fat, kindly lawyer whom his mother had retained to defend him, tell the judge that they were going to waive examination and consent to be held for the action of the grand jury.

"You see how it is, judge," simpered Hogan. "You'd have no choice but to hold my client on the officer's testimony. The easiest way is to waive examination and let the grand jury throw the case out of the window!"

Delany heard this announcement with intense relief, for it would relieve him from the dangerous necessity of testifying before Judge Harrison, and he could later spill the case before the grand jury when called before that august body. Moreover, he could tip off the district attorney in charge of the indictment bureau that the case was a lemon, and the latter would probably throw it out, of his own motion. The D. A.'s office didn't want any more rotten cases to prosecute than it could help. This seemed his one best bet, the only way to get his feet out of the flypaper. What a mess for a few pieces of rotten beef!

"You understand what is being done, do you?" inquired the keen-faced judge sharply. "You understand this means that, unless you give bail, you will have to stay in jail until the grand jury dismisses the case or finds an indictment against you?"

Underneath the cornice of the judge's dais Hogan patted his arm, and Tony, glancing for encouragement at the big friendly face above him, whispered "Yes."

So Tony went to the Tombs and was lodged in a cell next door to "Soko the Monk," who had nearly beaten a Chinaman to death with a pair of brass knuckles, from whom he learned much that was exciting, if not edifying.

Now, as Delany was wont to say for years thereafter, that damn Mathusek case just went bad on him. He had believed that in the comparative secrecy of the inquisitorial chamber he could easily pretend that he had originally made an honest mistake and was no longer positive of the defendant's identity, in which event when the grand jury threw out the case nobody would ever know the reason, and no chickens would come home to roost on him.

But when the cop visited the office of Deputy District Attorney Caput Magnus the next morning to inform him that this here window-breaking case was "a Messina," he found Mr. Nathan Asche already solidly there present, engaged in advising Mr. Magnus most emphatically to the exact contrary. Indeed the attorney was rhetorical in his insistence that this destruction of the property of law-abiding taxpayers must stop.

Mr. Asche was not a party to be trifled with. He was a rectangular person whom nothing could budge, and his very rectangularity bespoke his stubborn rectitude. His shoulders were massive and square, his chin and mouth were square, his burnsides were cut, and he had a square head and wore a square-topped derby. He looked like the family portrait of Uncle Amos Hardscrabble. When he sat down he remained until he had said his say. It was an unfortunate meeting for Delany, for Asche nailed him upon the spot and made him repeat to Caput Magnus the story of how he had seen Tony throw the brick, and then, for some fool reason, not being satisfied to let it go at that, he insisted on calling in a stenographer and having Delany swear to the yarn in affidavit form! This entirely spoiled any chance the policeman might otherwise have had of changing his testimony. He now had no choice but to go on and swear the case through before the grand jury—which he did.

Even so, that distinguished body of twenty-three representative citizens was not disposed to take the matter very seriously. Having heard what Delany had to say—and he made it good and strong under the circumstances—several of them remarked disgustedly that they did not understand why the district attorney saw fit to waste their valuable time with trivial cases of that sort. Boys would play ball, and boys would throw balls round; if not balls, then stones.

They were about to dismiss by an almost unanimous vote, when the case went bad again. The foreman, a distinguished person in braided broadcloth, arose and announced that he was very much interested to learn his fellow grand jurors' views upon this subject as he was the president of a casualty company, and he wished them to understand that thousands—if not hundreds of thousands—of dollars' worth of plate-glass windows were wantonly broken by young toughs every year, for which his and other insurance companies had to recoup the owners. In fact, he alleged heatedly, window breaking was a sign of peculiar viciousness. Incipient criminals usually started their infamous careers that way; you could read that in any book on penology. An example ought to be made. He'd bet this feller who threw the brick was a gangster.

So his twenty-two fellow grand jurymen politely permitted him to recall Officer Delany and ask him: "Say, officer, isn't it a fact— just tell us frankly now—if this feller Mathusek isn't a gangster?"

"Sure, he's a gangster. He was blowin' about it to me after I arrested him," swore Delany without hesitation.

The foreman swept the circle with a triumphant eye.

"What'd I tell you?" he demanded. "All in favor of indicting said Tony Mathusek for malicious destruction of property signify in the usual manner. Cont'ri-minded? It's a vote. Ring the bell, Simmons, and bring on the next case."

So Tony was indicted by the People of the State of New York for a felony, and a learned judge of the General Sessions set his bail at fifteen hundred dollars; and Hogan had his victim where he wanted him and where he could keep him, until he had bled his mother white of all she had or might ever hope to have in this world.

Everybody was satisfied,—Hogan, Simpkins, Asche, McGurk,

even Delany, because the fleas upon his back were satisfied and he was planning ultimately to get rid of the whole damn tangle by having the indictment quietly dismissed, when nobody was looking, by his friend O'Brien, to whom the case had been sent for trial. And everything being as it should be, and Tony being safely locked up in a cell, Mr. Joey Simpkins set himself to the task of extorting three hundred and fifty dollars more from Mrs. Mathusek, upon the plea that the great Mr. Hogan could not possibly conduct the case before a jury for less.

Now the relations of Mr. Assistant District Attorney O'Brien and the Hon. Raphael B. Hogan were distinctly friendly. At any rate, whenever Mr. Hogan asked for an adjournment in Mr. O'Brien's court he usually got it without conspicuous difficulty, and that is what occurred on the five several occasions that the case of The People vs. Antonio Mathusek came up on the trial calendar during the month following Tony's incarceration, on each of which Mr. Hogan with unctuous suavity rose and humbly requested that the case be put over at his client's earnest request in order that counsel might have adequate time in which to subpœna witnesses and prepare for a defense.

And each day Simpkins, who now assumed a threatening and fear-some demeanor toward Mrs. Mathusek, visited the heartsick woman in her flat and told her that Tony could and would rot in the Tombs until such time as she procured three hundred and fifty dollars. The first week she assigned her life-insurance money; the second she pawned the furniture; until at last she owed Hogan only sixty-five dollars. At intervals Hogan told Tony that he was trying to force the district attorney to try the case, but that the latter was insisting on delay.

In point of fact, O'Brien had never looked at the papers, much less made any effort to prepare the case; for if he had, he would have found that there was no case at all. And Delany's mind became at peace, because he perceived that at the proper psychological moment he could go to O'Brien and whisper: "Say, Mr. O'Brien, that Mathusek case. It's a turn-out! Better recommend it for dismissal," and O'Brien would do so, for the simple reason that he never did any more work than he was actually compelled to do.

But as chance would have it, three times out of the five, Mr. Ephraim Tutt happened to be in court when Mr. Hogan rose and made his request for an adjournment; and he remembered it because the offense charged was such an odd one,—breaking a window. Delany's simple plan was again defeated by Nemesis, who pursued him in the shape of the rectangular Mr. Asche. The latter shouldered himself into O'Brien's office during the fifth week of Tony's imprisonment and wanted to know why in hell he didn't try that Mathusek case and get rid of it. The assistant district attorney had just been called down by his official boss and, being still sore, was glad of a chance to take it out on someone else.

"D'you think I've nothin' better to do than try your damned old window-busting cases?" he sneered. "Who ever had the idea of indicting a boy for that sort of thing, anyhow?"

"That is no way to talk," answered Mr. Asche with firmness. "You're paid to prosecute whatever cases are sent to you. This is one of 'em. There's been too much delay. Our president will be annoyed."

"Oh, he will, will he?" retorted O'Brien, nevertheless coming to the instant decision that he had best find some other excuse than mere disinclination. "If he gets too shirty I'll tell him the case came in here without any preparation and, being in the nature of a private prosecution, we've been waiting for you to earn your fee. How'll you like that, eh?"

Mr. Asche became discolored.

"H'm!" he replied softly. "So that is it, is it? You won't have that excuse very long, even if you could get away with it now. I'll have a trial brief and affidavits from all the witnesses ready for you in forty-eight hours."

"All right, old top!" nodded O'Brien carelessly. "We always strive to please!"

So Mr. Asche got busy, while the very same day Mr. Hogan asked for and obtained another adjournment.

Some people resemble animals; others have a geometrical aspect. In each class the similarity tends to indicate character. So Mr. Asche, being rectilinear, was on the square; just as Mr. Hogan, being soft and round, was slippery and hard to hold. Three days passed, during which Mrs. Mathusek grew haggard and desperate. She was saving at the rate of two dollars a day, and at that rate she would be able to buy Tony a trial in five weeks more. She had exhausted her possibilities as a borrower. The indictment slept in O'Brien's tin file. Nobody but Tony, his mother and Hogan remembered that there was any such case, except Mr. Asche, who one afternoon appeared unexpectedly in the offices of Tutt & Tutt, the senior partner of which celebrated law firm happened to be advisory counsel to the Tornado Casualty Company.

"I just want you to look at these papers, Mr. Tutt," Mr. Asche said, and his jaw looked squarer than ever.

Mr. Tutt was reclining as usual in his swivel chair, his feet crossed upon the top of his ancient mahogany desk.

"Take a stog!" he remarked without getting up, and indicating with his toe the box, which lay open adjacent to the Code of Criminal Procedure. "What's your misery?"

"Hell's at work!" returned Mr. Asche, solemnly handing over a sheaf of affidavits. "I never smoke."

Mr. Tutt somewhat reluctantly altered his position from the horizontal to the vertical and reached for a fresh stogy. Then his eye caught the name of Raphael B. Hogan.

"Tutt, Tutt! Come in here!" shouted the head of the firm. "Mine enemy hath been delivered into mine hands!"

"Hey? What?" inquired Tutt, popping across the threshold. "Who —I mean——"

"Raphael B. Hogan!"

"The devil!" ejaculated Tutt.

"You've said it!" declared Mr. Asche devoutly.

That evening Mr. Ephraim Tutt, under cover of darkness, descended from a dilapidated taxi at the corner adjacent to Froelich's butcher-shop, and several hours later was whisked uptown again to the brownstone dwelling occupied by the Hon. Simeon Watkins, the venerable white-haired judge then presiding in Part I of the General Sessions, where he remained until what may be described either as a very late or a very early hour, and where, during the final period of his intercourse, he and that distinguished member of the judiciary emptied an ancient bottle containing a sparkling rose-colored liquid of great artistic beauty.

Then Mr. Tutt returned to his own library at the house on Twenty-third Street and paced up and down before the antiquated open grate, inhaling quantities of what Mr. Bonnie Doon irreverently called "hay smoke," and pondering deeply upon the evils that men do to one another, until the dawn peered through the windows and he bethought him of the all-night lunch-stand round the corner on Tenth Avenue, and there sought refreshment.

"Salvatore," he remarked to the smiling son of the olive groves who tended that bar of innocence, "the worst crook in the world is the man who does evil for mere money."

"*Si, Signor Tutti*," answered Salvatore with Latin perspicacity. "You gotta one, eh? You giva him hell?"

"*Si! Si!*" replied Mr. Tutt cheerily. "Even so! And of a truth, moreover!"

"People versus Mathusek?" inquired Judge Watkins some hours later on the call of the calendar, looking quite vaguely and as if he had never heard of the case before, around Part I, which was as usual crowded, hot, stuffy and smelling of unwashed linen and prisoners' lunch. "People versus Mathusek? What do you want done with this case, Mr. O'Brien?"

"Ready!" chanted the red-headed O'Brien, and, just as the judge had expected, the Hon. Raphael Hogan lumbered up in his slow, genial way and said: "If Your Honor please, the defendant would like a few days longer to get his witnesses. Will Your Honor kindly adjourn the case for one week?"

He did not notice that the stenographer was taking down everything that he said.

"I observe," remarked Judge Watkins with apparent amiability, "that you have had five adjournments already. If The People's witnesses are here I am inclined to direct you to proceed. The defendant has been under indictment for six weeks. That ought to be long enough to prepare your defense."

"But, Your Honor," returned Hogan with pathos, "our witnesses are very hard to find. They are working people. I have spent whole evenings chasing after them. Moreover, the defendant is perfectly satisfied to have the case go over. He is anxious for an adjournment!"

"When did you last see him?"

"Yesterday afternoon."

The judge unfolded the papers and appeared to be reading them for the first time. He wasn't such a bad old actor himself, for he had already learned from Mr. Tutt that Hogan had not been near Tony for three weeks.

"Um—um! Did you represent the defendant in the police court?"

"Yes, Your Honor."

"Why did you waive examination?"

Hogan suddenly felt a lump swelling in his pharynx. What in hell was it all about?

"I—er—there was no use in fighting the case there. I hoped the grand jury would throw it out," he stammered.

"Did anybody ask you to waive examination?"

The swelling in Hogan's fat neck grew larger. Suppose McGurk or Delany were trying to put something over on him!

"No! Certainly not!" he replied unconvincingly. He didn't want to make the wrong answer if he could help it.

"You have an—associate, have you not? A Mr. Simpkins?"

"Yes, Your Honor." Hogan was pale now and little beads were gathering over his eyebrows.

"Where is he?"

"Downstairs in the magistrate's court."

"Officer," ordered the judge, "send for Mr. Simpkins. We will suspend until he can get here."

Then His Honor occupied himself with some papers, leaving Hogan standing alone at the bar trying to work out what it all meant. He began to wish he had never touched the damn case. Everybody in the court room seemed to be looking at him and whispering. He was most uncomfortable. Suppose that crooked cop had welshed on him! At the same instant, in the back of the room, a similar thought flashed through the mind of Delany. Suppose Hogan should welsh on him! Coincidentally both scoundrels turned sick at heart. Then came to each the simultaneous realization that neither could gain anything by giving the other away, and that the only thing possible for either was to stand pat. No, they must hang together or assuredly hang separately. Then the door opened and a tall officer entered, followed by a very nervous Mr. Joey Simpkins.

"Come up here!" directed the judge. "You are Mr. Hogan's assistant, are you not?"

"Yes, sir!" quavered the anxious Simpkins.

"How much money have you taken from Mrs. Mathusek?"

"Four hundred and thirty-five dollars."

"For what?" sharply.

"For protecting her son."

"Where? How?"

"Why—from his arrest to the present time—and for his defense here in General Sessions."

"Have either you or Mr. Hogan done anything as yet—except to waive examination in the police court?"

Mr. Simpkins turned hastily to Mr. Hogan, who realized that things were going badly.

"Your Honor," he interposed thickly, "this money was an agreed fee for my services as counsel. This examination seems to me somewhat uncalled for and unfair."

"Call Tony Mathusek to the bar!" suddenly ordered the judge.

It was a dangerous play, but Hogan decided to bluff it through.

"I view of the fact that I have not received my fee I shall refuse to appear for the defendant!" he announced brazenly.

"Indeed!" retorted the judge with sarcasm. "Then I will assign Mr. Ephraim Tutt to the defense. You two gentlemen will please sit down—but not leave the court room. We may need you."

At that moment, just as the defendant was led to the bar, Mr. Tutt emerged from behind the jury box and took his stand at Tony's side. Nothing much to look at before, the boy was less so now, with the prison pallor on his sunken little face. There was something about the thin neck, the half-open mouth and the gaunt, blinking, hollow eyes that suggested those of a helpless fledgling.

"Impanel a jury!" continued the judge, and Mr. Tutt conducted Tony inside the rail and sat down beside him at the table reserved for the defendant.

"It's all right, Tony!" he whispered. "The frame-up isn't on you this time, my lad."

Cowering in the back of the room, Delany tried to hide himself among the spectators. Some devilish thing had gone wrong. He hadn't heard all that passed between the judge and Hogan, but he had caught enough to perceive that the whole case had gone flooy.

Judge Watkins was wise! He was going after Hogan, just as old Tutt would go after him, Delany. There was a singing in his head and the blood smarted in his eyes. He'd better beat it! Half-bent over he started sneaking for the door.

"Who is that man trying to go out?" shouted the judge in tones that shook Delany to the ankles. Hastily he tried to sit down.

"Bring that man to the bar!"

Half-blind with fear, Delany attempted to make a show of bravado and swagger to the rail.

"What is your name?"

"Delany. Officer attached to the Second Precinct."

"What were you leaving the room for?"

Delany could not answer. His wits were befogged, his throat numb. He simply stared vacuously at Judge Watkins, his lips vibrating with fear.

"Sit down. No; take the stand!" cried Judge Watkins. "I'll try this case myself."

As if his foot were already attached to a ball and chain, Delany dragged himself up—up—hundreds of feet up, it seemed—to the witness chair. As if from a mountain-side he saw dim forms moving into the jury box, heard the judge and Mr. Tutt exchanging meaningless remarks. The faces before him grinned and gibbered at him like a horde of monkeys. They had got him at last—all for a few pieces of rotten beef! That lean, old fox on the bench would tear his tongue out by the roots if he even opened his mouth; claw wide open his vitals. And old Tutt was fixing him with the eye of a basilisk and slowly turning him to stone. Somebody sure had welshed! He had once been in a side-show at Coney Island where the room simulated the motion of an ocean steamer. The court-room began to do the same—slanting this way and that and spinning obliquely round and round. Through the swirl of its gyrations he could see old Tutt's vulture eyes, growing bigger, fiercer, more sinister every instant. It was all up with him! It was an execution, and the crowd down below were thirsting for his blood, waiting to tear him to bits!

"You saw this boy throw a brick through Mr. Froelich's window, didn't you?" coaxed Judge Watkins insinuatingly. Delany sensed that the old white fox was trying to trick him—get him for perjury. No! He wouldn't perjure himself again! No! But what could he do? His head swung stupidly, swaying like a dazed bull's. The sweat poured from every pore in his vast bulk. A hoarse noise—like a death-rattle—came from his throat. The room dissolved in waves of white and black. Then, in a vertigo, he toppled forward and pitched headlong to the floor.

Deacon Terry, star reporter for the *Tribune*, who happened to be there, told his city editor at noon that he had never passed such a pleasant morning. What he saw and heard really constituted, he alleged, a great, big, full, front-page story "in a box"—though it got only four sticks on the eleventh page—being crowded out by a breach of promise suit. Why, he said, it was the damnedest thing ever! There had been no evidence against the defendant at all! And, after the cop had collapsed, Judge Watkins had refused to dismiss the case and had directed Mr. Tutt to go on in his own way.

The proceeding had resolved itself into a criminal trial of Hogan and Simpkins. Tony's good character had been established in three minutes, and then half a dozen reputable witnesses had testified that the brick had been thrown by an entirely different boy. Finally, Sussman and his assistant both swore positively that Delany had been in the back of the tobacco shop, with his back to the door, holding them up for cigars, when the crash came.

Terry wanted two columns; he almost cried when they cut his "great, big, full-page story" to:

SHYSTERS ACCUSED OF EXTORTION

A dramatic scene was enacted at the conclusion of a minor case in Part I of the General Sessions yesterday, when upon the motion of Ephraim Tutt, of the firm of Tutt & Tutt, Judge Simeon Watkins, sitting as a committing magistrate, held for the action of the grand jury Raphael B. Hogan and Joseph P. Simpkins, his assistant, for the crime of extortion, and directed that their case be referred to the Grievance Committee of the County Lawyers' Association, for the necessary action for their disbarment.

Earlier in the trial a police officer named Delany, the supposed chief witness for the prosecution, fainted and fell from the witness chair. Upon his recovery he was then and there committed for perjury, in default of ten thousand dollars bail. It is understood that he has signified his willingness to turn state's evidence, but that his offer has not been accepted. So far as can be ascertained, this is the first time either Hogan or Simpkins has been accused of a criminal offense. District Attorney Peckham stated that, in addition to separate indictments for extortion and perjury, he would ask for another, charging all three defendants with the crime of conspiracy to obstruct the due administration of the law.

At the conclusion of the proceedings Judge Watkins permitted a voluntary collection on behalf of the accused to be taken up by Mr. Tutt from among the jury, the court attendants and the spectators, which amounted to eleven hundred and eighty-nine dollars. In this connection the judge expressed the opinion that it was unfortunate that persons falsely accused of crime and unjustly imprisoned should have no financial redress other than by a special act of the legislature. The defendant in the case at bar had been locked up for six weeks. Among the contributions was found a new one-thousand-dollar bill.

"Talk about crime!" quoth the Deacon savagely to Charlie Still, of the *Sun*. "That feckless fool at the city desk committed assault, mayhem and murder on that story of mine!" Then he added pensively: "If I thought old man Tutt would slip me a thousand to soothe my injured feelings, I'd go down and retain his firm myself!"

"THAT SORT OF WOMAN"

"Judge not according to the appearance."—JOHN VII:24

"Tutt," said Mr. Tutt, "I see by the morning paper that Payson Clifford has departed this life."

"You don't say!" replied the smaller Tutt, glancing up from the letter he was writing. "Which one,—Payson, Senior, or Payson, Junior?"

"Payson, Senior."

"In that case, it's too bad."

"Why 'in that case'?" queried his partner.

"Oh, the son isn't so much of a much! I don't say the father was so much of a much, either. Payson Clifford was a good fellow—even if he wasn't our First Citizen—or likely to be a candidate for that position in the Hereafter. But that boy——"

"Shh!" reproved Mr. Tutt, shaking his head. "Remember that there's one thing worse than to speak ill of the dead, and that's to speak ill of a client!"

Mr. Payson Clifford, the client in question, was a commonplace young man, who had been carefully prepared for the changes and chances of this mortal life, first at a Fifth Avenue day school in New York City, afterwards at a select boarding school among the rock-ribbed hills of the Granite State, and finally at Cambridge, Massachusetts, in the cultured atmosphere of Harvard College. He emerged with a perhaps almost prudish distaste for the ugly, the vulgar, and the unclean,—and with distinct delusions of grandeur.

His mother had died when he was still a child and he preserved her memory as the most sacred treasure of his inner shrine. He could just recall her as a gentle and dignified presence, in contrast with whom his burly, loud-voiced father had always seemed crass and ordinary. And although it was that same father who had, for as long as he could remember, supplied him with a substantial check upon the first day of every month, and had thus enabled him to achieve that exalted state of intellectual and spiritual superiority

49

which he had in fact attained, nevertheless, Payson rather looked down on the old man, who palpably suffered from lack of the advantages which he had furnished to his son.

Payson, Sr., had never taken any particular pains to alter his son's opinion of himself. On the whole, he was more proud of him than otherwise, recognizing that, while he obviously suffered from an overdevelopment of the ego and an excessive fastidiousness in dress, he was at bottom clearly all right and a good sort. Still, he was forced to confess that there wasn't much between them. Payson, Jr., expressed the same thought more elegantly by regretting that his father "did not speak his language."

So, in the winter vacation, when Payson, Sr., fagged from his long day at the office sought the "Frolics" or the "Follies," Payson, Jr., might be seen at a chamber programme for the harpsichord and viola, or of Palestrina or the Earlier Gregorian Chants. Had he been less supercilious about it this story would never have been written,—doubtless no great loss at that. But it is the prerogative of youth to be arrogantly merciless in its judgment of the old. Its bright lexicon has no verdict "with mitigating circumstances." Youth is just when it is right; it is cruel when it is wrong; and it is inexorably in any case. If we are ever to be tried for our crimes, let us have juries of white-whiskered old boys who like tobacco, crab-flakes, light wines and musical comedy.

All of which leads up to the sad admission upon our part that Payson, Jr., was a prig. And in the very middle of his son's priggishness Payson, Sr., up and died, and Tutt and Mr. Tutt were called upon to administer his estate.

There may be concealed somewhere a few human beings who look back upon their treatment of their parents with honest satisfaction. I have never met any. It is the fate of those who bring others into the world to be chided for their manners, abused for their mistakes, and pilloried for their faults. Twenty years difference in age turns many an elegance into a barbarism; many a virtue into a vice-versa. I do not perform at breakfast, for the edification of my offspring, upon the mustache cup, but I chew my strawberry seeds, which they claim is worse. My grandpapa and grandmama used to pour the coffee from their cups and drink it from their saucers and they were—nevertheless—rated A1 in Boston's Back Bay Blue Book. No man is a hero to his children. He has far more chance with his valet,—if in these days he can afford to keep one.

His father's death was a shock to Payson, Jr., because he had not

supposed that people in active business like that ever did die,—
they "retired" instead, and after a discreet period of semi-seclusion,
disintegrated by appropriate stages. But Payson, Sr., simply died
right in the middle of everything—without any chance of a spiritual
understanding—"reconciliation" would be inaccurate—with his son.
So, Payson, Jr., protestingly acquired, by part cash and balance
credit, a complete suit of what he scathingly described as "the barbarous panoply of death" and followed Payson, Sr., to the grave.

Perhaps, after all we have been a bit hard on Payson, Jr. He was
fundamentally, as his father had perceived, good stuff, and wanted
to do the right thing. But what is the right thing? Really, it isn't
half so hard to be good as to know how.

As the orphaned Payson, ensconced in lonely state in one of the
funeral hacks, was carried at a fast trot down Broadway towards
the offices of Tutt & Tutt, he consoled himself for his loss with the
reflection that this was, probably, the last time he would ever have
to see any of his relatives. Never in his short life had he been face
to face with such a gathering of unattractive human beings. He
hadn't imagined that such people existed. They oughtn't to exist.
The earth should be a lovely place, its real estate occupied only by
cultured and lovely people.

These æsthetic considerations reminded him with a shock that,
just as he had been an utter stranger to them, so he had been a
stranger to his father—his poor, old, widowed father. What did he
really know about him?—not one thing! And he had never tried to
find out anything about him,—about his friends, his thoughts, his
manner of life,—content merely to cash his checks, under the unconscious assumption that the man who drew them ought to be equally
content to be the father of such a youth as himself. Up at Harvard,
he had stood rather grandly on his name—"Payson Clifford, Jr.,"—
with no questions asked about the "Senior" or anybody else. He
now perceived that he was to be thrown out into the world of fact,
where who and what his father had been might make a lot of difference. Rather anxiously he hoped the old gentleman would turn out
to have been all right;—and would have left enough of an estate so
that he could still go on cashing checks upon the first day of every
month!

It was one of the unwritten laws of the office of Tutt & Tutt
that Mr. Tutt was never to be bothered about the details of a probate matter, and it is more than doubtful whether, even if he had

tried, he could have correctly made out the inventory of an estate in the Surrogate's Court. For be it known that, while the senior member of the firm was long on the philosophy of the law and the subtleties of "restraints on alienation," "powers," "perpetuities" and the mysteries of "the next eventual estate," he was frankly short on the patience to add and subtract. So, while Mr. Tutt drew the clients' wills, it was Tutt who attempted to probate and execute them. Then, if by any chance, there was any trouble or some ungrateful relative thought he hadn't got enough, it was Mr. Tutt who reluctantly tossed away his stogy, strolled over to court and defended the will which he had drawn,—usually with success.

So it was the lesser Tutt who wrung the hand of Payson Clifford and gave him the leathern armchair by the window.

"And now about the will!" chirped Tutt, when, after a labored encomium upon the virtues of Payson, Senior, deceased, he took the liberty of lighting a cigarette before he commenced to read the instrument which lay in a brown envelope upon the desk before him. "I suppose you are already aware that your father has made you his executor and, after a few minor legacies, the residuary legatee of his entire estate?"

Payson shook his head mutely. He felt it more becoming under the circumstances to pretend to be ignorant of these things.

"Yes," continued Tutt cheerfully, taking up the envelope, "Mr. Tutt drew the will nearly fifteen years ago, and your father never thought necessary to change it. It's lain right there in our 'Will Box' without being disturbed more than once, and that was seven or eight years ago, when he came in one day and asked to be allowed to look at it,—I think he put a letter in with it. I found one there the other day."

Payson languidly took the will in his hand.

"How large an estate did he leave?" he inquired.

"As near as I can figure out, about seventy thousand dollars," answered Tutt. "But the transfer tax will not be heavy, and the legacies do not aggregate more than ten thousand."

The instrument was a short one, drawn with all Mr. Tutt's ability for compression, and filling only a single sheet. Payson's father had bequeathed seventy-six hundred dollars to his three cousins and their children, and everything else he had left to his son. After settling the bills against the estate, including that of Tutt & Tutt, he would probably get at least sixty thousand out of it. At the current rate he would continue to be quite comfortable,—more so in fact than heretofore. Still, it was less than he had expected. Perhaps his father had had expensive habits.

"Here's the letter," went on Tutt, handing it to Payson, who took out his pen-knife to open it the more neatly. "Probably a suggestion as to the disposal of personal effects,—remembrances or something of the sort. It's often done."

The envelope was a cheap one, ornamented in the upper lefthand corner with a wood-cut showing a stout goddess in a nightdress, evidently meant for Proserpina, pouring a Niagara of grain out of a cornucopia of plenty over a farmland stacked high with apples, corn, and pumpkins, and flooded by the beams of a rising sun with a real face. Beneath were the words:

> If not delivered in five days return to
> Clifford, Cobb & Weng,
> Grain Dealers and Produce
> 597 Water Street,
> N. Y. City,
> N. Y.

Even as his eye fell upon it Payson was conscious of its coarse vulgarity. "Weng"! Whoever heard of such a name? He certainly had not,—hadn't even known that his father had a partner with such an absurd cognomen! "—& Weng"! There was something terribly plebeian about it. As well as about the obvious desire for symmetry which had led to the addition of that superfluous "N. Y." below the entirely adequate "N. Y. City." But, of course, he'd be glad to do anything his father requested.

He forced the edge of the blade through the tough fibre of the envelope, drew forth the enclosed sheet, and unfolded it. In the middle of the top was a replica of the wood-cut upon the outside, only minus the "If not delivered in five days return to." Then Payson read in his father's customary bold scrawl the simple inscription, doomed to haunt him sleeping and waking for many moons:—

> In case of my sudden death I wish my executor to give twenty-five thousand dollars to my very dear friend Sadie Burch, of Hoboken, N. J.
>
> PAYSON CLIFFORD

For a brief—very brief—moment, a mist gathered over the letter in the son's hand. "My dear friend Sadie Burch!" He held back the exclamation of surprise that rose to his lips and endeavored to suppress any facial evidence of his inner feelings. "Twenty-five thousand!" Then he held out the letter more or less casually to Tutt.

"Wee-e-ll!" whistled the lawyer softly, with a quick glance from under his eyebrows.

"Oh, it isn't the money!" remarked Payson in a sickly tone, although of course he was lying. It *was* the money.

The idea of surrendering nearly half his father's estate to a stranger staggered him; yet to his eternal credit, in that first instant of bewildered agony no thought of disregarding his father's wishes entered his mind. It was a hard wallop, but he'd got to stand it.

"Oh, that's nothing!" remarked Tutt. "It's not binding. You don't need to pay any attention to it."

"Do you really mean that that paper hasn't any legal effect?" exclaimed the boy, with such a reaction of relief that for the moment the ethical aspect of the case was entirely obscured by the legal.

"None whatever!" returned Tutt definitely.

"But it's part of the will!" protested Payson. "It's in my father's own handwriting."

"That doesn't make any difference," declared the lawyer.

"Not even if it is put right in with the will?"

"Not a particle."

"But I've often heard of letters being put with wills."

"No doubt. But I'll wager you never heard of any one of them being probated."

Payson's legal experience in fact did not reach to this technical point.

"Look here!" he returned obstinately. "I'll be hanged if I understand. You say this paper has no legal value and yet it is in my father's own hand and practically attached to his will. Now, apart from any—er—moral question involved, just why isn't this letter binding on me?"

Tutt smiled leniently.

"For the reason that, when your father executed the original document, he went through every form required by the statute for making a will. If he hadn't, it wouldn't have been a will at all. If this paper, which never was witnessed by a single person, could be treated as a supplement or addition to the will, there would have been no use requiring the original will to be witnessed, either."

"That seems logical," agreed Payson. "But isn't it often customary to incorporate other papers by referring to them in a will?"

"It is sometimes done, and usually results in nothing but litigation. You see for yourself how absurd it would be to treat a paper, drawn or executed after a will was made, as part of it, for that would render the requirements of the statute nugatory."

"But suppose the letter was already in existence or was written at the same time as the will,—wouldn't that make a difference?" hesitated Payson.

"Not a bit! Not one bit!" chirped Tutt. "The law is settled that such a paper or writing can be given effect only under certain very special conditions and only to a limited extent. Anyhow, that question doesn't arise here."

"Why not?" queried the residuary legatee. "How do you know this letter wasn't written and placed inside the will when it was made? And that my father supposed that, of course, it would be given effect?"

"In that case why shouldn't he have incorporated the legacy in the will?" countered Tutt sharply.

"He—er—may not have wished Mr. Tutt to know about it," murmured Payson.

"Oh,—hardly!" protested Tutt. "We can be morally certain that this letter was written and placed with the will when your father came in here and asked to be allowed to see it, seven odd years ago. Mr. Tutt would have noticed it if your father had placed it with the will in the first instance, and would have warned him that nothing of the sort could possibly be effective."

"But," insisted Payson, "assuming for argument's sake that this letter was in fact written at the time the will was originally executed, what is the reason the law won't recognize it as a valid bequest?"

Tutt fumbled for another cigarette.

"My dear sir," he replied, "no paper could possibly be treated as part of a will—even if extant at the time the will was executed—unless distinctly referred to in the will itself. In a word, there must be a clear and unmistakable intention on the part of the testator to attempt to incorporate the extraneous paper by reference. Now, here, there is no reference to the paper in the will at all."

"That is true!" admitted Payson. "But——"

"But even if there were," went on Tutt, eagerly, "the law is settled in this State that where a testator—either through carelessness or a desire to economize space or effort, has referred in his will to extraneous papers or memoranda, either as fixing the names of beneficiaries of particular devises or bequests, or as fixing the amount or the manner in which the amount of such devises or bequests is to be ascertained, such a paper must not contain any testamentary disposition of property. In a word the testator having willed something can *identify* it by means of an extraneous paper if properly designated, but he cannot *will* the thing away by an extraneous paper, no matter how referred to. For example, if A wills to B 'all the stock covered by my agreement of May 1, with X' it merely describes and identifies the thing bequeathed,—and that is all right. The law will give effect to the identifying agreement, although it is separate from the will and unattested. But, if A's will read 'and I give such further bequests as appear in a paper filed herewith,' and the paper contained *a bequest* to B of 'all the stock covered by my agreement of May 1, with X' it would be *an attempted bequest outside of the will and so have no legal effect.*"

"Thanks," said Payson. "I understand. So in no event whatever could this letter have any legal effect?"

"Absolutely none whatever!—You're perfectly safe!" and Tutt leaned back with a comfortable smile.

But Payson did not smile in return. Neither was he comfortable. Be it said for him that while momentarily relieved at knowing that he had no legal obligation to carry out his father's wishes so far as Sadie Burch was concerned, his conscience was by no means easy and he had not at all liked the tone in which the paunchy little lawyer had used the phrase "you're perfectly safe."

"What do you mean by 'perfectly safe'?" he inquired rather coldly.

"Why, that Sadie Burch could never make you pay her the legacy, because it isn't a legal legacy. You can safely keep it. It's yours legally and morally."

"Well, is it?" asked Payson slowly. "Morally, isn't it my duty to pay over the money, no matter who she is?"

Tutt, who had tilted backward in his swivel-chair, brought both his feet to the floor with a bang.

"Of course it isn't!" he cried. "You'd be crazy to pay the slightest attention to any such vague and unexplained scrawl. Listen, young man! In the first place, you haven't any idea when your father wrote that paper, except that it was at least seven years ago. He may have changed his mind a dozen times since he wrote it. It may have been a mere passing whim or fancy, done in a moment of weakness or emotion or temporary irrationality. Indeed, it may have been made under duress. Nobody but a lawyer who has the most intimate knowledge of his clients' daily life and affairs has the remotest suspicion of— Oh, well, we won't go into that! But, the first proposition is that in no event is it possible for you to say that the request in that letter was the actual wish of your father at the time of his death. All you can say is that at some time or other it may have been his wish."

"I see!" agreed Payson. "Well, what other points are there?"

"Secondly," continued Tutt, "it must be presumed that, if your father took the trouble to retain a lawyer to have his will properly drawn and executed, he must have known: first, that it was necessary to do so in order to have his wishes carried out; and second, that no wish not properly incorporated in the will itself could have any legal effect. In other words, inferentially, he knew that this paper had no force and, therefore, it must be assumed that, if he made it that way, he intended that it should *have* no legal effect and did not intend that it should be carried out. Get me?"

"Why, yes, I think I do. Your point is that if a man knows the law and does a thing so it has no legal effect, he should be assumed to intend that it have no legal effect."

"Exactly," Tutt nodded with satisfaction. "The law is wise, based on generations of experience. It realizes the uncertainties, vagaries, and vacillations of the human mind and the opportunities afforded to designing people to take advantage of the momentary weaknesses of others, and hence, to prevent fraud and insure that only the actual final wishes of a man shall be carried out, it requires that those wishes shall be expressed in a particular, definite and formal way—in writing, signed and published before witnesses."

"You certainly make it very clear!" assented Payson. "What do executors usually do under such circumstances?"

"If they have sense, they leave matters alone and let the law take its course," answered Tutt with conviction. "I've known of more trouble—! Several instances right here in this office. In one case a widow found a paper with her husband's will expressing a wish that a certain amount of money should be given to a married woman living out in Duluth. There was nothing to indicate when the paper was written, although the will was executed only a month before he died. Apparently the deceased hadn't seen the lady in question for years. I told her to forget it, but nothing would suit her but that she should send the woman a money-order for the full amount—ten thousand dollars. She kept it, all right! Well, the widow found out afterwards that her husband had written that paper thirty years before, at a time when he was engaged to be married to that woman,

that they had changed their minds and each had married happily
and that the paper with some old love-letters had, as usually happens,
got mixed up with the will instead of having been destroyed as it
should have been.

"You know, it's astonishing, the junk people keep in their safe-
deposit boxes! I'll bet that ninety-nine out of a hundred are half full
of valueless and useless stuff, like old watches, grandpa's jet cuff-
buttons, the letters Uncle William wrote from the Holy Land, outlawed fire-insurance and correspondence that nobody will ever read,
and yet every paper a man leaves after his death is a possible source
of confusion or trouble. One can't tell how or why a person, at a
particular time, may come to express a wish in writing. It would be
most dangerous to pay attention to it. Suppose it was *not* in writing.
Morally, a wish is just as binding if spoken as if incorporated in a
letter. Would you waste any time on Sadie Burch, if she came in here
and told you that your father had expressed the desire that she should
have twenty-five thousand dollars? Not much!"

"I don't suppose so!" admitted Payson.

"Another thing!" said Tutt. "Remember this, the law would not
permit you, as executor of your father's will, to pay over this money,
if any other than yourself were the residuary legatee. You'd have
no right to take twenty-five thousand dollars out of the estate and
give it to Miss Burch at the expense of anybody else!"

"Then you say the law won't let me pay this money to Sadie
Burch, whether I am willing to or not?" asked Payson.

"Not as executor. As executor you're absolutely obliged to carry
out the terms of the will and disregard anything else. You must preserve the estate intact and turn it over unimpaired to the residuary
legatee!" repeated Tutt.

"But I am the residuary legatee!" said Payson.

"As executor, you've got to pay it over in full to yourself as
residuary legatee!" repeated Tutt, stubbornly, evading the issue.

"Well, where does that leave me?" asked his client.

"It gets you out of your difficulty, doesn't it?" asked Tutt. "Don't
borrow trouble! Don't—if you'll pardon my saying so—be an idiot!"

There was silence for several minutes, finally broken by the
lawyer, who came back to the charge with renewed vigor.

"Why, this sort of thing comes up all the time. Take this sort of
a case, for instance. The law only lets a man will away a certain
proportion of his property to charity,—says it isn't right for him
to do more, if he leaves a family. Now suppose your father had

given all his property to charity, would you feel obliged to impoverish yourself for the benefit of a Home for Aged Mariners?"

"Really," replied the bewildered Payson, "I don't know. But anyway, I'm satisfied you're quite right and I'm tremendously obliged. However," he added musingly, "I'd rather like to know who this Sadie Burch is!"

"If I were you, young man," advised the lawyer sagely, "I wouldn't try to find out!"

Mr. Payson Clifford left the offices of Tutt & Tutt more recalcitrant against fate and irritated with his family than when he had entered them. He had found himself much less comfortably provided for than he had expected, and the unpleasant impression created by the supposed paternal relatives at his father's funeral had been heightened by the letter regarding Sadie Burch. It would have been bad enough to have had to consider the propriety of paying over a large sum to a lady calling herself by an elegant, or at least debonair, name like Claire Desmond or Lillian Lamar,—but Sadie! And Burch! Ye gods! It was ignoble, sordid. That was a fine discovery to make about one's father!

As he walked slowly up Fifth Avenue to his hotel it must be confessed that his reflections upon that father's memory were far from filial. He told himself that he'd always suspected something furtive about the old man, who must have been under extraordinary obligations to a woman to ask his son to turn over twenty-five thousand dollars to her, when it was pretty nearly half his entire fortune! Would cut down his income from around four thousand to nearly two thousand! The more he pondered upon the matter, the more the lawyer's arguments seemed absolutely convincing. Lawyers knew more than other people about such things, anyway. You paid them for their advice, and he would doubtless have to pay Tutt for his upon this very subject, which, somehow, seemed to be rather a good reason for following it. No, he would dismiss Sadie Burch and the letter forever from his mind. Very likely she was dead anyway,—whoever she was. Four thousand a year! Not a bad income for a bachelor!

Now while our innocent young Launcelot hardened his heart against Sadie Burch, by chance that lady figured in a short but poignant conversation between Mr. Ephraim Tutt and Miss Minerva Wiggin on the threshold of the room from which he had just departed.

Miss Wiggin never trusted anybody but herself to lock up the offices, not even Mr. Tutt, and upon this particular evening she had made this an excuse to linger on, after the others had gone home, and waylay him. Such encounters were by no means infrequent and usually had a bearing upon the ethical aspect of some proposed course of legal procedure on the part of the firm.

Miss Minerva regarded Samuel Tutt as morally an abandoned and hopeless creature. Mr. Ephraim Tutt she loved with a devotion rare among a sex with whom devotion is happily a common trait, but there was a maternal quality in her affection accounted for by the fact that, although Mr. Tutt was, to be sure, an old man in years, he had occasionally an elfin, Puck-like perversity which was singularly boyish, at which times she felt it obligatory for her own self-respect to call him to order. Thus, whenever Tutt seemed to be incubating some evasion of law more subtly plausible than ordinary, she made it a point to call it to Mr. Tutt's attention. Also, whenever, as in the present case, she felt that by following the advice of the junior member a client was about to embark upon some dubious enterprise or questionable course of conduct, she endeavored to counteract his influence by appealing to the head of the firm.

During the interview between Tutt and Payson Clifford the door had been open and she had heard all of it; moreover, after Payson had gone away, Tutt had called her in and gone over the situation with her: and she regarded Tutt's advice to his client,—not the purely legal aspect of it, but the personal and persuasive part of it,—as an interference with that young gentleman's freedom of conscience.

"Dear me! I didn't know you were still here, Minerva!" exclaimed her employer as she confronted him in the outer office. "Is anything worrying you?"

"Not dangerously!" she replied with a smile. "And perhaps it's none of my business——"

"My business is thy business, my dear!" he answered. "Without you, Tutt & Tutt would not be Tutt & Tutt. My junior partner may be the eyes and legs of the firm and I may be some other portion of its anatomy, but you are its heart and its conscience. Out with it! What rascality portends? What bird of evil omen hovers above the offices of Tutt & Tutt? Has my shrewd associate counselled the robbery of a bank or the kidnapping from a widowed mother of her child?"

"Nothing quite so bad as that!" she retorted. "It's merely that

Mr. Samuel Tutt this afternoon tried to persuade a young man not to carry out his father's wishes—expressed in a legally ineffective way—and I think he succeeded, although I'm not quite sure."

"That must have been Payson Clifford," answered Mr. Tutt. "What were the paternal wishes?"

"Mr. Tutt found a letter in which the father asked the son to give twenty-five thousand dollars to a Miss Sadie Burch."

"Miss Sadie Burch!" repeated Mr. Tutt. "And who is she?"

"Nobody knows," said Miss Wiggin. "But whoever she is, our responsibility stops with advising Mr. Payson Clifford that the letter has no legal effect. Mr. Tutt went further and tried to induce Mr. Clifford not to respect the request contained in it. That, it seems to me, is going too far. Don't you think so?"

"Are you certain you never heard of this Miss Burch?" asked Mr. Tutt, peering at her sharply from beneath his shaggy eyebrows.

"Never," she replied.

"H'm!" ejaculated Mr. Tutt. "A woman in the case!"

"What sort of a young fellow is this Payson Clifford?" inquired Miss Wiggin after a moment.

"Oh, not so much of a much!" answered Mr. Tutt.

"And what was the father like?" she continued with a woman's curiosity.

"He wasn't so much of a much, either, evidently," answered Mr. Tutt.

We have previously had occasion to comment upon the fact that no client, male or female, consults a lawyer with regard to what he ought to do. Women, often having decided to do that which they ought not to do, attempt to secure counsel's approval of their contemplated course; but while a lawyer is sometimes called upon to bolster up a guilty conscience, rarely is he sincerely invited to act as spiritual adviser. Most men being worse than their lawyers, prefer not to have the latter find them out. If they have made up their minds to do a mean thing, they do not wish to run the chance of having their lawyer shame them out of it. That is their own business. And it should be! The law presents sufficiently perplexing problems for the lawyer without his seeking trouble in the dubious complexities of his client's morals!

The paradoxical aspect of the matter with Mr. Tutt was that, while he was known as a criminal lawyer, whenever he was asked for advice he concerned himself quite as much with his client's moral as his legal duty. The reason for this was probably to be found in the fact that, since he found the law so easy to circumvent, he preferred to disregard it entirely as a sanction of conduct and to ask himself merely, "Now is this what a sportsman and a gentleman would do?" The fact that a man was a technical criminal meant nothing to him at all; what interested him was whether the man was or was not a "mean" man. If he was, to hell with him! In a word, he applied to any given situation the law as it ought to be and not the law as it was. A very easy and flexible test! say you, sarcastically. Do you really think so? There may be forty different laws upon the same subject in as many different States of our political union, but how many differing points of view upon any single moral question would you find among as many citizens? The moral code of decent people is practically the same all over the terrestrial ball, and fundamentally it has not changed since the days of Hammurabi. The ideas of gentlemen and sportsmen as to what "is done" and "isn't done" haven't changed since Fabius Tullius caught snipe in the Pontine marshes.

Mr. Tutt was a crank on this general subject and he carried his enthusiasm so far that he was always tilting like Don Quixote at some imaginary windmill, dragging a very unwilling Sancho Panza after him, in the form of his reluctant partner. Moreover, he had a very keen sympathy for all kinds of outcasts, deeming most of them victims of the sins of their own, or somebody's else, fathers. Hence, when he learned from Miss Wiggin that Tutt had presumed to interfere with the financial prospects of the unknown Miss Sadie Burch, he was distinctly aggrieved. And, as luck would have it, the object of his grievance, having forgotten something, at that moment unexpectedly reentered the office to retrieve it.

"Hello, Mr. Tutt!" he exclaimed. "Not gone yet!"

His senior partner glanced at him sharply, while Miss Wiggin hastily sidestepped into the corridor.

"Look here, Tutt!" said Mr. Tutt. "I don't know just what you've been telling young Clifford, or how you've been interfering in his private affairs, but if you've been persuading him to disregard any wish of his father, plainly expressed in his own handwriting and incorporated with his will, you've gone further than you've any right to go."

"But," expostulated Tutt, "you know how dangerous it is to meddle with things like that. Our experience certainly shows that it's far wiser to let the law settle all doubtful questions than to try to guess what the final testamentary intention of a dead testator really was. Don't you remember the Dodworth case? A hypersensitive conscience cost our widowed client ten thousand dollars! I say, leave well enough alone."

" 'Well enough'! 'Well enough'!" retorted Mr. Tutt. "Are you going to constitute yourself the judge of what is 'well enough' for a young man's soul? I give you fair warning, Tutt: he's heard your side of it, but, before he gets through, he's going to hear mine as well!"

Samuel Tutt turned a faint pink in the region of his collar.

"Why, certainly, Mr. Tutt!" he stammered. "Do so, by all means!"

"You jolly well bet I will!" replied Mr. Tutt, jamming on his stovepipe.

Several days passed, however, without the subject being mentioned further, while the proper steps to probate the will were taken as usual. Payson Clifford's dilemma had no legal reaction. He had made up his mind and he was going to stick to it. He had taken the opinion of counsel and was fully satisfied with what he had done. Nobody was going to know anything about it, anyway. When the proper time came he would burn the Sadie Burch letter and forget Sadie Burch. That is, he thought he was going to and that he could. But —as Plautus says: "*Nihil est miserius quam animus hominis conscius.*"

You see, Payson Clifford, having been sent to a decent school and a decent college, irrespective of whether his father was a rotter or not, had imbibed something of a sense of humor. Struggle as he would against it, the shadow of Sadie Burch kept creeping athwart his mind. There were so many possibilities! Suppose she was in desperate straits? Hadn't he better look her up, anyhow? No, he most definitely didn't want to know anything about her! Supposing she really had rendered some service to his father for which she ought to be repaid as he had sought to repay her? These thoughts obtruded themselves upon Payson's attention when he least desired it, but they did not cause him to alter his intention to get his hooks into his father's whole residuary estate and keep it for himself. He had, you observe, a conscience, but it couldn't stand up against twenty-five thousand dollars reenforced by perfectly sound legal arguments.

No, he had a good excuse for not being a gentleman and a sportsman and he did not purpose to look for any reasons for being different. Then unexpectedly he was invited to dinner by Mr. Ephraim Tutt on West Twenty-third Street in a funny old ramshackle house with ornamental iron piazza railings covered with the withered stalks of long dead wistarias; and something happened to him. He had no suspicion, of course, what was coming to him when he went there, went merely because Mr. Tutt was one of the very few friends of his father whom he knew, and he held toward the old lawyer the same sort of patronizing attitude that he had had toward the old man. It would be a rotten dinner probably, followed by a deadly dull evening with a snuffy old fossil, who would tell him long-winded, rambling anecdotes of what New York had been like when there were wild goats in Central Park.

The snuffy old fossil, however, made no reference whatever to either old New York or wild goats,—the nearest he came to it being wild oats. Instead, he began the dreary evening by opening a cupboard on his library wall and disclosing three long bottles, from which he partially filled a shining silver receptacle containing cracked ice. This he shook with astonishing skill and vigor, meantime uttering loud outcries of "Miranda! Fetch up the mint!" Then a buxom colored lady in calico—with a grin like that which made "Aunt Sallie" famous—having appeared, panting, with two large glasses and a bundle of green herbage upon a silver salver, the old fossil poured out a seething decoction, performed an incantation over each glass with the odoriferous greens, smiled fondly upon the work of his hands and remarked with amiable hospitality, "Well, my son! Glad to see you!—Here's how!"

Almost immediately a benign animal magnetism pervaded the bosom of Payson Clifford, and from his bosom reached out through his arteries and veins, his arterioles and venioles, to the uttermost ends of his being. He perceived in an instant that Mr. Tutt was no ordinary man and his house no ordinary house; and this impression was intensified when, seated at his host's shining mahogany table with its heavy cut glass and queer old silver, he discovered that Miranda was no ordinary cook. He began to be inflated over having discovered this Mr. Tutt, who pressed succulent oysters and terrapin stew upon him, accompanied by a foaming bottle of Krug '98. He found himself possessed of an astounding appetite and a prodigious thirst.

After the terrapin, Miranda brought in a smoking wild turkey with two quail roasted inside of it, and served with currant jelly, rice-cakes, and sweet potatoes fried in melted sugar. Then, as in a dream, he heard a soul-satisfying pop and Miranda placed a tall, amber glass at his wrist and filled it with the creaming redrose wine of ancient Burgundy. He heard himself telling Mr. Tutt all about himself,—the most intimate secrets of his heart,—and saw Mr. Tutt listening attentively, almost reverently. He perceived that he was making an astonishing impression upon Mr. Tutt, who obviously thought him a great man; and after keeping him in reasonable doubt about it for a while he modestly admitted to Mr. Tutt that this was so. Then he drank several more glasses of Burgundy and ate an enormous pile of waffles covered with maple syrup. Lastly he had black coffee and some port.

It was an occasion, asserted Payson,—or—always goo' weather,— or somethin'—when goo' fellows got together! He declared with an emphasis which was quite unnecessary, but which, however, did not disturb him, that there were too few men like themselves in the world,—men with the advantage of education,—men of ideals. He told Mr. Tutt that he loved him. He no longer had a father, and, evidently relying on further similar entertainments, he wanted Mr. Tutt for one. Mr. Tutt generously assented to act in that capacity and, as the first step, assisted his guest upstairs to the library, where he opened the window a few inches.

Presently, Payson did not know how exactly, they got talking all about life, and Mr. Tutt said ruminatively that, after all, the only things that really counted were loyalty and courage and kindness, and that a little human sympathy, extended even in what sometimes seemed at first glance the wrong direction, often did more good— made more for real happiness—than the most efficient organized charity. He spoke of the loneliness of age, the inevitable loneliness of the human soul, the thirst for daily affection. And then they drifted off to college, and Mr. Tutt inquired casually if Payson had seen much of his father, who, he took occasion to remark, had been a good type of straightforward, honest, hard-working business man.

Payson, smoking his third cigar, and taking now and then a dash of cognac, began to think better of his old dad. He really hadn't paid him quite the proper attention. He admitted to Mr. Tutt— with the first genuine tears in his eyes since he had left Cambridge, that perhaps, if he had been more to him—. But Mr. Tutt veered off again, this time on university education; the invaluable function of the university being, he said, to preserve intact and untarnished in a materialistic age the spiritual ideals inherited from the past.

In this rather commonplace sentiment Payson agreed with him passionately. He further agreed with equal enthusiasm when his host advanced the doctrine that, after all, to preserve one's honor stainless was the only thing that much mattered. Absolutely! declared Payson, as he allowed Mr. Tutt to press another glass of port upon him.

Payson, in spite of the slight beading of his forehead and the blur about the gas-jets, began to feel very much of the man of the world, not a "six bottle man" perhaps, but—and he laughed complacently—a "two bottle man." If he'd lived back in the good old sporting days very likely he could have done better. But he'd taken care of two full bottles, hadn't he? Mr. Tutt replied that he'd taken care of them very well indeed. And with this opening the old lawyer launched into his favorite topic, to wit, that there were only two sorts of men in the world, gentlemen, and those who were not. What made a man a gentleman was gallantry and loyalty, the readiness to sacrifice everything—even life—to an ideal. The hero was the chap who never counted the cost to himself. That was why people revered the saints, acclaimed the cavalier, and admired the big-hearted gambler who was ready to stake his fortune on the turn of a card. There was even, he averted, an element of spirituality in the gambler's carelessness about money.

This theory greatly interested Payson, who held strongly with it, having always had a secret, sneaking fondness for gamblers. On the strength of it, he mentioned Charles James Fox—there was a true gentleman and sportsman for you! No mollycoddle—but a roaring, six bottle fellow with a big brain and a scrupulous sense of honor. Yes, sir! Charley Fox was the right sort! He managed to intimate successfully that Charley and he were very much the same breed of pup.

At this point Mr. Tutt, having carefully committed his guest to an ethical standard as far removed as possible from one based upon self-interest, opened the window a few more inches, sauntered over to the mantel, lit a fresh stogy and spread his long legs in front of the sea-coal fire, like an elongated Colossus of Rhodes. He commenced his dastardly countermining of his partner's advice by complimenting Payson on being a man whose words, manner and appearance proclaimed him to the world a true sport and a regular fellow. From which flattering prologue he slid naturally into said regular fellow's prospects and aims in life. He trusted that Payson Clifford, Senior, had left a sufficient estate to enable Payson, Junior, to complete his education at Harvard?—He forgot, he confessed, just what the residue amounted to.

Then he turned to the fire, kicked it, knocked the ash off the end of his stogy and waited—in order to give his guest a chance to come to himself,—for Mr. Payson Clifford had suddenly turned a curious color, due to the fact that he was unexpectedly confronted with the necessity of definitely deciding then and there whether he was going to line up with the regular fellows or the second-raters, the gentle-men or the cads. He realized that he had put himself at a disad-vantage, but he wasn't going to commit himself until he had had a good chance to think it all over carefully. In thirty seconds he was sober as a judge—and a sober judge at that.

"Mr. Tutt," he said in quite a different tone of voice, "I've been talking pretty big, I guess, bigger than I really am. The fact is, I've got a problem of my own that's bothering me a lot."

Mr. Tutt nodded understandingly.

"You mean Sadie Burch."

"Yes."

"Well, what's the problem? Your father wanted you to give her the money, didn't he?"

Payson hesitated. What he was about to say seemed so disin-genuous, even though it had originated with Tutt & Tutt.

"How do I know really what he wanted? He may have changed his mind a dozen times since he put that letter with his will."

"If he had he wouldn't have left it there, would he?" asked Mr. Tutt with a smile.

"But perhaps he forgot all about it,—didn't remember that it was there," persisted the youth, still clinging desperately to the lesser Tutt. "And, if he hadn't, would have torn it up."

"That might be equally true of the provisions of his will, might it not?" countered the lawyer.

"But," squirmed Payson, struggling to recall Tutt's arguments, previously so convincing, "he knew how a will ought to be executed and, since he deliberately neglected to execute the paper in a legal fashion, isn't it fair to presume that he did not intend it to have any legal force?"

"Yes," replied Mr. Tutt with entire equanimity, "I agree with you that it is fair to assume that he did not intend it to have any legal effect."

"Well, then!" exclaimed Payson exultantly.

"But," continued the lawyer, "that does not prove that he did not intend it to have a moral effect, and expect you to honor and respect his wishes, just as if he had whispered them to you with his dying breath."

There was something in his demeanor which, while courteous, had a touch of severity, that made Payson feel abashed. He perceived that he could not afford to let Mr. Tutt think him a cad, when he was really a sportsman. And in his mental floundering his brain came into contact with the only logical straw in the entire controversy.

"But," he said with an assumption of candor, "in that case, I should know positively that they were in fact my father's wishes."

"Exactly!" replied Mr. Tutt. "And then you'd carry them out without a moment's hesitation."

"Of course!" yielded Payson.

"Then the whole question is whether or not this paper does express a wish of his. That problem is a real problem, and it is for you alone to solve, and, of course, you're under the disadvantage of having a financial interest in the result, which makes it doubly hard."

"All the same," maintained the boy, "I want to be fair to myself."

"—And to him," added Mr. Tutt solemnly. "The fact that this wish is not expressed in such a way as to be legally obligatory makes it all the more binding. In a way, I suppose, that is your hard luck. You might, perhaps, fight a provision in the will. You can't fight this—or disregard it, either."

"I don't exactly see why this is any *more* binding than a provision in the will itself!" protested Payson.

Mr. Tutt threw his stogy into the fire.

"Maybe it isn't," he conceded, "but I've always liked that specious anecdote attributed to Sheridan, who paid his gambling debts and let his tailor wait. You remember it, of course? When the tailor demanded the reason for this, Sheridan told him that a gambling debt was a debt of honor and a tailor's bill was not, since his fortunate adversary at the card table had only his promise to pay, whereas the tailor possessed an action for an account, which he could prosecute in the courts.

" 'In that case,' declared the tailor, 'I'll tear up my bill!' which he did, and Sheridan thereupon promptly paid him. Have another nip of brandy?"

"No, thank you!" answered Payson. "It's getting late and I must be going. I've—I've had a perfectly—er—ripping time!"

"You must come again soon!" said Mr. Tutt warmly, from the top of the steps outside.

As Payson reached the sidewalk he looked back somewhat shame-facedly and said:

"Do you think it makes any difference what sort of a person this Sadie Burch is?"

In the yellow light of the street-lamp it seemed to the collegian as if the face of the old man bore for an instant a fleeting resemblance to that of his father.

"Not one particle!" he answered. "Good-night, my boy!"

But Payson Clifford did not have a good night by any manner of means. Instead of returning to his hotel he wandered, aimless and miserable, along the river front. He no longer had any doubt as to his duty. Mr. Tutt had demolished Tutt in a breath, and put the whole proposition clearly. Tutt had given, as it were, and Mr. Tutt had taken away. However, he told himself, that wasn't all there was to it; the money was his in law and no one could deprive him of it. Why not sit tight and let Mr. Tutt go to the devil? He need never see him again! And no one else would ever know! Twenty-five thousand dollars! It would take him years to earn such a staggering sum! Besides, there were two distinct sides to the question. Wasn't Tutt just as good a lawyer as Mr. Tutt? Couldn't he properly decide in favor of himself when the court was equally divided? And Tutt had said emphatically that he would be a fool to surrender the money.

As Payson Clifford trudged along the shadows of the docks he became obsessed with a curious feeling that Tutt and Mr. Tutt were both there before him; Mr. Tutt—a tall, benevolent figure carrying a torch in the shape of a huge, black, blazing stogy that beckoned him onward through the darkness; and behind him, Tutt—a little paunchy red devil with horns and a tail—who tweaked him by the coat and twittered, "Don't throw away twenty-five thousand dollars! The best way is to leave matters as they are and let the law settle everything. Then you take no chances!"

But in the end—along about a quarter to seven A.M.—Mr. Tutt won. Exhausted, but at peace with himself, Payson Clifford stumbled into the Harvard Club on Forty-fourth Street, ordered three fried eggs done on one side, two orders of bacon and a pot of coffee, and then wrote a letter which he dispatched by a messenger to Tutt & Tutt.

> Gentlemen, (it read): Will you kindly take immediate steps to find Miss Sarah Burch and pay over to her twenty-five thousand dollars from my father's residuary estate. I am entirely satisfied that this was his wish. I am returning to Cambridge to-day. If necessary you can communicate with me there.
> Yours very truly,
> PAYSON CLIFFORD.

One might suppose that a legatee to twenty-five thousand dollars could be readily found; but Miss Sadie Burch proved a most elusive person. No Burches grew in Hoboken according to either the telephone or the business directory, and Mr. Tutt's repeated advertisements in the newspapers of that city elicited no response. Three months went by and it began to look as if the lady had either died or permanently absented herself, and that Payson Clifford might be able to keep his twenty-five thousand with a clear conscience.

Then one day in May came a letter from a small town in the central part of New Jersey from Sadie Burch. She had, she said, only just learned, entirely by accident, that she was an object of interest to Messrs. Tutt & Tutt. Unfortunately, it was not convenient for her to come to New York City, but if she could be of any service to them she would be pleased, etc.

"I think I'll give the lady the once-over!" remarked Mr. Tutt, as he looked across the glittering bay to the shadowy hills of New Jersey. "It's a wonderful day, and there isn't much to do here. . . ."

"Sadie Burch? Sadie Burch? Sure, I know her!" answered the lanky man driving the tractor nearby, as he inspected the motor carrying Mr. Tutt. "She lives in the second house beyond the big elm—" and he started plowing again with a great clatter.

The road glared white in the late afternoon sun. On either side stretched miles of carefully cultivated fields, the air was hot, but sweet with magnolia, lilac and apple-blossoms. Miss Burch had obviously determined that, when she retired from the world of men, she would make a thorough job of it and expose herself to no temptation to return. It was eight miles from the nearest railroad. Just beyond the elms they slowed up alongside a white picket-fence enclosing an old-fashioned garden whence came the busy murmur of bees. Then they reached a gate that opened upon a red-tiled, box-bordered, moss-grown walk, leading to a small white house with blue-and-white-striped awnings. A green-and-gold lizard poked its head out of the hedge and eyed Mr. Tutt rather with curiosity than hostility.

"Does Miss Sarah Burch live here?" asked Mr. Tutt of the lizard.

"Yes!" answered a cheerful female voice from the veranda. "Won't you come up on the piazza?"

The voice was not the kind of voice Mr. Tutt had imagined as belonging to Sadie Burch. But neither was the lady on the piazza that kind of lady. In the shadow of the awning, in a comfortable rocking-chair, sat a white-haired, kindly-faced woman, knitting a baby-jacket. She looked up at him with a friendly smile.

"I'm Miss Burch," she said. "I suppose you're that lawyer I wrote to? Won't you come up and sit down?"

"Thanks," he replied, drawing nearer with an answering smile. "I can only stay a few moments and I've been sitting in the motor most of the day. I might as well come to the point at once. You have doubtless heard of the death of Mr. Payson Clifford, Senior?"

Miss Burch laid down the baby-jacket and her lips quivered. Then the tears welled in her faded blue eyes and she fumbled hastily in her bosom for her handkerchief.

"You must excuse me!" she said in a choked voice. "Yes, I read about it. He was the best friend I had in the world, except my brother John. The kindest, truest friend that ever lived!"

She looked out across the little garden and wiped her eyes again. Mr. Tutt sat down upon the moss-covered door-step beside her.

"I always thought he was a good man," he returned quietly. "He was an old client of mine, although I didn't know him very well."

"I owe this house to him," continued Miss Burch tenderly. "If it hadn't been for Mr. Clifford, I don't know what would have become of me. Now that John is dead and I'm all alone in the world this little place—with the flowers and the bees—is all I've got."

They were silent for several moments. Then Mr. Tutt said:

"No, it isn't all. Mr. Clifford left a letter with his will, in which he instructed his son to pay you twenty-five thousand dollars. I'm here to give it to you."

A puzzled look came over her face, and she shook her head.

"That was just like him!" she remarked. "But it's all a mistake. He paid me back that money five years ago. You see he persuaded John to go into some kind of a business scheme with him and they lost all they put into it—twenty-five thousand apiece. It was all we had. It wasn't his fault, but after John died Mr. Clifford made me—simply made me—let him give the money back. He must have written the letter before that and forgotten all about it!"

THE HAND IS QUICKER THAN THE EYE

"The hand is quicker than the eye."—THE MAN WITH THE THREE WALNUT SHELLS

"If any man can convince me and bring home to me that I do not think or act aright, gladly will I change; for I search after truth, by which man never yet was harmed. But he is harmed who abideth on still in his deception and ignorance."—MARCUS AURELIUS

Mr. Cephas McFee opened his safe-deposit box in the secrecy of the cubicle to which he had been escorted, and gazed with satisfaction upon its bulging contents. A warm glow rose through his fat little body at the sight of the equally fat packages of bonds and stock-certificates, and the thick bundles of notes and mortgages.

Slipped through the heavy rubber band encircling the topmost manila envelope was a roll of United States Government 4½ per cent short-term notes, which he had thrust there the week before—$25,000 of them. He remembered the amount exactly, for he had sold certain stocks upon which he had a profit of nearly $10,000, and invested the proceeds in the notes, which were practically as liquid as currency and could be disposed of anywhere at par. Then he had purchased some other securities at a lower price but equally desirable, and had paid for them with part of the notes, and he had had $25,000 of them left. He had counted them before he had slipped them under the band of the envelope, but he took them out and counted them again: $25,000.

Mr. McFee put the notes carefully in his pocket, closed the box, slid it back into its allotted resting-place among the tiers of similar receptacles in the vault outside, and climbed up to the light of day. It always gave him pleasure to visit the vault, for, no matter how his affairs had been going, the vision of his hoard not only reassured him but convinced him of his superiority to other men. In fact, his affairs never went otherwise than well, though sometimes he liked to pretend that they did, for the fun of discovering that he was mistaken.

Mr. McFee had what bankers call the "feel for money." Occasionally, it must be admitted, he felt it so hard that the Indians, buffaloes and other fauna engraved thereon squirmed in agony.

He saw everything, he remembered everything, he was sure of everything. Nobody could trick him. People often said of him, as some one once said of Macaulay, that they wished they could be as certain of anything as McFee was of everything.

In support of this general reputation for omniscience, and even for prescience, let it here be said that the day before he had figured out that Union Pacific was bound to go up, had bought two hundred shares through his brokers, Westbury & Wheatland, and had had the gratification of seeing it close at an advance of three points and a half. His visit to the vault had been for the purpose of paying for the stock with the $25,000 in 4½ per cent U. S. notes.

Mr. Westbury was reading the tape when Mr. McFee came in.

"Hello, early bird!" he exclaimed jocosely, for Mr. McFee was a valuable customer and Mr. Westbury liked to create an impression of intimacy. "Looking for worms?" Mr. McFee's thin mouth curved in the slightest suggestion of a smile.

"Nope," he answered. "I've got the worms already. Now I'm payin' for 'em."

He put his hand in his pocket and pulled out the notes.

"I wanta take up that two hundred U. P. I bought yesterday. Here's twenty-five thousand dollars in U. S. four and a halves. Gimme a receipt."

Then he ran his forefinger through the notes and counted them again.

"Twenty-five thousand," he repeated. "Take 'em!"

Mr. Westbury received the notes, counted them in turn, and nodded.

"Here, Prescott," he called to the anæmic cashier in the cage. "Here's twenty-five thousand dollars in U. S. four and a half per cents,—give Mr. McFee a receipt for them."

"Yes, sir!" responded Prescott with alacrity, for Mr. Westbury was a hard master.

He hurried forward, bowed politely to the customer, who paid no attention to him, received the notes from his employer, counted them, returned to the cage, and in a couple of minutes more came back and handed the receipt to Mr. McFee.

"I'll send the certificates over in a couple of days, as soon as we can get 'em transferred," said Mr. Westbury. "And meantime I'll dispose of the notes to our bank and credit you with the proceeds."

"Mind you don't charge me any commission!" cautioned Mr. McFee. "This ain't any stock-exchange transaction."

"Oh, that'll be all right!" agreed Mr. Westbury, smiling at the departing McFee. "Stingy little cockroach!" he added to himself.

Back in the cage, to which the light of day did not percolate, Prescott, the cashier, pinned the notes together and made the proper entries in the firm's books to cover the transaction. Then he put on his coat and hat, explained to Mr. Westbury that he was going to carry the notes over to the bank, and took the elevator to the first floor, where he went to a telephone booth and called up his wife. Their little daughter was sick and the doctor had not yet arrived when he had left for the office that morning, so he was anxious and worried. He did not like to telephone from the office because the other clerks could overhear what he said, and he was naturally sensitive.

"Is that you, Mollie! . . . Yes, it's me—Jim. How's Jennie?"

"Oh, Jim, the doctor says her temperature is a hundred and three and she may be going to have the flu, but he can't tell before noon. Couldn't you manage to get off?"

"Poor little Jennie!" he said. "I guess she'll be all right,—she's a strong kid. But I can't get away,—old Westbury would fire me if I asked him. I'll call up about twelve-thirty, though. Maybe I can sneak home at the noon hour."

His mind was full of little Jennie as he climbed up the marble steps of the Nordic Trust five minutes later and joined the surging line in front of the loan clerk's window. He was terribly sorry for Mollie, having to take care of the kid all alone. He'd noticed that Jennie's cheeks were flushed when he bent over the bed to kiss her good-by. That cursed flu—it killed people like flies—in a few hours. Jennie might die before he could get back to her! The sweat beaded his forehead under the thin hair of his half-bald head. Then the sharp voice of the loan clerk brought him abruptly to himself:

"What are you trying to do,—put something over?"

He glanced quickly up. He was in front of the window and the clerk was holding the notes which Prescott had automatically pushed through the bars.

"What do you mean?" he stammered.

"This ain't twenty-five thousand—it's only sixteen thousand," snapped the clerk. "Your slip says twenty-five thousand. Count 'em yourself. I haven't even taken the pin out."

Jim Prescott made no move to take the notes, for he could not see them. His whole body seemed suddenly to dissolve. His throat was like a thicket of nettles. He swayed—and clutched blindly at the bars of the window. Through blotches of black and yellow he saw a big marble clock dancing round in a sort of fox-trot. Eleven-fifty. The doctor would be almost there.

"Count 'em yourself, now. Get busy. Don't hold up the line all day."

Shaking, he yet managed to pull himself together sufficiently to count the notes. There was only $16,000—a ten-thousand-dollar note, a five and a one.

"Sixteen, ain't it?" demanded the clerk less harshly.

Jim nodded weakly and staggered back to the row of deposit desks against the wall opposite. He was short $9,000. The line moved forward.

"Buck up!" called the clerk over their heads, counting a bundle of certificates the while. "You'll find the other nine thousand on your desk."

But Jim knew otherwise. There was no other $9,000. Those three notes were the only notes that Mr. Westbury had given him. He must have miscounted them,—yet he had signed a receipt for $25,000. He was responsible for the money, even if he should not be accused of stealing it. He gasped for breath, struggling against a wave of nausea. He was done for,—had signed his own death warrant. He could not go back on his own signed receipt. Moreover, Mr. Westbury had also counted the notes. There was a hideous mistake somewhere. Time was needed to find it out. He mustn't lose the $16,000, anyhow. He stuffed the fist in which the notes were grasped into his pocket and held it there. Where should he go? Westbury he feared more than anybody in the world. Westbury would have him arrested. No, he must try Mr. McFee. Perhaps he, at least, would be reasonable about it and suggest some possible explanation. He couldn't tell Westbury; that would be suicide.

Yet upon the bare chance that, without knowing it, he might have left the $9,000 in notes somewhere in the cage, he sneaked back and began searching it hysterically.

"D'you turn over those notes?" inquired Westbury, going by.

"Yes, sir," stammered Jim in desperation. He must at all hazards conceal the situation from this Simon Legree.

But there was no sign of the notes upon the desk or anywhere in the cage. He got down on his hands and knees and ferreted round the floor like a pointer-dog. He looked in every possible place a dozen or twenty times. Then his nerves seemed to snap and he went wild—pulling open drawers and dumping out the contents, holding the ledgers upside down and shaking them—looking inside fastened bundles of folded papers. No,—he never had had any such notes! McFee—if he thought about it—would know that to be the fact.

He looked at the clock. It was his noon hour. He had never before in his life needed sustenance as he did now, but he had no time for food. He must find Mr. McFee at once. So he grabbed his hat and had rushed out onto the street before he realized that he did not know where the man's office was. A telephone book told him, and that suggested Mollie and the kid.

"The doctor's here now," came his wife's scared voice over the wire. "He says Jennie's got it,—but, if it don't turn into pneumonia, she'll pull through. Are you coming home?"

"What's her temperature?" he choked.

"One hundred and five," she answered. "Please come. Don't leave me alone!"

He groped his way out to the street, palsied with the fear of losing at one and the same time his child, his liberty and his honor.

Mr. McFee was not in his office, but had gone to his lunch club, they told him; and, after waiting about twenty minutes, the strain proved too great and Jim hurried over to that gloomy home of midday respectability on Pine Street known as the Down Town Association. Yes, Mr. McFee had come in, but he was lunching on the third floor with two other gentlemen.

"Please ask him to see me!" begged Prescott of the doorman, and his aspect was such that the members on their way out paused curiously to look at him. There was considerable delay before word was brought that Mr. McFee would see Jim in the top-floor hall, if he would come up.

"Well, well—what is it?" inquired McFee irritably, leading him into an empty private dining-room. "I'm right in the middle of my lunch. Couldn't you wait?"

"Mr. McFee," stuttered Jim, "are you sure you gave Mr. Westbury twenty-five thousand dollars this morning?"

McFee sprang backward, as if he had received a heavy blow.

"What! Am I sure? Of course I'm sure! I counted 'em. So did Westbury! What's more, I've got your receipt. Look here, young feller, what are you trying to put over on me?"

"I'm not trying to put over anything," pleaded Jim. "I took the notes to the bank and found there was only sixteen thousand dollars. I must have miscounted——"

Mr. McFee uttered an exclamation of derision.

"Miscounted 'em! Rats! You're short nine thousand dollars in your accounts, eh? You want to make it up out of me! Do I look like that kind of a sucker? Go tell that to the police!"

Jim swallowed hard, staring at McFee with smarting eyes. "But they're the same notes——"

"Look here," bellowed McFee. "I don't care anything about you, —you're only a marker. But I've got your receipt for twenty-five thousand dollars from Westbury & Wheatland. You want me to say they owe me only sixteen thousand dollars. What do you take me for,—a damn fool? Has Westbury sent you round here to work the baby act on me?"

"No," replied Jim faintly. "I haven't told Mr. Westbury yet."

"Why not?"

"Because I thought it was no use. He'd counted the notes. You had the receipt. If you couldn't help me, he couldn't."

"Well, he's goin' to know it almighty quick!" McFee's eye rapidly searched the room for a telephone. "There's only one person knows where that nine thousand dollars has disappeared to—and that's you. If I don't have the whole twenty-five thousand dollars back by three o'clock, I'll get a warrant out for your arrest. You've got just two hours to fix things up. Better make the most of your time."

The hard line of Cephas McFee's mouth looked like the closed door of a prison to poor Jim Prescott.

"Understand!" hissed McFee, "I mean it!"

Jim felt his way down the stairs with one hand against the wall. The jig was up. He had no defense. It was his own fault. They would claim that he had stolen the $9,000 between the office and the bank, and then invented the best excuse he could. It was certainly a hell of an excuse!

If he went back to the office, Westbury would browbeat, insult and humiliate him. Then he would be taken directly to the Tombs. If, instead, he went home he'd escape all that and have an hour at least with Mollie and his little Jennie. He'd telephone the office where they could find him. He'd forgot entirely the $16,000 in his pocket. Outside the club he started running. . . .

"Tutt," said Mr. Tutt, "after what happened in that tramp case last week I am tempted to paraphrase Ben Jonson's assertion that the Devil is an ass and declare that the Law is an ass."

"Where would that leave us lawyers?" queried Tutt dubiously. "However, I know a lot of attorneys——"

"Oh, I was only joking," returned his partner as he took a sip from his eleven-o'clock tumbler of malt extract. "However, it goes without saying that the law is archaic and more or less absurd. Anyhow, it's based on a fundamental error."

"What's that?" inquired his partner.

"Why," answered Mr. Tutt, "the idea that you can achieve justice in individual cases through the application of so-called general principles. You can't, and everybody knows you can't. No specific case ever yet fitted a general principle, any more than an individual face ever fitted a composite photograph."

"That's true," nodded Tutt. "Then again, the law draws a hard and fast line and says that everything on one side is right and everything on the other side is wrong, when really the line ought to wriggle round, and hop up and down, and make exceptions——"

"When really there oughtn't to be any line at all, you mean," retorted Mr. Tutt almost fiercely. "A thing can't be absolutely right or wrong, just or unjust, legal or illegal, any more than a human being can be absolutely good or absolutely bad. The law makes no allowances, except after a man has been convicted. We don't even have the French verdict of 'guilty under extenuating circumstances.'"

"Of course the whole idea of money damages is ridiculous," remarked Tutt, helping himself to a stogy. "Just as if the jury could compensate a mother, whose baby is run over by a fool motorist, by giving her a verdict of five or six hundred dollars!"

"Just fancy classifying a man as a criminal because he falls within some legislative definition, when another fellow ten times as bad happens not to do so," continued Mr. Tutt, ignoring the inadequacy of civil damages in favor of his particular hobby—the criminal law. "It's arrant nonsense. As an old preceptor of mine used to say, 'The code that puts one man in stripes and allows another to ride in a coach is purely artificial, and proves not a whit which is the better man.'"

"That's all right!" assented his partner. "When you come to think of it, it's pretty foolish for the law to make it murder to push a blind man off a cliff and not to make it any offense at all to let him walk over it, though by stretching out your hand you might prevent him."

"Omissions to act are almost never crimes," commented the senior partner. "You can let your neighbor's baby be run over by an oncoming train, even if you could easily snatch it out of danger and so save its life, and yet not be guilty of any offense whatever under the law."

"Or you could let your mother-in-law choke to death without sending for a doctor," grinned Tutt.

"Quite so," nodded Mr. Tutt. "It's a crime to defame a woman's character, if you write your accusation upon a slip of paper and pass it to some one else, but it's no crime—at least in New York State—to get up in a crowded meeting and ruin her forever by word of mouth."

"Yes, and it's a crime to steal a banana off a fruit-stand," contributed Tutt, "but it's no crime to borrow ten thousand dollars from a man, though you have no idea of returning it."

"You can be the meanest crook on earth and never go to jail," agreed Mr. Tutt. "Plain lying is not a crime, but lying under oath is a crime,—yet only provided it is done in a legal proceeding and relates to a material matter. Nobody on earth knows what is 'material' and what isn't."

"Yes," added Tutt eagerly. "If you steal four hundred and ninety-nine dollars out of a man's safe in the daytime it is grand larceny in the second degree and you can only get five years for it, but if you snitch a handkerchief out of the same man's pocket after sunset it is grand larceny in the first degree and you can get ten years."

"And if," commented his senior partner, "you take twenty-five dollars out of a bureau drawer it is petty larceny and you can only get a year for it."

"While a fellow who bumps into you on the street, if he has a friend with him, and grabs your cane, is guilty of robbery in the first degree—highway robbery—and can get twenty years," growled Tutt.

"But the same fellow can accuse you in print of the foulest depravity and damage your reputation beyond repair and be only guilty of a misdemeanor."

"Oh, we could sit here and knock the stuffing out of the law all day," mused Tutt. "But, since we get our living by it, we'd better leave some of it intact for next year."

Mr. Tutt smiled a little sadly.

"Jest as we may, I sometimes feel that an instrument as clumsy as the law might better be discarded entirely. Apart from the inconsequence of statutes and the absurdity of their distinctions, how can the law even pretend to dissect the delicate and complicated processes of the human brain or detect the subtle nuances that determine moral guilt or innocence? How can a jury possibly decide who is to blame as between a man and a woman, or two men or two women? Yet, in a lawsuit, one of the two has either to go to jail or give the other money. As if either of those things would heal a broken heart or even a slap in the face."

"And look at the jury," cried Tutt. "Just look at them! Ignorant, stupid, prejudiced—you wouldn't believe such people existed. But, even if they had brains, how on earth can they get at the real facts simply by listening to witnesses?"

"They can't!" ejaculated the elder.

"Now you've said something," agreed Tutt. "How can the jury decide anything? That's the whole point, so far as I'm concerned. There's no way of finding out which witnesses are telling the truth——"

"Even if they're trying to!" grumbled Mr. Tutt. "Which they generally aren't."

"I've discovered more things—after cases were all over!" mourned Tutt. "Honestly, the way some people will perjure themselves——"

"Or deceive themselves!"

"Or both," added Tutt. "Have you noticed how a woman will always testify to what she thinks ought to be so?"

"Which is entirely outside the merely physical limitations of all human testimony," supplemented Mr. Tutt. "In the first place, what a man actually sees and what he thinks he sees are two entirely different things. In the second place, he can't remember accurately what he thinks he saw; and, if he could, he never in the world would be able to tell anybody else."

"Quite right, Mr. Tutt," declared Tutt. "A thoroughgoing crook or just a plain damn fool isn't half so dangerous as a well-intentioned witness who is honestly mistaken as to what he thinks he heard or saw."

"Those are the fellows on whose testimony entirely innocent men sometimes go to jail," offered his partner.

"Look here!" said Tutt. "Speaking frankly, how much perfectly accurate testimony do you think is ever given in court?"

"None!" replied Mr. Tutt with conviction.

"I wonder, Mr. Tutt, if you would be willing to take a criminal case where there wouldn't be any prospect of a fee, simply to prevent a possible miscarriage of justice?" asked Miss Wiggin after lunch, stopping her employer on his way through the outer office. Mr. Tutt paused with his hand on the doorknob.

"That's what Tutt & Tutt are for," he answered genially. "But why do you think any injustice is likely to be done?"

"Because," replied Miss Wiggin, "I know the man and, what perhaps is even more important, I know his wife and child. They board in the same house with me."

"What is he charged with?"

"Stealing nine thousand dollars in United States four and a half per cent notes."

"If under those circumstances he still can't pay a fee, I should say that he was presumptively innocent!" remarked Mr. Tutt. "Where is he?"

"In the Tombs," answered Miss Wiggin. "He was arrested at four o'clock yesterday afternoon in his own rooms, where he had gone to be with his little girl, who was threatened with pneumonia— such a dear little child, Mr. Tutt."

The old man's face softened instantly.

"Got a little girl, has he? How old is she?"

"Only three,—with the loveliest head of yellow curls! Won't you defend him, Mr. Tutt?"

"Defend him? Of course I will," he replied. "How is the little girl?"

"Very sick indeed," answered Miss Wiggin. "He nearly went out of his mind when they took him away from her. And his wife is all alone and can't do anything for him."

"When is his case coming up?" inquired her employer.

"To-morrow morning at ten o'clock."

Mr. Tutt turned short on his heel.

"Get your hat," said he to Miss Wiggins simply, "and come along."

"You don't want me to go to the Tombs, do you?" she demanded. "I've plenty to do here."

"I'll get to the Tombs in time enough," he answered. "I want you to introduce me to that baby!"

Mr. Tutt did not return to the office until after five o'clock, and when he did he came alone. Under his instructions Miss Wiggin remained with Mrs. Prescott, to "keep her cheered up," as he said. Shortly after he had gone a trained nurse arrived, and later Mr. Tutt's own doctor happened casually in and took charge of things.

But while the feminine side of the office staff of Tutt & Tutt was ministering to the sick and needy, the old lawyer himself was very busy along other and different lines. Ten minutes' chat with Prescott had served to convince him of the latter's entire innocence as well as of the strength of the case against him. No element of proof apparently was lacking to demonstrate his guilt. Each link in the evidential chain seemed to be there.

In the first place a reputable business man had sworn out a warrant against the defendant charging him with the larceny of $9,000 in notes. Cephas McFee could have no motive in the world to make such an accusation against a stranger, if it were not true. Mr. Westbury had counted the notes. Jim had counted and receipted for them. He had lied to his employer when he told him that he had delivered the notes at the bank, and when he was arrested, having fled to his home without any explanation to his office associates, $16,000 of the original $25,000 was found still in his pocket. It was a practical confession. As old "Cap" Phelan would have said, "A dead open-and-shut case."

Yet Mr. Tutt knew that Prescott was innocent. He knew it because he had a greater faith in the man himself than in any logic or in any testimony, however damning the inference might appear. He knew it just as the general knows that his troops will win, no matter how outnumbered by the enemy divisions. But, like the general, he knew that he could not sit still and let the enemy attack; and, like the general, he set his staff instantly at work preparing for the battle of the morrow. Prescott could be as innocent as a babe unborn, but he would surely go to prison unless Mr. Tutt should be able to demonstrate that innocence.

How could he do so? That was his task, his problem. But, experienced as he was, he lost no time in taking certain preliminary steps. From a pay-station in a saloon on Lafayette Street opposite the Tombs he telephoned to the office and directed Tutt to procure immediately from a financial agency a report upon the financial status and responsibility of Cephas McFee. Bonnie Doon was ordered to cover McFee's office and not once to let that gentleman out of his sight until he retired to rest, and then to report all that said McFee had done—to Mr. Tutt personally in his library on Twenty-third Street, no matter what the hour; and Scraggs was instructed to take a ten-dollar bill and scrape an acquaintance with any one of Westbury & Wheatland's clerks who might be known to have a thirst for social intercourse.

Yet with all the definiteness of his preparations Mr. Tutt had not yet evolved any plan of campaign or decided what his line of defense was going to be. The case was coming up in the Police Court at ten o'clock next morning, and it was now five o'clock in the afternoon. Mr. Tutt lit a stogy and crossed the street to the Criminal Courts Building.

"Has Judge O'Hare gone home?" he asked of the attendant standing in the corridor.

"No, counsellor," returned the policeman, "he's still inside. He does a lot of work these days. Attends to all them probation cases himself." He held open the door. "He'll be glad to see you."

"Hello, Jo!" said Mr. Tutt a moment later to the white-haired man, who sat writing beneath the gas-light. "I want to talk to you about a case."

Judge O'Hare continued to write several seconds and then, looking up, remarked impassively, "Tutt—tutt! And yet again—Tutt!"

"It's on before you to-morrow morning," continued Mr. Tutt. "It's a curious sort of case."

"What is it?" The pen began scratching tentatively again.

"Broker's clerk charged with taking notes belonging to a customer. Evidence all against him, but—Jo, I know the boy's innocent."

"What do you want me to do?"

"Soak him, if you think he's guilty, but give me a little leeway in cross-examination."

Judge O'Hare definitely returned to his writing.

"Go as far as you like," he said shortly. "I'll give you every chance to prove his innocence."

Mr. Tutt uttered a snort. "Heavens! What a commentary on our system of administering criminal justice! You—a judge—sworn to presume the defendant innocent—talking of giving me every chance to prove it!"

It is an undoubted fact—which the older we grow becomes more and more apparent—that the mainsprings of human action are far less complicated than we are prone to think them. We may like to believe that we are actuated by a multitude of interrelated motives, but if we seriously attempt to analyze what has led us to follow any particular course, we shall usually discover that it was a single, rather simple, rudimentary desire, characteristic or ambition.

We are apt to scoff at the old-fashioned melodramas in which the various *dramatis personæ* seem little else than animated vices and virtues—some representing lust, jealousy or greed, and others honesty, loyalty and self-sacrifice. Yet the melodrama comes pretty near the truth,—nearer than we ordinarily suppose. The very fact that we used the word "characters" to describe the actors has significance. In ordinary life most of us trim our course by the polestar of some predominating trait; and make our haven or crash upon the rocks by virtue of some single saving grace or besetting sin. So when we crudely stigmatize Jones as a drunkard or a thief, a philanderer, a good sport or an honest man, we are really nearer hitting the mark than if we sought to dissect his animus after the fashion of Mr. Henry James.

The mainspring of Mr. Cephas McFee's life was his instinct for acquisition, for getting things and holding on to them. He called it "having his rights." And just as envy or anger will often lead men to do things which in calmer moments they would realize were subversive of their ends and even self-destructive, so McFee's acquisitiveness sometimes blinded him to the ultimate effects of his immediate acts, leading him to do on the impulse what in the long run actually militated against his interests. Thus it had not occurred to him for an instant that it could be otherwise than advantageous for him to have Prescott arrested. He told himself that that was the only right course for a virtuous citizen to pursue. The proper thing to do with thieves was to lock 'em up. He would expect his associates to do likewise in similar circumstances. But his real motive in arresting Prescott was the hope that by doing so he might force him to give back what he had stolen.

It was not enough that he had a perfectly good cause of action against Westbury & Wheatland. He didn't know what defenses their lawyers might not devise. He did know that you were never sure of anything unless you had got your hooks in it and had put it in the bank. Even then the bank might fail. It was better to have it in a mortgage. A mere claim, however good, against a pair of stockbrokers—even if they called themselves bankers—wasn't one-two-three with holding the threat of jail over a crook. That would get quick action—if the thief still had the notes. If not, McFee could still proceed against Westbury in the regular way. In a word, the criminal law offered a club to his hand which he eagerly snatched. The fact that he might be mistaken or that he might do an injustice was the merest straw swept down the mad current of his self-interest. He could have given a dozen good reasons why he had had

Prescott locked up, but there was really only one,—his vindictive purpose to make the clerk disgorge what he believed him to have taken.

But as the hours passed and the anticipated word from Prescott to the effect that if only he could get out of the Tombs he would gladly make restitution did not come, Cephas McFee began to feel not only grievously disappointed but also slightly upset, vaguely perceiving that having brought a criminal charge it was up to him to substantiate it. He even went round to his club and lost a dollar at backgammon to Frank Cassibeer, of Cassibeer & Fackenthal, in order to pump him about one's civil liabilities when one had another man arrested. He did it cleverly and Cassibeer did not suspect, but he made McFee uneasy by stating casually that one had to be sure that one had reasonable cause. Cephas wanted to ask what "reasonable cause" might be under varying circumstances, but refrained for fear that the lawyer might smell a rat.

Of course he had reasonable cause! If he hadn't, nobody ever had had. He'd counted the notes; so had Westbury; so had Prescott! And yet it certainly was, now that he came to think of it, a hell of a way to steal $9,000—give a receipt for $25,000 and then say you'd made a mistake; just after your employer had counted 'em, at that! It worried him. But the cuss had run away! Yet McFee knew that he hadn't run farther than his own home.

He began to wish he had not been quite so precipitate. He knew that he had had $25,000 in notes. He'd counted 'em in the vault. *Had* he counted 'em? A slight sweat broke out on his back. Could he swear he'd counted 'em? Of course he could! Anyhow, he'd seen Westbury count them. A strange and utterly unreasonable anxiety began to take hold of him. He was in the right—absolutely—knew he was in the right—and yet— Feverishly he called up Westbury at his house just before dinner.

The broker was very peevish. Why had McFee gone and made a mess of everything by arresting their cashier? Publicity like that was likely to damage their credit. If any arresting was to be done, it was Westbury & Wheatland's affair. They were responsible.

"But I thought I could make him cough up!" explained McFee, realizing that he had been somewhat inconsiderate in acting as he had without consulting the firm.

"Well, you didn't, did you?" snarled Westbury. "If he took the notes he's jolly well hung on to 'em, hasn't he?"

" 'If'!" bellowed Cephas through the telephone. "What d'you

mean by 'if he took the notes'?" Already he suspected some collusion between the broker and the clerk, by which he would be done out of his money. "You counted the notes, didn't you?"

"Yes, of course I did!" retorted Westbury, to McFee's intense relief. "The fact that we're liable to you for the nine thousand dollars is what makes me so sore about your having our man arrested. It'll be all over Wall Street to-morrow morning."

But still McFee was not satisfied! Down in the depths of his mean, mercenary little soul a horrible suspicion suddenly reared its head like a basilisk and turned him to stone. Suppose they had all been mistaken! There wasn't a chance in the world of it; the mere idea flouted the laws of reason; he had a signed admission of Prescott's guilt. But—if by some hocus-pocus the fellow shouldn't be convicted, he, McFee, would certainly be liable in damages. He'd heard that juries sometimes gave enormous verdicts. Pshaw!—a measly clerk! No need worrying! They'd all counted the notes! Westbury admitted liability. Nothing to worry about.

Yet in the middle of the night he awoke in a cold chill. Had he really had twenty-five thousand in notes? Had he really counted them when he took them out from under the rubber strap in his safe-deposit box? Had he in fact done anything more than glance over them? In the secrecy of his bed-chamber he admitted to himself that he had not! Had he counted them when he put them there? He tried to bring his mind back to the day when he had brought the notes to the vault, but he could not conjure up the picture. He was convinced that he had counted them upon that occasion,—but had he? The terrible thought came that perhaps he had not really counted them either time,—had only taken for granted that there were twenty-five thousand.

Frantically he got out of bed and paced the floor in his nightshirt, biting his nails. Well, he'd swear that he'd counted them, anyway! Nobody could contradict him. He had been alone in the vault. And of course there had been twenty-five thousand! Westbury had counted them. But suppose Westbury hadn't really counted them, either? The idea was preposterous! Yet, curiously enough, he began to wonder why he had originally assumed the notes to be of that amount. He turned on the electric light and started figuring out what the transactions had been that had left him with the notes in his possession. He was still hysterically at work when the maid knocked on the door and announced breakfast.

But McFee could not eat. He gulped half a cup of coffee and hurried downtown to his office. His books would show exactly how many notes he ought to have had.

At a quarter to ten he descended in the elevator, his face gray, and feeling rather sick, and as he stepped out into the corridor of the ground floor a thin young man handed him a subpœna signed by Magistrate O'Hare, ordering him forthwith to produce and bring with him to court "all books of account, records, documents and other papers relating in any way to the purchase or sale by you of any bonds, stocks or other securities during the past year."

He ducked back quickly into the elevator, dazed and horrified. Show his books? Disclose to the world his private affairs? Subject himself to hostile cross-examination in regard to all his business transactions? Risk official scrutiny of his Federal income-tax returns for the last five years? Lay himself open to the suspicion of having concealed his true financial status? And, worst of all perhaps, cast doubt upon the actual amount of the notes originally in his possession? Never! It was not to be thought of! Far better to withdraw the charge and let Prescott go! Gradually he got himself in hand and once more descended to the street.

Now just as the motives animating human action are not half so complicated as they are often made out to be, so what are termed "mysteries" are usually solved not by any highly elaborate or ingenious theorizing, but by some single pregnant isolated fact, which of itself settles the whole matter as a reagent clears a test-tube containing a cloudy mixture of chemicals. Novelists, playwrights and writers of short stories amuse themselves and their readers by the involutions of their inventiveness in devising a myriad of tiny clues which, when pieced together into a mosaic, present a beautiful picture of guilt or innocence.

In real life, however, a criminal case more likely turns on just one fact, seemingly insignificant, the importance of which in the beginning is quite apt to be overlooked. Was the cellar-door left locked or not? Did Maud leave her vanity-case in the taxi? Was it raining or not? How many bananas did Harry eat? Those are the mundane issues upon which a human life often hangs or by virtue of which a hundred-thousand-dollar verdict quite properly is rendered. Frequently, though they are almost self-evident, they are not thought of until the last witness has left the stand, in which event the case has to be reopened and the missing testimony supplied. Many a trial has been won by demonstrating as an afterthought that the chief witness was almost blind or deaf. Far more difficult is it to show that he was mistaken!

This, however, was the task Mr. Tutt had set himself if he would win his case. He must prove not only that Cephas McFee had been mistaken, but Westbury and Prescott as well. All the evening before, he had sat in front of the sea-coal fire in his library, smoking one stogy after another, nursing his chin in his hand and studying the various possibilities presented by the evidence as he knew it. He had derived no encouragement from any of his emissaries. The financial report upon McFee had been of no assistance; Scraggs had succeeded in accomplishing nothing except to get himself hopelessly drunk; and Bonnie Doon had telephoned that McFee had gone home before supper and apparently stayed there. Yet, after sitting motionless and wreathed in smoke for several hours, Mr. Tutt suddenly gave utterance to a sort of cluck, and slapped his knee with his right hand.

"What a fool I was not to have thought of that before!" he muttered. Then he poured out a sup of brandy from the cellaret, poked the fire, turned off the gas and climbed up stairs to bed.

When Cephas McFee reached the police-court the next morning he found Westbury already there in a state of fury.

"What d'you s'pose they've done?" demanded the broker angrily. "Subpœnaed all our books! You *have* made a mess of things! Why, it would take a truck to bring all our stuff over here, and meanwhile our business would simply go all to hell."

"Well, you needn't find fault with me about it. I didn't subpœna them. They've done the same thing to me!"

"That's nothing to what they *will* do to you!" snapped Westbury. McFee shivered.

"What do you mean?" he asked faintly.

"Haven't you ever heard of Tutt & Tutt?" inquired the broker.

"Y-e-es!" admitted the miserable McFee.

"Old Tutt will turn you inside out!" warned Westbury. "If you don't take care, he'll put you in jail. He doesn't stop at anything."

McFee looked at him helplessly.

"Well, I'm damned if I'll show him my books!" he ejaculated defiantly.

Westbury laughed heartlessly.

"A lot you'll have to say about it!" he retorted. "You'll show 'em all right or they'll lock you up!"

The room was stuffy, full of queer smells, reminding McFee of a zoo. This effect was heightened for McFee by the way the policemen acted, as if they were keepers of animals. The whole thing was terrible and disgusting. The cops would haul a man to the bar, the judge would chatter and roar at him like an old baboon, another smaller baboon would also chatter and roar somewhat less violently, and then the victim would be led away by the keeper behind a cage.

"Sit down there, you!" shouted a court officer, scowling, and the pair crouched upon the bench like two whipped setters.

What shocked McFee was the way people were bullied and ordered round. He had heard that the law was no respecter of persons, but he had never supposed that the law made a business of insulting people. Then there came a hiatus in the wretched procession of defendants, and McFee saw Jim Prescott standing almost in front of the baboon. Beside him was a tall, gaunt, old man with a wrinkled face.

An officer picked up a bundle of papers and called out in a raucous voice: "McFee! Cephas McFee! Take the stand!"

McFee rose and made his way forward through a gate in the bar which another officer held open for him.

"Be sworn!" directed the judge. "Hold up your right hand! No, the right hand! You do solemnly swear that in the matter of the People of the State of New York against James Prescott you will tell the truth, the whole truth and nothing but the truth so help you God? What have you to say?"

Cephas McFee found his throat very dry and his cheeks very hot. Standing on the platform with his hand in the air he felt like the statue of Liberty Enlightening the World.

"Is that your signature?" inquired the judge, who closer at hand seemed rather a kindly person.

McFee nodded.

"Don't nod your head! Speak out. The stenographer has to get what you say."

"Yes," answered McFee.

The judge ran over the complaint with his eye.

"You had twenty-five thousand dollars in U. S. four and one-half per cent notes, you delivered them to the defendant, and he

gave you a receipt—yes? Have you the receipt—yes? He has not
delivered the notes to the bank. You charge him with stealing them.
Is that correct?"

McFee started to nod again and then hastily stammered, "Yes.
Exactly."

"Well, that seems simple enough," remarked the judge. "Do you
wish to cross-examine, Mr. Tutt?"

The tall man stretched his arms.

"I certainly do!" he replied significantly, and McFee trembled.

"How do you know that you had twenty-five thousand dollars
in notes?" he asked.

"Because I counted them," answered McFee bravely.

"Where?"

"Once when I put them in my box in the vault, and again when
I took them out to give them to Westbury & Wheatland."

"Do you distinctly recall counting them on both occasions?"

"Yes," replied Cephas brazenly.

"Do you absolutely and unqualifiedly testify that you took each
note separately in your hands and counted it?"

The room clouded for a moment, then cleared.

"Yes," agreed McFee.

"You do, eh?" suddenly interjected the judge, bending forward
and fixing Cephas with his eye. "You distinctly recall counting the
individual notes?"

McFee swallowed.

"Ye-es. Yes, certainly, I do!"

A grim smile played for an instant about Mr. Tutt's mouth.

"You are aware that it is a crime to testify falsely in this or any
other legal proceeding?"

"Yes," admitted McFee, and again the room clouded.

Mr. Tutt pursed his thin lips.

"That is all—for the present," he remarked. "If Your Honor will
instruct the witness to remain, I may wish to question him further,
later on."

"Can't I get back to my office?" inquired McFee plaintively. "I
don't want to be kept dangling round all day. I——"

"You'll dangle just as long as you are needed!" chattered the
judge, looking as much like a baboon as he had in the beginning.
"Are there any more witnesses for the complainant?" He looked
round vaguely.

"There's Mr. Westbury," answered Cephas, who, though wilted, was eager to see the matter through. "He counted the notes."

Mr. Westbury came forward reluctantly while Mr. McFee took his vacant place on the settee.

"Did you count the notes?" asked His Honor.

"I did," affirmed Mr. Westbury with decision.

"How many were there?"

"Twenty-five thousand."

The judge raised his eyebrows and looked meaningly at Mr. Tutt.

"You are this man's employer, aren't you?" he continued.

"Yes, sir."

"Ever had any occasion to find fault with him?"

"No, sir."

"How long has he worked for you?"

"Twelve years this March."

"Has he handled large sums of money?"

"Every day."

"Have you ever missed any?"

"No, sir."

The judge leaned back.

"You may cross-examine, Mr. Tutt."

The old lawyer smiled at Mr. Westbury in a friendly fashion.

"I can see by your very frank answers," said he, "that you bear my client no ill will. I do not doubt your desire to be absolutely sincere. I only wish to ask you two questions. I think your replies will dispose of one side of this unfortunate case. The first is: Was your firm engaged very actively in dealing in four and one-half per cent notes?"

Mr. Westbury was delighted at the cordiality of the treatment accorded him, particularly as contrasted with that extended to McFee.

"Why, no, Mr. Tutt," he replied almost effusively; "we only had two or three transactions in them. In fact, this is the only one we have had for several weeks."

"You don't carry them on hand?" went on the lawyer.

"Oh, no," declared the witness. "We have no use for them ourselves. If a customer——"

"That is all I wanted to know. You had none on hand at this time?"

"Not that I know of."

The lawyer nodded as if satisfied.

"Now," he continued "you are absolutely positive there were twenty-five thousand dollars in notes?"

"Yes, absolutely!"

"Do you remember how many notes there were?" asked Mr. Tutt with solemn emphasis.

"Absolutely yes," answered Mr. Westbury. "There were three. Two ten-thousand-dollar notes and a five."

"You are sure there were three? Just as sure as that they totalled twenty-five thousand dollars?"

"Absolutely positive."

Mr. Tutt straightened up and gave a sigh of relief.

"Then, Your Honor, I move for the defendant's acquittal."

McFee almost stood up in his wrath. He knew they were going to try to put something over on him.

"How so?" queried the judge.

"Kindly let me see the notes that were found on the defendant's person," said Mr. Tutt to the clerk.

The lawyer took the notes which had been pinned together and turned each slowly, holding it up so that the judge could see it. There were three,—one for ten thousand dollars, one for five thousand and one for one thousand. Each was creased twice and all folded together neatly.

"These notes were found on the defendant. They amount to sixteen thousand dollars. The complainant, McFee, claims they are what remained after my client had abstracted nine thousand dollars in notes from the original twenty-five thousand. But Mr. Westbury testifies that there were only three notes,—two for ten thousand dollars and one for five thousand. Now if Mr. Westbury is correct, and is not the victim of an honest but natural mistake, as I claim that he is, my client must have substituted for one of the ten-thousand-dollar notes a one-thousand-dollar note. He could steal the nine thousand dollars in no other way. Where did he get that one-thousand-dollar note? The firm did not have any. Is it to be presumed that Prescott had procured one in anticipation of this very possibility? Moreover, the folds of the one-thousand-dollar note fit precisely the folds of the other notes. These three notes are the only notes that Mr. McFee had. He thought he had twenty-five thousand. He thought he counted them, but he mistook the one-thousand-dollar note, which was under the first ten-thousand-dollar note, for another ten. Turning the edges they look exactly alike. He told Mr. Westbury that there were twenty-five thousand in notes, and so impressed Mr. Westbury with that fact that he also made the same mistake.

"Prescott, being assured by both Mr. FcFee and Mr. Westbury that the notes amounted to twenty-five thousand, assumed their joint statement to be correct and in his hurry to give the receipt likewise miscounted them."

"It is an extraordinary illustration of self-deception," remarked the judge; "but the fact that there were only three notes would seem to be almost conclusive. As you say, it isn't to be presumed that Prescott had a one-thousand-dollar note all ready to substitute for a ten."

"Now you will understand why I wished to reserve a part of my cross-examination," explained Mr. Tutt. "I have subpœnaed Mr. McFee's books; they will of course show exactly whether he had twenty-five, or sixteen, thousand in four and one-half per cent notes, just as they would have if he had referred to them before having my client arrested. Mr. McFee, will you please resume the stand?"

For an instant Cephas McFee seriously contemplated flight, but the door of the zoo was guarded by a keeper, and every eye was fastened upon him. Very weak in the legs he climbed again to the witness-chair.

"Kindly let me see the book in which you entered the receipt of the notes that you placed in your vault," said the lawyer sternly.

"I—I haven't it here," choked McFee.

"Why not?" thundered Mr. Tutt.

"Be-cause I didn't propose that you should go prying into my private affairs," glared McFee.

"Oh! Not even if that involved sending an innocent man to prison! Your Honor, I ask for the commitment of this witness for contempt of court."

Just beside McFee the white-whiskered baboon suddenly began to gibber ferociously, and all the beasts in the menagerie started to roar in a deafening chorus.

He was lost! He knew it. Those lawyers! Why had he ever had Prescott arrested?

"Your Honor," he chattered, "I would like to withdraw the charge. There are so many possibilities of mistake——"

"You should have thought of that before!" shrieked the baboon. "Why didn't you look at your books?"

"I thought——"

"You thought!"

"What did you find," shouted Mr. Tutt, pointing an accusing finger at the wretched McFee, "when you looked at your books this morning? Tell the truth!"

McFee quaked and glanced uneasily this way and that.

"Answer!" roared the baboon, towering above him. "Answer, unless you want to go to jail for contempt."

Cephas McFee tottered and all but fell, while an officer supported him by the shoulder.

"I found that I had only sixteen thousand," he whispered faintly.

Then all the animals stood up on their hind legs and waved their paws and howled, and amid the pandemonium McFee heard the judge say to one of the policemen: "Hold this man on a short affidavit until I have time to consider his case more fully," and then to the world at large: "The defendant is discharged."

From the crowd upon the benches a young woman rushed forward and flung her arms hysterically about Prescott.

"Oh, Jim!" she cried wildly. "Oh, Jim!"

"Excuse her, Your Honor!" begged Prescott. "She's all upset!" He bent over her.

"How's Jennie?" he demanded.

"Jennie's all right," she cried. "She didn't have the pneumonia, after all."

Mr. Tutt leaned over and crossed his arms familiarly upon the judge's dais, while a paternal smile transfigured his gnarled old features.

"Jennie's their little girl," he explained. "And, Jo, she's the greatest kid you ever saw!"

THE BLOODHOUND

I

"Next!" The dejected file of prisoners beneath the glaring windows stiffened and limped forward. There were twelve of them—the same number as the minor prophets, the apostles, the tribes of Israel and the officers of King Solomon—a bullet-headed negro in a red sweater, charged with vivisection during a crap game, bringing up the rear. The line humped along beside the iron grating like a caterpillar, those behind butting forward those in front, turned the corner by the jury-box and disgorged two prisoners before the bar of judgment. It was the first Monday in January—pleading day.

"Next!" repeated Phelan, the court captain, standing inside the rail, to McNamara, his whipper-in. "Lively now!"

McNamara turned to the head of the line.

"You two there! Step up here!"

Mr. Dougherty, the tiny bald-headed clerk with the big mustaches that made him look like an animated mushroom, picked up the indictments on the top of the blue pile in front of him.

"Patrick Mooney and Daniel Mulligan," he intoned as if officiating at the high altar of the cathedral, "you are jointly indicted for the crime of burglary in the third degree, grand larceny in the first degree, assault in the first degree, receiving stolen goods and carrying concealed weapons. How say you? Do you plead guilty or not guilty?"

Neither of the two made reply.

"Have you counsel?" sang Dougherty.

"Got a lawyer?" interpreted Captain Phelan.

There was a slight bustle on one of the nearer benches as a heavily built man with sideburns came forward.

"I appear for both defendants, Your Honor," said he. "They plead not guilty. Will Your Honor set the case down for the twenty-first for trial?"

The judge nodded and made a note, and the stout lawyer turned away, about to resume his seat.

"Next!" shouted Phelan to the world at large. "Next!"

95

The taller of the two prisoners wheeled from the rail and started on the return trip. The other did not stir. He was a much smaller man, hardly five feet six, and of a different make altogether. He might have been your plumber, or electrician, or the grocer's clerk who takes your order at the side door; and though his demeanor was more timid than that of any of these, it was, nevertheless, defiant—some spark of courage, or at least resolution, still surviving after his year in Sing Sing.

"Judge—Your Honor," he said huskily, twisting his cap in his hands—"this man don't represent me. I haven't got any lawyer."

Old Judge Watkins peered down from the dais at him over his reading-glasses. He then looked after the retreating attorney.

"How's this, Mr. Hogan?" he asked. "I thought you said that you appeared for both defendants."

The attorney paused with a half-smile.

"So I did, Judge."

"The prisoner Mooney says you do not represent him."

"They're indicted together—for the same offense, committed at the same time. The defendant Mulligan's sister came to my office yesterday and retained me for both of 'em."

"Judge—Your Honor," repeated the man at the bar of justice stubbornly, "I don't know this lawyer and I don't know this man I'm indicted with. I never saw him before that night. I'm innocent, and I want a separate trial with my own lawyer."

Captain Phelan hoisted a blue shoulder and grinned at Mr. Dougherty. It was the old game—the ancient grandstand play—of seizing this opportunity to make a vigorous denial of guilt in the presence of the panel of jurors newly assembled for a month's service, in the hope that by so doing one might avoid going on the stand later at one's trial, and so escape the disagreeable necessity of submitting to cross-examination upon one's record and earlier history.

"Sunday night I was walking home," continued Mooney, "when this here defendant, Mulligan, came along with a bag and began talking to me. Just then a bull jumped out and drew his gun on us. He rapped for his side partner and they yanked us up to headquarters. See that lump on my forehead? Then the first cop said he found a gun on me. It's a plant, Judge, I didn't have one. What would I want with a gun, Judge? What I want is a chance to earn an honest living!"

He made his plea doggedly, yet with obvious hopelessness, for he no longer had any faith in "the course of justice."

Judge Watkins, sent down from Utica by his friend the Governor to hold a special criminal-trial term and so relieve the congestion in the Tombs Prison, beckoned to Mr. Dougherty, who elevated himself upon his glossy little tiptoes and held a whispered colloquy with His Honor across the edge of the dais. Behind the prisoner, on the first row of benches, a homely girl, her broad honest face covered with a screen of freckles, leaned forward hungrily. She had waited for Mooney over a year; she would wait ten more if need be, or until they carried her out in a box feet first. She, also, had lost all faith in the supposed equality of the law. For Paddy had been railroaded because he had swatted Micky Morrison over in Fagan's saloon, Micky being heir apparent of the lower East Side, a friend of Bloodhound O'Brien, the assistant district attorney, and honorary colonel of the Pearl Button Kids; while Paddy Mooney was a stationary fireman in an office building, without political affiliations, and not even a member of the union. This he now perceived to have been a grievous lapse, due, however, only to the reason that they had sought to bully him into it, and he wouldn't be bullied.

Judge Watkins looked searchingly around the court-room until his eye came to rest in a far corner.

"I will assign Mr. Ephraim Tutt to the case," said he, and at the summons the old lawyer arose from his seat and, stove-pipe hat in hand, approached the bar.

At that moment the door was pushed open violently and "Billy the Bloodhound," surrounded by his minions, entered. Ancient enemy faced ancient enemy.

II

William Francis O'Brien, the reader may recall, has hitherto been described in other pages as "the Yellow Dog of the District Attorney's Office." At any rate, he was one who viewed it as his duty to his God, his country, and himself to convict, by any means at his command, every hapless defendant brought to the bar of justice. Through his pertinacity, his resourcefulness, and his lack of scruple he had achieved great notoriety as a prosecutor. Lawyers feared him, defendants shuddered at the mere thought of facing his merciless cross-examination; for he was without consideration to the former or sympathy for the latter. He had no bowels or mercies.

To achieve his end he astutely made use of a veneer of apparent honesty, of naïve enthusiasm, that often made him seem, to juries, merely a blunt, well-meaning blunderer. Yet there was no guile of serpent he did not possess, no venom not in his teeth.

"Billy the Bloodhound," as he was called, was a more prominent figure in the Criminal Courts Building than District Attorney John Henry Peckham himself, who was content to have it so, since he shared the widespread belief that there had to be a crook in every law office, whether public or private. In fact, he found O'Brien more than a mere convenience, particularly because he could always count upon him for a conviction in any difficult case. As he used to say to his confidential friends: "If the Bloodhound hasn't got the necessary evidence,—he goes and gets it!"

Hence, because O'Brien was not only an asset but a valuable political go-between, the Honorable John Henry Peckham smothered his personal dislike for the dog and encouraged it to lick his hand. He also was forced to put up with his noise, and his overbearing and swashbuckling ways. For outside the court-room—as well as, to be accurate, sometimes inside it—Billy the Bloodhound was a swaggering, blustering sort of legal bravo,—preceded, surrounded, and followed wherever he went by a cohort of sycophants, clerks, process-servers, and police officers on special detail, who ran his errands, carried his books, bags, and papers, bought his theatre tickets, did his telephoning, acclaimed his coming and did him lip-service,—much as we may imagine some Roman senator of the same type to have been accompanied by his bodyguard of lictors who shoved the crowd aside at his approach. All this to Billy the Bloodhound was as the breath of life, and he played the part, bellowing down the corridors, shouting from the elevators, kicking his slaves in the shins and then handing them out cigars, whispering out of the corner of his mouth about "the big fellow" and "the one next," with so effective an air of mystery that he had everybody buffaloed; and the crowd all swore among themselves and to him that he was the greatest little man on earth.

He was thickset, bullet-headed, with closely cropped reddish hair and freckled sandy skin, and his short aquiline nose and square chin would have made the features of a cigar-store Indian—alas, poor redskin, he deserves an apology!—seem filled with the milk of human kindness.

Everybody feared and kowtowed to him. People who wanted

favors of Peckham went first to placate O'Brien, who was supposed to have the boss in his pocket; cops and detectives endeavored to have him handle their cases; judges were apt to try to conciliate him as a coming man politically, and as possibly the next district attorney. Whenever a "star case," a *cause célèbre*, or any matter attracting public attention came into the office, O'Brien sent to the chief clerk for the papers and grabbed it. He had even been known to send for the papers in a case already assigned to another assistant and grab that too. He gave out interviews to the papers, assumed the office of "acting district attorney" whenever Peckham absented himself, and frequently likewise when the latter was there, and constituted himself pretty much the whole show.

If one stood for him he wasn't so bad, and, if he hadn't been a crook, he might easily have been a power for good instead of a power for evil. It is not easy to overestimate that power, for he was the grand vizier of the most powerful public-office-holder in the United States, not even excepting the President himself. He could make or break a cop or blast at will the reputation of any man in the community. This the Honorable William Francis O'Brien!

Alas "the law's delay, the insolence of office, and the spurns that patient merit of the unworthy takes"! What price beside him, poor old Ephraim Tutt?

But wait! There is life in the old dog yet—old Tutt, we mean! So far, Billy the Bloodhound has but opened the door and entered the court-room, and Mr. Tutt has but turned to gaze at him. Let us reserve our lamentations until we see what will happen when they meet. Will not the gods lend courage and strength to the kindly old lawyer, who never yet did aught but good, although mayhap he may have done it in queer ways? And who never retired wholly vanquished from the field of honorable battle?

So, heralds, your fanfares! And summon all to the lists to behold the contest between the Bloodhound and the Knight of the Stovepipe Hat. Blow, bugles, blow! Set the echoes of the forum ringing for the legal joust! Court officers, bawl your best, with "Oyez! Oyez!" and "Hear ye! Hear ye!" Pound the railings and shout the honest burghers out of their hats and into their seats, make them move up and on, close the windows, lock the door so that none may escape, and let all who have business in our Honorable Court now with due deference draw near, give their attention, and let Mr. Tutt be heard!

III

Bill the Bloodhound strutted into the inclosure in front of the dais, bowed to the judge and preened himself before the gaping crowd—the little czar, the Pooh-Bah, the high-cockalorum of the Sessions—as the old lawyer was in the act of consulting his new client. Something about Mr. Tutt inspired Paddy Mooney with instant confidence, and, while the court waited, he hastily explained to him the circumstances surrounding his arrest. He had no witnesses, he said; he was being framed and he wanted to be tried at once. O'Brien swaggered to the bar.

"Well," he inquired roughly, "how do you plead? What are you going to do? You can't talk there forever."

Mr. Tutt smiled with the old-time courtesy he invoked when in his most dangerous mood.

"I am sorry to have unduly delayed the proceedings, Mr. O'Brien. We plead not guilty, and we ask an immediate trial."

It was at this moment that the Devil, in the shape of Delaney the cop, leaned over the rail and plucked the Bloodhound's sleeve.

"S-st, Mr. O'Brien! Put the screws on him and he'll plead guilty. We've got him cold. Here's the gun I took off him—loaded."

He shoved the revolver into O'Brien's hand, and the latter, always willing to oblige, slipped it into his pocket.

"Has he got a record?" he asked sideways.

"Sure! Just out of stir. Caught him with a valise full of swag he took out of a cigar-store. He's an old-timer—Gas House Gang. If he won't plead, stick him right on trial. It's a pipe!"

The Bloodhound nodded.

"Leave him to me! Here, you!"—addressing Mooney and Mr. Tutt together and as one—"plead guilty and I'll give you attempted grand in the second."

Mr. Tutt gravely shook his head.

"No," he replied, "I cannot let an innocent man falsely admit under any conditions that he is guilty."

O'Brien's face hardened.

"Suit yourself!" he snapped back. "If he doesn't, he'll get the limit."

"Not unless he's convicted!" murmured Mr. Tutt.

"Oh!" sneered his adversary. "You think you can get him off, do you? Don't fool yourself! It's a dead open-and-shut case. Will you or won't you? If you won't, he'll be on his way up the river by two o'clock."

Mr. Tutt's blood boiled and tingled.

"Mister District Attorney," he said sternly, "may I ask if you have examined into the merits of this case?"

"I've seen the only witness!" retorted O'Brien. "This man is an ex-convict. His picture is in the gallery. So are his thumb-tracks. He's guilty all right, all right! He's got no more chance than an icicle in Hades."

"Have you talked to him? Have you heard his story?" went on the old lawyer.

"I have not! And I don't intend to!" answered O'Brien shortly. "He can tell his story on the stand, and if there's anything to it the jury can acquit him."

"What chance has he got to have the jury believe him, if you bring out the fact that he has been in prison?" asked Mr. Tutt. "It will hopelessly prejudice them against him."

"That's why he'd better plead guilty!" grinned the Bloodhound.

"And you call that justice!" cried Mr. Tutt, his lips quivering. "Well, put him on trial—and be damned to you!"

"I will!" laughed O'Brien. "I'll put him on trial in ten minutes—as soon as the pleas are over. And then"—he bent over past Mooney and leered into Mr. Tutt's face—"and then be damned to *you!*"

As the court officer marched Mooney back to the pen a hand pulled Mr. Tutt by the coat tails. He turned and looked into the homely face of the freckled girl.

"Oh, sir," she begged, "for God's sake don't let them frame him! That brute Delaney was a witness against him on his first trial. He's Morrison's man. They've made up their minds to railroad him. Oh, sir! Save him! He's a brave, good lad that never harmed anyone. I know you're a big lawyer, but"—she lowered her voice to a whisper—"I've saved ninety dollars, and it's yours if you get him off!"

Mr. Tutt patted her arm.

"All right! All right!" he said soothingly. "I'll do my best, but not for your money! What's your name, my girl?"

"Annie Murphy."

"Do you know the man Paddy worked for before he was sent up?"

"Sure!"

"Go bring him here."

The girl hurried away and Mr. Tutt walked back to his seat.

"If I ever get that fellow to rights," he muttered, eyeing O'Brien as the latter swaggered at the rail, "may God have mercy on his soul!"

IV

In the good old mediæval days, our Teutonic relatives had a jovial habit of strapping any particularly unruly serf beneath the belly of a wild horse and then hunting him to death with dogs. The serf in this pleasant game had very little chance, but at any rate he had a fair start, and the horse did not have a ball and chain attached to his leg. But in the coming course, in which the dogs of law would run down Paddy Mooney if they could, he was handicapped in two ways: first, he had a ball and chain on his leg in the shape of his prison record; and second, in addition to the hatred which O'Brien entertained for all defendants, and particularly for those who had served terms in prison, he was the object of the prosecutor's special malignity because he was to be defended by Mr. Tutt, who on more than one celebrated occasion had shown the braggart up for what he was. To his ancient grudge, fed fat upon the old lawyer's part by years of successful opposition, was now added the smart of present insult. His rage against Mooney for not being willing to plead guilty fanned his fury against Mr. Tutt, and his hatred of Mr. Tutt transformed his anger against Mooney to poisonous serpents. To be in any way foiled made him a madman.

"Come here!" he growled at Delaney as he dragged him into the corridor. "Give me the goods on this fellow! I'll teach that sanctimonious old devil a lesson he won't forget in a hurry!"

The heart of Delaney leaped within him. He would have another conviction to add to his scroll of honor, and maybe the D. A. would write the Commissioner a letter of commendation, praising his services in sending up Mooney for another bit! Anyhow, Micky Morrison wouldn't forget it! Promotion dazzled him! He could have kissed O'Brien or licked his boots.

"Listen here!" he said, fawning upon the prosecutor. "It's a cinch. I caught this guy and another—Mulligan—wit' a bag of goods. I gave ye the cannon I took off him already. Mulligan'll turn state's evidence for a suspended sentence. Everybody's here! You'll eat him alive!"

"All right! Tell Mulligan I'll use him; and bring him up into one of the jury-rooms and go over his story with him. I don't want any slip-up now! I'm doing you a favor by trying this case myself."

"I know you are, Mr. O'Brien! I know you are!" declared Delaney. " 'Tis the next district attorney you're going to be!"

"Then get busy! Get busy!" ordered O'Brien, stalking back toward the court-room.

The reader might well be pardoned were he incredulous of what O'Brien and Delaney purposed to do. Fortunately such prosecutors are rare; but once in a generation—perhaps even more often—they arise; and against their villainy judges and lawyers are generally powerless, for their assassinations are hidden beneath the cloak of law and the pretense of public service. Little did the judge upon the bench wot of the proposed tragedy; had he done so he would have arisen and rent his official garments. But Mr. Tutt knew, and his heart turned faint within his old frock coat. O Justice, what crimes are sometimes committed in thy name!

V

The last disconsolate in the file of prisoners had pleaded not guilty and clumped back to the prison pen; the judge had listened to the manifold ingenious excuses urged upon him by talesmen reluctant to serve; the crowd in the court-room had thinned; it was twelve o'clock; the holocaust was about to begin.

The Bloodhound arose and strolled to the district attorney's table in front of the jury-box.

"Have you any case to move, Mister District Attorney?" asked His Honor, and, at O'Brien's nod, added to the clerk, "Fill the box, Mr. Dougherty."

"Take your places, gentlemen," called the latter, drawing twelve names rapidly from the wheel. "People against Mooney! Patrick Mooney, you are indicted for burglary in the third degree, grand larceny in the first degree, assault in the first degree, receiving stolen goods and carrying concealed weapons. If you desire to challenge any talesman you may do so now!" One almost expected to hear him continue "Or forever after hold your peace!"

But Mr. Tutt did not wish to challenge anybody, and smiled so genially at the double row of miscellaneous citizens, and with such an air of gratification declared "The jury is more than satisfactory," that every man of them expanded his chest and lifted his chin a fraction of an inch, convinced that Mr. Tutt was a man of parts, and became his friend for life.

Then the Bloodhound summoned them to their duty of sending men to prison. The defendant, he told them, had been caught in possession of the proceeds of a burglary committed but a few moments before his arrest. He had a loaded pistol in his pocket, which he had sought to draw upon the officer, who luckily had reduced him to a timely submission. His fellow criminal would take the stand and testify against him. It was a cut-and-dried case, a routine affair; and they would have nothing to do but to convict.

He called Delaney, whose immense blue bulk overflowed the witness-chair; and the cop made good the prosecutor's opening in every particular, describing Mooney's attempted flight, his effort to pull his gun and how he had frustrated it by felling him with his night-stick. He then identified the gun which O'Brien produced from his pocket.

Cross-examine!

Mr. Tutt asked but two questions:

"Do you know Micky Morrison?"

"I do."

"Do you belong to the same club?"

"I do!" defiantly.

"That is all!" And the old lawyer waved him from the stand.

Then Mulligan was brought up from the pen and put in the chair, and swore that everything that Delaney had said was gospel. He admitted that he was a professional burglar, but allowed that on occasions a burglar could tell the truth, and that this was one of them; and he supplemented the cop's story by describing in the most graphic detail how Mooney and he had planned and perpetrated the burglary of the cigar-store; but, his imagination being limited and his general intelligence even more so, he made a sorry exhibition of himself under Mr. Tutt's good-natured yet searching cross-examination. Indeed, he soon became so involved in contradictions as to Mooney's part in the affair that no man in his senses would have convicted a dog of the larceny of a bone upon his testimony.

One piece of evidence, however, remained unshaken,—Delaney's testimony that he had taken a loaded pistol from Mooney's pocket; and Delaney had not been in any way discredited under cross-examination. Quickly O'Brien shifted his position. As a strategist he had no equal.

"If Your Honor please," he said. "I do not feel that the jury should be permitted to convict the defendant of burglary or larceny on this character of testimony. The co-defendant Mulligan is an ex-convict, besides being confessedly guilty in this case, and his statement should not be received without stronger corroboration. I shall therefore ask Your Honor to withdraw from the consideration of the jury all the counts in the indictment except that for carrying a concealed weapon."

He spoke as if with an earnest hope for salvation—and the jury viewed him with approbation. The fox! He knew that Mooney could not meet the charge without taking the stand and admitting that he had been in prison, while, had all the counts been left in the indictment, the jury might well have been led to render a general verdict of acquittal, owing to the obvious unreliability of Mulligan's testimony.

"The People rest," said O'Brien.

The jury turned to the defense.

"Take the stand, Mr. Mooney," directed Mr. Tutt, while the Bloodhound licked his lips.

Paddy Mooney felt his way around behind the jury-box and to the witness-chair. He knew that he was innocent, but he knew that he was going to be pilloried on cross-examination and utterly discredited. He was an ex-convict. That would be enough to send him up again. But, unless he took the stand and denied that the weapon was his, the jury would have no choice—would have to convict him. It was a slim chance but it was worth taking. No use giving up without a fight!

Doggedly, under Mr. Tutt's lead, he denied everything that had been testified to against him, including that he had, or ever had had, a revolver. Mulligan had joined him, he swore, unsolicited, and when Delaney had appeared, he had made no attempt whatever to escape. Why should he have? He had done nothing.

"Your witness!" said Mr. Tutt with a bow toward the jury-box.

The Bloodhound crept toward the witness-chair with the stealth of a panther about to spring. At three feet he sprang!

"Mister Mooney, have you ever been convicted of a crime?"

"Yes," answered the defendant in a husky voice.

"Of what crime?"

"Assault."

"Ah! And you say you are a peaceable sort of person?"

"Yes."

"When did you get out of jail?"

"Last week."

The jury looked at one another. The poison had begun to work.

But the dose might be too small. O'Brien intended to take no chances. As he would have expressed it, he was going to "give him the gaff." He beckoned Delaney to the rail.

"What have you got on him?" he asked. "Give it to me quick."

"He's an old-timer," stammered the cop. "Gas House Gang. Cracked safes and done most everything."

O'Brien knew he was lying, but he had a right to take an officer's word for a thing like that.

"Go up to my office," he ordered Delaney, "and bring me down Jones' *Professional Criminals of America.*"

The cop hesitated.

"He ain't in it!" he ventured.

"Did you hear what I said?" shouted O'Brien. "Go get it!"

While Delaney is waiting for the elevator, to do his master's bidding, let it be explained that when a criminal, or anybody else for that matter, goes upon the witness-stand to testify, he may be asked upon cross-examination by the opposing counsel any fact as to himself or his past which may tend to discredit him, for if he be a rascal and unworthy of credence the jury are entitled to know it so as to be guided by that knowledge in the performance of their holy office. Now there are only two limitations upon this sacred right of cross-examination as to credibility—the discretion of the presiding judge and the fact that, if the matter inquired about is not directly connected with the issue involved, the lawyer asking the question is bound by the witness' answer and is not permitted to show in rebuttal that it is false.

Yet neither of these limitations in fact amounts to anything, and the latter, instead of being a handicap to a prosecutor, is really an advantage; for often a lawyer asks a question from which the jury infers something which is not true and which the lawyer could not prove to be true if he were allowed to try to do so in rebuttal. For example: If a reputable prosecuting attorney should ask a colored defendant, charged with stealing A's chickens on Friday, if it were not a fact that he had stolen B's chickens on Saturday and the colored defendant denied it, the jury would doubtless accept the interrogation of the prosecutor as true and assume that the luckless negro had stolen chickens from both A and B upon consecutive days. Yet, if the prosecutor were at liberty to prove that the negro was lying when the latter denied he had stolen B's poultry, he might find it exceedingly hard to do so. Thus the law's restriction, which is apparently an advantage to the defendant, in reality works against him, in the same way that the "right" to take the stand in fact compels him to do so or suffer the penalty of refusal in the form of the jury's natural assumption that he is guilty. Of this great principle the Bloodhound now proposed to avail himself to the utter annihilation of Paddy Mooney and Mr. Tutt, who he was resolved should together plunge down into the abyss of discredibility.

For he knew that, because he held a public office of large responsibility, any question put by him to Mooney would in the jury's eyes be tantamount to an accusation; particularly after he had evinced such an apparent fairmindedness by asking the judge to quash the burglary, the receiving and the larceny counts in the indictment.

The issue now hung in the balance.

A police officer had sworn to finding a loaded pistol on the prisoner, and a self-confessed crook had corroborated him; the defendant had vehemently denied it, although the force of his denial had been somewhat tempered by his admission of having been previously convicted of assault: but, in view of the judge's admonition that the burden of proof would be on the prosecution to prove its case beyond a reasonable doubt, the jury might acquit. Something must be done.

O'Brien did not hesitate. He would "smear" Mooney so that nobody would pay the slightest attention to his denials, however convincing under other circumstances they might have been. It would not be difficult. Any hint or suggestion that Mooney was a professional "gun"—the slightest innuendo to that effect, probably —would be enough; even if he didn't look it. For look it he certainly did not, as he sat motionless on the witness-chair,—more like a clay statue than a man, his chalky face set and his narrow shoulders foursquare to the world,—an impotent yet defiant creature, like a wild animal driven into a hole or fettered to a stake. Only when his eyes met those of Annie Murphy over Mr. Tutt's shoulders did his stubborn expression soften.

O'Brien caught the looks that passed between them, and scowled. That sort of thing always had a bad effect on the jury. He must "can" it somehow. He strolled back to his place and faced Mooney again.

"You come from the Gas House district, don't you?" he asked.

"No," replied Mooney.

"Ever hear of the Gas House Gang?"

"Yes, but I'm not one of them."

"Oh, you're not, eh? I didn't ask you that. Why did you hurry so to slip that in?"

"I object!" interposed Mr. Tutt. "Such a suggestion is improper and prejudicial."

Judge Watkins, who despised technicalities, waved him aside.

"I will permit the question. The witness volunteered a statement. He may be examined upon it."

Mr. Tutt subsided.

"Because," retorted Mooney, "you were trying to make the jury think I was."

"Maybe you're right!" countered the Bloodhound, with a grin at the jury-box. "Now, how many times have you been convicted of crime in other States?"

"Never!" cried Mooney. "And you can't prove it, either."

"Well, maybe I can't prove it," admitted O'Brien easily, "but," he added insinuatingly, "I can inquire how many times you have committed burglaries—say, in New Jersey?"

Mooney grasped the arms of his chair so tightly that his hands went white. He turned indignantly to the judge.

"Your Honor," he protested, "has this man got the right——"

"Answer the question!" admonished His Honor. "This is proper cross-examination."

"Well?" sneered O'Brien.

"I never committed any burglary!"

"No burglaries! What kind of crimes, then, have you committed?"

"I never committed any crimes!"

Mooney thrust forward in his seat toward his torturer and clinched his jaws. It was all nuts for O'Brien.

"Oh!" he laughed. "You didn't, eh? I thought you were just out of Sing Sing!"

"But I hadn't committed any crime."

"So you were innocent that time? Just as you claim to be now!"

"Delaney railroaded me for Micky Morrison!"

The Bloodhound reddened with anger.

"Strike that out!" ordered Judge Watkins. "Don't volunteer. Answer only the questions put to you. Were you innocent that time?"

"Yes—I was!" declared Mooney with such obvious sincerity that O'Brien wished he had not asked the question. So far he had not scored heavily, although his adversary was getting groggy. At that instant Delaney re-entered the room and approached the rail with a large book in his hand.

"S-st!" he whispered to O'Brien, handing over the book. "Ast him if last December he didn't smash Sugar Grady's nose wit' a blackjack down on Hudson Street; an', say, ast him if he wasn't one o' the bunch 'at beat up Inspector Boyle with brass knuckles over behind the engine-house."

The Bloodhound's eyes gleamed. Real stuff! He put the questions to Mooney, receiving with an indulgent grimace the latter's emphatic denials, and the jury, who had seen his conference with the police officer, felt sure that a desperate thug was seated before them, while Mr. Tutt, a satiric smile playing about his withered lips, vowed vengeance deep and dire upon the unscrupulous O'Brien.

But the Bloodhound, frenzied at the scent of human gore, was now resolved to rend Mooney limb from limb. With all the gleeful malice of a Spanish inquisitor about to tear out his victim's beating heart with a pair of incandescent pincers, this charming understudy of Satan sauntered nonchalantly up to the witness and, holding the *Professional Criminals of America* so that the jury could plainly read the title, opened the book and running his finger down a page as if to mark the place—and looking up from time to time as he apparently read what he had found there—put to the hapless being with the moral death-chair before him, as if solemnly declaring the accompanying accusation to be true, the following question:

"Did you not, on September 6, 1927—in company with 'Red' Burke, alias the Roach, Tony Savelli, otherwise known as Tony the Greaser, and 'Dynamite' Tom Meeghan—crack the safe of the American Railway Express at Rahway, New Jersey, and get away with six thousand dollars?"

There was no doubt about O'Brien's having caught the jury now. Just as John Hancock signed his name to the Declaration of Independence so large that no one need use spectacles to read it, so Paddy Mooney screamed his outraged denial so loud that even the dead might well have heard him.

"It's a lie!" he yelled, jumping up and shaking his fist at O'Brien. "I never knew any such people. And I never was in Rahway."

"So *you* say!" the Bloodhound taunted him. "But don't you know that both 'the Roach' and 'the Greaser' testified at their trials that you were there?"

"Wait a moment!" interpolated Judge Watkins. "Do not answer

until your counsel has time to object. Mr. Tutt, do you object to the question? If you do, I will exclude it."

But Mr. Tutt gravely shook his head.

"I prefer to have him answer it," he said.

"I know nothing about it at all!" protested Mooney. Once more he turned to the bench. "Your Honor," he cried, "he's framin' me! I——"

Judge Watkins banged his gavel.

"You will have your chance to explain on the redirect," he remarked coldly, for he, too, was now convinced that the witness was a desperate criminal.

"That is all!" declared O'Brien, as with an air of triumph he threw the book ostentatiously on the table in front of the jury-box. The defendant was cooked. That question about Red Burke had done the trick, driven the last nail into the lid of his coffin. He sank gloatingly into his chair. He had 'em on the run. The jury could convict without leaving the box. There was nothing left for old Tutt to do but try to extract additional denials from his already discredited client.

But the old lawyer made no such move. Instead, he remarked:

"Mr. Mooney, you were asked whether you had not been previously convicted of assault, and you replied in the affirmative. I now ask you whom you were charged with assaulting?"

"Micky Morrison."

"Who arrested you for the alleged offense?"

"Officer Delaney."

"You mean this same officer who has just sworn that he found a pistol in your pocket?"

"Yes, sir."

Mr. Tutt drew in his lips.

"That is all!" he said, without further attempt to rehabilitate his client. Then as Mooney left the stand Mr. Tutt addressed Judge Watkins:

"If Your Honor please, I had intended calling a character witness—a former employer—in behalf of the defendant, but what has transpired would seem to make any such testimony immaterial." He hesitated for an instant, and to O'Brien came the sudden thought that the old lawyer might be going to throw up the sponge and plead his client guilty after all. But to his astonishment he heard Mr. Tutt say: "There is one thing, however, to which I invite the court's attention. The prosecutor has produced a loaded pistol here which he claims was found in my client's possession. It is the basis of the charge against him. Yet the district attorney, for some reason best known to himself, has not offered it in evidence. Unless this is done, in view of the fact that the pistol has been exhibited to the jury, I shall ask for a dismissal."

O'Brien rose languidly to his feet.

"The merest oversight, Your Honor. Here is the pistol. I offer it in evidence."

"I object," said Mr. Tutt—"unless it appears on the record from whose custody it is produced, how it got here, and that it is in the same condition as when received."

"Mr. Tutt is technically correct," nodded His Honor.

The Bloodhound's lips curled.

"I got it from Officer Delaney this morning, and have had it in my pocket all the time. It is exactly as I received it. Does that satisfy you?"

"Not unless you so testify upon the stand," answered the old lawyer, looking fixedly at O'Brien, who experienced a curiously sickening sensation.

"If Mr. Tutt insists, you will have to be sworn," ruled His Honor. "But it is a rather unusual demand for any lawyer to make, under the circumstances."

"This is a rather unusual case," retorted Mr. Tutt, unperturbed.

O'Brien shifted his feet uneasily. He did not like the idea of facing Mr. Tutt from the witness-chair,—not in the least! Still there was no help for it.

With the pistol in his hand he ascended the stand, took the oath and without sitting down repeated in a rather shaky voice what he had just said.

"Have you any cross-examination?" asked Judge Watkins.

"I have," replied Mr. Tutt amid a sudden silence. What could the old codger be up to?

"You are one of the public prosecutors of this county?"

"I am," shot back the Bloodhound.

"And you are sworn to uphold the law?"

"Yes."

"To prosecute those of whose guilt you are satisfied through the introduction of legal evidence in a legal manner?"

"Of course." O'Brien's uneasiness was growing. But Mr. Tutt's next question momentarily allayed his anxiety while arousing his irritation.

"Where were you born?"

"New York City."

Judge Watkins frowned at the question. This procedure was not at all according to Hoyle.

"Gas House section?"

One of the jury sniggered. His Honor raised his hand in gentle admonition.

"Is this revelant, Mr. Tutt? I do not wish to criticise, but your question seems rather trivial."

Mr. Tutt bowed.

"This is cross-examination," he replied. "However, I will withdraw it. Do you know one Micky Morrison, Mr. O'Brien?"

"Yes," scowled the Bloodhound.

"How much did you pay him for your appointment as assistant district attorney?"

O'Brien turned first red, then white. Judge Watkins brought down his gavel.

"That will do!" he remarked. "The jury will disregard the question!"

"If Your Honor please," replied Mr. Tutt quietly, "I have as much right to attack this witness' credibility as he had to attack that of my client. I press the question in another form:

"Did you not pay six thousand dollars to Michael McGurk to be delivered to Micky Morrison in consideration for his securing your appointment as assistant district attorney?"

"I did not!" shouted O'Brien. "And you know it! Your Honor, are you going to permit me to be insulted in this way?"

But a puzzled, if not actually bewildered look, had settled upon the learned justice's countenance.

"Do you know 'Red' Burke, alias the Roach; Tony Savelli, otherwise known as the Greaser; and 'Dynamite' Tom Meeghan?"

"Mr. Tutt," expostulated Judge Watkins, "you may have a technical right to test the witness' credibility, but the matter is within my discretion and——"

"That is the precise question he asked my client," replied Mr. Tutt coolly. "What is sauce for the goose should be sauce for the gander."

"He may answer your question, if you press it," acquiesced His Honor, "but there must be a limit to this sort of thing."

"Only a few more questions, Your Honor. Mr. O'Brien, have you ever been convicted of crime?"

"No!" valiantly answered the prosecutor, now gray as a ghost, for he saw his doom advancing upon him.

"Have you ever committed one?"

O'Brien choked.

"I won't force you to answer that!" threw in Mr. Tutt gallantly.

"Have you any basis for that question?" demanded His Honor sharply.

Mr. Tutt smiled first at the jury and then at Judge Watkins.

"Your Honor," he replied in his most engaging manner, "you and I perhaps belong to a generation which has old-fashioned ideas of honor. I admit that I have had no basis for any of the questions which I have just asked the witness. Honor demands that I should do so; yet, in a sense, honor demanded that I should ask them, although I might later have to disown their sincerity. But, sir"—and his old voice rose high and vibrant—"but, sir, I do not abandon my attack upon this witness' credibility. I have but one more question to ask of him, and upon his answer I stake my client's liberty. Let this witness but answer any way he may see fit—yes or no, I care not which—give any reply at all that may be officially recorded here and not hereafter be disputed or denied by him—and these twelve men may return a verdict against my client."

Judge Watkins was gazing intently at Mr. Tutt. The faces in the court-room surged up and down like ocean waves beneath O'Brien's smarting eyes. He was gaffed, himself.

"Sir!" thundered Mr. Tutt, pointing an accusing finger at the miserable apology for a man now cowering upon the stand. "Sir! *When you took this book in your hand*"—he lifted Jones' *Professional Criminals* from where it lay upon the table—"*and pretended to read from its pages, were you reading something that was printed there or not? YES—OR NO?*"

In the silence all could distinctly hear the ticking of the clock upon the rear wall of the court-room.

"Tick-tock! Tick-tock! Tick-tock! Yes—no! Yes—no! Yes—no!" it went.

O'Brien squirmed, looked down at the rocking floor, and turned faint.

"Tick-tock! Tick-tock!" alternated the clock.

"Yes—no! Yes—no!" answered O'Brien's pulse.

Everything was going black and white, and great pulpy gray spiders seemed grabbing at him from the circumambient air. If he put the thing through and answered "Yes"—insisted that he had been reading from the book, that old gray wolf down there would put the book in evidence and prove him a perjurer, send him up! A band of sweat oozed from beneath his red skullcap of hair. Yet if he answered "No"—admitted that he had made the whole thing up —that there was not a word in the book about Mooney at all—it would be almost as bad!

In his agony, he nearly clutched the flimsy legal straw of refusing to answer on the ground that his reply might tend to degrade or incriminate him! But this would leave him in an even worse position. No, he must answer!

"Tick-tock! Yes—no! Tick-tock! Yes—no! Which—what!"

He moistened his lips and swallowed twice. He coughed—for time; and fumbled for his handkerchief. After all, he had done nothing that was not strictly legal. He had not charged that Mooney was a professional crook; he had only asked him the question. That didn't commit him to anything! You could ask what you chose and you were bound by the witness' answer. A gleam like sunrise flashed across his seething brain. Ah, that would save him, perhaps! Old Tutt would be bound by his answer. And then he saw himself tricked again! Yes, Tutt might be bound in the case at bar—although his muddy mind wasn't quite sure whether he would be or not—but he himself would be forever bound by the written record. He could never get rid of the millstone that his *yes* or *no*—no matter which —would hang about his neck! Old Tutt, like the Old Man of the Sea, would forever be upon his back!

"No," he muttered at last in a woolly voice, so low and thick as to be hardly audible. "I was not—reading from the book."

He bowed his head as if awaiting the headsman's stroke. A hiss —a score of hisses—writhed through the air toward him from the benches. Captain Phelan made no attempt to stop them.

"You mean—" began Judge Watkins incredulously. Then, with a look of disgust, he turned his back upon O'Brien.

Mr. Tutt gazed at the jury. The Lord had delivered his enemy into his hands.

"Now, gentlemen," he said, with a deprecating smile, "you may convict my client if you wish."

There was a moment's puzzled silence, broken by the foreman.

"Not much we won't!" he exploded. "The fellow we want to convict is O'Brien!"

And in a flurry of involuntary applause which followed, the ancient Dougherty was heard to murmur:

"Hearken unto your verdict as it stands recorded. You say the defendant is *not guilty*—and so say you all!"

"MR. TUTT, TAKE THE STAND!"

Mr. Ephraim Tutt, after an exhausting day at the office, had just reached his old-fashioned house on West 23d Street and ensconced himself in the horsehair rocker before the sea-coal fire in his library, when a series of bloodcurdling screams echoed from the basement below.

"Help! Help! Oh, Lawdy! Murder! He-e-elp!" rose in smothered shrieks from the kitchen. "Help! Murder! He-e-elp!" The voice was that of Mandy, his colored cook.

The kitchen was two flights below, in the rear, and whether murder, arson, burglary or mayhem was in progress, instant action seemed imperative. The old man hurled open the window.

"Police!" he shouted. "Police! Help! Police!"

Seizing the poker, he hurried down the first flight of stairs toward the front hall, but before he could reach it, two officers burst in and, hearing the hullabaloo, threw themselves, without pausing for inquiry, down the lower flight leading to the kitchen. Mr. Tutt followed. The fact that the street door had been ajar corroborated his fear of burglary.

"Help! Help! Oh, thank de Lawd!" Mandy's shrill bellow tapered off to a gasping lamentation like the dying wail of a steam siren. The officers were putting their guns back into their holsters as Mr. Tutt crossed the threshold.

Mandy, her two hundred and fifty pounds swathed in an antique white nightgown and wearing a ruffled nightcap, her eyes popping with fright, stood beside the range with her arms elevated above her head. Upon the kitchen table was a flour bag from which protruded a partially consumed leg of lamb, and near by a bottle of milk, a can of tomato soup, a loaf of bread, an orange and a couple of bananas. Flat upon its back, motionless, with outspread arms, lay the body of a man—of a slender young man with emaciated cheeks and hollow eyes—either dead or in a faint.

"All right, auntie. You can take down your arms," said the first cop. "What's it all about?"

Cautiously, her ample bosom heaving hysterically, Mandy subsided into a chair.

"What on earth has happened, Mandy?" panted Mr. Tutt.

"Oh, Lawdy! I nebber had such a scare! I come down to git mah dream book, an' no sooner I reach de do' dan I see de light burnin', an' dis man, he popped out'n de closit wif a pistol in his hand. 'Stick 'em up!' he says. 'Don't say nuff'n!' But I could'n' help it, an' I screamed an' hollered. I called on de Lawd Jesus, and he done save me! Right 'fo' my eyes, Lawd Jesus struck him down an' he fell dead in his tracks whar he is!"

The first cop ran his hands over the body and looked about the floor.

"He ain't got no gun!" he announced. "Mebbe he used this"— holding up a plated table knife. He put his head to the man's chest. "He ain't dead either. He's just passed out. Funny! Must 'a' had a stroke or sumthin'." He took out a notebook and pencil.

"What's your name, auntie?"

"Miranda Washington."

"You the cook?"

"Sho, Ise de cook."

"What did you say you was doin' when this guy tried to stick you up?"

"Lookin' fo' mah dream book."

" 'Dream book'!"

"Pardon me," interrupted Mr. Tutt, who had now recovered his equanimity. "I can probably save you trouble. This is my house. Mandy is my cook. I did not dine at home this evening and so she went upstairs early, before I came home, leaving me to lock up. Then, having got undressed and ready for bed, she discovered that she had left her dream book downstairs. Mandy is a great believer in dreams, although she belongs to the school of Pharaoh rather than that of Freud. Meanwhile this fellow, seeing that the lower stories were no longer lighted, effected an entrance. When Mandy unexpectedly disturbed him, he threatened her with the handle of that knife, which she naturally mistook for a pistol. Isn't that about it, Mandy?"

"Hit sho is!" agreed Mandy. "An' de Lawd in his wrath struck him down!"

The figure on the floor had not stirred. The second and taller cop now took a hand.

"Well, auntie, you can go back to your dreams. . . . Look after the prisoner, Pat, while I send for the wagon. . . . Got a phone handy?"

"Right overhead in the pantry," answered Mr. Tutt.

The first cop unloosened the man's shirt. He had no collar and the sinews of his neck below a week's growth of beard stood out like the cords of a hoist. He was dressed only in a pair of ragged trousers and torn black sweater. Stockingless feet showed through the burst sides of shapeless shoes. His pockets yielded a piece of string, a half-smoked cigarette and two sulphur matches.

"Bring down a decanter of brandy," directed Mr. Tutt. "We must do what we can to revive him."

"Doc Levine'll bring him to, all right, when the wagon gets here," remarked the cop, peeling one of the bananas and biting it in two. "Say, it's luck fer this here guy he didn't have no gun. Breakin' and enterin' an occupied dwelling in the nighttime with intent to commit a crime if armed with a dangerous weapon, is first degree burglary. The judge could give him life. Otherwise, it's burglary in the second, and ten years is the limit. I got it! It's also burglary in the first if he armed himself inside after the break! A knife is a dangerous weapon. He was threatenin' the cook wid the knife when he passed out." He nodded with satisfaction. "Sure, he can get life!"

As Mr. Tutt forced the brandy through the pale, parched lips of the unconscious derelict upon the floor, he wondered if, in that case, life were worth bringing back.

"I understand you want to withdraw your complaint?"

Hiram T. Backus, acting district attorney of New York County, balanced his cigar carefully upon the edge of the mahogany desk and took up an indictment endorsed "The People of the State of New York versus Kaplan."

He was a tall, shaggy-headed man who prided himself on a fancied resemblance to Abraham Lincoln.

"That is hardly a correct statement," answered Mr. Tutt. "This defendant was indicted directly by the grand jury, without any preliminary hearing in the police court. Strictly speaking, there is no complainant. Certainly I am not."

"The People of the State of New York are—is the complainant," replied Mr. Backus impressively. "Your name, however, appears upon the back of this indictment as the chief witness. It amounts to the same thing."

"Pardon me if I differ with you. Had I been in any way consulted, I should never have made a complaint against this defendant."

The acting district attorney retrieved his cigar and leaned back in his revolving chair.

"How about your duty as a citizen? The evidence, including your own, has been heard and weighed by the grand jury, which, after careful deliberation, has indicted him for burglary in the first degree. This man is clearly a dangerous criminal. What would people say if I deliberately permitted this indictment to be dismissed or the case to go by default?"

Mr. Tutt smiled one of the gentlest of benign smiles.

"They would undoubtedly say that you were a wise and upright public servant who knew how to temper justice with mercy."

"I have no right to temper justice with mercy. I am sworn to uphold the law. If there is any mercy coming to this defendant, it must be from the judge presiding at the trial, after a jury has convicted him."

Mr. Tutt shrugged.

"You know what that means?"

"I know that there are no criminal judges more fair-minded than ours," haughtily returned Mr. Backus.

"Of course! Of course!" said Mr. Tutt hastily. "But this man has been indicted for burglary in the first degree, on the theory that he was armed. What is the evidence? Merely that he pointed a plated table knife at my cook, pretending it to be a dangerous weapon, and told her to throw up her hands."

"Dillinger did that very thing!"

Mr. Tutt suppressed an inclination toward murder in the first. What was the use! But he must control himself.

"If this defendant is brought into court under an indictment for burglary in the first degree, backed by all the prestige of the district attorney's office, what chance has he got to receive a punishment to fit his actual offense? The jury will naturally think, 'If Hiram T. Backus says this man is guilty of burglary in the first degree, who are we to question it? He must be so! Away with him!'"

"Oh, it's not so bad as that!" protested Backus modestly, but titillated.

"You don't realize your own tremendous influence," continued Mr. Tutt. "Swayed by that influence, the jury will convict less upon the evidence than upon their confidence in you as the acting district attorney of this county."

"But the judge can remedy any injustice that may have been done," argued Backus.

"He can. But the judge shares with the jury this well-deserved confidence in your wisdom and integrity. He will say—just as you have—that Dillinger did the same thing. But he will mean it seriously —not as you do—in a Pickwickian sense."

"What do you mean—not as I do?"

"You know that this man isn't really a burglar."

"I don't know any such thing! I never heard of the case before."

"Ah!" exclaimed Mr. Tutt. "That is why I am here. Once you have had the facts really brought to your attention, I am certain that you will agree with me that this is no case to be pressed to trial."

"And why not?" asked Mr. Backus, a trifle suspiciously.

Mr. Tutt cut off the end of a stogy and borrowed a light. He was making progress.

"This is a most unusual and pitiful case. The prisoner, Ludwig Kaplan, a carpenter, has been out of work for nearly three years. He is married and has four children, one fifteen months old. There is another on the way. His wife is nervously ill and two of the children are tubercular. When his savings were exhausted, he applied in due course for unemployment relief, but was turned down on the ground that his father-in-law, also unemployed and who lived with them, was drawing a small pension as a Spanish War veteran. For two years they scraped along as best they could. About five weeks ago, the father-in-law was run over and killed by a motor truck. The pension stopped, they now had nothing to live on, and again Kaplan applied for relief. The usual investigation followed. Twelve days later the application received preliminary approval, but still the family sat waiting for the ponderous relief machinery to begin to move.

"On the night of the alleged burglary, Kaplan had had nothing to eat for more than twelve hours. His wife was delirious. The children were crying for bread. The baby needed milk. He had walked all the way to the Bronx to look for a job which was non-existent. He was desperate, nearly out of his mind. Just inside those doors on 23d Street there were well-filled ice boxes, closets crammed with foodstuffs. The lower floor of my house was dark, the upper windows lighted. He crept into the kitchen and, without thinking of his own hunger, made up a little pile of meat, canned goods, fruit, bread and milk. Just as he was about to put them in a flour bag and take them away, my colored cook came in. He was so terrified that, not knowing what else to do, he instinctively picked up a table knife and, thrusting the handle toward her hysterically, imitated what he had read about in the papers and seen in the movies. He said, 'Stick 'em up!' And then he collapsed in a dead faint due to hunger and shock, from which he did not recover until he had been placed in the prison hospital ward.

"Now, I ask you as a matter of simple humanity not to prosecute that unfortunate human being for burglary in the first degree, for which he could be sent to prison for life. He did not commit that crime. I will guarantee to see to it that he and all his family shall be sent to the country and properly cared for there until he can find work. Abraham Lincoln would have pardoned this man. May you follow his example!"

Mr. Backus nursed his chin. He entirely agreed with everything that Mr. Tutt had said as to how people regarded him, and, accordingly, he thought highly of Mr. Tutt. Yes, undoubtedly—if what the latter said were true—Lincoln would have let this prisoner go.

"It certainly seems a hard case," he admitted. "Still, technically he is undoubtedly guilty of burglary in the first degree. Under the decisions, a table knife is a dangerous weapon. However——"

He pressed a button.

"Ask Mr. Gogarty to come in here," he directed the officer who answered.

Instantly Mr. Tutt's old heart sank into his congress shoes. One of the toughest birds in the district attorney's office! What pity could be expected of him!

"May I ask why you are sending for Mr. Gogarty?"

"It's his case, I must ask his opinion, as a matter of courtesy if nothing else," replied the other uneasily.

Entered a fascist—Mr. Gogarty.

"Well, Backus," he barked, hardly glancing at Mr. Tutt, "what is it?"

"People against Kaplan. The complainant wants to withdraw. How about it?"

"That's that holdup case, isn't it? It's airtight. The defendant's halfway up the river already. Of course, the complainant can't withdraw!"

"It is a very hard case, Mr. Gogarty," interposed Mr. Tutt, trying to put the conversation on a less official key.

"Every case is a hard case—for somebody," retorted Gogarty.

"These complainants are all hell-bent to get their man arrested, but as soon as he goes to jail, they turn chickenhearted."

"When the alleged crime was committed, this defendant had had nothing to eat for over twelve hours. He fainted from exhaustion and lack of food."

"One of those 'stole to keep the children from starving' cases?" sneered Gogarty.

"Precisely and literally that. There is no doubt as to the facts. I have looked into them personally and I only wish you would do the same."

"Mr. Tutt offers to send the defendant and his family to the country and keep them there until he can get work, provided we dismiss the indictment or accept a plea to illegal entry and recommend a suspended sentence," explained Backus.

"Suspended sentence, my hat! In a first-degree-burglary case? Who the hell is this complainant?"

Gogarty picked up the indictment and examined the list of witnesses upon its reverse side.

Then he stared with a half grin at Mr. Tutt.

"So you're not the defendant's lawyer, as I naturally assumed; you're the complainant!"

"I am neither the complainant nor the defendant's attorney. The alleged offense for which he is indicted occurred in my house, but I would be glad to see the prosecution dropped. I am not the complainant in this case."

"Just a Good Samaritan, eh? Makes no difference. You're the chief witness for the State—the only one, in fact, except the two cops and this nigger, Miranda Washington. Who is his lawyer?" He glanced at the face of the indictment. "H'm! Don't seem to have any. Well, the court will have to assign counsel."

Mr. Tutt faced the prosecutors.

"What do you propose to do?"

"I can't very well go counter to the advice of Mr. Gogarty," answered Backus weakly.

Mr. Tutt arose.

"Mr. Gogarty," he said solemnly, "I may as well tell you frankly that I do not care to testify against this man."

"The hell you don't! Well, you've got to testify whether you like it or not!"

Mr. Tutt's lips trembled.

"Unless you accept my suggestion to accept a plea to illegal entry, you will never secure a conviction in this case."

Gogarty's jaw shot out.

"Oh, that's it!" He snatched a yellow slip from the corner of the desk and rapidly filled it with his fountain pen. Then he handed it to the old man. It was a subpœna requiring Ephraim Tutt's appearance as a witness at the trial of Ludwig Kaplan for burglary the next day but one.

"I guess that fixes it. If you don't come to court voluntarily in obedience to this subpœna, we'll bring you there in a hurry-up wagon."

Mr. Tutt slowly tore the paper into fragments and scattered them upon the floor. His face was stern.

"For the last time, will you accept a plea in the case of the People versus Kaplan to illegal entry and recommend him to mercy?"

Gogarty leered at him.

"No, grandpa, we won't! And you can do your damndest!"

Mr. Tutt reached for his stove-pipe hat.

"In that case, I will!" he said.

There are two sorts of cases in the District Attorney's Office: the one known as a "big case"—usually murder—where a squad of deputies brief the law and the facts for the trial assistant, aided by detectives and officers on special detail; the other, the ordinary knock-down-and-drag-out, run-of-mine offense, which the prosecutor "tries off the papers," with no special preparation, calling the witnesses who have already testified before the grand jury in the order in which they appear upon the back of the indictment. The People versus Kaplan was of the latter sort.

The cops had told Gogarty all about it—how they had caught the defendant red-handed, and how both Mr. Tutt and his cook had been there throughout the whole affair, seen all there was to be seen, heard all there was to be heard. It was, in police parlance, a "pipe." This was "nuts" to Gogarty, who never did a stroke of work for himself unless it was absolutely necessary. He had always hated Mr. Tutt, and he proposed to teach the old geezer a lesson for interfering, by convicting Kaplan of the highest degree of crime possible and giving him the limit.

One of the minor intermediate steps by which he proposed to achieve his unholy end was by inducing his friend, the Hon. Aloysius McCann, to assign as counsel to the prisoner one Sammy Grossbaum, the most inefficient shyster hanging about the courtroom, who would make a farce of the defense. He had, in fact, already spoken to Sammy, tipped him off, given him a couple of cigars and promised not to forget him. No preparation would be necessary except to make sure that the witnesses had been properly subpœnaed and were in court. He had subpœnaed Mr. Tutt himself, and the names of Officer Patrick O'Grady and Officer William Sheehan had been ticked off on his working calendar, showing that they were on hand. Miranda Washington had not yet put in an appearance, but the head process server had stated that she had been duly subpœnaed. No doubt she was on the way, and, anyhow, even if she did not arrive on time, Tutt, who had seen the whole show, together with the cops, would be enough to convict. Everything was O. K. He could fire when ready. His ancient enemy, helpless under oath in the witness chair, would be compelled to testify against the man he had sought to save. The very defense was to be conducted by a stool pigeon.

His annoyance may therefore be imagined when, the case having been called, Ludwig Kaplan was led in from the prison pen and Mr. Ephraim Tutt arose from where he had been sitting and took his place at the defendant's side.

"Mr. Clerk, please indorse my name upon the indictment as counsel for the prisoner," he said quietly. Then, turning to his client: "Sit down, Ludwig. You have nothing to fear. Everything is going to be all right."

Gogarty was struck dumb. Old Tutt couldn't act as counsel for the defense! How could any prosecutor try a case in which the State's chief witness appeared as attorney for the prisoner? No such thing had ever before happened or even been thought of! However, he supposed there was no legal reason against it. After all, a witness was a witness, obliged upon his oath to tell all he knew. And if he chose to defend the man he testified against, it would certainly put him in a very awkward position—open to the suspicion of soft-pedalling his testimony for the benefit of his client. All the same, Gogarty didn't like it. Could the old codger have something up his sleeve, of which this was but a forerunner? And the defendant! Old Tutt had rigged him out in a nice new blue serge suit, so that he didn't look like a gangster at all! Gogarty was so angry that, almost before he was aware of it, a jury had been sworn and the case was on.

"You may open to the jury, Mr. Gogarty," directed the court;

and the prosecutor, with his professional smile of ingratiation, approached the box and, looking familiarly down upon the twelve faces, began:

"Gentlemen of the jury: I shall not detain you with any lengthy preview of the evidence in this case. The witnesses will speak for themselves—and how! This defendant was caught red-handed, about nine o'clock at night, burglarizing a house on West 23d Street, in the course of which, being surprised in his preparations to make way with his loot, he attempted to hold up one of the servants with a knife. Unfortunately for him, either by Divine act or some mysterious force of Nature, he fell insensible in a fainting fit or collapse before he could carry out his threatened assault. That is all there is to this case." He hesitated. "All but one curious coincidence—namely, that the burglar has retained as his lawyer the chief witness against him; for what reason I can safely leave to your own imaginations."

He was about to call one of the policemen, when Judge McCann beckoned to him.

"Say, Bill, what is this? Tutt can't defend and prosecute at the same time!"

"Damn if I know whether he can or not," replied Gogarty. "But he's been working to get this fellow off ever since he was indicted. Maybe he's tryin' to hide something."

"What sort of case have you?"

"Ironclad. You heard my statement."

"Well, don't let him get away with it," warned McCann. "Give him the works." Gogarty turned toward the courtroom.

"Officer Patrick O'Grady, take the witness chair!"

"You are a member of the police force of the City of New York," rattled off Gogarty. "Were you on duty at or about nine o'clock on the night of April seventeenth last on West 23d Street?"

Officer O'Grady shoved his gum into the corner of his mouth and replied self-consciously that he was. He was a large man and had difficulty in squeezing his huge bulk into the chair.

"Tell us what happened."

"On the night of April seventeenth last," repeated O'Grady, like an automatic machine, "I was on post on 23d Street. Officer Sheehan was just relieving me when we heard some one holler 'Police.' We both ran up the block. As we approached this here house we heard screams, and went in to see what was the trouble. This gentleman here"—pointing at Mr. Tutt—"was coming down the stairs with a poker in his hand. Some one was yelling bloody murder on the floor below, and we beat it down to the kitchen as fast as we could. A colored woman was standing by the stove with her hands in the air, screaming at the top of her voice. On the floor was this here defendant. He'd fainted or something. I frisked him, but he had nothing in the way of gun. Then this gentleman"—again indicating Mr. Tutt—"came in. He asked the colored woman——"

"I object," said Mr. Tutt. "The officer cannot testify to what I asked or what may have been said in reply."

"This was in the presence of the defendant, wasn't it?" inquired the court. "I'll allow it."

"One moment, Your Honor!" Mr. Tutt got up. "Statements made in the presence of a defendant are admitted—if admitted at all—on the theory that they may call for a reply, which, if not made, may be tantamount to acquiescence or even confession. Otherwise they would be pure hearsay. Now, it is obvious that if a defendant is insensible, as the officer testifies was the case here, he could not reply, any more than if he were bound and gagged, drugged or dead. He could not even hear what was said. Hence his silence could not give consent, no inference can be drawn from it, and nothing said in his presence can be used as evidence against him."

"I hadn't thought of that," admitted McCann, looking quickly at Gogarty. "Unless Mr. Gogarty can answer your point, I shall reverse my ruling and sustain the objection."

Gogarty tried again: "Well, did Mr. Tutt say something?"

"He did."

"And did the cook say something?"

"She did."

"And this was in the presence of the defendant?"

"He was there."

"What was said?"

"I object," said Mr. Tutt.

"Sustained."

Gogarty looked helplessly at McCann. Of course, it wasn't admissible. What the hell was he to do? He sparred for time:

"Did you find anything on the floor?"

"I found a plated table knife and half a banana."

"Is this the knife?"

"It is."

"I offer it in evidence," said Gogarty.

"Received," said McCann. "It may be marked 'People's Exhibit A.'"

"Haven't you got the banana?" inquired Mr. Tutt innocently, and the jury laughed, to Gogarty's fury. He couldn't think of anything more to ask.

"Well, what—what happened then?"

"Officer Sheehan telephoned for the wagon, and while he was gone, this gentleman tried to make the defendant swallow some brandy, but he couldn't. Then the wagon came and we took the prisoner first to the station house and then to the hospital."

"Did you have any talk with him at any time?"

"No, he was insensible."

"What happened to the cook?"

"I don't know."

"And that's all you know about the case?"

"That's all."

"Your witness," said Gogarty, with a grimace toward the bench, and Mr. Tutt arose. The jury looked at him expectantly, almost affectionately. There must be some good reason why he should be defending the youth who had robbed his house—if, in fact, the latter had done so.

"Officer O'Grady," began the old man gently, "did you have any difficulty in getting into my house?"

"None at all. The door was open."

"I did not open it for you?"

"No. You was still coming down the flight above."

"Thank you, Officer. Now, you say that the cook was screaming?"

"Sure. She was scared stiff."

"And there was apparently a young man dead, dying or at least insensible on the floor near her?"

"Yes. He was like a corpse."

"She had her hands raised to heaven?"

"They was up in the air."

"As you have seen negroes raise their arms when praying?"

"She weren't prayin'. This feller had stuck her up."

"I move that the answer be stricken out as unresponsive," said Mr. Tutt.

"Strike it out," ordered the court. . . . "Answer the question, Officer."

"How do I know how niggers raise their arms?"

"Was there anything about the way she held her arms that of itself would indicate whether she were praying or merely frightened?"

"Maybe she was both."

"Maybe she was," agreed Mr. Tutt. "Were you in the kitchen when she raised her arms?"

"I was not."

"Then you don't know whether she lifted them before or after the young man had his collapse?"

"I do not."

"Did you see the defendant enter the house?"

"No."

"Then you cannot testify from your own observation that this woman did not let him in?"

"No."

"Or offer him the food that was on the table?"

"No. I wasn't there."

Mr. Tutt sat down. Then he added with the utmost good nature: "And although I couldn't get the defendant to drink any brandy, I had no difficulty on that score with you, did I?"

Officer O'Grady grinned sheepishly without replying.

"Pretty good brandy, wasn't it?"

"Best I ever tasted!"

"That is all, Officer. Thank you."

The foreman smiled at Mr. Tutt.

"Got any on your hip?" he whispered *sotto voce*.

"I object to the juror conversing with counsel!" snapped Gogarty, choking with rage, thereby alienating the foreman forever.

Officer Sheehan proved of no more aid to the prosecution than his comrade, O'Grady. Whenever he started to tell what either Miranda or Mr. Tutt had said upon the momentous evening, he was instantly stopped. Apart from what he had learned from them, it was obvious that he could shed no light whatever upon the defendant's presence in the house or what had occurred after the latter's arrival there.

McCann was getting restive. Fundamentally, he had no more regard for Gogarty than Gogarty had for him. Their alliance was strictly one of business. They hunted in the same leash after the same game. Both wanted a reputation for convictions, and McCann had no inclination to see his court turned into a monkey house, which Mr. Tutt appeared to be doing with some success. Again he beckoned to the prosecutor.

"You're getting your neck in a noose!" he warned. "First thing you know you won't be able to make a case."

"All right! All right!" retorted Gogarty truculently. "Give me a break! Of course, I can make a case. These cops don't know anything. I'm going to call my real witnesses now. . . . Miranda Washington, take the stand!"

No one stood up. There was naught but silence.

"Call her in the hall," ordered Gogarty. "She was subpœnaed all right! She must be here!"

"Miranda Washington! Miranda Washington!" could be heard booming through the corridors.

The doorkeeper thrust in his head.

"Witness doesn't answer."

Gogarty stepped to the rail and whispered angrily to a process server.

"I served her myself yesterday afternoon, boss," the latter assured him. "Honest, I did!"

"Well, send out a 'forthwith' for her! Telephone the nearest police station!"

Fuming, he retraced his steps to his place before the jury box. He wasn't done yet. Now the Old Fox would have to tell what he knew.

"Mr. Tutt, take the stand."

"With pleasure," beamed the old man, bowing to the court and seating himself in the witness chair.

Gogarty, realizing that he must exercise more control, aped an air of easy amiability.

"Mr. Tutt, you live at —— West 23d Street, don't you?"

"I have lived there for thirty years."

"What time did you go home on April seventeenth last?"

"About nine o'clock."

"How did you get in?"

"With my latchkey."

"Where was your colored cook, Miranda Washington, at that time?"

"I do not know."

"Where did you go after you let yourself in?"

"I went to my library, sat down, opened a bottle of Burgundy and started to read."

"Did anything attract your attention?"

"Yes. I heard Miranda scream."

"What was she screaming about?"

"She was calling upon the Lord for help."

"What did you do?"

"I threw open the window, yelled for the police, grabbed the poker, and ran downstairs."

"You didn't know what might have happened?"

"I did not. I only knew that Mandy must be very much frightened."

"Were the officers ahead of you?"

"They were—by a few feet."

"And when you reached the kitchen what did you see?"

"Exactly what has been already described—Mandy with her arms raised to heaven, an apparently dead man upon the floor."

"Did you have any conversation with your cook?"

"Yes."

"What was it?"

"I object to that question, as the defendant cannot possibly be bound by the answer," returned the witness-lawyer.

"Sustained!" McCann was scowling at Gogarty.

"Was anything missing out of your house?"

"On the contrary, nothing had been taken."

"Didn't you testify before the grand jury that Mandy said——"

"Bang!" went McCann's gavel.

"What this witness testified before the grand jury is not evidence here!" he declared severely.

Gogarty, grinding his teeth, see-sawed from one leg to the other.

"Have you had any conversation with the defendant about that night? How he got into your house and why he went there?"

"Any conversations I have had with the defendant are privileged, as between lawyer and client."

"You should know that, Mr. Gogarty," admonished the court.

"How do I know when this witness became the attorney for the defense?" returned Gogarty.

"I will tell you," replied Mr. Tutt. "I offered him my services the day before yesterday, after learning from you that he had no counsel."

Gogarty looked disgusted. "Do you know where this precious cook of yours is at the present moment?"

Mr. Tutt, pressing the tips of his long fingers together, smiled genially at Gogarty:

"I haven't the faintest idea."

"When did you last see her?"

"Night before last. I knew that she had been hoping to visit some relatives in the South and, as I intended to move over to the club for a week or so, I told her that she could have that time to herself. If she is not at my house, I do not know where to suggest that you look for her."

"Didn't you know perfectly well that she would be needed as a witness in this case?" flared Gogarty.

"It did not occur to me that I need concern myself about the requirements of a prosecuting attorney so celebrated for the careful preparation of his cases as yourself, Mr. Gogarty," replied Mr. Tutt. "Besides which, did I not understand you to say that she had been duly subpœnaed?"

Gogarty slumped into his chair.

"That's all!" he ejaculated, waving his hand to indicate that Mr. Tutt was at liberty to leave the stand. But the old man did not move.

"Have you concluded your examination, sir?" he inquired with elaborate politeness.

"Sure. You may step down," answered Gogarty.

"I do not wish to step down," returned Mr. Tutt. "Now that you are through your direct, I propose to exercise the privilege of cross-examining myself."

The twelve in the box, taking this as one of Mr. Tutt's jokes, grinned. No. 6 guffawed. Mr. Tutt, however, cleared his throat and with utmost seriousness propounded himself a question:

"Mr. Tutt," asked Mr. Tutt, "did you close and lock the door of your house on your return home the evening of April seventeenth last?"

Gogarty sprang up.

"Hold on there! You can't do that!"

Mr. Tutt blandly regarded him.

"Why not?"

"It's nonsense! Whoever heard of a witness cross-examining himself?"

"I have done so a great many times," replied the old man. "While it may be somewhat unusual, it is, under the circumstances, correct legal procedure."

"There's too many unusual things in this case!" growled Gogarty. He looked angrily toward the bench. "Your Honor, I object to defendant's counsel sitting up there and talking to the jury under the guise of asking himself questions."

Now, although Mr. Tutt's statement as to the legality of what he proposed to do was entirely sound, it so happened that such a thing had never occurred in McCann's experience. On the other hand, he was thoroughly disgusted with Gogarty's lack of preparation and general conduct of the case. So he hedged.

"What you propose is certainly rather novel, isn't it, Mr. Tutt?" he commented. "How can a witness cross-examine himself? It is hardly possible for him to act as both a witness and a lawyer at one and the same time."

"With the greatest deference to what may appear to be Your Honor's opinion," answered Mr. Tutt, "it is not only possible but often absolutely necessary. A moment's reflection will convince Your Honor that this must be so. It cannot be the law that a defendant may be deprived of the right of cross-examining any witness who may be called against him. Even were I a witness for the defense instead of the chief witness for the prosecution——"

"You!" grunted Gogarty. "You're a swell witness for the prosecution!"

"I repeat," said Mr. Tutt, "that even were I a witness for the defense, it would not occur to the prosecutor that he could prevent my testifying in behalf of my client merely because I happened to be the prisoner's attorney. That would be, obviously, a perversion of justice. But here he has called me as a witness himself! What is sauce for the gander is sauce for the"—he peered whimsically at Gogarty—"the—er—goose. He must fish or cut bait. He cannot have his cake and eat it. In a word, he cannot avail himself of my testimony and at same time deprive the defendant of one of his most fundamental rights—that of cross-examination."

"What you are saying seems to make good sense," agreed McCann. "I confess that at first blush the idea of a witness cross-examining himself seemed to be somewhat ludicrous. The difficulty——"

"—— is hardly worthy of such a designation, Your Honor. That there is no one to question me on behalf of the defendant but myself is the merest accident. Had I an associate, of course, he would be at liberty to do so. Moreover, a defendant may always act as his own counsel, and should he see fit, could cross-examine me now. There is no reason, however, in law or practice, why I should not relieve him of that burden and cross-examine myself."

"I do not see any," answered McCann. "You may proceed."

Mr. Tutt bowed. "Where was I? . . . Oh, yes! The question was as to whether I closed and locked my door that night. My answer is:

"I do not recall doing so. As I grow older, my memory becomes less and less reliable. It is more than likely that I forgot to close it after me—in which case"—he looked up at McCann—"if I may, ex officio, so to speak, resume my capacity of defendant's counsel, my client could not be guilty of burglary, but only of illegal entry."

McCann nodded. Gogarty was out, so far as he was concerned. Mr. Tutt continued to question himself:

"Mr. Tutt, do you know of your own knowledge whether this defendant entered your house by himself through the open door or rang and was admitted by your cook?

"I do not.

"Do you know of your own knowledge whether this defendant was a friend of your cook or an intruder?

"I do not.

"Do you know of your own knowledge whether or not your cook voluntarily procured the food upon the kitchen table for the purpose of giving it to the defendant to take with him?

"I do not.

"Do you know of your own knowledge whether this defendant collapsed before or after your cook screamed?

"I do not."

Gogarty had thrown himself, sulking, into his chair.

"Go ahead," he snorted. "Ask yourself anything you like!"

"I have finished. Is there any redirect examination?" inquired Mr. Tutt.

"No. That is the People's case."

Mr. Tutt descended from the witness stand and returned to the counsel table, followed by the puzzled eyes of the jury.

"The defense rests," he said. "I move that the court direct a verdict of acquittal."

"Do you want an adjournment in order to locate your missing witness?" asked McCann.

But Gogarty had had enough. The woman was probably in Louisiana by this time! The sooner the whole thing was over the better.

"Hell, no!" he growled. "Go ahead and throw the damn case out!"

McCann rapped for order.

"Gentlemen of the jury," he said: "In the case at bar there has been, for one reason or another, what appears to the Court to be an entire failure of competent evidence to establish the elements of the crime with which this defendant stands indicted. There is nothing to show—so far as the record goes—that this defendant was not voluntarily admitted to the house of Miranda Washington either as a friend or as a beggar, that she did not voluntarily assemble the food upon the table either for him to eat or as a gift to his family, and that her screams when he collapsed were not merely those of fright and alarm at his unfortunate condition. For that reason I must direct an acquittal; although, were it not for the rules of evidence by which the Court is bound, we should no doubt have heard quite a different story. . . . Mr. Clerk, you may take the verdict."

As the jury crowded around Mr. Tutt to learn what it was all about, Gogarty sidled to the bench.

"I forgot that point about him being insensible," lamely explained the brilliant prosecutor.

"I know who was insensible!" scathingly remarked McCann.

Just at that moment a stout negro woman in a flamboyant calico dress with a sash of baby blue pushed her way to the bar.

" 'Scuse me!" she said, with a wide smile full of white teeth. "Ise Mandy Washington. Was any one lookin' fo' me?"

"Are we looking for you?" shouted Gogarty. "I'll say we are! Where have you been all this time? Don't you know the judge can send you to jail for staying away from court after you have been subpœnaed?"

Miranda faced him defiantly, her hands on her ample hips. Then her eye caught Mr. Tutt's and, in spite of herself, she giggled.

"Ah's been comin' all de time, Mistah Man! De jedge can't do nuff'n to me! Ah's been on mah way!"

THE MEANEST MAN

I

Ever since old "Doc" Barrows had swindled the Somerset County agriculturists by selling them worthless bonds, and Squire Hezekiah Mason, the then local prosecutor, in spite of the fact that Doc was known to be a harmless old nut, had insisted on sending him to Sing Sing for so doing, his widowed daughter, "Ma" Best, had been paying back her father's victims little by little—all except Mason himself, and to him, at his own suggestion, she had given a mortgage on the Phœnix Hotel for twice the amount involved. Doc had been sixty years old when Mason had sent him up—a cheery old soak with an insane glitter in his watery eye whenever the conversation touched upon diamond mines, gushers, or the wonderful way you could distill gold out of sea-water—"Seen 'em do it myself, I tell ye!" He had staggered out of prison ten years later, the glitter gone, a broken old man, rambling on, until he died, about the days when he had been on intimate terms with "the Morgins," the "Rocky-fellers," and "Johnny W. Gates."

In the sixteen years which had elapsed since Doc's conviction, Ma had wiped out the major part of his indebtedness.

There was a certain justice in the voluntarily assumed obligation, for part of the Phœnix Hotel had originally been built out of Doc's ill-gotten gains, and Ma continued to run it for the benefit of those whom he had defrauded, most of them people of small means. She would have wiped out all of it, had she not been paying double interest to Mason.

The loss of the five thousand dollars which Doc had enticed from the horny clutch of this country Shylock had cruelly hurt the latter's pride. He still had the bonds—beautiful pink securities engraved with the effigies of Indians, chasing herds of buffalo off prairie railroad-tracks in order, apparently, to enable them to escape the onward rush of a locomotive with a cuspidor-shaped smokestack —gold refunding general-mortgage bonds, bearing 8 per cent, and not due until 1967! He had bought them from Doc at 89⅞, under the impression that the latter, being a mental defective, did not know what they were worth, only to find a few months later that no such bonds had ever been issued. Doc, who had put the money, meantime, into the second floor of the hotel, insisted that the railroad's assertion was sheer nonsense.

"Morgin handed me those bonds himself, he did! 'Doc,' he says, 'you kin just put 'em away and fergit about 'em, an' you'll have sumpthin' to fall back on in your old age,' he says. 'They'll sell at 200 some day, Doc,' he says. . . . How kin you tell they won't, Mr. Mason?"

"What did you give Mr. Morgan for 'em?" demanded Mason, with his eye on the jury, which half an hour later found Doc guilty.

"I give him a half interest in my patent."

"What patent?"

"My sea-water patent fer makin' gold."

And the jury had convicted Doc under the common misapprehension that such was their duty if he owed the complainant money.

That evening the prosecutor had called upon "Ma" Best in the kitchen of the Phœnix Hotel.

"Judge Tompkins is going to sentence your father to-morrow morning, Mrs. Best," he said with an ominous ring in his gritty voice. "What I say will have consid'r'ble influence. As you know, your dad was convicted for stealin' two thousand dollars from 'Toggery Bill' Gookin by falsely representing them bonds to be legal obligations of the corporation issuin' the same. He kin get anywheres from one to ten years. There's another indictment chargin' him with stealin' five thousand dollars from me. I kin have it tried or not, ez I see fit. But I guess your dad kin get punished all that's necessary in Toggery's case. Now my money went into the hotel, so why not give me a mortgage on it? Ten thousand dollars would be about right, I guess. I figure I lost more'n that. You see the bonds was worth two hundred, accordin' to what your dad told me, and I had five of 'em. That in itself makes ten thousand. And then there's loss of interest, and expenses, and what I might 'a' made in something else if I'd kept my money. I don't see why Tompkins needs to be so awful hard on Doc, in view of his condition, 'specially if——"

He got the mortgage; Doc got ten years. And Ma had been paying the Squire eight hundred dollars annually for sixteen years—a total of twelve thousand eight hundred—and still owed Mason the principal of ten thousand.

"All the same, father did get five thousand dollars from him,"

Ma had protested to Sheriff Moses Higgins, in defense of her action, when he had expostulated with her.

"I wish Doc had taken all he had, durn his soul!" returned Mose indignantly.

That was also the way all the inhabitants of Pottsville felt about it, for there was no more unpopular man in the whole upper tier of New York counties than Squire—"Stinker"—Hezekiah Mason, whose mortgage on the Phœnix Hotel was but one in his sheaf of nearly a hundred that covered the farms of Somerset County.

For ten years Ma had worked herself to the bone trying to make enough profit out of the precarious transient business to pay the Squire his usurious interest and have something left for more deserving sufferers. But the roads were bad, trade was light, and the only really good seasons were while the County Fair was on in the autumn, the winter term of court, and during the trout season in the spring, when Lawyer Ephraim Tutt, and a few other sapient ones, hied themselves to the Mohawk Valley to whip the whirling waters of Chasm Brook or the quieter inlet of Turkey Pond.

At that time the Phœnix, although famous for its cooking, was known as a three-dollar house—namely, room, a dollar-fifty; dinner, a dollar; supper, seventy-five cents; breakfast, fifty. Thus, if you took board by the day you saved a whole seventy-five cents! There was electric light, but no running water in the rooms; the beds had wooden slats, and towels were changed only on demand. Ma cooked the meals, her small daughter Betty waited on the table, assisted by a miscellaneous negro boy named Ulysses, and the upstairs work "got done somehow," a hand-to-mouth enterprise which paid its way because expenses were reduced to a minimum and there were no bad debts. In fine, during those first ten years "Ma" Best ran the Phœnix Hotel for the benefit of Squire Mason, who cracked the lash of labor over her back and took ninety-five per cent of the profits.

And then the motor brought Prosperity with a gigantic *P* to Pottsville and the Phœnix Hotel. Where the eye of the traveller had originally been met only by a sign in faded lettering above the pillars of a sagging piazza and rickety porte-cochère, now swung the creaking silhouette of a flamingo-colored bird in full flight—rivalling in size the fabled roc—and alleged by the artist, "Cy" Pennypacker, of the Art Foto Salon, to be an accurate representation of a phœnix arising from its ashes. The pillars gained self-respect and stood erect. Bright blue replaced the weatherworn white of the façade. And Ulysses, arrayed in a uniform of smart green with pill-box cap of the same, lolled superciliously beneath the porte-cochère to open the doors of the line of waiting motors and pass the occupants on to the head-waiter—erstwhile Deputy Sheriff Sam Bellows, who stood in white ducks beside the door and waved the motorists into the dining-room at two-fifty per head.

The Perfect Tour had put Pottsville on the map, and the Phœnix, by virtue of its vermilion and blue trappings, became a palace hotel. For three miles in both directions, up and down the valley, the appetite of the approaching motorist was titillated by similar scarlet phœnixes, suspended at intervals above the roadway, each bearing a single magic word. From these signs, taken tandem, successively, *in toto*, *en masse* and *ensemble*, the wayfarer, provided his eyesight was unimpaired by the strident color, would be gradually educated in crescendo to the gastronomical possibilities awaiting him in Pottsville.

EAT—EAT—EAT at the PHŒNIX HOTEL—EAT—EAT!
Famous for its Chicken and Lobster Dinners.
Fresh Corn—Beans—Peas—Cider—Waffles—Flapjacks.
EVERY MODERN CONVENIENCE
Hot Baths.
Golf—Tennis—Hunting—Fishing
EAT—EAT—EAT at the PHŒNIX HOTEL—EAT—EAT!

Ma admitted that the references to sport were slightly exaggerated, and that the final *s* on the word "Baths" was nearly a fib, but she said she reckoned if folks wanted to hunt and play "golluf" there wasn't anything to stop 'em, and anybody who wanted to pay for the privilege could take plural baths instead of one.

Anyhow, the point is that they came, joyously leaving two-fifty per behind them and cramming the white-gloved palms of Sam Bellows and Ulysses with silver quarters and half-dollars; and many of them stayed overnight and bought picture-postals, and nut sundaes, and the genuine Indian moccasins and curios which Ma ordered from New York and sold in the hotel lobby, and crowded into the Pottsville Palace cinema, and "just loved being in the country—I mean the real country!"

So Ma replaced the slats with box-springs and put up her prices—room, six-fifty; dinner, two-fifty; supper, two-fifty; breakfast, one-fifty; garage, two-fifty. The Phœnix became a twelve-dollar-a-day house, and the citizens of Pottsville pointed with pride to Ma's new filling-station, with its green lattice covered with artificial crimson ramblers and its row of scarlet and blue pumps.

"I only wish dad could ha' lived to see this day!" she sighed frequently as the money kept on pouring into her lap. "There's more gold in oil than in sea-water!"

Her success was wormwood to Squire Mason's soul, since he regarded the hotel as by rights belonging to him. He'd paid for most of it, hadn't he? He ground his yellow teeth at the thought that the mortgage had but one year more to run. Ma tried to pay it off, but he would not let her.

"No, I'm in no hurry. I'm satisfied with my interest and my security," he snarled.

Distrustful of him, she offered, if he would cancel the mortgage then and there, to pay a bonus of five hundred dollars; but, although sorely tempted, he refused.

"I'll git that hotel yet!" he swore to himself. "All these fixings cost a pile o' money; p'r'aps she'll go bust! Or mebbe when the mortgage falls due, I kin fix it so she can't raise the cash to pay, and I'll have the chance to foreclose! Lots of things can happen in a year!"

So, having installed running water in the bedrooms and added a couple of baths, a new dining-room with plate-glass windows, an architectural chimneypiece and a radio, Ma, indulging in a sort of second blooming, walked into Sheriff Moses Higgins' automobile agency one morning and bought herself a dandy little new sedan to trundle her old bones around in.

To Mason it was the last straw. He, who had always been too mean to buy a car himself, was sick with envy of the woman who paid him eight hundred dollars a year voluntarily and out of a sense of justice. The yellow-eyed monster perched upon his shoulder and whispered in his hairy ear.

It was he that should have had that car! The woman had bought it out of his money! He almost persuaded himself that if she had a spark of common decency she would offer to give it to him. And then it slowly dawned upon his jaundiced intelligence that there was no real reason why he should not own a car himself, instead of sponging on anybody who happened to be going in his direction.

Cautiously he let it become known that he was thinkin' some

of gettin' a car later on, mebbe, and on the strength of it had several hundred miles of tryouts and demonstrations in both Pottsville and Patterson. All winter long he studied catalogues, canvassed thoroughly the used-car question, debated exhaustively with Sheriff Higgins the relative desirability of various types, and at last, when the latter's patience was almost exhausted, broached the proposition which he had been maturing in his mind.

The Honorable Hezekiah had for twenty years been consumed with a devouring social ambition—that of being elected a member of the Pottsville herd of the Sacred Camels of King Menelik, the benevolent order of which Sheriff Higgins was probably the most influential Dromedary. Thrice had he foisted his name upon the election committee of the local lodge of The Brotherhood of Abyssinian Mysteries, to which the herd belonged, and thrice had he been unanimously blackballed. Yet he was not discouraged. Every man had his price. Tit for tat! It would only need a little log-rolling. If he purchased the contemplated car from Sheriff Higgins, why should not the latter procure his longed-for election to the Abyssinian Brotherhood?

"Well, Sheriff!" he remarked, strolling into the show-room one evening early in April, "I've 'most decided to order one of your Silent Silver Sixes; provided, of course, you're willing to split your commission with me. But there's just one little matter I wanted to talk over with ye first—so's there wouldn't be any misunderstanding later."

"Wal, what is it?" inquired Mose suspiciously.

"You're still Grand Supreme Patriarch of the Sacred Camels, ain't ye?"

The sheriff's face became grim.

"I don't know what you have reference to!" he replied stiffly.

"Bunk!" retorted the Squire. "What's the use bein' so mysterious 'bout something everyone knows! Don't I watch you going into the P. and H. Hall every Friday night? I kin see you, right through the window, setting up there in your purple nightgown a-holding your gold spear!"

The Grand Supreme Patriarch of the Sacred Camels of King Menelik restrained a homicidal impulse in view of the prospective sale of the Silent Silver Six.

"Speakin' seriously, Mose, what I want to ask you is this: What chance have I got of being took into the brotherhood? I know all the boys, and there ain't nothin' agin me, so far as I know. Why can't you get me in?"

The sheriff turned contemptuously on the hard-visaged lawyer.

"Mason," he said frankly, "you've about as much chance to get into any fraternal organization as a celluloid cat to get outer hell. They wouldn't elect ye into the Boy Scouts, the Total Abstinence League, or the Society for the Prevention of Cruelty to Animals."

As the Squire stalked out of the store Mose almost suffered a relapse.

"Durn it all!" he muttered. "I've lost that sale all right! Now, sure as shootin' he'll go over to Job Allen at Patterson and buy one o' them Humming Highjackers!"

But the Honorable Hezekiah fooled 'em all! Contrary to the firmly established and universally accepted moral tenet that every patriotic citizen should buy his car from his own local dealer, the measly skinflint committed the one unpardonable sin. Just to show 'em, he sneaked off to Utiky and bought a four-thousand-dollar Cytherea sedan on the installment plan, b'gosh!

Hate was not the only motivating cause of the Squire's extravagance, for the dealer who sold him the Cytherea had done so at a sacrifice, the car having been originally ordered by Miss Judy Josclyn of the Scarlet Sinners Number 3 Road Company, and never paid for. As Miss Josclyn's taste had expressed itself in a special paint job estimated at seven hundred and seventy-five dollars, involving yellow body and wheels, mud-guards, wheel-caps and rims, with vermilion trimmings, prospective customers, who as motorists desired to remain modestly inconspicuous, had rather shied from it. Not so Squire Mason! Here was his chance to parade, not only his wealth, but his independence of his fellow townsmen. Keep him out of the Sacred Camels, would they? He would let them see that he could get along quite well without them. He would teach 'em that they could not treat him with indifference and at the same time expect to get his money! He'd make 'em set up and take notice!

"Who's that in the big fancy car?" he could hear the yokels exclaiming to one another.

"That? Don't you know who that is? Why, that's Squire Hezekiah Mason, richest man in Somerset County!"

What they really said was: "Say, Bill, seen Mason's circus parade? He might as well 'a' bought a lion-cage and steam-calliope!"

But, of course, he trowed not of this, the only fly in the ointment of his satisfaction being the obvious fact that "Ma" Best's sedan was nearly as big as his.

II

Came then the great and never-to-be-forgotten day, a scarlet day compensating the citizens of Pottsville and of Patterson tenfold—nay, a thousandfold!—for all that they had ever suffered at Hezekiah Mason's hands—a purple day, the fame of which was destined to go echoing down the corridors of time until no true son or daughter of Pottsville could afford to admit, without losing caste, that he or she had failed to be one of those present and assisting in the dénouement. And since a precise knowledge of the *locus in quo* will contribute toward a fuller enjoyment of the adventure about to be recounted, let us now invite the attention of the jury—as did Squire Mason upon the day of the trial—to a somewhat detailed description of the whereabouts.

Know then, all of ye, that between Pottsville and Patterson Corners runs a highroad that at one point, for a hundred yards or so, borders the turbid overflow from Turkey Pond, forming as it were a causeway, or dike. In winter the boys skate there, but as the spring advances the waters recede and the pond becomes a swamp of black mud, thick or fluid, depending upon the character of the season's rainfall. Now, at a point about halfway across this swamp and at the foot of a slight declivity, another road emerges from the woods directly at right angles to the highway. It is a dangerous spot, since a motor coming downhill cannot be seen from the road below, which has no fence or barrier to protect it from the swamp. The road is the road of prosperity for the local inhabitants, who have spared neither labor nor money to make it straight, hard and smooth, and there is no true knight of the open road, whose eye alights upon that gray ribbon flowing so alluringly into the azure distance, but is irresistibly impelled to put his foot down and "step on it."

And now, gentlemen, having accurately described to you the place where the accident occurred, I must direct your attention to the time, the weather, the *dramatis personæ*, and what is commonly known as the *res gestæ*.

It is not my purpose, gentlemen of the jury, to attempt in any way to palliate the fault of my client, Mrs. Best. What she did, she did!—albeit unintentionally. But it is my duty to place within your reach all of the facts, in order that you may have a full understanding of the case and may be thus enabled, without confusion, fear or favor, to reach a proper decision.

My client, "Ma" Best—that good sweet soul—having at first utilized the services of the versatile Ulysses as her chauffeur—when he was not otherwise engaged—and observing the ease and dexterity with which he manipulated the wheel, decided before long to essay driving the car herself. Can you really blame her? Even if she had thoughtlessly neglected to take out a license? Imagine for yourselves, gentlemen, that beautiful spring afternoon, on Friday, May thirteenth last, with all Nature smiling, the birds singing, the great outdoors luring, as well as the commendable humanitarian desire to call upon your old friend Abigail Dix up on Beech Knoll, and inquire after her lumbago. Ulysses is busy at the filling-station. Your Silent Silver Six is awaiting you under the porte-cochère of the hotel. Propelled by an irresistible philanthropic urge, you seat yourself, release the brakes, push the self-starter, listen to its fascinating whir, and gently move off into the sunshine.

III

At about half-past four on that same afternoon Hezekiah Mason, having some interest to collect from a farmer who lived a few miles beyond Patterson Corners, closed his desk, shut and locked the door of his law office and descended the stairs. His beautiful yellow and vermilion Cytherea was awaiting him at the curb, new, glorious and uninsured,—for Hezekiah was a thrifty man and regarded insurance as a pure waste of good money. Seating himself in the sedan, he started her up and gingerly let in the clutch.

The birds were singing, all Nature smiling, and so on, and so on. But Hezekiah did not smile. Nature did not amuse him. Carefully—at not more than fifteen miles an hour—he started along the highroad toward Patterson Corners. Just ahead of him, in a dilapidated flivver which he had purchased for thirty dollars, rattled along one Oscar Giddings. As he gained the causeway, the said Oscar, tempted by the smooth surface, put on speed.

Hezekiah, filled with natural contempt for the wretched junk-shop drawing so rapidly away from him, and not desiring to be left behind, accelerated his own pace. They were about fifty yards apart and going at approximately thirty-five miles an hour as they approached the intersection of the crossroad leading from the knoll. No other cars were in sight. Oscar, unaware that there was a motor behind him, having run by the crossroad, suddenly decided, for no reason at all, to back and turn up it. Without extending his hand, looking around, or giving any other warning, he stopped abruptly, and throwing the gears into reverse, shot backward toward the onrushing and unsuspecting Squire, who, thinking only of how he should collect his interest, was paying no attention to the car in front of him, when he suddenly perceived that the flivver, instead of going in the same direction as himself, was backing toward him and that a collision was apparently inevitable.

Meanwhile "Ma" Best, who had somehow managed to negotiate the Beech Knoll Road, had satisfied her curiosity about Abigail's lumbago and had started upon her return trip. Half-way down the hill she realized to her horror that the car was out of her control. Hanging for dear life to the wheel, she could but try to steer and call upon the Lord. She did this loudly, as the Silent Six, at forty miles an hour, bounded down the slope towards the causeway, just as Oscar was slowing up at the entrance of the crossroad and the oncoming Squire had jammed on his emergency.

Swinging to the right in a vain effort to clear the flivver, "Ma" struck the Cytherea square in the midriff at the very instant when the Honorable Hezekiah was congratulating himself on his miraculous escape.

There was no justice in it! Squire Mason hadn't done a single thing he oughtn't to have done. He was driving well within the speed limit and was exercising due care; Oscar had deliberately stopped and backed without warning; "Ma" had no license, and didn't know how to drive anyhow. By every rule of right and equity one or both of the two latter miscreants should have suffered.

But they did not! As fate would have it, the bumper of the Silent Six caught the Cytherea at some mysterious point in its equilibrium, and with a crash that could have been heard in Utica, drove the Squire clear off the causeway and into the swamp, as neatly as a drop-kick planted squarely between goal-posts. "Ma" was knocked breathless against the steering-wheel, but otherwise unharmed; the Silent Six stopped, with a bent bumper, in its tracks. Oscar, hearing the smash, awoke to the realities in time to see the Cytherea lying upon its side in the mud and the Honorable Hezekiah Mason frantically struggling to climb through a badly damaged door.

"For heaven's sake, help a feller, can't ye?" he yelled. "Gol ding it, we're sinkin'!"

He spoke the truth! Beyond peradventure the Cytherea was slowly disappearing into the swamp,—sinking by the head in some hole or quicksand.

"Do somethin' quick, can't ye?" bawled the Squire, as he squeezed himself through the door and stood erect and apparently uninjured upon the side of the car.

"What kin I do?" inquired the dumfounded Oscar. "If she's sinkin', she'll sink! I ain't got no way to stop her."

"Haven't you got an emergency chain?"

"No. Haven't you?"

The Squire made no reply. He had discarded the idea of an emergency chain as extravagant.

Clouds of steam, accompanied by a fierce hissing, arose from the unfortunate Cytherea.

"Better come ashore!" suggested Oscar.

"How'm I goin' to git ashore?" roared the Squire. "This here is quicksand."

"If only there was a fence. I'd throw y' a rail, but there ain't none," Oscar informed him.

"If only there was a brick, I'd throw it at your head!" yelled the desperate attorney. "Why don't you go fer help, instead of standin' there like a pair of idiots doin' nothin'?"

At this moment two other cars drew up and the occupants thereof, observing the woebegone Squire, extended their derisive sympathy. The Cytherea was now a yellow Atlantis in a black and slimy ocean, which was creeping up over the wheels with the inevitability of Judgment Day. A truckload of farm-hands rumbling across the dike, stopped, gaped and burst into a hymn of hate. Other cars appeared from both directions.

People sprouted mysteriously out of the ground, and the Pottsville fire-alarm began to sound its tocsin. Soon the causeway was lined with jeering spectators feasting their eyes upon the Squire in his extremity, but making no move to help him. They had waited a lifetime for this opportunity and were going to make the most of it. Their witticisms were both mordant and heartless. But the Squire, who had at first ground his teeth in impotent rage, was by this time too terrified either to resent or properly to evaluate them.

"Jump in, Squire! The water's warm!"

"Swim fer it, old mud-turtle!"

"What'll you take for the old bus?"

"Can't y' walk on the water?"

Above the chorus of catcalls was now heard the frenzied clanging of a bell, as the Pottsville Hook and Ladder Company came clattering across the causeway. Over on Turtle Pond the whistle of Sampson's Steam Lumber Mill added its shrill voice to the infernal clamor. The red-hatted firemen, led by Grand Supreme Dromedary Mose Higgins, piled off the truck and rushed to the edge of the swamp.

"Hey, Squire!" called the sheriff. "Want to buy a nice, new car, if I'll split commissions with ye?"

"Got one'll float?" inquired "Toggery Bill" Gookin.

"Sell him a marine policy!" suggested someone else.

At that point the Cytherea gave a slight lurch and vanished, leaving the Squire protruding from the swamp like a red-faced statue of liberty ankle-deep in mud.

"Ye ain't goin' to stand there and let me drown, be ye?" he shrieked. "I'll give any feller two dollars that'll throw me a rope."

"Don't be extravagant! It ain't worth it!" retorted one of the onlookers.

"Make it two-fifty!" urged another. "Them pants alone must 'a' cost two dollars!"

Ma, who had been feeling a little faint and generally discombobulated, suddenly revived and burst into song:

> "*Throw out the life-line!*
> *Throw out the life-line!*
> *Somebody's sinking out there!*"

They all joined in the chorus.

The mud was now up to the Squire's knees. Clearly of the opinion that they would deliberately let him drown, he raised imploring hands clasped as in prayer.

"Save me!" he begged hoarsely. "Have some pity, can't ye? I know most of you folks has it in fer me, but if you get me out of this, I swear——"

"Don't swear, Squire!" advised the sheriff. "And don't make no rash promises! We're goin' to save you. We need somethin' to amuse us durin' the long winter evenings!"

He hurled an improvised lasso at the cowering figure. It dropped over the Squire's shoulders and he clutched at it desperately.

"Now then, boys!" And with cries of joy the Sacred Camels of King Menelik laid hold upon the line and rushed with it across the road. It tightened. The Honorable Hezekiah Mason tried to move his feet, failed, and at the next tug toppled forward face down in the mud.

"All together!"

Thus ignominiously did they pull him ashore upon his belly. Coated with slime and weeds, as it might have been with tar and feathers, he staggered to his feet upon the causeway. Shaking his fist at his rescuers and spitting out eel-grass, he shouted:

"I'll have the law on all of ye for this! An' ye'll pay well for it! Damages, special damages, and exemplary damages! Ye'll be sorry ye ever pulled me out!"

"We knew that when we did it," replied the sheriff. "But we thought suffocatin' was too easy a death for ye. We're savin' you for somethin' 'special and exemplary'! An' when we git through with ye, we're going to have ye stuffed!"

IV

It was not without due warning, therefore, that the Honorable Hezekiah commenced his famous one-hundred-thousand-dollar action for personal injuries against "Ma" Best, the Town of Pottsville and Oscar Giddings.

Alleging quite properly that through their joint acts and negligences he had been severely bruised, contused and otherwise damaged, and had suffered severe internal injuries of a permanently disabling character, together with great physical pain and mental agony, and had lost his new Cytherea sedan car, and put his gold watch on the blink, and spoiled his pants and his hat and what not, and so forth, and of a truth, moreover, and then some, and again, and even so—and they were every one of 'em equally responsible, each having contributed to the debacle, viz, *sic* and to wit:

(A) The defendant Best, because she had negligently run into him, while driving without a license; (B) the defendant Giddings, because he had negligently backed without giving any warning, and thus forced him, Mason, the said plaintiff, into the position where he was hit; and (C) the defendant Town of Pottsville, because it had negligently failed to maintain a proper wall, fence or other barrier at the side of the road, as a result of which he had been knocked into the swamp and pecuniarily damaged as to his health and person and belongings, as follows:

Five thousand by the loss of his car, five hundred for his watch, one hundred for his clothes, three and a half for his hat, fifty cents for being taken back to Pottsville, and one hundred thousand for his bodily injuries, external, internal, real and imaginary, past, present and future, with costs, and interest, and disbursements to date, amounting in all to the sum of one hundred and seventeen thousand, nine hundred and ninety-nine dollars and eighty-seven cents, *sic transit gloria mundi, quod erat demonstrandum, in loco parentis,* and God save the State of New York. Signed, Hezekiah Mason, Attorney and Counsellor at Law; Office and Post-office Address; Five Cents Savings Bank Block, Pottsville, Somerset County, New York.

Mr. Tutt, who had arrived at the Phœnix Hotel on his annual spring fishing-trip upon the very day the complaint was served, perused the monstrous thing with keen attention. He loved Pottsville and the Phœnix—even in its new war-paint—and he adored "Ma" Best, and he quickly perceived how the crafty Squire intended to divert the sweet uses of adversity into an opportunity to get Ma's little patrimony away from her, by securing a substantial judgment, too large for her to pay in cash, and foreclosing on his mortgages. A clever Dick, this Machiavellian country squire! Even had the Pottsville treasury contained enough money to satisfy a reasonable judgment—which it did not—it could not satisfy Mason. What he was hungering to get his clutches on was the Phœnix Hotel with its growing trade. Hence, for all practical purposes, Ma was the only defendant.

"Who's this Oscar Thingamyjig?" asked Mr. Tutt as he handed her back the paper.

"Oscar Giddings? Oh, he's just a poor farmer who does odd jobs around Campson's Mill. His wife's always been sick and they have a whole flock of small children. I don't s'pose Oscar's got ten dollars in cash in the world."

"Does Mason know that?"

"Sure. 'Course, he knows it!"

Mr. Tutt canted his stogy towards the ceiling and studied the insects decorating the new electric globe that had replaced the ancient kerosene lamp.

"Could you get him over here in such a way that he wouldn't be seen?"

"Yes, I can get hold of him easily enough. He always stops in to Colson's for his mail about five o'clock. I'll speak to him this afternoon and ask him to call here after supper."

Promptly at 7:30 o'clock Oscar Giddings arrived. Obviously poor in more senses than one—in goods, in health and in appearance—it was fantastic to suppose that Mason honestly expected to squeeze any money out of him.

He now stood by the door, twisting his cap and evidently expecting a word-lashing from Mr. Tutt for having been the fundamental cause of the accident. In this he was agreeably surprised.

"Come in and sit down, Oscar," remarked Mr. Tutt genially. "Have a cigar? And how about a piece of pie and a cup of coffee?"

"Sounds pretty good to me!" replied Giddings, thus encouraged.

"How are you getting on?"

"Fair to middlin'. Leastways, I was until this accident happened. I s'pose now I'll have to hire a lawyer, and that'll take all the money I've saved up."

"I don't suppose you'd fancy having Squire Mason get a judgment against you for a hundred thousand dollars?"

Giddings, in the act of elevating a large piece of apple-pie, paused and grinned.

"It wouldn't make a mite of difference to me how big it was, if it was over eight dollars. That's all I've got. Say!" he added, "he can't put me in jail, can he?"

"No—although you ought to be there," replied the old lawyer. "He can't put you in jail, owing to the unfortunate fact that nobody was killed. If the Squire had been drowned you might have been convicted of manslaughter in the second degree."

"I sure was careless!" freely admitted Oscar. "It's mostly my fault. If I hadn't backed up, the Squire wouldn't have had to slow down, and if he hadn't slowed down, he wouldn't have been where Ma could hit him."

"You know what he's after?" continued Mr. Tutt. "He wants to get a judgment against Ma so big that she can't pay his mortgage when it comes due next year, and he can foreclose."

"Then why is he suing me?"

"Perhaps because he thinks that he may somehow squeeze something out of you or hopes, by dropping the case against you, to induce you to testify in his behalf against Ma."

"He's got another guess coming to him if he thinks that!" declared Giddings.

Mr. Tutt handed him a stogy. "You'd like to help Ma?"

"You bet! Anyways I can!"

"Then I wish you'd go to Mason and, without letting him know that you've seen me, try to settle his personal claim against you."

"What with?"

Mr. Tutt took a hundred-dollar bill from his wallet and gave it to him.

"Go to Mason and tell him that you have no use for lawyers, and don't want to waste what little money you have by paying an attorney what you really ought to turn over to *him* in settlement of his claim. That'll appeal to him! Tell him you've only got five dollars cash of your own, but that, if he'll settle with you for forty or fifty dollars, you'll try and borrow the difference. He'll probably jump at the chance. Make a date with him for the next day. Then get this bill changed over at the bank, and when you go into Mason's office, before giving him the amount agreed upon, demand a release. He will be quite ready to give you one, and will probably start to fill in a printed form. At this point you must begin to show signs of uneasiness. Just imagine that you're one of these actor fellows. 'Mr. Mason,' you will say, 'I don't know anything about law and I'm not much on reading and writing.' You can pretend that for once, whether it's accurate or not. 'Your receipt may be all right, but I'd rather you'd sign one I can understand. I wrote this out in my own hand. If it suits you, it will suit me.' If he signs, you can pay him the money; not otherwise."

"Where will I get the receipt?"

"I'll make one out for you. Have you got any writing-paper at your house? Fine! Use a pencil and be careful to copy the spelling exactly—whether it looks right to you or not. And you can keep all you can save out of the hundred dollars."

"Fair enough!"

"You might give Mason to understand that if he settles with you in this way, it won't do him any harm on the trial and may do him some good. He's a crook, and a crook is always ready to believe everyone else is crooked too."

"Well," returned Oscar, "I'm glad I came over here."

"The pleasure is mutual," said Mr. Tutt. "I wonder if you could stage another little act for me? Before you first go to see Mason, I should like you to have an open-air quarrel with Ma over who was to blame for the accident. Select the most public place in town and a time when plenty of folks are around. I promise that whatever profanity you use will be freely forgiven you."

V

The great fight between "Ma" Best and Oscar Giddings is still discussed as one of the historic events of Somerset County, and to this day neither party is quite sure just how far the other was making believe. It started at five o'clock on Saturday afternoon in front of Colson's Grocery, and inside of ten minutes Oscar had lost his collar and necktie and Ma her false front. By 5.20 the entire voting population, including dogs and small boys, were participating in the row, and it was still being carried on vicariously long after the principal actors had been carried off the field. Yes, it was a great success in every way, including the accidental presence of the Honorable Hezekiah Mason himself, who, on crutches and with his arm in a sling, happened to be limping by just in time to see Ma lambasting Oscar over the cocoanut with one of old Colson's brooms. In fact, rumor hath it that so keen was his delight in the spectacle that at its conclusion he offered to make good to old Colson the cost-price of the broom—"s'long as it was spiled anyhow"—if he'd send the relic over to the office.

Ma, who did not know in the least what it was all about, looked forward to the trial with apprehension, particularly in view of Mr. Tutt's open admission that her chance was slim. The most they could hope for on the undisputed facts, was that the jury would render a verdict small enough for her to pay and at the same time have enough left to meet the Squire's mortgage. The whole Valley of the Mohawk, from Amsterdam in the east to Utiky in the west, was agog over the approaching trial, for the tidings had penetrated to the remotest hamlet that Mr. Tutt was going to sacrifice his vacation and defend "Ma" Best, and that Squire Mason intended to try his own case. For the Honorable Hezekiah's object was clear to all,—his iniquitous purpose, under guise of an innocent action for personal injuries, to gain title to and possession of the Phœnix Hotel, rake in the shekels as lord proprietor thereof, and compel Ma to work for him *de jure* as she now did *de facto*.

Ma confessed to Mr. Tutt that with any sort of a verdict the Squire would probably be able to accomplish his fell design, for the truth was that the Phœnix was overextended. Ma had been coining money, yes; but the blue and white paint, the new plumbing system, the garage, the vermilion birds and Ulysses' green livery had not all yet been paid for. And the trouble was, she had no defense! To go driving around without a license was *res ipsa loquitur* —negligence *per se!* Irrespective of brakes or anything else, it shifted the burden to her of proving that she was not to blame, when everybody knew that she was, at least in part. It was darned hard luck for her that Oscar Giddings had taken it into his head to go backing around that way, but, if Ma hadn't been driving a motor-car when she had no legal right to so, the Squire would not have been knocked into the swamp. And as to damages! The Cytherea had vanished forever. *"Spurlos versenkt!"* No derrick or wrecking-machine was of the slightest use when you couldn't find hide or hair of the remains! Apparently, although no one had ever so suspected, the hole in the swamp went clear through to Chiny! Perhaps some Mongol emperor or Tibetan llama was even now racing around the Gobi Desert in that gorgeous chariot.

So it was reasonably clear that the Squire was entitled as matter of law to the Cytherea's replacement value—four thousand dollars anyway. And there were his costs and disbursements—say two hundred and fifty dollars more—and his minor property damages, watch, trousers, hat, and so on—say fifty—before you even got to the scratches on his epidermis and those permanent internal injuries which the old fox was parading so publicly. The Squire, as his own attorney, might have a fool for a client, but he was certainly taking all the steps to insure getting a verdict.

Already one surgeon and two gastro-intestinal specialists from Utica had engaged rooms at the Phœnix for the duration of the trial, and it was asserted by those who were backing the plaintiff—the odds over at Colson's were quoted at 2½ to 1, no bet received over ten cents—that the Squire could prove positively that since, and directly owing to, the accident he had (1) lost appetite, (2) been unable to sleep, or if he did, suffered from agonizing dreams in which he was being hurled naked over a precipice, (3) was afflicted with constant headaches, (4) found his eyesight growing dim, (5) could not freely use his right hand, (6) discovered one leg had become shorter than the other, (7) experienced sudden fits of nervousness, (8) was constantly afflicted with shooting pains in and about, adjacent and appertainin' to, the groin and abdomen, (9) had damaged his coccyx, his *sartorius longus* and his *pons asinorum*, (10) had great difficulty in breathing, and (11) suffered from unexplained attacks of nausea on arising in the morning,—by reason of all of which his health and earning capacity had been permanently impaired to the tune of $100,000.

Anyhow, all agreed that—no matter how much of a liar he was!—he was sure of a verdict unless the jury deliberately violated their oaths, which they certainly would not do. For Pottsville prided itself upon its application of a legal system that did justice to rich and poor, beloved or despised, Jew and Gentile, even Republican and

Democrat, alike. The very fact that Mason was suing his native town, and that the jury would be composed largely of Sacred Camels, would only make 'em tend to lean over backward.

And then Mason made his great gesture! He publicly announced that, in spite of the town's negligence in failing to provide a proper protection upon the open, or swamp, side of the causeway, he had no intention of penalizing his fellow citizens who had so remotely contributed to the result. He would confine himself to the two defendants, who by their joint, direct and coöperative acts had smashed him up. In a word, even if there had been a fence to prevent his being precipitated into the swamp, "Ma" Best would have crashed into the Cytherea just the same, and it was possible that the soft mud had saved him from greater injuries—if that were possible. So the Squire indulged in his little stage play, discontinued his action against the town, and went to trial against the two joint tort-feasors— "Ma" Best and Oscar Giddings.

The case drew the biggest gate ever known in Somerset County, for everybody knew that it was really a fight for the Phœnix Hotel. Besides, they all were eager to hear the Squire's account of those terrible experiences that had given him the cramps and injured his coccyx. Even if the result was to be a foregone conclusion, the gathering agriculturists—sea-lawyers all of them—licked their chops at the prospect of hearing Old Man Tutt cross-examine the wily Hezekiah. It was sure to be a battle royal.

The rising sun disclosed hanging over the roads leading to Pottsville a sinuous dust-cloud beneath which jangled, coughed and rattled every known make of motor vehicle in use since the erection of the Dewey Arch. There wasn't an inch of parking space left on Main Street. Every room at the Phœnix was taken and by five A. M. the cue waiting at the door of the courthouse reached all the way to "Toggery Bill" Gookin's Gents' Furnishing Store. "Ma" Best, who had been unable to snatch a wink of sleep all night, seized what she pessimistically believed would be a last opportunity, to drive a brisk trade in coffee and doughnuts with these early birds. More distinguished, or more favored, visitors she indulged, in the Phœnix Hotel dining-room, on breakfast food, griddle-cakes, hot rolls, bacon and eggs, for a dollar and a quarter per, and she had taken in two hundred and ninety dollars by nine o'clock, when Sheriff Mose Higgins crossed the street to the courthouse and unlocked the door.

Instantly the assembled throng burst in, filling every seat, and in five minutes there wasn't available space left upon the floor for another pair of high boots. Even the windows were lined with faces of small boys, many of the owners of which were more or less suspended in mid-air, or at least lying head down on the roof above, where any self-respecting cat would have found difficulty in securing a foothold. In a word, and speaking by the book, there was a jam so big that Sheriff Higgins swore in another deputy—vice present-headwaiter Sam Bellows resigned—to keep the crowd in front of the steps moving, and to see that the principal actors and the witnesses gained admission without physical injury—or even *damnum absque injuria*.

But although Mr. Tutt had dined and slept at the hotel the night before, he had now utterly and unaccountably disappeared, and nobody had the remotest idea what had become of him. Gone fishin', prob'ly! Could he have forgotten all about this momentous occasion? Could anything have happened to him? And if he did not arrive, would old Judge Tompkins grant Ma an adjournment?

By 9:45 everything was set. Squire Mason, bandaged as to one arm, and using a cane, limped up the steps and made his way to the counsel table amid an ominous silence. Sheriff Higgins, chewing the official gum, glared around the crowded room.

"If I hear any more hissing," quoth he, "I'll throw everybody out!" And thereupon everyone hissed!

The clock on the rear wall of the court room moved imperceptibly to ten o'clock, Judge Tompkins ascended the bench, the roll of the jury was called, and still no Mr. Tutt! Ma was in despair.

"Mason versus Town of Pottsville, *et al.*," called out His Honor.

"Ready for the plaintiff," responded Squire Mason, laboring to his feet by means of his cane. "The action has been discontinued against all parties except the defendant Best. I am ready to proceed."

Judge Tompkins looked inquiringly at Ma.

"I see that you are represented by Mr. Ephraim Tutt," said he. "Do you expect him to be here?"

"He promised to come," she replied. "I don't know where he can be!"

"When did you see him last?"

"Last evenin' at suppertime," answered Ma helplessly. "I guess he must of gone off fishing!"

"Well," declared His Honor, "I don't see how we can force you to trial without counsel. Do you, Squire Mason?"

"You oughtn't to hold me responsible for his not bein' here," replied Mason wrathfully. "If Mr. Tutt isn't enough interested in this case to stop fishing for a few hours, the defendant had better substitute other counsel for him. There's just as good lawyers in this town as there are in New York!"

"That's all right!" retorted His Honor. "But I'm not going to penalize the defendant either. I'll grant an adjournment——"

"Hold on a minute!" shouted Mason, waving his arms and obviously forgetting in his excitement that he was supposed to be disabled. "To adjourn the case would work a great hardship on me. I have brought expert medical witnesses from a long distance and at much expense!" He pointed to the three graybeards sitting in a row on the front bench. "I have subpœnaed some twenty local witnesses as to the facts. It wouldn't be fair to make me bring 'em all here over again when—as everybody knows—there's no defense. Mrs. Best won't deny that she was driving her car without a license when she run into me. . . . Ask her! The only question is one of damages, and any lawyer could cross-examine my witnesses, if he had a couple of hours' preparation. Why not call the case, put a jury in the box, and then adjourn until two o'clock? Mrs. Best can retain a lawyer in the meantime."

"There is a good deal of force in what Squire Mason says," remarked Judge Tompkins. "What do you think, Mrs. Best? It is highly desirable that we should not bring all these witnesses here again. Will you try and get another lawyer by afternoon?"

Ma looked flustered and said nothing. Squire Mason nodded and beamed.

"We'll try to make a little headway," said His Honor. "Fill the jury-box, Mr. Wadhams, and let Squire Mason examine the talesmen, so that those who are disqualified for any reason, need not be detained any longer than is necessary."

"Perhaps I'd better make a general statement about the nature of the case," said Mason, confident that things were going his way, and that the tide in his affairs, if taken at the flood, would lead on to fortune. If he could only rush the case through before Mr. Tutt got back, it might mean thousands of dollars in his pocket.

"It may save time. I see no objection. Go ahead!" said His Honor. "I should be glad to learn something of the case myself."

The Squire turned to the assembled talesmen.

"Gentlemen of the jury," he began, "this is an action for dam——"

He stopped short. From outside came a burst of cheers: "Hurray for Mr. Tutt!"—"Soak it to the old skinflint!"—"Lambaste the son of a gun!" came through the windows, creating, strangely enough, no confusion whatever in the minds of the spectators as to whom these latter admonitions referred to. Speech, for once, failed the Squire. It was hard luck for him if Tutt had come back, but after all, he consoled himself, it wasn't going to make any difference in the result.

"Hurray! Hurray for Mr. Tutt!" yelled the crowd, stampeding for the door of the court room and bearing the old lawyer helplessly along with them.

"For dam—ages," finished the Squire inaudibly, as Old Man Tutt appeared in the doorway arrayed in full fishing regalia, including khaki jacket, rubber waders, creel, net and rod. Removing his ancient gray felt hat, he made his way to the rail.

"Good-morning, Your Honor! . . . Good-morning, Squire! . . . I crave your pardon for being late, but the fact is I was unexpectedly, and unavoidably detained. If, however, you will forgive my appearance, I am quite ready to proceed with the case."

"Well, I've no objection, if your adversary hasn't," smiled Judge Tompkins. "Go ahead, Squire Mason, and select your jury. No, I forgot! Go on with your remarks!"

But the Squire seemed to have lost interest in his contemplated speech.

"We might as well proceed in the usual way," he said rather feebly.

So the box was filled with twelve good and true hard-boiled citizens, who without exception solemnly assured Squire Mason that they were lovers of all mankind, including himself, without regard to character, business or profession, religion or politics, and that it would be a cinch for them to do perfect justice between him and "Ma" Best, and that they could treat a Democrat as well as a Republican, and would not favor the defendant because she was a woman, and that they had heard nothing whatever about the case, or about the Brotherhood of Abyssinian Mysteries or the Sacred Camels of King Menelik—whatever that may have had to do with it—and that they had never stopped over to, or taken a meal at, the Phœnix House or spoken to the defendant "Ma"—Mrs.—Best, or been convicted of a crime or done anything they should not have done, or heard anything whatever which would prejudice them against the unfortunate plaintiff whose damages they would be called upon to assess.

"I'll take the first twelve that come along!" said Mr. Tutt, nodding to the triple quartet of supermen in the box. "Go right ahead, Squire, and expound your wrongs!"

Accordingly the jury were sworn and Squire Mason once more arose and, while Mr. Tutt feigned to fall fast asleep—as perhaps he really was!—recounted the story of his misfortunes, including the injuries to his *sartorius longus* and *pons asinorum*, and then requested permission to reverse the order of proof and to call his witnesses a little out of order, so that they might get back to their patients as soon as possible. "Doctor Dignum, step up here, please!"

Doctor Dignum was a sour-visaged, desiccated medico with a soiled, rattish-yellow beard, who looked as if he had stepped out of the Eden Musée, but as a witness he proved to be an unqualified "wow." He had attended practically all the universities and medical schools in the known world, had read everything in every language, including the Scandinavian, and there was nothing connected with therapeutics, biology, microbiology, surgery, immunology, or psychoanalysis that he did not know intimately. He was not one of those of whom it could be said that:

> *A pancreas on the human rim*
> *A yellow pancreas was to him*
> *And it was nothing more.*

Far from it! If injured, said pancreas became instantly to Doctor Dignum the basis of a one-hundred-thousand-dollar suit for damages. He swore not only that he had examined the Squire's gastrointestinal tract and analyzed the contents thereof, but had studied his entire anatomy as well, including his coccyx, and that in his expert opinion, as a result of the shock, of the collision, and being knocked into the swamp, the Honorable Hezekiah would be permanently disabled and his earning capacity impaired for the rest of his natural life.

In similar fashion Doctors Watts and Tuzzy gave evidence, estimating the Squire's damages just referred to as nearly equal to that of the Johnstown Flood, throughout all of which testimony Mr. Tutt gently dozed and, some said, mildly snored, to awake only at the judge's query of:

"Have you anything to ask in cross-examination?"

"Nothing!" murmured Mr. Tutt sleepily.

"Then may my witnesses go back to Utica?" inquired the Squire in some surprise.

"They may go to—Utica!" said Mr. Tutt, winking at the jury.

VI

At last the crucial moment arrived when Squire Mason, somewhat nervously it must be confessed, ascended the witness-chair, and in a weak and permanently injured voice told the sad story of the catastrophe of Friday, the thirteenth day of May.

"Will you concede that your client was driving without a license?" asked Judge Tompkins, addressing the defense.

"Certainly," replied Mr. Tutt.

His Honor raised his eyebrows.

"Merely for the purpose of shortening the trial, may I inquire if you are willing to concede that she was guilty of negligence and that the plaintiff was exercising due care?"

"I am," agreed Mr. Tutt, while the jury stared at him, and the crowd on the benches breathed hard. He must be asleep, to concede away his case like that!

"Then am I to understand that this proceeding is merely in the nature of an inquest to assess damages?"

"Not at all!"

Judge Tompkins sank back.

"Very well, then! Cross-examine."

Mr. Tutt stood up and faced the Honorable Hezekiah. The two ancient adversaries looked into each other's eyes.

"Mr. Mason," began Mr. Tutt, "I gather from your opening address and subsequent testimony that you claim this unfortunate accident was due to the joint negligence of the town of Pottsville, of one Oscar Giddings, and of my client, Mrs. Best?"

"I do," answered the Squire, his confidence once more regained. "However, I've discontinued the action so far as the town and Giddings are concerned."

"I am aware of that. How long have you known Mr. Giddings?"

"A long time—ten years anyhow."

"He is a very poor man, isn't he?"

"Yes. That's the reason I didn't want to be too hard on him."

"You didn't think it would be worth while, did you?"

"Partly that."

"You didn't entertain any such charitable sentiment toward my client, Mrs. Best?"

"No, she's a rich woman!" snapped the Squire.

"Owns the Phœnix Hotel?"

"I believe so."

"A valuable property?"

"So-so."

"You've got a mortgage on it for ten thousand dollars which falls due next May?"

"Yep."

"What was the consideration given by you for that mortgage?"

Squire Mason addressed the court. "I object. What's that got to do with it?"

"I will allow it—on the question of possible bias."

The Honorable Hezekiah compressed his lips.

"I took it in settlement of my claim against her father, 'Doc' Barrows; he swindled me."

"Out of how much?"

"I reckon he cost me over ten thousand dollars."

"Isn't it the fact that you only lost five thousand, and that you blackmailed my client out of the balance by threatening to send her father to prison?"

"I did not. He was goin' anyway!"

The old lawyer shrugged his high shoulders.

"H'm! He *went* anyway! I concede that!"

Mr. Tutt took a sip of water from the tumbler beside him, then fumbled in his trousers pockets and drew forth a wrinkled piece of paper.

"Did you make an independent settlement with Giddings?"

The Squire flushed slightly.

"I did," he admitted cautiously.

"How much did you get out of him?"

"I let him off for sixty-five dollars."

"Didn't think you could squeeze any more out of him, did you?"

The Honorable Hezekiah once more appealed to the judge.

"I object to that question!" he snapped.

"You needn't answer it, then!" bowed Mr. Tutt.

"Did you, in return for Giddings' sixty-five dollars, give him a receipt?"

"I did."

"Is this it?" Mr. Tutt smoothed out the paper and stepped toward the witness.

"Let me see it," interjected Judge Tompkins, holding out his hand.

Silence ensued while he perused the document. Squire Mason tried to look unconcerned.

"Is this the receipt you gave to Giddings?" asked the judge finally.

"I guess so. Looks familiar!" replied Mason, in a vain attempt at jocularity.

"I offer it in evidence," announced Mr. Tutt.

"Received."

Judge Tompkins was squinting at Mason over his spectacles. The audience sensed that there was a nigger in the woodpile somewhere.

"Gentlemen of the jury," said Mr. Tutt, showing the foreman the paper, "please examine this exhibit with care. I pay Squire Mason the compliment of assuming that it is not in his handwriting. . . . Am I right, Squire? . . . I thought so! However, that does not affect its validity." He read it slowly so that all could hear:

> i hereby sertify Oscar Giddings has give me sixti five dollres in full settlement of his libility for the damage he done me in the axident on may 13
>
> HEZEKIAH MASON.

"You gave that written satisfaction to Oscar Giddings for a valuable consideration?" continued Mr. Tutt gravely, once more returning to the witness.

"Sure," replied the Squire uneasily, beginning to realize that something was wrong, but not knowing what it was.

"I move that the complaint in this action be dismissed!" said Mr. Tutt quietly.

The judge swung around toward the bewildered attorney in the witness-chair.

"Squire Mason, what have you to say to that?"

The Honorable Hezekiah gaped at him.

"I dunno—what I—should say!" he stammered.

"Don't you realize that in accepting sixty-five dollars from Giddings in full satisfaction of his liability you released all parties?"

The Squire grabbed tight the arms of his chair. For a moment he thought the court must be joking with him.

"How do you mean—'all parties'?"

"Are you not aware of the rule of law whereby a release and satisfaction to one of several joint tort-feasors operates to release all?"

"No-o," he stammered. "I never heard of it!"

"Evidently not! Well, whether you have or not, that's the law!" Judge Tompkins turned to the amazed jury.

"It is an ancient and well-established rule, almost without exception in England and America, that for a single injury there can be but one recompense. When more than one unite in the commission of a wrong, each is responsible for the acts of all and for the whole damage. Also, when separate and independent acts of negligence by different people concur in perpetrating a single injury, each is fully responsible for the trespass. Courts will not undertake to apportion the damages in such cases among the joint wrongdoers. The injured party has at his election his remedy against all or any number. He may elect to look to one only, and, if he accepts from that one a benefit or property in satisfaction and release, he can go no further. He cannot have a second satisfaction. Having had reparation from one, who was responsible for all the damage, and released him, all others who were jointly, or jointly and severally, liable are also released. One satisfaction is a bar to further proceedings in the same cause of action. The plaintiff in this case, having elected to look to the defendant Giddings for his remedy and released him, cannot proceed further. He has—er—unintentionally perhaps—released the defendant Best as well. The complaint is therefore dismissed. You are discharged with the thanks of the court. Clear the box, Sheriff. Is there anything else on the calendar?"

"No, Yerroner," replied the Grand Supreme Exalted Patriarch of the Sacred Camels. "I kinder think this is enough for one day."

"Then adjourn court."

There was a wild rush forward upon the part of those present, to congratulate "Ma" Best upon her unexpected victory. Squire Mason seized the opportunity to escape unostentatiously from the court room, and those who noticed him on his way out commented upon the fact that he walked with a vigor which showed no sign of being impaired. Judge Tompkins, in spite of the adjournment, had remained upon the bench to glance over some papers.

Mr. Tutt coughed interrogatively.

"If Your Honor please, since the court is no longer in session, may I make an announcement?"

"Go as far as you like," answered the court.

Mr. Tutt faced the audience.

"Ladies and gentlemen, Sons and Daughters of King Menelik, Brother Camels, visiting firemen, and all strangers within the gates of Pottsville, on behalf of my client, Mrs. Best, I take pleasure in stating that as soon as she can change her duds and get into a calico apron, a dole of coffee and doughnuts will be served gratis at the Phœnix Hotel to all comers, from now until three o'clock. Come and eat your fill, free from the distressing thought that in so doing you are benefiting our worthy friend, Squire Mason. I thank you!"

"But how can I ever thank *you*, Mr. Tutt!" exclaimed Ma, as the crowd poured out, whooping, into the street. "How can I pay you for what you've done for me? There isn't anything in the world I wouldn't do for you."

"You can do one thing for me!" replied Mr. Tutt.

"Please mention it!"

"Take down all those dog-gone vermilion birds you've got hanging from the trees between here and Patterson—'eat signs,' I believe they're called—and rip that green uniform off Ulysses, and paint out the blue strips on the front of the Phœnix, and put a muffler on the radio. Modern comfort isn't half so good as the old-fashioned kind. Don't you agree with me, Judge?"

"Er—what was that?" inquired His Honor, looking up from the document before him. Then he sniffed and wrinkled his nose. "For Pete's sake, Eph, what's that infernal—pugh!—smell?"

Mr. Tutt somewhat shamefacedly lifted his creel from beneath the table. "Darn if I didn't forget all about those trout!" he explained.

"What made you so late?"

Mr. Tutt pulled out a couple of stogies and handed one to the judge.

"Do you know that big pool halfway up Chasm Brook?"

"Do I!" retorted His Honor, lighting one of the stogies.

"Well," went on Mr. Tutt, lighting the other stogy, "we were driving over the hill on our way back this morning, and I just couldn't resist trying a cast or two. So I sneaked up to the pool and—gosh, you should 'a' seen the rise I got!"

"Hook him?" demanded Tompkins excitedly.

"Sure, I hooked him! But," he added ruefully, "he got away!"

Judge Tompkins regarded his friend thoughtfully.

"Say, Eph," he remarked, "I knew there was something I wanted to ask you. How do you spell 'certify'?"

"That depends!" said Mr. Tutt.

THAT OLD GRAY MARE

"The old gray mare, she ain't what she used to be——"

Mr. Tutt yanked his long, rubber-booted legs out of the muddy ooze of Turtle Pond, unjointed his rod, looked in his creel, grunted and started slowly across the fields toward Pottsville. He had had no luck and he was very tired; he wasn't so young as he used to be, and the time was probably not far off when he must give up fishing forever. He was in truth a has-been; he belonged to a bygone era.

Thus ruminating, he noticed that a ragged circular tent had been erected in the middle of the otherwise deserted fair grounds and that a dozen or more horses were tethered on the baseball field. Near by stood an obsolete democrat wagon, a sailcloth-covered truck, and a large yellow van upon which was painted in ornamental letters of bright blue: DOC ROBINSON'S ALL-HEALING SALVE AND PAIN CURE. A couple of negro boys were shooting craps in the pitcher's box. It was obviously a caravan belonging to one of that well-nigh extinct species, the old-fashioned itinerant horse dealer. Although common enough in his youth, Mr. Tutt had not encountered one in years.

The sight cheered him somewhat, bearing witness as it did to the fact that he was not the only anachronism in this supposedly horseless age. Across the road, two men were lounging on a bench in front of the primitive wooden jail. One of them was Mose Higgins, sheriff of the county and ex-officio Grand Past Master of the Sacred Camels of King Menelik.

"Howd'y', Mr. Tutt," he called, closing his jack-knife and strolling over to meet the lawyer. "Ketch anythin'?"

Mr. Tutt shook his head.

"No, they wouldn't rise. Guess they knew it was a holiday. What's the encampment over there?"

"That belongs to Doc Robinson. Been there two weeks. You remember him, don't you?"

"I don't seem to. Who is he?"

"That's him over there on the bench. He's my prisoner."

"Your prisoner?"

"Yes, durn him! He's an old trader comes through here every few years. He's got to stand trial day after tomorrow for hoss stealin'. I'll be glad when it's over. He's given me a peck of trouble, but he ain't such a bad feller. . . . Hey, Doc! Come on over."

Doc Robinson, whose sitting posture at the moment resembled that of a grasshopper, hitched to his feet and slouched toward them. He was spare and tall—almost as tall as Mr. Tutt—with a brown, leathery skin, watery, pale-blue eyes and a drooping walrus mustache. This, together with his hair, which he wore long over his collar, was jet-black, except at the roots. He was clad in a greasy frock coat, soiled red waistcoat with tarnished silver buttons, and much-shrunken, checked trousers pulled over high boots. A brown rivulet followed the wrinkles from the corner of his mouth downward toward his chin.

"Howd'y', brother," he said in a pleasant drawl.

Mr. Tutt took his hand.

"I hope my friend the sheriff is extending you proper hospitality," he answered. "Stogy?"

Doc took the stogy, bit off the end, expelling it through the air in a skillful parabola, and accepted a light.

"I ain't got nuthin' at all to complain of, thank y'," he replied. "In fact, this here calaboose is one of the most comfortable I ever stayed in. It ain't myself I'm worried about; it's my hosses, and what's goin' to become of 'em. There's one or two that's kind of ailin' and need care. The sheriff's mighty kind and lets me go over every day an' doctor 'em up, but if I should—after I leave here— You know what I mean?"

Mr. Tutt nodded. Surely there must be something good about an old fellow who had the well-being of his animals so much at heart.

"Well, cheer up! You can cross that bridge when you came to it."

"I'll be crossin' it pretty quick—trial's day after tomorrer. You see, if I was to be sent to the county jail it wouldn't be so bad. I could keep an eye on 'em. But if I have to go to state prison—way up to Dannemora—God knows what'll happen. Those niggers'll sure neglect 'em. I dunno!"

He took off his five-gallon hat and ran his fingers through his forelock.

"Come! Come!" Mr. Tutt encouraged him. "Why anticipate any such thing?"

"The folks around here don't like me," answered Doc simply.

"Horse traders never has been popular in this part of the country," agreed the sheriff. "Still, Doc swears he's innocent."

Doc put both hands on the old lawyer's shoulders and looked him straight in the eye. "Listen!" he said with an intensity that carried conviction. "I don't know who you be, but you look well-meanin' and fair-minded. I'm tellin' you God's truth when I say I never touched that hoss—never saw it agin, once I sold it. The hoss they found over in the shack wasn't the same hoss at all." His walrus mustache trembled and there was moisture in the faded eyes.

"Y'see," explained Mose, "this here Jake Sowerbutt, who bought the hoss from Doc, had it stole right out of his barn the very same night. So he come straight down here next mornin' and found it— or he says he did—over back of the grandstand; swears to it positive."

"It wasn't the same hoss!" reiterated Doc. "Honest, it weren't! Why, I had that same hoss nearly a month. My boys'll testify to that."

"The jury won't pay much attention to niggers," commented Mose. "And they're not likely to believe Doc either, especially since, bein' he hadn't got money to pay a lawyer, the judge assigned Squire Mason to defend him, and you know how much interest that old skinflint'll take if he ain't gettin' paid nuthin'."

"The squire's a good lawyer," conceded Mr. Tutt generously.

Doc scratched his head.

"I guess it looks kinder bad fer me! I ain't sayin' this Sowerbutt isn't sincere about it. Them hosses do look alike—mighty alike. He's jest honestly mistaken. After all, he only had that mare a few hours. You can't really get to know a hoss in as short a time as that. There weren't no particular marks on her nor nuthin'. It looks as if I was the victim of circumstances. I don't care for myself. I'm an old man. I ain't got any one dependent on me. If it weren't fer my hosses——"

"Well, Doc, I reckon it's time fer me to lock you in," interrupted the sheriff. He winked at Mr. Tutt. "Jest a formality. Doc wouldn't run away. Couldn't if he wanted to. We'd ketch him inside of three miles." He fitted his key into the door, motioned Doc Robinson inside, and locked it.

"I ain't got nowheres to run to," agreed Doc through the barred hole. "Good night, folks."

"It's the doggonedest case I ever come acrost!" asserted the sheriff, as he and Mr. Tutt walked toward the town. "A gol-blasted nuisance! Doc's kind of a nice old feller, even if he is a hoss trader, but I'm not bothered so much about him as I am what do with all these hosses and niggers."

"What about them?" asked Mr. Tutt.

"Payin' fer their keep an' all. The law don't help none. I can't find anythin' in the statutes to cover it—nary a word. Neither can Pettingill, the district attorney,—only that ain't sayin' nuthin'. In the fust place, it costs nearly eighty-five cents a day to feed Doc; then I'm required by law to impound the stolen hoss as evidence, and the county hez to foot the bill on account of Sowerbutt bein' deprived of the use of it until after the trial—that comes to five dollars a week more. Then there's the durn caravan. Pettingill's put the two niggers under detention as necessary witnesses, and they claim they're entitled to an allowance fer board and lodging, and I suspect mebbe they're right; and then there's fourteen more hosses. Yes, sir, this case is eatin' up a sight of money. Y'know, we allus let the gypsies and trippers use the fair grounds fer campin', an' last summer we put in runnin' water to attract the tourist trade. It did too. So when Doc came along this time, we naturally allowed him to set up his tent and graze his hosses there."

"A sort of tenant by sufferance?"

"Wors'n that, accordin' to Squire Mason. He claims Doc is a guest of the town and that, so long's we've put him in jail, we're responsible fer the hosses—at least so long as their feed don't come to more'n their worth. I don't dare take a chance on it, either. They eat a sack of oats a day; and as fer hay, they make a load look sick in a week! Gosh, I dunno how long we kin keep it up."

Mr. Tutt chuckled.

"Well, this terrible drain on the town's resources will be over in a day or two."

"I hope so, but that's a question. If the jury convicts Doc of grand larceny, the judge can send him to state prison and the county will be rid of him and his hosses fer good and all—that is, I think it will —but if they only find him guilty of petty larceny, he'll come right back to the county jail and I'll have to run a boardin' house and livery stable fer another year."

"What did Sowerbutt pay for the horse?" inquired Mr. Tutt.

"Ninety-eight dollars. That's the itch. It's three dollars short of the amount required to constitute grand larceny in the second degree under the statute. 'Property of the value of over one hundred dollars,' it says. But I guess they'll find the hoss was worth over a hundred, all right."

"They probably will, under the circumstances," agreed Mr. Tutt. "How long a sentence can he get in that case?"

"Five years."

"And what kind of a horse was it?" mused the old lawyer.

"An old gray mare," answered Mose.

Mr. Tutt bade good night to the sheriff and trudged back to the Phœnix Hotel, but in spite of Ma Best's sausages and waffles, he could not get Doc Robinson and his horses out of his mind. Time was when you might meet such a one almost anywhere in the rural districts, driving along at the head of his little cavalcade of equine nondescripts acquired by purchase, barter or possibly more dubious methods, following the sun, the county fairs and horse sales, the first true exponent of interstate commerce, existing by virtue of that law of human nature according to which every adult male is convinced that he can build a fire better than any one else, take his friends' money playing poker and—formerly—sting the other fellow every time in a horse trade.

The horse dealer flourished because horse trading, to the average countryman, represented sport, adventure, profit. It took the place of war. The sagas and epics of the corner store all had an equine flavor. Famous horse trades made state history. Every horse in the county was for sale—at a price. Every man, no matter how highly he valued his nag, was ready at a moment's notice to swap him for another. Horse trading had its own laws and rules of ethics—*caveat emptor*. The deacon, concluding his exhortation to a higher life with a peroration upon the value of honesty and fair dealing in business, would gather the skirts of his frock coat about his shanks, step out to the buggy sheds and make Ananias and Sapphira look like pikers. The horse trader's hand was against every man's and every man's hand against him. He had no friends, no legal rights that a jury felt bound to respect.

What chance, then, for old Doc Robinson? Despised and rejected by men whose business ethics were in practice no higher than his, who would gladly have cheated him if they could, three dollars in the jury's estimate of the gray mare's value would make a difference of four years in his prison sentence. Would they hesitate? Not much!

Poor old cuss! But why not "poor old Tutt"? Were not both of them childless, lonely old men, plugging along at their jobs in default of anything else to do until their summons came? After all, the lawyer asked himself, was there so much difference between them? Were the tricks of Doc's trade any worse than his own? He had pulled some pretty fast ones in his time, even if they had always been in the cause of justice. Had he been a horse trader instead of a lawyer, might he not easily have found himself in precisely the same unfortunate situation as Old Doc?

"There, but for the grace of God, goes Ephraim Tutt," he muttered. "By jumping Jehoshaphat! If I can do anything for that old fellow, I will. I only wish it was my case."

But although it wasn't and the trout had suddenly begun to rise again, Mr. Tutt could not bring himself to go fishing on the day of Doc's trial. He could see at first glance, as he entered the courtroom, that the stage was set for a legal lynching. The jury, composed largely of the Sacred Camels of King Menelik, had already been sworn, and the district attorney, the Honorable Abner Pettingill, was about to open the case. He was a pale-faced, chinless, pimply young man, renowned for his elocutionary prowess, with political ambitions, a cockatoo's comb and a roving Adam's apple. Old Doc Robinson, sitting beside Squire Mason and wearing a look of helpless resignation, was going to be railroaded to make a Roman holiday. With his drooping mustaches, he was the counterfeit presentiment of the woodcut upon the label of his own bottles of horse medicine.

"You may proceed, Mr. District Attorney," said Judge Tompkins, and the Honorable Abner, shaking his forefinger in the direction of the counsel table, burst into a torrent of invective against the prisoner. The defendant was, he declared, the meanest of all criminals—a hoss thief. Had God given the hoss strength, had He, in the words of Job, "clothed his neck with thunder," in order that a quack, a crook, a rogue, like this miserable specimen at the bar, might make use of that noble animal to defraud his unsuspecting fellow men? The Almighty forbid! No hoss—in Somerset County, at any rate—should be put to such base uses unless the miscreant paid the full penalty of the law.

The defendant had been indicted for grand larceny in the second degree—there was, to be sure, a count for petty larceny, but the jury could disregard that for the time being; for stealing property worth more than a hundred dollars, to wit, one gray mare. The crime was of peculiar boldness and duplicity. This wretched thief had sold the mare in question to Jake Sowerbutt, an honest Republican farmer over Corinth way, and had gone back that very same night and stolen it out of the barn. Pretty slick, eh? Took a perfessional to do a thing like that, eh? Almost kinda funny. Like the story of the feller who hired his small boy to go to bed without his supper and then, when the kid was asleep, had gone upstairs and stole the money. Hah! So the defendant was smiling, was he? Well, let him smile! He'd smile on the other side of his mouth before this trial was over! Did not the "immortal bard"—the Honorable Abner referred to that great author, William Shakespeare—say that a man "may smile, and smile, and be a villain"? He certainly did!

Perspiring, the Honorable Abner flung his hand heavenward in a final appeal to the Goddess of Justice and called Jacob Sowerbutt, the owner of the mare, to take the stand.

Mr. Sowerbutt, a small man with a husky voice, arrayed in a costume akin to that of a Coney Island barker, thereupon came forward and solemnly swore upon Holy Writ to tell the truth, the whole truth and nothing but the truth, so help him God. He had, he stated, been sitting on his front porch about one o'clock, after dinner, when this feller—pointing at the defendant—had come driving along, accompanied by a nigger boy in a democrat wagon to which was hitched a gray mare—a kind of whitish-gray, with a white mane and white bobbed tail—and asked if he'd like to buy it. Did Mr. Sowerbutt know this man? Sure he knew him; the feller'd been comin' through that part of the county fer years. Wa-al, they got to talkin', and the upshot of it was that, since his own hoss had just died of the colic, he tried out the mare for a mile or two and bought her fer ninety-eight dollars cash money, put her in the barn, and the defendant drove off.

Wa-al, that night after supper he had to go over acrost the road, and while he was behind the woodpile he heard some one come along and kind of slow up. He peeked over the top and seen it was Doc Robinson with his nigger boy in the same democrat wagon, and he heard Doc say, "That's the place! That's where the mare is!" Then they drove on. Next morning he found the barn door open and the animal gone.

"Did you ever see that mare again?" inquired the Honorable Abner in a portentous voice.

"You bet I did!" retorted Mr. Sowerbutt eagerly. "I knew who'd stolen her, all right. So I got Sam Hinkley, one of my neighbors, to drive me over here in his automobile. We went straight out to the fair grounds to where this here feller had put up his tent. I didn't see him nowhere, but there was another nigger loafin' around, and I asked him could I look at the hosses. He said sure, so we walked around, and at fust I didn't see nuthin' that looked like my hoss—only a lot of roans and bays. Then all of a suddint I caught sight of a head stickin' out of a shed. I could see the nigger didn't want me to go over there, but I walked right up and threw open the door, and there was the gray mare."

"Your hoss?"

"My hoss."

"Are you proof positive it was your hoss?"

"Absolutely. At first I wasn't quite certain, because this here hoss had a long white tail while the mare I had bought had only a stub. Then I noticed something queer about her rump—some sticky stuff around the top of the tail. I was just goin' to feel of it when in comes the defendant.

"'You better not touch that mare,' he says to me. 'She's sick—got the glanders.'

"'Oh, has she?' I says. 'She seemed all right when you sold her to me.'

"'What do you mean, sold her to you?' he says. 'I never sold you that mare. The mare you bought was a different one.'

"'It looks mighty like her to me,' I says.

"'They was a team of matched grays,' he says. 'I bought 'em down Herkimer way. I sold you the off mare. This is the nigh one.'

"'Seems kind of funny,' I says, 'if they was a team of matched grays, how this one has a tail and mine didn't.'

"'That was just a whim of the owner,' he says. 'He bought 'em that way. They passed the law agin' bobbin' hosses' tails jest about that time. He had bought the mare I sold you before that; then he found this one, which was a perfect match except fer the tail, but he couldn't cut it off on account the law.'

"'That was too durn bad,' I says, reachin' out behind me fer the tail, and before he could stop me I gave it a yank an' off it come! It was holler and fitted right over the stump, but the glue wasn't quite dry."

"The tail came off?"

"Yes, sir. Off it come!"

The Honorable Abner bent over and lifted up what appeared to be the long white tail of a horse.

"Is this the tail to which you refer?"

Mr. Sowerbutt examined the tail with conscientious care.

"That's the tail," he declared definitively.

"I offer the tail in evidence," said the district attorney.

"Received. Mark it People's Exhibit A," nodded the judge.

"Wa-al," continued Mr. Sowerbutt, "that was enough fer me, as I guess 'twould 'a' been fer anybody. So I swore out a warrant and had him locked up."

"What became of the gray mare?"

"The sheriff impounded her as evidence."

"Do you know something about the value of horses?"

"I've bought and sold 'em all my life."

"What, in your opinion, was the value of the mare you bought from the defendant?"

Mr. Sowerbutt frowned with the intensity of his cerebration.

"In my opinion, that mare wasn't worth a cent less than a hundred and fifty dollars."

"You got her cheap."

"That's the idea. I got her cheap."

The Honorable Abner paused and cleared his throat.

"If Your Honor please," he said, "the mare for the stealing of which the defendant is on trial is now outside the courthouse. I should be glad if the jury could be given opportunity for a view, to aid in determining the animal's value."

"If the jury wish to examine her, they may do so," agreed Judge Tompkins. "We will adjourn court for ten minutes for that purpose. . . . Mr. Sheriff, you will keep the jury together and not permit them to converse either among themselves or with strangers."

The spectators poured out of the courtroom, and the jury, accompanied by Sheriff Higgins, Squire Mason, Mr. Tutt and Doc Robinson, followed them into the open air and joined the circle of Pottsvillians gathered about the dejected creature, which, with lowered head, was standing in the middle of the village square. Pot-bellied, sway-backed, with thick fetlocks, an obvious spavin on the off hind hock, well-defined collar marks on the chest and withers, and projecting yellowed teeth, this old gray mare was clearly not what she used to be, whatever that may have been. As David Harum might have said, the only evidence that it was a horse was the fact that it was not something else.

"She's fifteen years old if she's a day! Durn if I'd give twenty-five dollars for her!" declared "Toggery Bill" Gookin, who, having once owned a part of a trotting horse, regarded himself as an authority.

"Shut up!" shouted the sheriff. "Didn't you hear what the judge said?"

"I ain't talkin' to the jury!" retorted Toggery. "Besides, he said you wasn't to let the jury talk to strangers. I ain't no stranger."

This floored the sheriff.

"Wa-al," he said, "looked at her enough? I reckon it's ten minutes. I'm going to take ye all back, anyway. Come along now. Step lively."

So they all filed in again, Mr. Sowerbutt took the witness chair, and Squire Mason arose to cross-examine.

Did Mr. Sowerbutt regard himself as an expert on hosses, he inquired. . . . Mr. Sowerbutt allowed he knew quite somethin' about 'em. . . . Was there any particular way that the witness could identify this hoss as his hoss? . . . Yes, sir, there was! He could 'a' told that mare anywheres by the spavin on the off hind hock and the collar marks, let alone her size, conformation and general appearance. . . . Only owned her a few hours, didn't he? . . . Yes, but that was enough! . . . Squire Mason wiped his forehead and made one last effort: How could the witness be sure that the hoss hadn't just walked out of the barn by itself? Mr. Sowerbutt retorted that he had put the bar across the door and then gone out by the rear. In the morning the bar was down and, although Mr. Sowerbutt had seen some pretty smart hosses, he'd never met one that could take down a bar. This sally was received with loud guffaws from the jury.

"No more questions," gloomed the squire.

"The People rest," chirped the Honorable Abner.

It had been quick work.

"Mr. Robinson, please take the stand," directed Mason, adjusting his spectacles and clearing his throat.

Old Doc's defense, which he gave with an air of bewildered innocence, consisted of the same explanation that he had made to Sowerbutt when the latter had accused him. He had bought a team of gray mares from a farmer in Herkimer who was closing out his stock preparatory to moving to New York. He could not just remember the man's name—Smith, he thought it was. The mare he had sold to the complainant was the off mare, the one outside in the square was the nigh mare, a different mare altogether.

The Honorable Abner gathered himself to tear the witness to pieces.

"Where were you born?" he challenged, as if to imply that the witness might never have been born at all.

"I don't know," answered Doc. "My folks travelled with a circus."

"Got any address?"

"Not exactly. I turn up in the same places 'bout every year or so."

"Have you a license to practice veterinary medicine?"

"No, sir."

"You hold yourself out as a doctor, don't you?"

"No, sir."

The Honorable Abner brandished a bottle of Doc Robinson's All-Healing Salve.

"This is one of your bottles, ain't it?"

"Yes, sir."

"What does the 'Doc' stand for?"

"Just Doc. What everybody calls me."

"Don't you sell this stuff to any one who will buy it?"

"Yes, sir. And it will cure everythin' the label says it does."

"And don't you go around doctoring horses for money?"

"No, sir. I just sell the medicine, but I know a good deal about sick animals and I give my customers the benefit of it."

"You're a horse trader, aren't you?"

"Yes, sir," answered Doc simply. "I've swapped hosses for nigh onto fifty years."

"Make a good thing out of it?"

"No, sir. Hardly a living."

"Where were you the night Mr. Sowerbutt's mare was stolen?"

"Right here all the time, except when I drove by his house a little after sundown, just as he says, and called my boy's attention to the fact that that was where we had sold the mare; but we didn't stop and we didn't go back."

"And you haven't any idea who stole the mare you sold to Mr. Sowerbutt?"

"No, sir. Some hoss thief, I guess."

"Some other hoss thief, you mean?"

Jeers from the spectators and a rap for order from the judge. Excluded.

"Why did you put a false tail on?"

"To make her look better."

"To fool some innocent buyer?"

Old Doc straightened up.

"I don't reckon it would fool many of the folks in these parts. There ain't none slicker at a hoss trade anywheres I know of."

"So you had two gray mares when you passed through Corinth only three weeks ago?" cooed the Honorable Abner.

"Yes, sir."

"Have you brought any one here to court to testify to that fact?"

"No, sir."

"Why haven't you?"

"I didn't imagine any one would be likely to remember. They'd only just recall I had a bunch of hosses."

"You also came through Myrtle Grove and Wayland and Grafton with your two gray mares, didn't you? Couldn't you find somebody to come here and say so?"

"I don't believe so," returned Doc helplessly.

The Honorable Abner glanced significantly at the jury.

"You don't, eh? That's all!"

Old Doc climbed down and was followed by the two negro boys—one a spindling with a peanut-shaped head and the other a roly-poly gnome, who admitted to having been in the reformatory. They corroborated Doc's testimony in every particular. The Honorable Abner waved them disdainfully from the stand. Case closed. "You may go to the jury, gentlemen." They went—Squire Mason, in a halting, ineffectual argument based on the well-known possibilities of mistaken identity, and the district attorney on the wings of an impassioned appeal calculated to land him, trailing clouds of oratorical glory, in the senatorial chamber of the state capital. In conclusion he begged his fellow citizens not to be misled by sympathy into rendering a verdict for mere petty larceny as a result of which the defendant might become a guest of the county for an entire year, whereas, if convicted of grand larceny—to wit, of property more than one hundred dollars in value—he would be sent to state prison, thus relieving the local taxpayers of the necessity of his support. Sowerbutt was a good judge of hoss flesh and he had testified that the mare was worth a hundred and fifty. Even should the jury accept the price paid—ninety-eight dollars—as evidence of value, they must bear in mind that the defendant had stolen a halter, blanket and four horseshoes as well, which, taken together, would make up the required amount.

Judge Tompkins then charged that the rule was well established that possession of property recently stolen creates an inference that such possession is a guilty one and casts upon the defendant the burden of explaining it to the satisfaction of the jury—see People versus Rogan, 223 Appellate Division 242—and that the question as to whether possession of stolen property by a person accused of larceny establishes his guilt is one of fact for the jury—see People versus McCallum, 103 New York 587—and their verdict would be either guilty of grand larceny in the second degree, guilty of petty larceny, or not guilty. "You may retire, gentlemen."

The jury straggled out, Judge Tompkins vanished into his chambers, old Doc was taken back to the prison pen, and the spectators drifted into the square, from which the gray mare had already been removed to the livery stable.

Mr. Tutt was left alone in the otherwise empty courtroom. A verdict of guilty was a foregone conclusion. Yet, in spite of the evidence and Doc's exceedingly vague defense, the old lawyer was convinced of his innocence. He might be a scalawag, might be up to any sharp trick in a horse trade—and let him who was without sin cast the first stone—but at bottom he loved animals, and no man who loved animals ought to go to jail. Lighting a stogy, the old man strolled into the corridor upon which the jury room opened and where Sheriff Higgins sat on duty. Sounds of altercation floated through the open transom. A verbal riot was in progress.

"Sh-h!" whispered Mose. "They won't be long now. They've found him guilty already, but they can't decide on the degree."

"That old bonebag ain't worth fifteen dollars!" came the shrill voice of Pete Colson, the groceryman. "I'm for petty larceny."

"And have him roostin' over in the jail fer a whole year at our expense? Not by a damn sight!" yelled Meecham, the foreman. "Grand larceny!"

"But we've got to give him the benefit of the doubt, ain't we? Well, I got one! Petty larceny!"

"Tell ye what!" proposed Meecham. "We're 'bout evenly divided. Let's roll for it. Fust feller gits a natural kin hev the say. How about it?"

The proposition apparently met with approval, for silence descended, presently followed by the sound of rolling dice.

"I win!" shouted Meecham. "Grand larceny in the second. All agreed? Then it's a verdict!"

There was a pounding upon the other side of the door.

"Y' better beat it afore they come out!" admonished the sheriff, and Mr. Tutt beat it.

"Have you anything to say why judgment should not be pronounced against you?" inquired Judge Tompkins two days later,
looking down over the rim of his spectacles at Old Doc Robinson,
who stood at the bar of justice.

Mr. Tutt took his place beside the prisoner.

"If the court please," he said, "Squire Mason has very generously consented that I be substituted for him as attorney for the
defendant. Will your Honor kindly make an order to that effect?"

"I see no objection, if that is the defendant's wish," replied the
judge.

"It is," answered Doc. "If I kin hev Mr. Tutt, I want him to look
out for me from now on."

"So ordered. Are you ready for sentence?"

Mr. Tutt stepped inside the rail.

"We are not, Your Honor. I wish to make a motion in arrest of
judgment and for a new trial on newly discovered evidence. I ask
the court to set this day week for the hearing and to issue a subpœna for the witness, Jacob Sowerbutt, returnable upon that day."

The Honorable Abner, who had fully expected that by that time
Doc Robinson would be on his way to Dannemora, sprang to his
feet.

"This defendant was convicted of a state-prison offense after a
fair trial!" he snapped. "On the face of it, Mr. Tutt can't have any
new evidence. If he has, let's hear what it is. I don't see why this
defendant should be quartered on the town any longer, so that
counsel can dig up more excuses for delay."

"Mr. Tutt has just come into the case," replied Judge Tompkins.
"I shall grant his request. The prisoner is remanded until this day
week. . . . Mr. Clerk, you may issue as many subpœnas as Mr. Tutt
desires."

Mr. Tutt's self-projection into the case aroused considerable mis-
giving in the Honorable Abner, who could not help feeling that he
had, perhaps, gone rather far in his appeal for a verdict of felony
upon economic grounds. It was true that Squire Mason hadn't entered any objection to his remarks, and exceptions must be taken
at the time to have any legal validity. All the same, he felt sure
that Old Man Tutt would find some way of making trouble for
him. He felt more sure of it when Mr. Tutt entered his office after
the court's adjournment that afternoon, sat down, tendered him a
stogy and said:

"Mr. Pettingill, I must congratulate you on the skill with which you conducted the case against my client. Your address to the jury was a masterpiece. You should go far, young man! Very far!"

"Oh, I dunno," cautiously returned Abner. "I did the best I could."

"On the other hand," continued Mr. Tutt meditatively, "nothing helps a man in a public career so much as a reputation for safe-guarding the rights of the underdog."

"I guess that's true," agreed the D. A.

"In that connection, have you considered what a favorable effect it might produce if you should consent to have the verdict against Robinson set aside and the indictment against him dismissed?"

"Wha-at?" stammered the Honorable Abner. "You must be crazy!"

"Not at all," replied the old man. "Your whole procedure has been irregular from start to finish. The verdict is against the weight of evidence; in spite of its eloquence, your address to the jury was seriously prejudicial to the defendant's rights and violated your prerogatives as a prosecutor; and the case was not decided by a fair expression of opinion on the part of the jurors, as required by law. In short, I shall not have the slightest difficulty in getting the court to set the verdict aside and order a new trial. It will be much better for you to appear to do this out of a sense of fair play and of your own volition."

"Poppycock!" exploded the district attorney.

"But I am not going to be content with that. I want you to dismiss the indictment against him."

The Honorable Abner bounced from his chair in righteous wrath.

"I never heard such gall!" he declared. "Dismiss the indictment! Why, for heaven's sake?"

"Because the defendant is not guilty of the crime charged against him. He did not steal the gray mare he sold to Sowerbutt."

"Tell that to the marines!" sneered Pettingill.

"I'll tell it to the world!" answered Mr. Tutt.

Calm descended upon the county of Patterson and the village of Pottsville, if not upon the conscience of the Honorable Abner Pettingill. The Robinson trial was over, the defendant had been convicted, and there was nothing now left but that he should be sentenced—as he so richly deserved—to prison. Not one of the entire Brotherhood of Sacred Camels—though regretting Mr. Tutt's misdirected sympathy—but regarded the latter's appearance on be-half of old Doc as a mere legal gesture. Anyhow, it must be so, they all concluded, since he did not miss a day's fishing during the

entire following week. It was, however, only the calm which tra-
ditionally precedes the tempest.

When at last the morning set for the argument upon Mr. Tutt's
motion for a new trial dawned, such Pottsvillians as were awake
rubbed their eyes in amazement, wondering if a circus had unexpectedly come to town. Then they hastily donned their clothes and
hurried out into the street. The Honorable Abner, motoring into
Pottsville shortly before ten o'clock, suddenly perceived that the
whole place was full of horses—gray horses. It was, as the saying
goes, "lousy" with 'em. He had never seen so many horses of one
color in his life. They were everywhere—hitched along the streets,
grazing in vacant lots, and being driven up and down in buggies
and farm wagons; there were even vans over by the "deppo" and in
adjacent alleys from which protruded surprised and mildly protesting heads; so that the Honorable Abner was obliged to park his car
in the only space available, which was three blocks away.

Inside the crowded courtroom, the heavy atmosphere of expec-
tancy was strongly tainted with the pungent smell of ammonia which
drifted in through the open windows. Judge Tompkins was already
on the bench and Mr. Tutt just getting to his feet as the Honorable
Abner entered.

"If the court please," began the old lawyer, "in lieu of presenting
a complicated affidavit, I should like to recall Mr. Sowerbutt for
further examination."

"I object," gasped the Honorable Abner, struggling to recover
his breath. "The statute explicitly states that in order to grant a new
trial, the court must have evidence before it which could not have
been hitherto produced. This witness was thoroughly cross-examined
and his testimony cannot now be attacked."

"Generally speaking, you are quite right, Mr. Pettingill," replied
His Honor, "but Mr. Tutt did not represent the defendant at the
trial and I am inclined to be lenient in the matter. Let's hear what
he wants to prove and what the witness may say. If his testimony is
not sufficient, I shall, of course, deny his motion."

"Mr. Sowerbutt," said Mr. Tutt, after the rather flustered complaining witness had been once more sworn, "when you identified
the gray mare which you found in the defendant's possession, you
had no doubt whatever but that it was yours?"

"Not fer a minute! I could have told that mare anywheres," declared Mr. Sowerbutt.

"Does that hold true now?"

"It sure does! I kin tell that mare, no matter where I see it, just as well as I could then."

"That I do not question for a moment," bowed Mr. Tutt. "Do you know where the mare is?"

"Over to Fernald's Livery Stable."

"Have you any objection to stepping over there and pointing her out to his Honor?"

Sowerbutt looked at Judge Tompkins.

"I reckon not, if he wants me to."

"As I cannot very well ask to have the mare brought into the courtroom, may we adjourn to the livery stable?" suggested Mr. Tutt.

"I don't mind," said His Honor. "It will give us time for a smoke. I'd rather like to have a look at that old gray mare again myself."

The crowd in the courtroom, apparently infected with the same idea, stampeded in the direction of Fernald's Livery, where most of the citizenry of Pottsville were soon gathered. Indeed, so great was the mob milling about the door that the officials had considerable difficulty in forcing their way inside.

"Where is this horse?" inquired his Honor.

Sheriff Higgins waved toward a row of stalls, from the nearest of which projected the sunken rumps, gaunt hind legs and frayed bobbed tails of three gray scarecrows.

"She's over thar, Jedge."

"Which is she, Mr. Sowerbutt?" inquired His Honor. "Please show her to me."

Mr. Sowerbutt, pursing his lips, carefully scrutinized the three cadaverous rumps and ran his hands down the knobbled legs. Then he solemnly unhitched each one and led her out on the stable floor for further examination.

"Got ter git more light," he explained.

"What's the matter, Jake?" yelled some one. "Can't you tell your own hoss?"

"Keep still, can't ye?" ordered the sheriff. "Or I'll put ye under arrest."

Sowerbutt scratched his head.

"Kin I hev 'em all out here together," he asked, "so's I kin study 'em better?"

"Certainly," agreed His Honor, and the three mares were placed side by side. Each had saddle marks on the withers, each a spavin on the off hind hock.

Mr. Sowerbutt studiously inspected each mare from all angles.

"Durn if I kin tell one from t'other!" he at length confessed.

"You say now that you cannot identify the mare which you say was stolen from you?"

"I'm afraid I can't, Judge. I only owned her a few hours. Nat'cherly, I didn't photograph the harness marks. These doggoned mares all look 'bout the same to me. Anyhow, I can't swear which is mine."

"By gum, they're triplets!" chortled Toggery Bill from his place of safety outside the door. "I wouldn't give fifty dollars for the lot!"

"Whose are the other two mares?" asked His Honor suspiciously.

"Mr. Tutt's," answered the sheriff. "Leastwise he brought 'em here 'bout an hour ago and asked me to stall 'em alongside the Sowerbutt mare. I didn't see no harm in it, so I did as he said."

"Which of these are his?"

"Hanged if I know now," answered Mose. "I did when I first put 'em in there, but with all this shufflin' 'round, they've got kind of mixed up and I don't know for sure which is which."

"Neither do I," remarked Mr. Tutt. "Won't you have a stogy, Judge? I heard you say you'd like a smoke."

Once more in the courtroom, Judge Tompkins, his kindly old face a study in mixed emotions, rapped for order.

"Mr. District Attorney," he said, "thanks to Mr. Tutt, we have had, it seems to me, a pretty conclusive illustration of the unreliability of human testimony. It is quite obvious that, should I grant a new trial, Mr. Sowerbutt's evidence as to the identity of the mare found in the possession of the defendant would be quite valueless. As you have pointed out, however, what has occurred this morning is not, strictly speaking, in the eyes of the law, newly discovered evidence. It merely argues a lack of ingenuity on the part of the former counsel for the defendant. The witness' capacity should have been tested upon his original cross-examination; not at this late date. I regret that it is not in my power to grant this defendant a new trial."

"You can, Your Honor," said Mr. Tutt quietly. "Under Section 465 of the Code of Criminal Procedure, you have the power to grant a new trial in any criminal case where the verdict has been decided by lot. The sheriff here can testify that the jury in this case actually shot craps to determine the degree of crime of which the defendant should be convicted."

"Is that so, Sheriff?" demanded Judge Tompkins.

"It suttinly is," answered Mose, feeling in his vest pocket for what the late Justice Oliver Wendell Holmes once referred to as "the implements of decision." "I not only heard 'em but I found these on the table after they'd left the jury room. I'm sure the boys didn't mean no harm."

"Well, Mr. District Attorney!" said His Honor sternly. "What have you to say to that?"

The Honorable Abner rubbed what passed for his chin.

"I really don't know," he stammered. "This is all most surprising to me—very surprising, indeed. I suppose, under the statute, Your Honor will have to grant a new trial."

"Undoubtedly," agreed Tompkins significantly. "Is there anything else which, under the circumstances, occurs to you might be done?"

The Honorable Abner hesitated. Of course there wouldn't be the slightest use trying old Doc a second time. In a flash of mental illumination he perceived the truth of Mr. Tutt's remarks about his future career. Why not turn his defeat into a political asset? Conscious that every eye in the courtroom was upon him, the Honorable Abner thrust one hand into his vest and ran the other in a heroic gesture through his coxcomb.

"If Your Honor please," he declaimed in a voice that was unctuous with the milk of human kindness, "no one more than myself desires to see justice tempered with mercy. I realize that, as public prosecutor of this county, I represent not only the people at large but the defendant as well. I ask that the indictment against him be dismissed."

"I so order," said Tompkins. . . . "Mr. Robinson, you are discharged. I regret that through an honest mistake you have been put to so much inconvenience."

"Oh, I ain't minded it much, thank you, Jedge," answered old Doc politely. "Kin I go now? I want to look after my hosses."

Sheriff Higgins followed His Honor into the latter's chambers.

"Take an eyeful of that, Judge," he said, pointing to a box on the front page of the Pottsville Weekly Clarion, out the afternoon before. "There was one like it in every paper in Somerset County. And the niggers was distributin' handbills all day yestiddy."

Judge Tompkins adjusted his spectacles and reached mechanically for the frayed butt of the stogy donated to the cause of Justice by Mr. Tutt. He read:

WANTED: A whitish-gray mare, fifteen hands three inches high, weighing about 1,300 lbs. Must be at least twelve years old, with sway-back, potbelly, tail bobbed, collar marks on withers and chest, and a spavin on off hind hock. Will pay cash for same if delivered between the hours of 6 and 8 A.M. in front of Pottsville Courthouse, Thursday, June 10. Ephraim Tutt.

"That old feller's pretty cute now, ain't he?" commented Mose.

"Yes, Eph's pretty cute," agreed His Honor. "But hang it all! What I'd like to know is who stole Sowerbutt's mare."

"Doc," said Mr. Tutt that evening, as the two old men sat together on the veranda of the Phœnix Hotel while the two darkies rolled their bones on the lighted path leading to the kitchen, "take another drink and tell me why you didn't bring some witness from Corinth, or any of the other towns you passed through, to testify that you had two gray mares. It would have been so easy and saved you such a lot of inconvenience."

Doc wiped his mouth with the back of his hand and lit a fresh stogy.

"Wa-al," he drawled, "it wouldn't have been so easy, at that. You see, I got that team of mares under rather—er—peculiar circumstances. In fact, it didn't seem exactly advisable to let the owner know I had 'em. So I dyed 'em. They was piebalds until we got to Corinth, and then I cleaned up the nigh one and sold her to Sowerbutt. After I got into Pottsville I fixed up the other one that same night—put a nice tail on her and all, ready to sell. Fust thing I knew, along come Sowerbutt next mornin' and claimed her for his. But she weren't!"

"I see," mused Mr. Tutt. "They were piebalds as far as Corinth and then they became gray mares again. Well, anyhow, you didn't steal either of 'em from Sowerbutt."

Old Doc's watery eyes gleamed momentarily in the darkness.

"Not from Sowerbutt."

MR. TUTT IS NO GENTLEMAN

I

Mr. Ephraim Tutt had just come out of the clubhouse and was standing, rod in hand, on the bank of the Santapedia beside his guest, Mr. Bonnie Doon, preparatory to the evening's fishing, when a canoe appeared unexpectedly around the bend a third of a mile downstream.

"By Lazarus, if it ain't Judge Quelch!" Donald McKay expelled a thin brown stream over the bank in the direction of the approaching canoe. "He's got them same two hairy outlaws a-guidin' him he had last season! The gol-blasted old trouble maker!"

Mr. Tutt would have tolerated no such disrespectful allusion to a regular member of the club in good standing from any guide except old Donald, and not from him save and excepting with regard to the aforesaid member of the judiciary. But the judge could hardly be said to be in good standing, except technically, and there was no gainsaying that he was a trouble maker—even a curse!

"Do you suppose he's coming here?" asked Mr. Tutt hopelessly.

"He can't be goin' nowheres else," commented Angus Ogilvy, the old lawyer's bowman. "There's nowheres else fer him to go, 'cept to Push-and-be-Damned, and there ain't no fish there."

"He's a slick one," growled old Donald. "He was up here fust thing in May, the minute the season opened, and killed a thirty-two pounder. It gave him his third leg on the trophy—which was all he needed. So he saved the rest of his time in case any one else should go him one better. He's got five days left. He must have heard about Mr. Warburton landin' that thirty-five-pound fish on Saturday. That spoiled his chance for the Golden Salmon, so now he's comin' back again."

"That's right!" agreed Mr. Tutt. "The judge had the trophy hog-tied until Saturday. By jumping Jehoshaphat! I'd like to swang-dangle that old fellow!"

"He telephoned up last night to ask who was here," volunteered Angus. "He knows the clubhouse is full. They told him Mr. Warburton was goin' out day after tomorrow. He could have waited perfectly well until next week."

"He's following up that fresh run of fish," alleged Donald shrewdly. "They was at Two Brooks night before last. They'll probably reach here by tomorrow."

The canoe, bearing amidships a tall, saturnine man, was rapidly heading for the landing. Mr. Tutt scrambled down to meet it.

"Hello, Judge!" he cried out genially. "How are you? Hope you've had good luck!"

The occupant of the canoe vouchsafed no reply until it had grounded and the bowman had spiked his paddle and leaped out. Then he arose stiffly and stepped ashore.

"I understand that you have a guest," he announced in a hostile tone, without replying to the old lawyer's greeting. "Of course, you are acquainted with the rule which provides that no guest shall occupy a room in the clubhouse if it is required by a member."

"Of course, I know the rule, Judge," replied Mr. Tutt. "But I had no idea that you wished to stay here until just now when I saw you coming up the river. If you had only telephoned——"

Judge Quelch turned to his guides.

"Take those duffel bags up to the veranda," he ordered. "We shall be here the best part of a week." Then addressing Mr. Tutt, he added: "The clubhouse is for the members who pay the dues, not for visitors who contribute nothing."

"Mr. Warburton is going out on Tuesday," answered Mr. Tutt, controlling his temper as well as he could. "If you would be willing to use one of the other camps farther up the river—Push-and-be-Damned, for instance—until then——"

"I intend to fish here!" snapped Quelch, making his way up the bank.

"Allow me to present my guest, Mr. Doon," interposed Mr. Tutt. Bonnie stepped forward, but Quelch barely nodded to him.

"The camp at Burnt Hill is vacant, if you and your friend want to go there, or you might try Push-and-be-Damned yourself," he shot back, following his dunnage toward the clubhouse. "I have no intention of going anywhere else."

"Very well!" said Mr. Tutt shortly. "I will sleep with the guides until Tuesday. You can occupy my room. I hope you will enjoy it!"

II

The Golden Salmon is the trophy donated by the Rt. Rev. Lionel Charteris, Bishop of St. Albans, the beloved founder of the Wanic Club, which, as every fisherman knows, owns the best water on the Santapedia, one of the great salmon rivers of New Brunswick, if not of the world. Here, on a grassy bluff below the forks over-looking what is known as the Home Pool, stands the low, wide-eaved bungalow where six of the finest gentlemen and grandest sports in the world, including Ephraim Tutt, have spent many of their happiest days—that is, they had spent them there until dear old Bishop Charteris had died at the age of eighty-nine and his small estate, including most unfortunately his share in the Wanic Club, had passed into the hands of a relative whom he had never seen, the Honorable Philo Utterbach Quelch.

The Golden Salmon, under the terms of its gift, was to become the property of whichever member should kill the largest fish in the Home Pool in three seasons. It stood in a case of crystal on the mantelpiece of the big fireplace in the sitting room, under the mounted carcass of Leviathan, the famous fifty-pound salmon that the bishop had killed the last season he had spent there, after having hooked it the year before on a Parmachenee Belle and lost it, and after Mr. Tutt had rehooked it the following spring on a Silver Doctor, only to lose it in his turn—which is an entirely different yarn, though true. Very different! For this particular narrative deals with the morals and manners traditional among sportsmen and gentlemen—that is, among real ones, but not to include, of course, the Honorable Philo—curse him—Utterbach Quelch.

Up to the interjection among them by law, so to speak, of the said Utterbach, the half dozen gentlemen now comprising the Wanic membership had fished the Santapedia together in the utmost har-mony, eagerly looking forward each year to the moment when, the cares of office or of business laid aside, they could resume their sport upon the sunlit reaches of the river and cement their ancient friend-ships around the camp fire. But with the arrival of the Honorable Utterbach, everything was changed in the twinkling of an eye and a black cloud o'erspread the sunset of their lives. And now, by thunder, the fellow had two legs on the Golden Salmon!

To get the exact picture of the consequences of his eruption upon their peaceful clubhouse, one must comprehend that the Wanic is a rather swell affair. To receive an invitation to cast a fly there is the dream of every salmon fisherman, but such invitations are in inverse ratio to the eagerness with which they are sought after. The Prince of Wales has fished there—for a goose egg—and so has the Maharajah of Bhurtpore, the King of the Belgians, Will Rogers,

Douglas Fairbanks, and a limited number of other potentates, pan-
jandrums and the popular pals thereof; but they are the great exceptions.

An ordinary human being could no more pry himself into the
social circle of the Wanic Club than he could into the family dining
room at Buckingham Palace. Those old boys have known one another for more than half a century. They went to school together,
some of them. Mr. Tutt is the only person ever distinguished with
an honorary, or elective, membership. They are all the personifica-
tion of gentleness and courtesy. It is their pleasure to give way to
one another's preferences and to oblige one another in all things,
since there is fishing enough for all and to spare.

It had never occurred to them to pay any attention to their legal
rights, if they had any, or even to the printed rules of the club,
which, to all intents and purposes, had been forgotten ever since
they had been drawn up twenty-five years before. Yet no sooner
had the Honorable Philo Utterbach Quelch made his appearance
than they were rudely awakened to the undeniable fact that a share
in a salmon-fishing club is property governed by the laws apper-
taining to the same, and that the rules and by-laws of such a corporation have a like force and effect.

Quelch was a cadaverous man with a coffin-shaped face, a querulous, rasping voice, and a legal manner, which, perhaps, was only
natural considering his profession. Yet a legal manner is a poor
manner among sportsmen; as is too great a regard for the technical
niceties of one's rights. He had, moreover, an affliction of some sort
which, when he spoke, made him stutter, squawk, strangle and
explode so that he could be heard all over the camp; and at night
he coughed, hawked and snored so that even the wild beasts, which
had come down from the hills to nuzzle the garbage cans, fled
back to their fastnesses in terror.

The strange thing about Quelch, like many other unpleasant persons, was that he could be perfectly agreeable when he chose to
be so. He was highly cultivated, had read much, traveled widely,
and was learned in piscatorial as in other branches of the law. But
there was something about him which made others dislike him more
when he was trying to be affable than when he was being frankly
nasty, which was most of the time. For in the woods it is better to
be detestable than to be a bore. Quelch was both. The interminable,
strangulated orations with which he regaled his fellow members

upon the veranda after meals, in which he retailed his various exploits in the world of sport, drove his fellow members nearly wild. The news that Quelch was coming was inevitably a signal for the hasty exodus of every one else, and, in consequence, he usually had the clubhouse to himself.

But this was different—the Golden Salmon was at stake! For a brief space, Mr. Tutt considered accepting the Honorable Quelch's suggestion to move to Burnt Hill or Push-and-be-Damned, but Bonnie Doon had never been salmon fishing before, there was a fresh run on its way up the river, and—curse the fellow!—Old Man Tutt hated to be bullied by a lawyer half a dozen years younger than he was himself, even if he were a judge. So he went over and slept with the guides.

Having thus coolly ousted Mr. Tutt from his room in the clubhouse, Judge Quelch proceeded to make himself at home there, appropriating the seat at the head of the dining table, the best easy-chair next the fireplace, and the only hammock upon the veranda, acting as if in so doing he was but exercising the prerogatives inherited from his distinguished half uncle. He also indulged in a practice anathema to all campers, preëmpting all the pegs and hooks on the outside of the clubhouse for his personal belongings, distributing his under and over garments everywhere, including a particularly dirty pair of ancient blue overalls, which he hung just outside the door of the living room, so that no one who either went in or out could fail to be reminded of his presence.

Being, therefore, in what was for him a genial frame of mind, he proceeded, after supper, to elucidate, for the edification of his fellow members, the law governing the ownership of wild game.

"There is," he announced, "a great deal of confusion in the minds of most sportsmen as to the rights which they can acquire in what the law calls *feræ naturæ*, or wild animals. There are, in fact, no property rights in wild animals, including fish, until the latter are reduced to actual manual possession by the hunter or fisherman, or are so wounded or confined as to be within his absolute control."

"Do you mean to say that the salmon we kill in front of our clubhouse don't belong to any one until they're actually landed?" asked Ives.

Judge Quelch flourished his cigar as if it were a gavel.

"That is precisely what I mean, sir. Ever since the Magna Charta of King John, it has been firmly established that in England the King owns all wild game not legally reduced to possession, and in

America that the state in its sovereign capacity exercises the same ownership. That is the reason we all have to take out fishing licenses and pay a fee to the state. Our ownership of the banks of the river gives us only an exclusive right to fish in the waters beside us. While it is true that our right of fishery is enough to enable us to keep off trespassers and appropriate any fish they have killed in our own waters, it would not be sufficient to permit us to follow a poacher who had hooked a fish in front of the clubhouse and to take it away from him after he had killed it in waters other than our own."

Donald McKay, who was whittling at the other end of the veranda, looked up.

"Are you sayin', Judge, that it's the law if a poacher comes on our waters and hooks a salmon, and it runs down stream and he kills it beyond our boundary, we can't take the fish away from him?"

"Exactly. We have only an exclusive privilege of taking the salmon while it is in our water. The moment the fish passes beyond our boundaries we lose that right of fishery and the fish becomes subject to the poacher's superior right of absolute manual possession, although we could, of course, bring an action against him for trespass."

"By Lazarus! That's news to me!" declared Donald. "And it'll be news to a lot of other fellers."

Judge Quelch grinned in what he intended to be a benign fashion, but which merely approximated the smile of a hyena.

"Laymen—including guides like yourself—are not supposed to be familiar with the technical rules of law in such matters. There is a fundamental difference between owning a fish outright and having merely the exclusive privilege of trying to catch it on one's own waters."

"They had a funny case like that downriver about a deer," volunteered Donald. "One man wounded it pretty bad and, while it was runnin', another feller shot it through the heart an' killed it. They had a kind of moot court in the camp and gave it to the feller that wounded it first."

"Entirely wrong!" asserted Quelch authoritatively. "The law is absolutely settled that under such circumstances the animal belonged to the one who killed it—reduced it to actual possession. I can, in fact, cite you an exact precedent—Pierson versus Post, 3 Caines Cases 175, if I remember correctly."

"I'm sure you always remember correctly," said Mr. Tutt.

"It was a case about foxes. There had been a hunt, and the hounds were about to make a kill, when a farmer, seeing that the fox was cornered, shot and made off with it. The court held that he was perfectly within his right. I can recall the exact words of the decision: 'An action will not lie against a man for killing and taking a wild animal pursued by and in view of the person who originally found, started, chased it, and was on the point of seizing it.' There are innumerable cases on the subject. They cover bear, deer, seals, birds——"

"Are there any about salmon?" asked Mr. Tutt quietly.

"Er—perhaps not specifically about salmon," conceded Judge Quelch, "but by analogy——"

"Do you contend that if two men are fishing a stream and one hooks a salmon, the other has a legal right to gaff and take it, on the ground that he was the one to reduce it to actual possession?"

"I most certainly do!" answered the judge. "Most of us know to our cost that our chances of ultimate possession of a salmon on the end of a hundred yards of line are exceedingly precarious, to say the least. The fish belongs to the one who gets him."

"Humph!" snorted the president of the British Columbian Railways. "What would you think of a man who gaffed another man's fish?"

"As a judge," replied the Honorable Philo, "my task, should such a case come before me, would be solely to interpret and apply the law according to my best lights."

"Don't you agree that there's a great deal of difference between the chances of reducing to possession a deer that has been wounded by a bullet and a salmon which has been solidly hooked, and is attached to a No. 1 leader the end of a twenty-four pound test line?" asked Mr. Tutt.

"I do not!" snapped the judge. "The line or leader may break."

"In any case," continued the old lawyer, "I understand your position to be that hooking a salmon gives a fisherman no right to the fish that is superior to any one else's. So that if another fisherman hooked the same fish foul, it would belong to whichever could manage to land him?"

"That is not only my position but it is the law!" affirmed the Honorable Philo.

"Don't you think that among sportsmen such a performance would justly be regarded as contemptible?" demanded Warburton.

The Honorable Philo Utterbach Quelch turned a pale orb upon his questioner.

"It is time that sportsmen, so-called, realized that they are governed by the rules of law like everybody else," he remarked.

"So you'd take another man's fish if you hooked him foul?" inquired Mr. Tutt.

"That would depend—on circumstances. I only say that under the law I would have the right to do so, if I chose," replied Quelch.

"But do you think any man calling himself a gentleman would do a thing like that?" persisted Mr. Tutt.

"A gentleman!" repeated Quelch sarcastically. "Will you kindly inform me in what respect a person calling himself a gentleman differs from any one else?"

"The word has had a pretty well defined meaning for several hundred years," mused Mr. Tutt. "You may have heard the phrase 'on my honor as a gentleman,' perhaps?"

"I have heard it, and I fail to see how the honor of a gentleman differs from the honor of any other citizen," sneered Quelch. "Honor is honor, and law is law. Every nation and every religion in the world has a different standard of morals. The only basic test of the rightfulness or wrongfulness of an action is whether that action is legal or illegal."

The president of the Royal Bank of Canada leaned forward.

"The by-laws of practically every club provide that a member may be expelled for conduct unbecoming a gentleman. Why is that, if it means nothing?" he remarked.

"That's all it does mean!" snorted Quelch. "Nothing! Such provisions have no validity in the courts. The member of a club cannot be expelled for anything he had a legal right to do. I'm sure I've no idea of what is meant by a gentleman."

"I can well believe it," murmured Mr. Tutt.

"Hear! Hear!" came from the other end of the veranda.

Quelch's eye swept the circle of disgusted sportsmen.

"Well, come on; tell me! What is a gentleman?" he demanded.

"I don't wonder you ask!" commented Mr. Arbuthnot.

"Trying to define a gentleman has been a favorite parlor game so long as I can remember," said Quelch. "It can't be done, for the simple reason that the word is entirely vague, a meaningless term. It belongs in the same category as questions like 'What is art?' and 'What is beauty?' If you ask me——"

"We do ask you!" Ives shot at him.

"As a man of considerable experience of the world, who has listened to countless litigated disputes, I say that, in the final analysis, the only satisfactory test of a gentleman is whether or not he is willing to infringe the legal rights of others. Any other gauge of human conduct is hopelessly confused. If one applies the purely legal test, everything becomes clear and definite. For example—and I cite this as an excellent and most apropos illustration—when I arrived here, this evening, I found that Mr. Tutt had invited a guest to fish with him—a right derived by him solely from our by-laws; but those very same by-laws provide that no guest can occupy a room in the clubhouse if it is required by a member. Now, I have two legs on the trophy presented to the club by my uncle, Bishop Charteris, and I am entitled to five more days' fishing at the Forks. To attempt to exclude me from the club and to prevent me from securing the trophy, if I can, would certainly not be a gentlemanly course of procedure. But what is the test? The law as expressed in our rules. Should I, out of some mistaken idea of courtesy, waive my rights in this instance, I should not only be unjust to myself but open the door to every sort of abuse. The clubhouse might easily become filled with guests who would prevent the regular members from getting any fishing at all. We must uphold the rules. The true gentleman is he who is willing to suffer criticism for the ultimate good of all."

Mr. Tutt produced and lit a stogy.

"What you say—coming, as it does, from the lips of Gamaliel, so to speak—interests me extremely," he remarked. "But I can easily see that questions might arise even under our by-laws which would be very hard to settle by purely legal reasoning and which might have to be determined by an appeal to some less rigid test!"

"Indeed!" remarked the Honorable Quelch. "What, for example?"

"Well," drawled Mr. Tutt, "my very dear old friend, your half-uncle, Bishop Charteris, bequeathed the trophy to whomsoever should kill the biggest salmon in the Home Pool during three seasons. Now, suppose I hooked a fish in Push-and-be-Damned, say, and it carried me down to the Home Pool and I killed it there—would I come within the requirements?"

"Certainly not!" ejaculated Quelch. "To qualify for the trophy, the fish must be hooked in the Home Pool by the member having the right to fish there at the time."

"And where do you get that?" inquired Ives.

"That is my judicial interpretation of the paragraph of my uncle's will," answered Quelch. "And I am ready to gamble my professional reputation that it would be sustained by any of the higher courts of New Brunswick."

"Suppose I hooked a fish in Push-and-be-Damned and it carried me down to the Home Pool, what would you do if you were fishing there?"

"If I had drawn the Home Pool under the provisions of the by-laws and were fishing it, I should require you to move along."

"Suppose I couldn't? Suppose the salmon wanted to stay there?"

"You'd have no right to remain and spoil my fishing," declared Quelch. "Whoever draws the Home Pool has the right to the undisturbed possession of it. All others are trespassers. In fact," he added, "a proper construction of the by-laws would give me the right to hook and take the fish—in which case it could properly be regarded as having been killed in the Home Pool."

"I merely wanted to know," explained Mr. Tutt. "After all, applying technical legal rules rather simplifies things, as you say. . . . By jumping Jehoshaphat, it's half past six!"

"Time we were pushing off!" interrupted Norton, adding something under his breath inaudible to the Honorable Philo.

"Did you hear what the judge said, Donald?" asked Mr. Tutt with his gentlest smile as he climbed into the canoe.

"I heard him!" answered Donald, picking up his paddle. "And also his reference to guides in general! Wouldn't it be the gol-blastedest thing if the old scalawag managed to cinch the Golden Salmon?"

"He won't if I can help it!" asserted Mr. Tutt.

III

The pools at the Wanic Club are drawn by lot each day and, as luck would have it, during the next four days the Honorable Philo, although a redoubtable fisherman, did not improve his position with respect to the Golden Salmon. He still had two legs on it, but no more. Mr. Warburton's thirty-five-pound fish remained the largest taken from the Home Pool that year. Then, on the last day of the five upon which he was still entitled to fish, the judge proceeded to draw the Home Pool for both morning and evening. It was a heavy blow to the other members, for the fresh run of fish that had been on their way up the river had just arrived and that particular pool was boiling. Every one agreed that it would be just Quelch's luck to kill a forty-pound fish at the last minute and carry off the trophy.

The Wanic Club stands at the Forks of the Santapedia. There are six pools in all: The Home Pool just in front of the clubhouse —where a sand pit lying in mid-river divides the current, part of which having flowed past the spit turns upstream in a back eddy, rejoining the rapids again above the bar—the Cocktail, the Corkscrew, and the Wildcat on the half-mile stretch below. Above the forks are two others—Push-and-be-Damned, which, being a mile away, has a camp of its own; and lower down, a couple of hundred yards above the Wanic clubhouse, one of the very best pools of all— Donald's Leap—where, in his younger days, Donald McKay had jumped a full twelve feet from the bank to a rock in midstream to gaff a salmon entangled among the driftwood.

The Honorable Philo's last day dawned auspiciously, one of those perfect days for fishing that come but once or twice in a season. The water was neither too high nor too low, the sun was bright and hot, there was enough of a breeze to ruffle the surface without making it difficult to cast. Mr. Tutt had killed two salmon weighing more than thirty pounds each in the Home Pool the evening before, and the wardens had reported that they had seen several big fish, estimated at upwards of forty pounds, moving upstream toward the Forks. And, of course, it had to be the Honorable Philo who drew the Home Pool that day, and, of course, before breakfast he had already killed a thirty-three pounder on a Jock Scot. He came in arrogantly, consuming a trencher of oatmeal, two large platters of corn cakes and maple sirup, and several cups of coffee, after which he proceeded to expatiate magniloquently upon his chances of winning the trophy. Even if he didn't kill the biggest fish that year, he pointed out, his chances were still three to one as against any one else. Clearly, in his opinion, the Golden Salmon was already as good as his.

The limit to the number of fish a member may kill in one day is six, so that Quelch could take but four more and, if he were to capture the trophy, one of these must exceed the weight of Warburton's thirty-five pounder taken the previous week. Now Quelch belonged to that variety of fisherman whose ambition is to kill as many fish as possible. He was inevitably on his pool by five in the morning and kept casting, casting, casting, until darkness rendered it no longer possible to do so. He had even been known to go on fishing when he could no longer see his fly. But if one is not trying to catch more than his competitors, but merely a bigger fish, the greater number he catches without achieving his object the worse it is for him, since it reduces his final chances.

"By Lazarus!" exclaimed old Donald as Mr. Tutt emerged from the clubhouse after lunch. "I've just seen something I wouldn't have believed possible, if it weren't fer Angus to corroborate me. I take my oath I saw the judge hook and play a salmon out there, and when he most brought him in and saw he was only twenty pounds or so, he had one of his hairy sons-of-guns cut the leader and let him go! Is that within the rules?"

"I suppose so," answered the old lawyer wryly. "A member may kill only six fish, and a fish that is released isn't technically killed, even if it dies afterwards."

Donald spat contemptuously.

"That's on a par with what he did up to the Headwater Pool last year. You know, all the fish that pass by here go up there to spawn. They're so hungry they'll pretty near jump at the bare hook, let alone a fly. A member is only allowed to stay there two days and kill a dozen fish."

"What did Quelch do?"

"I'll tell ye what he did, and I've made affidavit of it too. He and them two dog-faced boys from Boiestown went up there last September and hooked and landed seventy fish. They kep' twelve of 'em and threw back fifty-eight. You know how much chance for life a salmon has, once he's been hooked and landed. But the judge claimed he was within the rules!"

"Donald," he said, "something must be done about this man Quelch."

But luck was with the Judge. All that afternoon, in spite of the protests of the other members, he turned the Home Pool into a piscatorial slaughterhouse, hooking salmon, playing them nearly dead and, because they were not large enough, letting them go. By five o'clock he had hooked nine and kept only four; thus, as he contended, still maintaining the legal right to kill two more. He worked like an automaton, standing in his waders on the sand spit and whipping every inch of water from the point where the Santapedia shoots through a flume of rocks in an almost solid column of brown amber into the rapids, across the deep, oily stretches between the bar and the high banks in front of the clubhouse, to where the river broadens into dimpling shallows before part of it swirls onward into the Cocktail and the rest swings into a back eddy that circles around the bar and rejoins the main stream again. Crouched beside his canoe were the two hairy apes from Boiestown, ready to shove off and follow any fish that might seek to escape down river. And still he cast, quartering the pool with every variety of fly in his book, determined before night to land a salmon bigger than Warburton's thirty-five pounder.

Concededly, his chances were good. There were forty-pound fish in the pool and at any moment one of them might take his fly. Ives, Norton and Arbuthnot, who had drawn the Cocktail, the Corkscrew and the Wild Cat, respectively, had given up and were smoking their pipes on the veranda. No doubt about it, the fish were all in the Home Pool. Mr. Tutt and Bonnie Doon, with Donald and Angus, had gone up to Donald's Leap and were fishing it from the banks.

A portentous silence hung over the Forks. No sound disturbed the tranquillity of the late afternoon, save the murmur of the river, the occasional splash of a kingfisher or the sound of expectoration from one or the other of Quelch's hairy guides. The shadows began to lengthen and the golden light to creep higher and higher toward the tops of the pines. Dusk was falling fast—that indeterminate translucent veil which, like a mist, screens and magnifies, transforming even the commonest of objects. That, perhaps, is why the late fishing is best, since the gathering darkness helps to deceive the salmon when he sees what he takes to be a fly. Such was the hour, and big with Fate. Now, if ever, Quelch might expect to raise and kill his winning fish.

Suddenly, from far above the Forks, came a distant shouting. Something exciting was going on up there, and it could mean but one thing. Mr. Tutt—or possibly Mr. Doon—had hooked a mighty fish. Instantly the river became alive. The hullabaloo increased, growing momentarily louder, so that the members left the veranda and gathered on the bank to see what was going to happen. The guides and cook came running from the camp and cookhouse.

First, Donald appeared, gaff in hand, jumping from rock to rock, closely followed by Angus and Bonnie Doon. Then, upstream, struggling with all his might, Old Man Tutt came into view, his rod bent in a half circle, butt against belly, his reel screeching, his line taut as a telegraph wire attached to race horse. Obviously, he had hooked a salmon in Donald's Leap and, do what he would, it was pulling him down the river.

It was a precarious situation, for above the Forks the Santapedia goes sweeping around jagged boulders, over sharp ledges and

past tangled piles of logs and driftwood which offer every opportunity for the line to catch and the fish to break away. But although
Mr. Tutt had already been dragged a hundred yards, he had, nevertheless, managed to hang fast to his fish, which, accompanied by a
chorus of yells from Donald, Angus and Bonnie Doon, was making
its away straight for the falls above the Home Pool. Any such view
halloo is inevitably the signal for every member to leave what he is
doing, no matter where or what, and to come hurrying to watch the
kill. But Quelch did not budge. Stolidly he went on with his casting,
hardly vouchsafing so much as a look upstream.

They were all there now. Warburton, who had come back to see
the finish, Ives, Norton, Arbuthnot, the two wardens, the cook, his
helpers, and half a dozen guides were strung along the bluff, for they
knew, from the way that Mr. Tutt, Donald and Angus acted, that
this was indeed no ordinary fish.

"By Godfrey!" muttered Ives. "That salmon is sure coming down
into the Home Pool, and if it does—so help me Quelch!—there's
going to be a cat fight before we get through."

"Thar he goes!" shouted Angus hysterically, as a black streak
slithered over the falls. "He's a whale! Forty-five pounds if he's
an ounce!"

"Fifty, by Lazarus!" yelled old Donald. "I never seen one as big
—not even the bishop's!"

"What did you raise him with?" called out the methodical Norton.

"A Griswold Gray. He only riz once—and took it solid!"

"Did you see his tail?"

"Looked like the stern of an ocean liner!"

Mr. Tutt was staggering in midstream, reeling bravely as opportunity offered and struggling to gain the bank above the falls,
whence he might hope to exercise some control over the fish at the
end of his ninety yards of line. But the current is powerful here,
hurling itself like a mill race against the high dune in front of the
clubhouse and whirling deep, black and foamflecked along the edge
of the pool, so that even a small fish has a good chance of escape.
Naturally, the salmon made for this point of least resistance, pulling
out more and more line as Mr. Tutt scrambled over the rocks and
came running after it along the shore.

"Get a canoe!" ordered Norton, and Donald and Angus plunged
down the shelving gravel and, clambering in, pushed off into the
center of the pool, ready to follow should the salmon make another
break for lower down.

The fish was now hanging directly opposite, about a hundred feet from the sand bar from which Quelch was casting. Looking across at Mr. Tutt, he called harshly:

"Get off my water!"

"I can't!" answered the old lawyer. "I'm fast to a salmon."

"Makes no difference! I've the exclusive right to fish this pool. You're a trespasser! Order your guides ashore!"

Just then Mr. Tutt's line slackened for a moment and a black back rose to sight, only instantly to disappear again. Mr. Tutt reeled frantically.

"I tell you to get off my water!" bellowed Quelch.

"I'm going to land my fish first!"

"You have no right to kill a salmon in this pool!"

"I'm going to, all the same!" replied Mr. Tutt. . . . "Hey, there, Angus! Push out into the shallows!"

"If you kill a salmon here, I shall claim him as mine!" warned Quelch.

"Nonsense!" declared Arbuthnot. "You can't prevent another member from following a fish into your water."

"The courts will decide that!" retorted Quelch.

The black object rose once more to the surface some twenty-odd feet lower down the pool. At the same instant Quelch raised his rod. It was a long cast—forty yards at least—but the judge was an expert and could hit a leaf unerringly at that distance. Ping! His line became taut, his rod whipped into a half circle, and with a leer of elation he began to reel in. Incredible as it seemed, he had succeeded in hooking Mr. Tutt's fish foul at the first cast. An outcry of protest came from the spectators upon the bank.

"That's the dirtiest trick I've ever seen done on a river!" asserted Ives.

"I'm fully within my rights!" retorted Quelch. "No matter who lands this fish, it is mine—and counts for the trophy!"

Both old men were now fast to the same salmon—the one by the mouth, the other by the tail—and favored by the swiftness of the current, it was making headway against both of them.

"I hooked this fish!" panted Mr. Tutt.

"That gives you no legal claim. You haven't reduced him to possession! A salmon is *feræ naturæ*——"

"*Feræ naturæ* be damned!" bawled the old lawyer, as, at that precise instant, his line parted and his rod straightened so that he nearly fell over backward. A grin of triumph gathered upon the

face of the Honorable Utterbach at the realization that the gods had
thus unexpectedly intervened in his behalf. All he had to do now
was to land his fish, and the trophy would be his; for he felt convinced that he was fast to the biggest salmon of the season, if not of
all time. But landing a salmon foul is no easy task, as the Judge
well knew. It often means an endurance contest—requiring hours of
hard work to tire him out.

So the Honorable Philo sat down carefully on his sand spit,
propped his heels against a rock, inserted the butt of his rod in the
socket of his leather belt, and dug himself in with his line leading
directly into the centre of the pool where the fish was now apparently sulking.

Ives, Warburton, Norton and Arbuthnot had gathered about
Mr. Tutt in earnest consultation. Presently Arbuthnot came down
to the edge of the landing.

"We have held a meeting of the club members, Judge Quelch,"
he announced acidly, "and you have been expelled for conduct that
was unbecoming a gentleman."

"Rot!" returned the Honorable Philo. "You can't expel me!
Besides, your meeting was not properly called. The law will respect
my rights, even if you do not!"

He was about to add something more, but his reel began to sing
as the salmon made for the end of the pool, so that he scrambled
hastily to his feet and followed along the sand spit. Quelch was a
good fisherman and knew that even if he could not hold his fish in
the swift water, he might be able to steer it into the back eddy; so
he let it run the length of the pool and then swung it across the
current. It was a daring and clever manœuvre—and it succeeded.
Back came the salmon upstream into the dead water on the other
side of the bar and, with the strain on the line thus relieved, Quelch
reeled in until he had shortened his line by fifty or more feet. Making a complete circle around the sand spit, the fish reëntered the
Home Pool and, taking advantage of the rapids below the falls and
the powerful current in front of the clubhouse, made for the lower
river, running out the line again until Quelch's reel was all but
stripped.

Once more, however, the judge turned him just in the nick of
time and nursed his fish into the backwater again, around the head
of the spit and into the Home Pool. Already an hour had gone by,
it was almost dark, but the salmon seemed as fresh as ever. With
every passing minute, the Judge's time was running out and, unless

he could land his fish, he would have lost his chance, for that year at least, of capturing the Golden Salmon. The lamps had been lighted in the clubhouse, but, although supper was ready, Tobias, the cook, did not announce it, preferring to stand with the others and watch the finish fight going on below.

"If he don't land him next trip, it's all over!" declared Norton, as the judge once again steered his quarry into the backwater. "It'll be pitch black inside of ten minutes."

This time, however, it became obvious that the judge meant to bring the struggle to an end, for when the salmon again followed the current of the back eddy into the main pool, he began to reel in with all his strength. Slowly the line shortened.

"Dammit! I believe he's got him!" swore Ives.

One of the hirsute guides had climbed into the canoe and swung it across the end of the spit in order to intercept the salmon, should it make a final rush; the other waded into the water with his gaff held in readiness to strike.

Inch by inch, the salmon came in, not, as usual, turning over so as to exhibit its belly, but with its back flush with the surface.

Quelch walked to the river's edge.

"Now!" he yelled. "Let him have it!"

They all watched breathlessly as, amid a silence like the vacuum between two worlds, the guide reached forward with his gaff and struck. Generally, under such circumstances, the salmon puts up a frantic battle for life, floundering about and scattering the water in every direction. Many a fish has been lost owing to the desperate character of its last minute's struggle. But in this instance nothing of the sort occurred. The gaff encountered no resistance and, with but slight effort, Quelch's guide lifted his quarry from the water. Quickly he dropped it—but not before a chorus of jeers and catcalls had arisen from the opposite bank. Shamefacedly he waded backward toward the spit, dragging behind him—a waterlogged pair of blue overalls! Quelch stared at them stupidly. Gingerly he picked them up by one leg. They were his own!

Slowly, while the crowd upon the bank hugged themselves with delight, the Honorable Utterbach dismounted his rod and got into his canoe.

Arbuthnot met him at the landing.

"I call to your attention," said he severely, "that since you arrived in the afternoon, your five days are already up and that you are no longer entitled to remain here. Your room has accordingly been turned over to Mr. Tutt."

"You are correct according to the by-laws," conceded the judge. "I will pack up my things, and after supper——"

"You are not entitled to supper," interrupted Arbuthnot coldly. "You got here at five o'clock and you have already exceeded your time by two hours. Member or no member, you will move on at once."

The judge turned to his guides.

"Get ready to go to Push-and-be-Damned," he said shortly. "We'll have supper when we reach camp."

"And be damned!" echoed some one.

Ten minutes later he was gone.

"How did you ever come to think of it, Mr. Tutt?" asked Norton as they all sat around the camp fire that evening.

"Well," admitted the old lawyer as he lit a fresh stogy and tossed the rest of those in his case to the guides, "the fact is I did the very same thing last year at Burnt Hill—with a pair of overalls too. A strong current is very deceptive and will make a small fish act like a big one at any time. I saw Warburton go ashore to land a half-pound chub in front of the clubhouse only last Monday. I figured that if I waited until it was nearly dark, I could make most anything act like a salmon."

"I'll say you did!" commented Ives. "You had me fooled to the last second."

"And then, you see," continued Mr. Tutt, "I already had Quelch's assurance as to what he would do under the circumstances. He ran true to form and lived up to his principles—such as they are. I've no doubt he considers himself more sinned against than sinning."

"I caught a wash boiler once down to Henshaw's, and I saw a feller play an old shoe for half an hour at Two Brooks," said Old Donald. "I've seen the same sort of thing happen half a dozen times!"

They all smoked in silence for a while. It was broken by Angus.

"And they was his own pants at that!" he chuckled.

The Honorable Utterbach sat disconsolately, after a supper of cold beans, upon the rough porch of Push-and-be-Damned under a leering moon. The two hairy apes from Boiestown lolled at a distance against the veranda, spitting alternately in a disdainful manner at an adjacent stump. Overalls! The Judge's moose lip quivered and something suspiciously like water glistened on his lower lids. Cæsar, Alexander, Napoleon—even Bismarck—may have wept, but there is no record of it. And, after all, they were iron men.

The Honorable Utterbach felt very much alone. He was not a man of iron. What could be the trouble? He was a judge, wasn't he? And the law was the law? He had only acted according to his lights. Yes, he had been treated outrageously. Outrageously! And he had lost the Golden Salmon—for that year anyway! Pulling out a huge silk handkerchief, he blew his nose with a blast that might have echoed to the Forks. Then, with his lips still quivering, he looked up at the moon.

"Mr. Tutt is no gentleman!" he declared.

THE VIKING'S DAUGHTER

I

BAR HARBOR, Mt. Desert, Maine.
Desire retain your services in important matter. Please come at once. All expenses paid. Money no object.
ALLISON DINGLE.

The telegram had arrived at a moment when Mr. Tutt—the rest of the office force, with the exception of Miss Sondheim and Bonnie Doon, having departed for a vacation—was feeling particularly old and lonely.

"Dingle? Dingle? Ever hear of him, Bonnie?" He tossed the yellow sheet toward the ambulance chaser. "Look him up in *Who's Who*."

Mr. Doon reached for the unwieldy red volume that always stood on the end of the table alongside the Bible, the *World Almanac*, *Burke's Peerage*, *Bartlett's Familiar Quotations*, the *Shakespearean Concordance*, *Bibby's Pocket Dictionary* and *Ploetz's Manual of Universal History*.

"Dingal—Dingball—Dingbat—Dingel—here he is: 'Dingle, Allison; b. Yonkers, N. Y., Sept. 30, 1870; s. Thomas and Sarah Jane D.; m. Mary Haskell, of Brooklyn, N. Y., April 15, 1904.' Gee! This guy certainly hates himself! They write their own obituaries, you know! Claims he's a manufacturer, financier, author, genealogist, agrostologist——"

"What's that?" asked Mr. Tutt.

"Got me!" answered Bonnie. "But whatever it is, he says he's it!"

"What clubs or societies does he belong to?"

"Union League, Yale, Sons of the Revolution, Society of American Wars, United Order of Americans, President of the Breakfast Food Manufacturers' Association, Vice-President of the Nordic Society—there's nearly a page of it!"

"He's everything but a Blue Goose and a Sacred Camel!" declared Mr. Tutt.

"Anyhow, I guess he's good for a ticket to Bar Harbor." Bonnie replaced the book. "If you don't feel like taking such a long trip this hot weather, I——"

Now, although Mr. Tutt had always insisted that New York was par excellence the finest summer resort upon the American continent, he was at this particular juncture yearning to get out of it. In the first place, there was absolutely nothing doing in the office of Tutt & Tutt; in the second, the weather had been unspeakably hot; thirdly and lastly, he hated to be left there all by himself when everybody else was off having a good time, and even the Saturday-night meetings of the "Bible Class" at the Colophon Club, where they played deuces wild and everybody raised on a red and black nine, had been temporarily suspended.

Besides, strange as it may seem, in spite of the fact that Mr. Tutt was by birth a New Englander and had fished most of the inland waters of the state of Maine, he had never visited the sea-coast, although he probably knew more of its early history than most of the native inhabitants. He had passed many a winter evening beside his sea-coal fire in his musty old library on Twenty-third Street, smoking innumerable stogies and reading of the earlier expeditions from France and England to the North Atlantic coast nearly two decades before the Pilgrims landed at Plymouth in 1620.

Champlain was one of his favorite heroes, and he was familiar with the fact of his picturesque but ill-starred expedition, which, under the charter of Henry of Navarre, King of France, and the leadership of Pierre de Guast, Sieur de Monts, had visited the coast of Maine in 1603, discovered the island of Mt. Desert, and attempted unsuccessfully to establish a colony at the mouth of the St. Croix River, where most of his followers had fallen victims to starvation, scurvy and Indian arrows. Hence Mr. Tutt's interest in Mt. Desert was not social, nor even professional, but historic.

He had always wanted to go to Mt. Desert; and now the chance was being offered him—all expenses paid—by the distinguished Mr. Allison Dingle. Send Bonnie Doon in his place? Perish the thought! It made no difference who or what Mr. Dingle might be, or the nature of the matter in which the latter desired to retain him. "Service" was the motto of Tutt & Tutt.

So Mr. Tutt gave Bonnie Doon a paternal smile.

"It is very kind of you to suggest going in my place," he said. "But as I read his telegram, Mr. Dingbat demands my personal attention."

"Dingle is the name," corrected Mr. Doon with hauteur.

His employer arose.

"I shall honor the call of this patriotic manufacturer of dry cereals," he announced. "You and Miss Sondheim can hold down the office furniture while I am gone."

Thus it was that Mr. Tutt, at five o'clock next morning, had found himself in the wilds of Maine. He had gone via Boston and debouched at Bangor, tired and rather cross, after a sleepless night in the Pullman; but having snatched a cup of coffee at the station restaurant and transferred himself to the back platform of the train, he had begun to revive. As he rattled down the single track to Ellsworth and the Mt. Desert ferry, Mr. Tutt, breathing into his tobacco-tanned lungs the cold air in which the balsam of pine forests was mingled with the breath of the ever-nearing sea, revived more and more.

Later he had stood clinging to his hat in the bow of the "Norumbega" as it churned across the bay toward the mountains that ranged themselves like a row of gigantic elephants over the island of Mt. Desert, passed through a narrow channel between some small spruce-covered islands, called The Porcupines, and threading its way among the yachts lying in the harbor, bumped at length against the Bar Harbor pier. Mr. Tutt had enjoyed every minute of that beautiful sail, and it was by reason of his desire not to miss anything, and his consequent commanding position in the bow of the steamer, that he was the only passenger to observe the tableau at that moment being enacted upon a neighboring float at which lay a small stubby white launch.

A girl in khaki overalls and blue jersey, her yellow hair cupped by a round blue worsted cap, was standing in the stern, evidently engaged in saying good-by to a white-flanneled young man upon the float, who seemed disinclined to let go her hand. They evidently had a great deal of importance to say to each other, and they were much too engrossed to notice either the approach of the "Norumbega," or the inquiring presence of Mr. Tutt.

"All ashore that's going ashore!" yelled the mate as the hawser looped one of the piles; and Mr. Tutt, grasping his carpetbag, descended the plank.

Reaching the pier, he turned to see what further might have happened. The launch was by this time a couple of hundred yards from the float, scudding for the open bay, the girl looking back, one hand upon the wheel, and waving good-by with the other.

A trimly gaitered chauffeur relieved Mr. Tutt of his carpetbag, conducted him to a shining limousine, whirled him through the town and up a half-mile of curving bluestone drive to a château surrounded by pines upon the summit of a neighboring hill.

It was a sparkling day, one of Stevenson's "green days in forests, blue days at sea." The odor of roses drifted from the garden near by; across the tree tops he caught the glint of the ocean.

Mr. Tutt would have liked to throw himself down on the lawn, stick his face into the hot grass, and maybe roll about and kick his old heels in the air; but a portly, pink-faced manservant was standing upon the marble step beneath the porte-cochère.

"Mr. Dingle wished me to say that he will be down in a few minutes," he said. "Breakfast is at nine o'clock. Shall I show you to your room, sir?"

So Mr. Tutt turned his back on the sunlight outside and followed the butler through a shadowed entrance hall, hung with armor and mounted trophies, and up the heavily carpeted stairs, to a vast white bedchamber, adjoining an equally vast bathroom, resplendent in tile and gleaming nickel.

At the door of this natatorium, Mr. Griffin, the gentleman in waiting, paused.

"How do you like your bath, sir?"

"Er—medium, I guess," temporized the old lawyer.

The eyes of the stately one enfiladed Mr. Tutt's congress shoes, string tie and rusty old frock coat. Elevating the carpetbag upon a supercilious finger, he inquired unhopefully, "Shall I lay out some other clothes for you, sir?"

Mr. Tutt, who had thrown himself at full length upon a lounge and was feeling in his pockets for a match, waved him aside.

"No," he replied. "In point of fact, I haven't got any. And you needn't bother to open that bag, either. There's nothing in it but a toothbrush, a pair of socks, a bundle of stogies and my last copy of the *Influence of Wealth in Imperial Rome*."

"Very good, sir. Thank you, sir," said Mr. Griffin.

"Not at all!" said Mr. Tutt.

II

"I'm a Nordic," said Mr. Allison Dingle, half an hour later, with one eye on the butler. "And," he added with a significant nod at Mr. Tutt across the breakfast table, "we Nordics must hang to-

gether." He drained his cup of coffee nervously and poured half a
pitcher of cream over the cereal on the plate before him. "Oh, I'm
not a pessimist! All I mean is that we Nordics, who furnish most of
the back-bone, muscle and moral character to the American nation,
ought to present a solid front to any attempted relaxation of the
immigration laws. America ought to be for the American—the real
ones! We ought to breed true," he waved a stubby arm, "particularly since we live in a country where the really good elements in
the stock have a chance to rise to the top. There's where we put it
all over the English and the Germans, who weaken the strain by
inter-marriage within an artificial nobility already run to seed!"

An egg-shaped spoon jingled. Mr. Dingle was addressing an
imaginary audience of thousands.

"Yes, sir! 'Out of a democracy of opportunity we have created
an aristocracy of achievement!' There is no wealth, no honor, no
public position which is not within the grasp of any man who has it
in him. Look at the Vanderbilts, the Astors; at Rockefeller, at Car-
negie, at Ford—and, in a more modest degree, myself! These men
had nothing except their natural inheritance of brains and moral
fibre, and the other dominant characteristics of our race."

He leaned back in his wicker chair, which creaked ominously, a
short, snugly-tailored fat man with restless gray eyes.

"When did you come over?"

Mr. Tutt regarded him abstractedly.

"Me? The ferry landed me at the Bar Harbor pier about twenty
minutes ago."

"I know that—I meant your people. When did they come to
America?"

"I haven't the remotest idea."

Mr. Dingle refused to be placed in the position of entertaining a
mongrel.

" 'Tutt' sounds like a Scotch name," he mused, ignoring his guest's
admission of ignorance. "We Dingles are Scotch. 'Dingwell' the
name was originally, until it was unfortunately corrupted over here
to 'Dingle.' There is a barony in the family. The first Lord Dingwell
dates from 1609. My personal forbears were naturally not in the
direct line, but were merely of good, honest yeoman stock, who
came over somewhere toward the beginning of the last century. I
find genealogy rather interesting to play with. Everybody should
have a hobby, don't you think?"

"I certainly do," agreed Mr. Tutt.

Mr. Dingle cast his other eye at the tall Englishman who was fussing at the side-table.

"That will be all, Griffin," he said impatiently. "You needn't wait." Griffin reluctantly retired, and his master arose and closed both doors leading off the breakfast porch.

"We may as well get down to business," continued Mr. Dingle as he sat down again. "Your time is valuable and so is mine—and I have a golf engagement at ten o'clock. Try one of these." He extended a gold case containing a row of oversized cigarettes, each bearing the initials "A. D." surmounted by a discreet crest.

Mr. Tutt produced a withered stogy.

"I'll smoke my own brand, if you don't mind."

Mr. Dingle helped himself and returned the case to his pocket.

"Well, the fact is I'm up against a delicate situation. Every rich man has to face the possibility of blackmail, I suppose, but this is different from the ordinary run. . . . The trouble is Robert insists on marrying the girl. He's only twenty-two, and still in college. All my hopes are centered on him. I want him to take my place in the business world—to start where I leave off—and so far, he has come right up to scratch. But last Sunday he broke the news to me that he wanted to get married. At first, naturally, I supposed that it was some girl friend of his whom I knew, whose parents come up here in the summer—from New York, Philadelphia or Boston. Then I discovered that this woman had been a waitress at the village tea-room, and that she is the daughter of a—of a lobsterman."

Mr. Dingle paused to allow the full horror of the disclosure to sink in.

"Yes, sir! The daughter of a common fisherman—a man who gets his living by catching lobsters. Imagine my son tied up for life to a woman like that! It would ruin him socially—and in a business way too. Ridicule is the one thing that kills a man. Lobsters! It would spoil all my daughter's chances of making a proper match. There is a young Englishman of title over here just now, who is quite attentive to her. If he knew about this lobster business he'd run like a rabbit!"

Mr. Tutt nodded.

"No doubt he would. . . . Have you seen the young lady?"

"No! And I don't want to. Whatever she looks like—and I assume that she must be good-looking or Robert wouldn't have fallen for her—such a marriage would be preposterous—a calamity."

"Do you know anything against her except that she is a lobster-man's daughter?"

"That's all I want to know. I don't want to be allied with that sort of people."

"What's her name?"

"Her name?" Mr. Dingle's gray eyes held the glint of ice. "Her name," he announced, "is Dizzy Zucker—and she comes from Mud Island!"

Mr. Tutt experienced a certain sympathy for his dogmatic host. Dizzy Zucker of Mud Island! It certainly sounded like bad news! "What do you want me to do?" he asked.

"Go there and buy her off."

"But suppose she won't be bought off?"

"Every woman has her price. I'll pay her anything she asks, so long as it doesn't get into the papers; buy the whole island rather than have my only son married to a lobsterman's daughter! Can't you see the headlines? Mud Island! There'd be photographers and reporters swarming all over it! I've no idea what kind of a name Zucker is—Italian probably, or maybe it's Portuguese—there are a lot of them scattered along the coast. But that's the least of my troubles. I could even swallow Mud Island! What I can't stomach is the lobsters—and the girl's front name! Dizzy might mean anything. I can't find out from Robert whether it's her surname, her Christian name—if she is a Christian—or a nickname. If it's the last, she probably drinks. I don't know how a girl would get a name like that in any other ways—unless she was an acrobat or suffered from vertigo. Some of these islanders are a tough lot." He leaned back and patted his forehead with his napkin. "Dizzy! Lobsters!" he muttered.

"Where is this Mud Island?"

"Thirty miles offshore from Bass Harbor Light. I'll send you over, when you're ready, in my motorboat. You'll get there in a couple of hours. If money won't turn the trick, maybe your powers of persuasion will. I appreciate that what I'm asking you to do for me is a bit unusual, and I'll not forget it. Do whatever is necessary, and if you're successful, you can fill out your own check and I'll sign it without looking to see how much it's for. I've a lot of other business—and my present attorney isn't altogether satisfactory."

He was the kind of client all lawyers dream about.

"I've only one suggestion," said Mr. Tutt, "and that is that you go with me. It would be much safer if you were on hand to sign your check and close the transaction yourself. If I went alone, the girl might change her mind while I was making my report to you, or perhaps tell your son."

"There's something in that," agreed Mr. Dingle. "We'll go together, and start after luncheon. Now I must hustle off to the golf club. Meantime try to amuse yourself."

"I'd like a chance to talk to your son before we go," said the old lawyer. "It might be wise to get a slant on the young lady through him."

"All right. But you'll find him very obstinate. He simply won't talk to me! In fact we're barely on speaking terms. However—see you at one o'clock. Ta-ta!"

III

From where Mr. Tutt stood on the veranda, awaiting the arrival of the Younger Dingle, he could see the whole grand sweep of Frenchman's Bay. Eastward stretched the hundred-harbored coast, promontory after promontory lying in echelon. Behind him, on the hill, crows summoned one another to council in the pines, squirrels scampered over carpets of pine needles. The air was tonic to the old lawyer's soul.

"What a place to live!" he exclaimed as, with his eyes wandering over the horizon festooned with the smoke of distant steamers bound for Halifax or New York, his thoughts flew back three hundred years to the day when Champlain in his *patache*, a tiny open boat with lateen sails and oars, had come coasting by the reefs and rocks, the bays and harbors of the then unknown coast, until he had sighted the bare summits of *Les monte déserts* from which the island took its name. Hardy explorers those, who, braving shipwreck, starvation and savage enemies, had come in their tiny shallops to found a new empire for the King of France!

The seascape shifted its lights and shadows to suit the play of the old man's fancy. The low-lying islands became the shelter of Spanish buccaneers, their rakish schooners hiding behind clumps of trees to swoop down upon the unconscious fishermen,—that far-off sloop, carrying its load of lumber from Eastport to Boston, changed to a Portuguese caravel, a Norse trireme, a shallop of the Cabots, or the quaint bark of the brave De Guast with his motley company of nobles and vagabonds,—a crew of whom François Villon would have loved to sing—of gamblers, cutthroats, gay young blades of Paris, bloods of the court of Henry IV, and thieves fleeing the torture of the galleys. Mr. Tutt knew the stories of all of them. Under the

still, blue, burning sky he saw the mists enveloping De Guast's
fragile vessel amid the crags of the long-sought islands; heard the
surf roaring along the barren granite shores; watched the creaming
of the sunken reefs, the flapping sails of the pinnace; heard the boom
of cannon above the songs of Lescarbot and the patter of Latin pray-
ers. Did Dingle suspect the debt he owed De Guast?

"How do you do, sir?" The words, in a clear, boyish voice,
brought Mr. Tutt to himself. Robert Dingle, tall, brown, was extending his hand. Mr. Tutt recalled the scene on the float. It was thus
that he had first seen him. His heart warmed to the young man.
Was Dingle, Sr., on the right track, after all? In his self-assumed
capacity of adjuster-general of the universe, Mr. Tutt resolved to
get at the bottom of the matter.

"How about a walk in the woods?" he suggested, with his gentlest smile. "I don't often get such a chance as this— That is, unless
you have an engagement."

The boy shook his head.

"No," he replied; "as it happens, I've nothing whatever to do
this morning. I'll be delighted to show you a little of Mt. Desert."

They wandered up the hill back of the house, through the pines,
to an open sunny spot on the very crest covered with gray reindeer-
moss.

Mr. Tutt made no effort to force the conversation, but there was
something so sympathetic about the old man's kindly face and
courteous manner, that they had not rested there twenty minutes
before Robert had told him the whole story of his love-affair with
Dizzy Zucker.

"It all seems so foolish and unnecessary!" declared the boy, as he
lay on the bed of moss with his hands locked behind his head, looking up at Mr. Tutt. "If Father would only just see Dizzy once, and
talk to her—but he won't even let me bring her to the house! It
isn't as if she were an uneducated girl,—Dizzy goes to college. You
see, I'm on our college glee club and we gave a concert at Colby,
winter before last. Dizzy was on their reception committee. I
thought she was the grandest girl I'd ever met, so honest and capable
and lovely to look at. I guess she liked me pretty well, too, although
she didn't say so.

"I went back to college, but I used to think of her a lot, and once
I sent her a book of poetry—Yeats, you know—and got a letter
from her, saying she hoped we'd meet again sometime—nothing
much, but very friendly and nice. Well, the following summer Dad

rented this place here in Bar Harbor in order to give my sister a chance to meet what he calls the 'right sort' of people, and when I got here I found that Dizzy had taken a job in the village tea-room. Of course, after that, I saw her all the time."

"That was a year ago?"

"Yes. I didn't see her but once all last winter. You see, Dizzy's father died a long time ago, and she has always lived with her mother and her grandfather on the island, except when she has been away at school and college, or working. Last March her grandfather was taken sick with pneumonia and they sent for her to go back. He died, and she stayed on there to look after her mother, who is quite an old lady and can't be left alone. I saw Dizzy for a couple of days during the Christmas vacation while she was visiting her brother in Boston. I want her to go back to college again this autumn, but she says she ought not to leave her mother; and that, anyhow, they couldn't afford it unless she makes a lot of money this summer lobstering. It makes me feel like a perfect rotter to be hanging around here doing nothing, while she's hard at work over on the island.

"I suppose Dad would like me to marry the daughter of somebody just like himself, who'd made a few millions in mining, or insurance, or electric lighting, or canned goods, and is satisfied to spend three or four months here in the summer going out to a lot of fat luncheons and dinner parties. He talks a lot about wanting to have me begin where he leaves off. Well, where is he leaving off? As far as I can make out, it's at the Kebo golf course and the Pot and Kettle Club. I don't mind coming up here in my college vacations and swinging a golf club for a week or so, in order to be near him, but I'd a darn sight rather be off camping in the woods, or taking a walking trip in Switzerland, or putting in a couple of months with Grenfell in Labrador.

"Perhaps Dad shouldn't have sent me to college if he wanted me to be the perfect type of American business go-getter. It isn't that I don't like business. I do. I really enjoy it a lot. I'm pretty good at figures and I've taken a lot of courses in economics and banking. But I've taken others, too—in philosophy and fine arts—and I think there's something in life besides money." He considered a moment. "I want to be perfectly fair to Dad. I'm not sure he really values money any more than I do, but he confuses the kick he gets out of making it—it's his form of sport, you see!—with the thing itself. That's his fallacy. He says he judges people by what they've done, whereas he really judges them by what they've got. I agree that manufacturing breakfast-food is a high and honorable calling, only I don't see why the man who makes it is any better than the woman who passes it around the table.

"And then, of course—speaking confidentially—Dad is bugs on this Nordic business. To hear him you'd think the present generation of Dingles were of undiluted English blood. You got all this talk of his about our being merely 'good honest yeoman stock'? Well, I looked that good old yeoman stock up, and the first Dingle to come over was a ticket-of-leave man whose family had to pay his debts to get him out of jail. And Dad's paternal grandmother was a French Creole born in Martinique. I don't suppose he counts her in at all!

"He's just as muddled in his theories about racial inheritance as he is over that democracy-of-opportunity-and-aristocracy-of-achievement bunk of his, in which he measures achievement simply by how much money a man has got. It seems to me that it's not how much a man has got, but how he gets it that counts. I'm ready to become an aristocrat by achievement in the breakfast-food business and carry on the prestige of the Dingle family, but I'm going to marry whom I choose!

"I don't regard it as any particular favor to me for Dad to load me up with all his money. I'd enjoy life exactly as much as a retailer as if I were a wholesaler,—selling athletic goods, writing ads or raising chickens, so long as I do it with the right girl. From what Dizzy tells me, there's a lot of excitement in the lobster business. Dad is too pig-headed even to look at her! Once I told him her name and where she came from, he shut up like a clam. He won't even let me use the launch to go to see her. . . . Can you keep a secret?" Mr. Tutt nodded solemnly. "So she has to come over here to Bar Harbor to see me!"

"How does she get here?"

"In her own motorboat. She can make it in four hours and a half. . . . I haven't any money of my own, but I can work. If Dad won't give his consent to our marriage I can marry without it. I'm fond of Dad, but he doesn't need a lawyer half so much as a little broad-mindedness. He at least ought to be willing to listen to me."

"I'll do my best to see that he listens to me," said Mr. Tutt.

IV

It is a scant mile from the top of Malvern Hill, where the millionaires live, to the boat wharf, where the real life of Bar Harbor centres,—the steam-laundry, the bakery, Hodgkins' fish-market, Nickerson & Spratt's feed-store, Mr. Angelo's peanut-stand, Charlie Parker's canoe-float and supply-store, and the Dirigo landing, where once in a blue moon you can find an old-time Portugee seaman with rings in his ears. Thither it was that Mr. Tutt, who always gravitated toward the genuine rather than the artificial, leaving behind him the gray-stone château of good old yeoman Dingle, took his way. From the bluestone drive he emerged upon a broad concrete highway lined with flower-bedecked stone walls and, smoking a contemplative stogy, strolled down West Street toward the harbor.

Here descending a hill, he passed a small grocery store where prominent in the window stood a pyramid of parti-colored packages labeled Dingle's Korn Pops. America was surely the land of opportunity! Contemplatively, he continued, pausing to buy a package of peanuts from Mr. Angelo, and arriving eventually at the steamboat wharf, where he sat down on one of the piles.

Engrossed in the view and otherwise fully occupied in eating his peanuts, he was rudely accosted from below: "Avast there! What ye doin' with them shells?"

Directly beneath him lay an exquisite mahogany launch nearly a hundred feet in length. Flags fluttered at her bow and stern, her brass blazed in the sunlight and the waves reflected themselves in dancing ripples on the green of her shining water-line.

Her red-faced captain, no less immaculate, glared up at the old lawyer.

"Don't y' s'pose I've got suthin' better to do than pick up your peanut shells?" he demanded.

"Sorry. Very careless of me. . . . Have a peanut?"

"No, I won't!"

"Sorry. My mistake. . . . Nice launch you've got there. . . . Have a cigar?"

The captain's austerity melted, as did that of most people when Mr. Tutt was around.

"Thanks, don't mind if I do." He made a fair catch. "Yes, she's a pretty good boat."

"Who does it belong to?"

"Feller named Dingle."

"Don't say! I've heard of him."

"Like to come aboard?"

"I sure would!"

Thus it was Mr. Tutt made another friend.

V

The bell of the launch jangled, the dial registered "Full Speed—Reverse," and the "Arrow" churned back into a whirlpool of seething foam.

The launch, bearing the two elderly men on their cynical adventure, had raced seaward for an hour, slicing through the rollers, while the silhouette of Mt. Desert sank lower and lower over the stern. Then on the uttermost purple rim had lifted a gray shadow, growing in definition each instant as they leaped toward it, until it had become an island with ruddy granite cliffs and fir-capped promontories; lonely, yet beautiful, and seemingly uninhabited save by the snowy gulls that spotted its rocky shores or flickered against the background of its black pines.

"That's Mud," announced the captain. "Nothin' much else between us an' Lisbon."

At that moment he observed a jagged, barnacle-covered rock, not quite awash, apparently rushing directly at the "Arrow," and gave a frenzied jingle.

"That was a close one!" he ejaculated, gazing anxiously at the island across the maelstrom created by the "Arrow's" abrupt retrocession. "It's been some time since I was over here."

He slipped the lever to "Ahead" and the launch hummed in a sweeping half-circle around the nearest promontory.

"That's the harbor—such as it is."

They were at the mouth of a narrow cove the shores of which, littered with buoys, nets and lobster-pots, rose everywhere in steep gravel banks to where it joined the meadow. At the farther end, a few weatherbeaten gray shanties clustered about a sagging wharf. Unless one wanted to shin up the slimy piles, it was difficult to see how one could get up there.

"Tide's goin' out. I'll have to set you ashore in the tender," the captain allowed. "I'll run in ez fur ez I darst."

With her engines at "Slow" the "Arrow" nosed a hundred yards or so in toward the wharf, the anchor was dropped, the dinghy lowered.

"Wait for us, captain," ordered Mr. Dingle, as he climbed in, followed by Mr. Tutt. "We'll be back inside an hour."

"All right, sir. I can't stay in here 'count of the tide, but I'll hang around close as I kin. I'll be watchin' out fer ye."

Mr. Tutt looked about him, sniffing the reek of tar and seaweed.

So this was Mud Island! Again the grim suspicion came creeping over him that, after all, Mr. Dingle might be right. How could any girl who lived in such a place, even if she had gone to college, make a suitable wife for a young man of Robert Dingle's tradition and environment? Well, they would see. But first, how were they ever going to climb up that almost perpendicular bank? Slipping and sliding, his congress shoes filled with loose gravel, Mr. Tutt, followed by his fat client, scrambled up the slope and collapsed panting on a bed of juniper at the top. There was no suggestion of a road; no sign of life except the footpath that straggled around the cove to the group of houses on the opposite side. There was not even a cow in sight.

"This is a hell of a place!" grunted the perspiring Mr. Dingle. "That girl must live over in one of those hovels."

They walked along the path, which presently ducked over the dune and quartered the stony beach left bare by the receding tide. A grizzled gaffer with incredible ringlets was searching among the stones, watched from a distance by a small freckle-faced boy. The ancient one looked up at their approach.

"Ain't seen a knife-blade, have ye?" he cackled at Mr. Dingle. "I lost one here some'res ever so long ago. I dunno where it is." The cracked voice was plaintive.

"I have not!" snapped Mr. Dingle, stepping aside into a mudhole.

"He's all right!" called out the small guardian, approaching. "That's only old Pop Mullins. He's cracked, but he won't hurt nobody. Been lookin' for that knife-blade for the last thirty years. He's eighty-seven. Folks never dies here. . . . Dizzy Zucker? Sure, I know where she lives. You keep on this path round the cove, an' up over that hill thar, an' through the grove, an' you'll see it. Big yaller house."

It was a glittering afternoon. About them the meadow was sprinkled with daisies and wild roses. Beyond the reddish rocks of the headland they could see myriads of white horses racing shoreward across a bay of indigo. The air was full of grassy smells, pungent with the odor of thyme, juniper and sun-dried moss, the breeze fragrant of fir and balsam. From overhead the sun burned hot upon their backs. Through the drone of bees and the rasping of locusts came the faint syncopated tinkle of unseen cowbells, the occasional bleat of sheep.

"It's a fine afternoon," admitted Mr. Dingle. "These folks have a pretty nice place to live in—if they are able to appreciate it."

The path led up the hill, traversed a grove, and unexpectedly

emerged upon the other side of the promontory. A horizon of un-
broken ocean encircled them. From the beach below came the roar
and rattle of the breakers. A solidly built two-story house with a
cupola, surrounded by tall pines, faced the sea a hundred yards back
from the edge of the cliff. Beside the open door of a shed, piled high
with birch logs, a hatchet lay upon a wood-block, the ground littered with white chips. Smoke was rising from the kitchen chimney.

"Go ahead. You must do the talking," directed Mr. Dingle.

Mr. Tutt knocked on the kitchen door, which was opened by a
pleasant-faced woman, spotless in white calico.

"Does Miss Dizzy Zucker live here?" he asked.

"Yes," answered the woman, "here's where she lives. She's out at
present. But if you want to bargain for lobsters, it isn't any use, for
she's all contracted up with Gains & Foster down to Boston."

"We're not looking for lobsters," answered Mr. Dingle stiffly.
"We want to see her about something else."

"Well, if you want to try to find her, she's gone over to read to
old Captain Freeman. He's stone-blind. She reads to him 'most every
afternoon. You can follow the path right along the cliff."

They strolled on and entered the fragrant woods again, pausing
frequently to enjoy the ocean-glimpses through the trees.

"Say!" unexpectedly exclaimed Mr. Dingle, as they gazed through
a framework of spruce and hemlock at the blue white-flecked bay.
"This would be some site for a summer cottage, wouldn't it? Just
look at that view! A fellow could buy one of these islands and have
it all to himself. Don't suppose it would cost hardly anything to
speak of. He could have a regular place over at Bar Harbor, with
all the society he wanted, and come over here every day or so to—
to——"

"——to live?" suggested Mr. Tutt.

The path circled back through the pines and they found themselves once more on the edge of the meadow overlooking the cove.

Here, in a patch of sun, a tall old man with snow-white hair and
beard was sitting with closed eyes, his head resting against a pine
trunk. Beside him, flat on her stomach, lay a girl reading aloud—
the girl Mr. Tutt had seen that morning on the float. She lifted her
eyes at their approach.

"I beg your pardon," said he. "Are you Miss Zucker?"

"Yes," she said, without moving, "that is my name."

"Would it be convenient for you to have a few moments' talk
with us—on a matter of business?"

"That's all right, Dizzy," boomed from the old man's lips. "Don't you bother about me. You must 'a' read more'n an hour already. Go ahead and talk to these folks."

Miss Zucker scrambled to her feet. She was still dressed in her khaki overalls. She had presented a pretty enough picture in the early morning as she stood in the stern of the launch with her hand upon the wheel; now, close at hand, Mr. Tutt perceived that she had real beauty.

"What do you want to speak to me about?"

Mr. Tutt, ignorant as he was of all feminine artifices, could not but wonder whether the blue cap and jersey had not been selected with an eye to contrast, for against them her bobbed yellow locks and clear sunburned skin looked almost golden. They made her eyes sky blue, her white teeth whiter. She stood easily erect, with her head thrown slightly back as if she were looking out to sea. Although her shoulders in the tight jersey looked absurdly small, she was only half a head shorter than Mr. Tutt—and Mr. Tutt was a tall man. Her expression was frank and direct.

"I haven't any lobsters—if that's what you want," she added.

Mr. Dingle rubbed his chin and looked at his companion.

"Allow me to introduce myself." The old lawyer bowed. "My name is Tutt—Ephraim Tutt—and this is Mr. Allison Dingle."

Miss Zucker flushed under her tan—flushed to the top of her temples, the tips of her ears.

"Tutt—Dingle? I never knew anybody by those names," interjected Captain Freeman. "You're not island men, are you?"

Mr. Tutt, repressing a natural desire to explain that they were Nordics of good old yeoman stock, admitted that unfortunately they were not island men.

A moment of mutual embarrassment followed, relieved by a totally unexpected diversion.

Miss Zucker pointed suddenly to the cove.

"If that's your launch, she's in trouble!" she exclaimed. "Looks to me as if she were aground."

A single glance was enough to satisfy them that the "Arrow" was, indeed, in trouble, for she lay canted on her side high out of water in mid-channel, surrounded by a flotilla of skiffs and lobster boats, while Captain Hull waved his arms and shouted ineffectually at the cosmos.

"Never ought to have come in on ebb tide," interjected the blind man, towering to his feet. "It's plumb crazy. You don't know much about this coast, I reckon."

"Better come along and see if we can't get her off!" cried the girl, running swiftly down the hill, followed by Mr. Tutt and his client.

"She's hard and fast on the bar!" she shouted to them over her shoulder, as she climbed into a dory and pushed off.

"Say," panted Mr. Dingle, "this is awkward!"

A crowd of perhaps twenty islanders was gathered on the beach, yelling encouragement and jocularities at the unfortunate Hull, who, waist-high in the water and assisted by the mate, was attempting to lift the bow clear of the mud.

"I got trapped just like a lobster, b'gosh!" he shouted. "We come into the dog-goned cove all right, but when I went to turn around to git out, I got stuck on this here dog-goned mudbank. Tide must 'a' dropped jist enough to ketch us."

He grasped the bow in his arms and heaved. The thin mahogany cracked.

"Look out! You'll rip the engines out of her!" warned the girl. "You can't move until the tide comes in."

"And when will that be?" inquired Mr. Dingle.

"About six to-morrow morning."

"Dear me, this *is* awkward!" repeated Mr. Dingle.

The girl, who had been surveying the situation from a dory, came rowing toward them.

"Your launch is all right," she said. "Lucky the bottom where she went aground is soft and level, and will distribute the weight of the engines so that they won't tear through. She'll lie there safe enough until morning."

"Isn't there any way for me to get back to Mt. Desert?" inquired Mr. Dingle, addressing Dizzy for the first time directly.

"Cap'n Higgins might take you over in his dory. He puts on an outboard motor—she makes nearly six knots."

"How long would it take?"

"About six hours."

"But I wouldn't get home until one o'clock to-morrow morning!"

"Besides which, you haven't as yet accomplished your purpose in coming here," warned Mr. Tutt.

"Looks as if we'd have to spend the night. Do you know of anybody who would put us up?" asked Mr. Dingle.

"The Duncans might take you in. They sometimes accommodate people," she replied. "Shall we go there and see?"

They followed the duck board that constituted the main street toward a frame house planted in the middle of a field. Four adults, three men and one woman, rocking on the porch and regarding the horizon with studied unconcern, stolidly awaited their approach. The men were all in their shirtsleeves and collarless, apparently taking turns spitting over the crazy balustrade.

"Good-evening, Mrs. Duncan," said Dizzy. "These gentlemen want to spend the night. Can you accommodate them?"

Mrs. Duncan seemed to be suffering from acute indigestion.

"No, I can't!" she snapped, after a lengthy silence.

"She can't!" echoed the last spitter. "School-teacher's stayin' here."

"I'm sorry. We'll try Mrs. Godkin."

The man at the other end of the row spat joyously.

"She's full too. The coastwise missionary's got her only room."

Mrs. Duncan's turtle eye was fixed upon a tin can containing one dingy geranium.

"Why don't you take him in yourself?" she inquired, adding enigmatically, "I guess what's good enough for one is good enough for another."

Dizzy turned to her companions.

"Do stay with us. Mother will be delighted to have you," she said cordially.

Already the sun's red ball was rolling on the purple horizon and the shadows of the pines were shooting across the field. A wind chill from the mists of the Bay of Fundy drew down the hill.

"Really, this is most embarrassing," said Mr. Dingle in an aside to Mr. Tutt. "What the dickens are we going to do?"

"Unless you want to sleep out here in the meadow, I guess you are going to spend the night at Mrs. Zucker's," succinctly replied Mr. Tutt to Mr. Dingle.

The shipwrecked Son of the Revolution turned humbly to the daughter of the islands.

"Er—really, I hardly know what to say," he stammered. "I—er—hate to impose upon your mother; but if there's nowhere else——"

"There isn't!" she laughed. "You will be entirely welcome. If you can amuse yourselves looking around the town for a few minutes, I'll dash ahead and get things ready."

"Well—it's awfully good of you," began Mr. Dingle, but already the girl had turned and was running light-footedly up the hill.

He stared helplessly at Mr. Tutt.

"Say!" he ejaculated. "I wouldn't have had this happen for a million dollars!"

VI

Mr. Tutt and Mr. Dingle watched Dizzy Zucker disappear among the pine trees.

"No, sir! I wouldn't have had this happen for a million dollars," repeated the manufacturer miserably. "Imagine coming over here to try to buy off a—er—blackmailer, and then finding yourself forced to accept her hospitality and spend the night in her house! It's—it's grotesque!"

"Oh, it isn't so bad as all that," Mr. Tutt encouraged him. "In fact, it seems to me to be almost providential. It puts us on a solid and amicable footing at the very start, and gives us plenty of time to feel our way along instead of hurrying roughshod through negotiations that will probably require very delicate handling. In fairness to the girl herself, you ought to find out something about her, first hand; anyhow, that will be necessary in order to make up our minds what to offer her."

"Well, as I told you before we started," replied Mr. Dingle doggedly, "I'll buy the whole damned island before I'll let my son marry into a lobsterman's family. It doesn't look as if it would cost much either. I don't believe the land is worth over fifty dollars an acre cleared, if that; and uncleared, it's practically worthless. What bothers me is how you are going to broach the subject. She might take it into her head to get mad and throw us out of the house, and then where would we be?"

"Right here in this meadow," admitted Mr. Tutt.

"You'll have to wait until morning before you try to talk business with her," warned Mr. Dingle. "Anyhow, as you say, the more we know about her, the better we'll be able to calculate what to offer. How about giving the village the once-over, as she suggested? What a wretched-looking place! I don't believe they've even got a church! How do you suppose they manage to make a living?"

"From the sea, I suppose," answered Mr. Tutt. "Don't you think we'd better go back and try to arrange to have Captain Hull and your crew taken care of for the night? They can't sleep on the "Arrow.' "

Captain Hull and the engineer were just coming ashore in the dinghy as Mr. Tutt and Mr. Dingle reached the beach, where a reception committee composed of the entire population of Mud Island, including old Pop Mullins, was awaiting their arrival. The sand-bar on which the "Arrow" had gone aground was now clear out of water, and she lay high and dry across the mouth of the cove.

"Darned if I had any notion there was any such tide here as that!" declared Captain Hull in extenuation of his error, as he climbed shamefacedly out of the dinghy. "Must be over two fathoms if it's an inch!"

"Tide averages eleven foot," replied Captain Freeman, who had seated himself on a tar barrel and was interrogating the witnesses to the disaster. "There won't be a part'cle o' water in this cove two hours from now. You kin walk acrost it anywheres."

"I was diggin' clams this mornin' right where your propeller lies," announced another ancient mariner.

"Say, Joe, you didn't see nuthin' o' that knife-blade of mine out thar, did ye?" inquired Pop Mullins. "I lost it ever so many years ago, an' I've been lookin' fer it ever since."

"Sorry, Pop, but I didn't," answered the other old man in a kindly tone. "I heard you lost one and I'll keep an eye out fer it."

"What sort of a knife was it?" asked Mr. Tutt.

"It were an oyster knife—a new one," replied Pop. "That is, it were a new one when I lost it. I guess it would be kind o' rusty by this time."

"Come up to the store and I'll buy you another," volunteered the lawyer.

Pop appeared overwhelmed by such munificence.

"Wa-ll, na-ow, that's kind of ye, I'm sure," he said with an embarrassed smile. "I don't know ez I ought ter let ye do so much for me."

"It won't do no good," declared Captain Freeman. "Dizzy buys him a new knife every six weeks or so, and he just puts 'em away somewheres and goes on lookin' for the old one."

"No matter," said Mr. Tutt. "I'd like to buy him a knife."

"Go along, Pop," urged the crowd. "Let him git ye a new one."

Headed by Pop Mullins, Mr. Tutt and Mr. Dingle, the crowd moved in single file along the duck board toward the group of shanties constituting the village. A flight of steps, so high as to seem almost like a ladder, led up to the door of a weatherbeaten combination post-office and grocery store which stood on the side of the hill. Two little girls and a wizened old man with a nutcracker face stood staring down at the approaching throng.

"Hi, Henery!" yelled someone. "This man's goin' to buy Pop a new knife. Got one?"

"Reckon I hev," mumbled Henery. "Come on up an' I'll see what there is."

"Henery's postmaster," explained Pop as they laboriously climbed the steps. "He's been postmaster pretty nigh ez long's I kin remember. He come from Lowell, Massachusetts, time of the war—didn't ye, Henery?"

"I sure did, Pop," answered the wizened one. "I come here the year President Lincoln signed the Emancipation Proclamation. Lowell was my home. I used to know Gen. Benjamin F. Butler well. But I had a hankerin' fer the sea, an' this seemed a likely place. . . . How'll one o' them do ye?"

"How much is it?" asked Mr. Tutt.

"A quarter. It's the kind Dizzy allus gits fer him."

"Thank you very much," said Pop, pocketing the knife. "You'll find Henery a very interesting man."

"You say you came here during the Civil War?" challenged Mr. Dingle suspiciously. "How old are you, may I ask?"

"I'll be eighty-nine next month," said Henery. He lifted off his ragged wig, disclosing an entirely bald skull. "This ain't my own haar, ye see. But there's plenty o' folks livin' on this island older'n I be. Take old Captain Higgins—he's nearly a hundred."

"Where does he live? I'd like to meet him," said Mr. Tutt.

"First house to the right at the end of the street," replied the postmaster. "Pop will be glad to show ye."

The sun had sunk below the horizon, leaving behind it a fan of gold. Overhead the sky was dappled with pink clouds. The reflected light bathed the weather-beaten sheds and dwellings, and the no less weather-beaten faces of the old folks about them, in a magic sheen. The pines upon the promontory stood like bronze pillars against the deep blue. Mr. Dingle felt as if he were in a strange mysterious world, unlike anything which he had ever known before and in which nothing was real. They bade the postmaster good-night and walked on. Standing apart a hundred yards up the hill was a shanty no bigger than a large doll's house.

"That's whar Cap'n Higgins lives," said Pop. "He most allus goes to bed at sundown, but I'll rout him out. He'll be glad to see ye."

The doll's house was perhaps eight feet high by seven feet square, with tiny windows, surrounded by a fence inclosing a miniature garden of phlox, sunflowers and hollyhocks.

Pop pounded on the closed door with his fist.

"Ahoy, Cap'n Higgins!" he cackled. "Got visitors fer ye! Let down your companionway!"

A muffled bellow came from somewhere under the roof, there was a heavy creaking, the door opened a crack, and a huge white beard protruded from it.

"Who's thar?"

"It's me—an' some men from the mainland," explained Pop.

The door opened wider, a shaggy head appeared in the aperture, and its owner came forth, stooping, and stood up. Erect, he was nearly as tall as the rooftree of his house.

"Glad to see ye," he said in a deep husky voice, extending a gnarled, blue-veined hand, first to the manufacturer and then to Mr. Tutt. "I can't ask ye to come in, 'cause there ain't room. There's hardly space fer the cats after I get in."

"What a delightful house you have!" remarked Mr. Tutt. "It's the smallest one I ever saw."

"Yes, it's a pretty good house. I built it myself," agreed Captain Higgins, obviously pleased at the compliment. "When I gave up the sea about twenty years ago I had to have some place to live, an' havin' no family and not wantin' to go to any o' them seamen's homes or such places, I set to and built myself this house. I've lived here ever since."

"May I peek in?" begged Mr. Tutt.

"Sure! Look all ye want."

Captain Higgins picked up the white kitten that was purring between his ankles, and stepped to one side. Mr. Tutt bent his head and thrust it through the door. A rag carpet covered the floor, white dimity curtains hung across the windows, the unpainted walls were gay with lithographs. One side was completely filled with a modern, highly polished stove. There was a rocking-chair, but no bed. A ladder led upward to a manhole in the ceiling.

"Where do you sleep?" inquired the lawyer.

"I bunks 'tween decks," explained Captain Higgins. "There's just room for my mattress under the keel—I mean the ridgepole. I tried to make it ez much like my old quarters aboard the 'Sarah N. Higgins'—my old barkentine—ez I could. Below decks, I've got my little galley and cabin, and I've got my berth above. It's mighty snug and shipshape. It wasn't allus ez pretty ez it is now, though. Miss Zucker, a young lady who lives here—she's quite a near neighbor o' mine—gave me the picters and put up the curtains for me."

"We are spending the night at her mother's," explained Mr. Tutt.

"Wa-al, ye couldn't have a nicer place to stay!" declared Captain Higgins warmly. "The Zuckers are jest about the finest people on this island, or anywheres else, I reckon. They was among the first to come here way back in the time when nobody knew whether these islands belonged to France or England. I sailed with her father an' her gran'ther an' her great-gran'ther. They was all deep-sea men who could take a ship around the Horn or through the Strait of Malacca when there weren't no lighthouses or markin's on the reefs—just crammed full sail on her and sent her boomin' through."

"Do they still breed good sailors hereabouts?" asked Mr. Tutt provocatively.

"They do that—men an' women! I don't want to see any man handle a boat prettier than this here Dizzy Zucker, the young lady I spoke of. You know how Deer Island men rate, I reckon. They won't have none but them to sail the big international cup races. Well, Deer Isle is only eleven miles south of here, and the men on all these islands rate as Deer Island men. It's in the blood—they're loyal. They'll see ye through and they'll stick by ye. Now take Dizzy. She's one of the smartest girls ever I see—college-eddicated an' able. She could go anywheres an' be welcome—be an ornament to any society. But would she go away an' leave her mother? Not she! Lor' bless ye, she looks after every sick woman and child on this island! And that's sayin' suthin' when there ain't a nurse or a doctor or a midwife nearer than Swan's Plantation—fourteen mile by water. Dizzy's one of our selectmen now. She was elected unanimous last November."

"Indeed!" exclaimed Mr. Tutt. "Is there much party feeling here?"

"Pretty strong. We've got thirty-seven voters, with a reg'lar Republican majority of five. It hasn't changed, so fur ez I know, in ten years. Dizzy was on both tickets."

"What an extraordinary old man!" declared Mr. Dingle as they said good-night and walked on. "And a very garrulous one. He seems to have a rather high opinion of the Zucker family."

"Well, can you blame him?" mused Mr. Tutt.

VII

It was dark by the time they reached the top of the hill, and they found their way through the grove to the house by the light shining through its windows. Perhaps, thought Mr. Tutt, it was by the light from those same windows that Captain Freeman and Captain

Higgins had shaped their homeward courses on their return from far-distant ports across the seas. Inside, they could see Mrs. Zucker moving about her shining kitchen, and from the crack of the window came a pleasant smell of cooking.

"I don't know how you feel about it," growled Mr. Dingle, "but I've never been more embarrassed in my life. I don't see how I can partake of that woman's bread and salt, and then turn right around and offer her money to keep her hands off my son. I'd rather not take a bite to eat. But to be honest, I'm as hungry as a bear."

"I'm glad the situation has not deprived you of your appetite," replied Mr. Tutt. "I think we are exceedingly fortunate in having such a comfortable place in which to spend the night. I'm quite hungry myself."

"Well, knock and get it over with," said Mr. Dingle, and Mr. Tutt knocked.

"No trouble at all," declared their hostess, leading them into the kitchen. "No trouble at all. I'm always glad to have any friends of Dizzy's stay with us—that is, if there ain't too many of 'em. Only I'll have to ask you to wait a few minutes more while I get supper. You just make yourselves comfortable there around the stove. . . . Sure, smoke all you want to. A sea-captain's wife is used to tobacco."

Dizzy was not in evidence, but from the darkness outside came the sound of chopping, and presently she came in bearing an armful of wood.

"I'll just run down to the car and get a few lobsters," she said, depositing the wood and picking up the lantern which she had left beside the door. "I won't be five minutes."

"It's certainly most hospitable of you," murmured Mr. Dingle, as he took off his overcoat and settled himself as near the fire as seemed reasonably safe. "You really needn't cook any lobsters on my account."

"Oh, that's all right! Lobsters take the place of chickens with us," explained Mrs. Zucker. "I hope you both like 'em. Chicken feed is so high these days—an egg is quite a luxury. But lobsters take care of themselves. Thank God for the lobster, I say! When my great-grandfather, Isaac Weyman, moved over here from Swan's Plantation in 1823, these islands were all covered with fine farms. Salt was hard to get in those days and the islanders used to trade with any French or English vessels that came along—two pounds of fresh beef or mutton for one of salt. Think of that! They didn't do nearly so much fishing as you'd think. That came later. They were real homesteaders. I've heard Gran'ther say that folks along the coast—including Boston and New York and Philadelphia—all lived just about the same—not much difference between city and country."

"I take it that your husband was a deep-sea sailor," commented Mr. Tutt.

"Yes; he and his father and gran'ther before him," she answered. "They all followed the sea. My husband was drowned when Dizzy was five years old, so Gran'ther Zucker came to live with us. He was a pretty old man by that time, so he took up lobsterin'. He died of the pneumony last winter."

She paused and sighed. From the stove arose the sound of sizzling, accompanied by a delicious aroma.

"Gran'ther Zucker was a wonderful old gentleman," she continued. "He'd been most everywhere in the world. Him and Cap'n Freeman, his chum, sailed round the Horn together in 1871. They most always shipped in the same vessel when they could. . . . Gran'ther was terrible fond of Dizzy. Summers he taught her how to sail an' trawl an' make lobster pots, and winters he taught her out of books. 'Twas him prepared her for college. She's a senior now at Colby."

"Do many of the young people from the island go to college?" asked the lawyer.

"Most all the boys and girls that's fit to go. I don't hold with educating the whole kit and caboodle. But the general run goes either to Colby or Bates or the University of Maine. They work summers and go to college in winters."

"And then what?" suddenly inquired Mr. Dingle, who was gradually shedding his embarrassment.

"The majority of 'em become doctors or lawyers or business men, and the girls get married and settle down in the cities. It's a great shame!"

"How do you mean—a shame?" Mr. Dingle leaned forward.

"I hold they ain't near so happy, nor don't begin to live near so well as they would if they stayed right here on the island. My husband, Captain Zucker, said he'd sailed all over the globe, up and down, crisscross and sideways, and there weren't any prettier place than the Maine coast—and no climate anywheres that could touch it."

"That was your idea, too, in settling on Mt. Desert, wasn't it, Mr. Dingle?" said Mr. Tutt innocently.

"Why, yes—certainly," agreed Mr. Dingle.

"And look how much it costs to live in those places!" she rattled on with the volubility of one who rarely had a chance to talk herself out. "My son Lester, who's a doctor in Boston, he can't lay by anything. He's smart too. But what with a wife and four children, he's never been able to contribute toward sending Dizzy to college. She's earned her way—every cent of it—waiting on table, an' clerkin' an' teachin'. She's a real smart girl, if I am her mother."

"Did you say she was in the lobster business?" inquired Mr. Dingle timidly.

"I don't know as I said it, but she is," answered his hostess. "Gran'ther Zucker had a fine string of traps, and when he died last winter it took all Dizzy's savings to pay for his illness and the funeral. D'y' know, there weren't a decent coffin this side of Bass Harbor? Anyhow, I was left all alone here, so she came back and carried on the business. She's doing well too—makes all her own traps an' everything. Next winter she aims to take me along to live with her, while she finishes her course and gets her degree."

"Don't you look forward to seeing her married?" hazarded Mr. Tutt.

"I haven't seen anybody near good enough for her yet," declared Mrs. Zucker, turning to the stove.

At that moment the young lady herself entered the kitchen, carrying a basket.

"Aren't they beauties?" she demanded, throwing back the cover. Mr. Dingle looked in. He seemed fascinated.

"Are those lobsters?" he exclaimed. "I always supposed they were red."

"You're learning," Mr. Tutt informed him.

As he watched Dizzy standing so unselfconsciously in the lamplight in her brown overalls, her cheeks flushed from running uphill and damp with the mist that clung in hundreds of tiny drops to her hair and eyelashes, he wished that he had a daughter like her. Did they breed girls of such sort in cities? He wondered what his client thought about it. He continued to wonder when, ten minutes later, she came downstairs dressed in a trim, one-piece frock of dark-blue worsted edged with white, and began deftly to set the table.

The old lawyer had never eaten a more savory meal—broiled live lobsters with drawn butter, hot muffins, new potatoes in their jackets, fresh corn on the cob, griddlecakes and maple sirup, blueberries and cream, coffee.

"I'm supposed to be dieting," announced the manufacturer rue-fully. "But I'm going to cut loose for once. I wish my chef could cook like this."

Replete, they sat and smoked in the spotless kitchen, while the two women cleaned up and washed the dishes. Just as they finished, Captain Freeman entered.

"Heard you men were here," he said. "Wa-al, you kin rest easy. Your boat seems all right and your crew are over to Putnam's. Thought you might like to know where they was. Anyhow, a 'gam' with a strange vessel is always agreeable."

"Glad to see you, Captain Freeman," cried Dizzy, leading the blind man to a chair. "Did you have any trouble finding your way across the lot?"

"Nary a bit! I see as well by night as by day. I been walkin' that path now nigh on seventy years."

"May I offer you a stogy?" asked Mr. Tutt.

"No, thanks. I never got used to seegars," replied the old man. "Yes, sirs! I kin remember when old Captain Lester Zucker built this house—Dizzy's great-gran'ther. That was in 1849, when every-body was all het up over the gold in Californy. He must 'a' been around ninety at that time. He run the blockade during Revolu-tionary days, fit the Barbary pirates, an' was with Commodore Perry in 1812. Yes, born right here on this island. His great-gran'ther settled here in 1698. He's buried up thar in the grove—spelled his name L-e-i-c-e-s-t-e-r. Unless the marble cutter made a mistake, he spelled Zucker different too—Z-o-o-k-e."

"That's right," nodded Mrs. Zucker. "They used to spell it that way, but they changed it, 'cause folks always mispronounced it."

Captain Freeman exhaled a cloud of smoke rivaling in size that of Mr. Tutt.

"There used to be an *h* in it, somehow. Wa-al, it don't make no difference. But Captain Lester, he was quite interested in things like that. Told me he went somewheres in London once and paid to have it all looked up. But his son, Cap'n Isaac, never bothered about it none."

"We don't pay much attention to names around here," commented Mrs. Zucker. "Maybe we do spell it wrong, but what of it? A name don't mean anything, when you come to study it. There's Miss Duncan—she's always so ashamed because her great-great-great-great-grandmother was a full-blooded Kennebec Indian. I figured out she's only a one-sixty-fourth part."

"Zactly!" agreed Captain Freeman. "And if the Indian had been a buck instead of a squaw, Miss Duncan might have inherited his name, spite o' the fact that she had sixty-three other ancestors, just as closely related to her, named entirely different."

Dizzy had been scribbling on the back of a paper bag.

"On that basis," she remarked, "and allowing four generations to a century, a person who traced his ancestry back three hundred years would have 4,096 ancestors, from any one of whom he might have got his name."

Mr. Dingle showed signs of interest.

"I really never thought of that before," he ruminated. "But, of course, it's quite true."

"Three hundred years ain't such a long time," mused Captain Freeman, "albeit a good many changes kin take place. I remember when all these islands was populated thick. Every inch of shore line was took up with farms, although no one did much farming. What they did was to build boats. You could hear the calkin' irons ringin' all the way from Calais to Biddeford Pool. I've seen sixty-two vessels built right in this very cove where you ran aground—brigs, barkentines, schooners an' full-rigged ships. Every man was a sailor, an' his ambition was to sail his own ship. There was a heavy coastwise trade in salt cod an' lumber, an' to the Bahamas and West Indies. Occasionally a feller would take a sportin' chance and try Madeira, Lisbon, Algiers and Constantinople. The islanders was rich then. If a man died, his widow would invest what he left, in a ship—one thirty-second or one sixty-fourth."

"The lumber trade was a very active one," contributed Mr. Tutt.

" 'Twas so!" agreed Captain Freeman. "An' a good deal of lumber that started for Boston an' New York never got farther than the captain's farm. There's lots of houses on this island built from lumber that was dumped ashore on the way by, an' paid for the consignor as lost at sea."

"There must have been a lot more goin' on here in those days than there is now," said Mrs. Zucker.

"Oh, them was lively times!" declared the captain. "We had a lot of social life—corn-huskin's, clambakes an' quiltin's. Folks was always visitin' around. I remember rowin' a girl fourteen miles to a huskin' over on Dog Island once."

"Dizzy's father and I sailed and rowed twenty-five to find a preacher to marry us," said Mrs. Zucker. "Took us all day to get there—and then he was out! He'd rowed eleven miles to Duck Island to bury a man."

"Conditions haven't improved much in that respect," said Dizzy. "There isn't a doctor or an undertaker nearer than fourteen miles by water. Of course, now that there are motorboats, it isn't so bad."

"Not unless there's a storm on," qualified her mother. "There's been many a soul passed out, and many a child born, on this island without assistance from doctors. But, of course, gasoline has made a big difference."

Mr. Dingle had been listening attentively.

"What you say, Captain Freeman, interests me extremely," he remarked. "What has been the reason for the decline of prosperity on these islands?"

"Steam," answered the old sailor. "It killed the coastwise trade, just as it did the overseas. There weren't no use building brigs an' schooners when one tug could tow a string o' barges half a mile long. So we quit ship-buildin'. Ever since then the folks on these islands has been livin' on their hump, more or less, although the hump don't amount to nothin' to speak of."

"That's when we began lobsterin'," said Mrs. Zucker. "If steam took away our carryin' trade, it enabled us to market our fresh fish and lobsters."

"What does it cost per pound to ship from here to Boston?" asked Mr. Dingle.

"Six cents," answered Dizzy. "Three cents to Rockland, and three more to Boston. A power-smack calls here a couple of times a week. I can sell direct for thirty-five cents a pound, or pay freight and try to profit by the fluctuations in price."

"We couldn't do no sech thing before steam," said Captain Freeman. "Some folks is inclined to lament modern inventions, but I hold there's a good deal to be said for 'em. . . . Don't y'want to turn on the radio, Diz, before I go?"

Dizzy vanished into the adjoining room and presently through the open door came the strains of "Valencia."

"That's Russell's orchestra over at the Swimming Club in Bar Harbor," she said. "I tried New York and Boston, but there was nothing interesting."

"Wa-al, I must be gettin' along an' give you folks a chance to git to bed," said Captain Freeman, after the music had stopped. "Glad to have met you."

"I tell you it's a great comfort on a winter's night when there's a storm ragin', to sit here snug an' warm an' listen to a concert or an opry or a good speech, just like the folks on the mainland," remarked Mrs. Zucker appreciatively. "Makes you forget you're miles out to sea. We heard the President's speech just as clear as if he was upstairs. . . . Wouldn't you like to turn in?"

Mr. Tutt and Mr. Dingle agreed it would not be a bad idea at all.

Lamp in hand, high above her head, the girl guided the two men up the narrow stairs.

"This was Gran'ther's room," she said, throwing open a door. "I hope you won't mind sleeping in the same bed." She put down the lamp, lingering for a moment to make sure that they had everything they might need.

It was a square, high-ceiled corner room, curtained with old-fashioned English chintz and furnished in heavy San Domingo mahogany. Upon the mantel stood an elaborate model of a Chinese junk, done entirely in ivory. A seaman's brass-bound chest stood in one corner, a tall secretary in the other, and upon the walls hung several prints of vessels under full sail. Mr. Dingle commented upon the beauty of the furniture, admiring the grain and polish of the mahogany. Her grandfather had brought it all himself from San Domingo more than sixty years ago, Dizzy said, and there were a lot of curious old things downstairs in the parlor collected by the great-grandfather who had been interested in family history. So far, Robert had not been mentioned, neither had there been any reference to the business which had brought them there. As she closed the door softly behind her, Mr. Dingle said, "I wonder what that girl thinks of us."

"I don't know what she thinks of us," answered Mr. Tutt. "But I know what I think of her," he added as if to himself.

VIII

It soon became obvious that the night in Gran'ther Zucker's bed was not going to be a success. Neither of them was used to sleeping with anybody else, a ghostly light pervaded the room, the patch-work quilt was too hot, and something was evidently preying upon the Dingle mind. The manufacturer tossed restlessly from side to side, sighing and groaning, and occasionally giving vent to distraught outcries. The lobsters had evidently been too much for him.

Mr. Tutt stood it as long as he could. At last he arose. A gibbous moon hung low over the pines. From the beach below the house came a muffled roar. From Gran'ther Zucker's bed came a roar equally muffled, hollow and unearthly. Mr. Tutt stood shivering by the window, for the air that came through it was chill.

" 'It is a nipping and an eager air,' " quoted the lawyer as he slipped on his frock coat. " 'The glowworm shows the matin to be near, And 'gins to pale his ineffectual fire.' " He tiptoed to the door. " 'Rest, rest, perturbed spirit'!" he remarked to the huddled form.

Downstairs it was warm and cozy, and the range shone red. Mr. Tutt, lighting first a lamp, then a stogy, started on a voyage of exploration. His first survey of Great-gran'ther Leicester's collection of curios proved disappointing—nothing more than a glass case containing a few Indian relics, a stuffed and rather mangy sea-otter, a small brass cannon. Mr. Tutt placed the lamp on the center table holding the radio, and sat down. A little reading perhaps might soothe his weary nerves enough to induce sleep. But he could see nothing to read. There was not even a magazine lying about. Usually people left something on the center table, if only a photograph album. He glanced beneath it. Stacked against the legs was a row of books evidently removed to make room for the radio—a copy of *Chambers' Miscellany of Useful and Entertaining Facts*, which Mr. Tutt knew by heart; *Ben Hur*, the *Christmas Carol*, *Webster's Dictionary*, and a heavy volume bound in black leather and held by an iron clasp. He picked it up, blew off the dust and lifted the cover.

"To the most high and mighty Prince James, by the grace of God, King of Great Britain, France and Ireland, defender of the faith, etc., the translators of the Bible wish grace, mercy and peace, through Jesus Christ our Lord." One of the original copies of the King James version.

Mr. Tutt, with the volume upon his lap, turned to its faded record of births and marriages. The first entry was barely decipherable:

Our Lady's Day, 1639, Leicester Bayard Villiers Zouche married to Mary Cavendish Montagu Drummond, of Eastlake, Hants.

Followed page upon page of births, deaths and marriages, during which the name Zouche became in turn Zouke, Zooke, Zooker, and finally Zucker. Two Christian names appeared over and over again —among the men, that of Leicester; among the women, that of Desire. The final entry was:

Sept. 6, 1903, born to Abner and Mary Zucker, a daughter—Desire.

The creaking of the staircase awakened the old man from the reveries conjured by the record, and he looked up to see Desire herself standing in the doorway with a lantern in her hand, dressed in oilskins, a sou'wester and rubber boots.

"Good-morning, Desire," he accosted her. "Where are you going at such an early hour?"

"It's not early," she replied. "It's after one. I have to go and pull my traps. . . . I'm sorry you couldn't sleep."

"What do you know about this?" he asked, pointing to the first entry in the family Bible.

"Yes, that is the way the name used to be spelled. Great-gran'ther went into it all very carefully. There's a family tree over in the corner which carries it back ever so much farther."

She reached behind the bookcase and pulled forth a great scroll which he helped her to unwind.

At the top of the trunk, opposite the date 1308, appeared the name Zouche of Haryngworth; at the bottom, among a hundred or more tiny leaves, that of Leicester Bayard Villiers Zouche.

"The oldest barony in England," mused the old man.

"Is it?" she inquired. "Well, that's where the Zuckers came from, and"—she laughed—"the way we figured it out to-night, I must be nearly one ten-millionth part of a Haryngworth!"

"Whatever the percentage, you're all wool and a yard wide, my dear," he answered.

"Well, none of those things count much around here," she commented.

At the moment there was a noise from above. Mr. Tutt hurriedly rolled up the scroll and replaced the book as Mr. Dingle sleepily made his appearance.

"What are you two making such a noise about?" yawned the manufacturer.

"I was just going to ask Mr. Tutt if he wouldn't like to come out and help me pull my lobster traps," answered the girl.

"Sure, I'll come! Why don't you join the party, Dingle?"

"Do!" cried Desire. "There's going to be a lovely sunrise."

Mr. Dingle hesitated.

"Well, I'll go—as far as the beach," said he.

"Oh, come on!" urged Mr. Tutt. "Be a Nordic!"

IX

The moon had set, and in place of it a pale luminosity yielded the sleeping islands as, swinging her lantern, Desire led the way across the meadow to the wharf, where a fifteen-foot motorboat was made fast. Here she unlocked a small shanty and brought out two sets of oilskins, which in the case of Mr. Tutt just reached to his knees and in that of Mr. Dingle trailed upon the ground—the long and the short of it. The latter climbed in dubiously.

"If we upset I'd have a swell chance to float in these things!" he muttered, wedging himself in the stern between two half barrels, dimly visible by the light of the lantern which the girl had placed near the winch-head amidships. Down there underneath the piles, it was pitch black, clammy as a charnel-house,—the boat, a ferry for lost souls. He meditated flight, but, during the instant that pride withheld him, the engine started with a sputter and they chugged swiftly out into the darkness.

Too late! His heart sank. On its way down it encountered his stomach.

"Ugh!" he groaned. "What on earth is in those barrels?"

"Bait," answered the girl laconically.

Mr. Dingle pinched his nose between his fingers. "Wad sord of baid?"

"Refuse from the sardine factory."

So far the water had been smooth; now, as they neared the mouth of the cove, the launch began to rock gently but ominously.

"Ugh!" groaned Mr. Dingle again. He could see nothing—it was as if his sight had gone entirely into his nose. He felt that all would soon be lost. Once around the promontory, the full force of the ocean-swell struck the launch, tossing it about like a chip, while an icy breeze smote him in the face and whisked away his outcries. In the darkness he clung to the barrels like a frenzied cat, as amid lashings of spray and spin-drift the frail cockleshell that stood between him and death reared, hung in mid-air and plunged with an angry roaring of the propeller downward again into bottomless black craters. He entirely forgot the terrible odor from the barrels. They were headed straight for Spain! The end could not be delayed for long!

"H-how far out are y-you g-going?" he shouted in agony to the girl, who stood calmly holding the tiller.

"A couple of miles. If you set your traps on a rocky lee shore like this, you lose most of 'em in the winter. The big storms toss 'em around and smash 'em to bits. So I go out where I can get good clear bottom."

Two miles? They would not outride such a sea for a hundred yards! And then a whiff from the sardines upset his universe. He leaned weakly against the nearer barrel, clasping it with convulsive tenderness.

Unexpectedly and without preliminary, the sea turned lead color instead of black-green. Between plunges, he could see Mr. Tutt clutching at his sou'wester in the bow. The sight gave him comfort. They were literally both in the same boat, anyhow! But with the coming daylight the waves seemed even more mountainous. It was incredible that the launch could climb—climb—climb to their awful summits or survive the never-ending coast down into eternity. And then, with an abandonment of all hope, he realized that they were beyond sight of land. They were in a wilderness of waters. On every side, within arm's length, death yawned for him with gigantic, hissing, foam-flecked jaws.

"Isn't this—far—enough?" he gasped.

Suppose this was really to be the end! What a useless and utterly absurd way to die! Just to put out to sea for no purpose whatsoever —on a sort of bet—and be drowned! A ridiculous performance! Not even in his own boat! His life simply thrown away before he'd had half a chance to enjoy his money and the position that he'd made for himself! What good his fine house over at Bar Harbor, his apartment in New York, his fine car, his chef—Griffin? He could not die and lose everything like that! And yet he felt sure that drown he would. He realized that he was miserably afraid.

In that black moment in which he clung face to face with death, he was forced to acknowledge that, so far as he was concerned, he was no more a Nordic than he was a Latin or a Celt. The ghost of his Creole grandmother arose from the waves and shook an admonitory finger at the little man paralyzed with terror. Why had he always tried to gloss her over? His own grandmother! What was the use of pretending that one was anything in particular, when, as that girl had proved last evening, one had had four thousand ancestors only three hundred years back?—and millions before that? As he prepared to meet his God, Mr. Dingle confessed that he was a fraud. And there was Robert! He could not leave Robert yet— so young, so inexperienced—to face life alone. If, before he died, he could only see him safely married to the right girl!

At that instant the sun broke through the gray bank of cloud upon the eastern horizon and the leaden world became one of purple and bronze. It shone through Desire's wind-tossed hair, turning it and her oilskins to bright gold. All that had been vague, vast and mysterious became definite, close at hand and natural. They were

not out of sight of land, after all! Somewhere off there to the right
he could see the island cliffs. Desire looked at him and smiled. Suddenly Mr. Dingle felt an immense and reposeful confidence in the
stalwart, erect, fearless young figure beside him. She was strong
and brave and resourceful. She would not let him drown! And she
was gentle and kind. She wished him no evil. How easily she could
have disposed of him had she been so minded! Instead she had protected him—saved his life! He experienced an unbounded admiration for her capacity—as he already had for her lithe beauty.

"Hold on tight now!" she cried as she ran the launch up into the
wind and shut off the engine. "There's one of my pots!"

They were drifting rapidly astern toward a white object that
bobbed and ducked. Desire threw over the wheel, seized a gaff,
and pulling in the buoy, tossed the warp over the davit-block, took
a turn around the winchhead and started the engine again. Then, as
the line ran up over the side, she coiled it deftly in the bottom of
the launch.

"Here it comes!"

Leaning down below the davit, she heaved aboard the main trap.
The winch rumbled again and she drew in another,—the bridle trap.
With the two traps dripping on the stern sheets, she once more shut
off the engine. The main trap was empty, the second contained three
greenish monsters. Desire swiftly unfastened the button that closed
the door below the guy line, removed the bait bag, tossed the contents overboard and refilled it with a handful of the sardine refuse
from the barrel in front of Mr. Dingle. Then, thrusting the trap
overboard, she opened the other, reached in and took out the lobsters, threw one into the water and the two others into an empty
keg, rebaited the trap and shoved it after its fellow, all before the
six fathoms of warp that held the two traps together had run out.

"Wish I could do anything as well as that," thought Mr. Dingle
admiringly. "She's as sure as Helen Wills!"

Her nonchalance communicated itself to him. He no longer believed death to be so imminent.

"Why did you throw one of 'em overboard?" he asked.

"That was a seed lobster," she announced—"a female. Of course
we mustn't keep those. And one of the others was a shedder."

"A what?" bellowed Mr. Tutt from the bow.

"A shedder—a lobster that has shed its shell. Every year they
crawl down into the mud and rocks and do that, beginning from the
middle of July to the first of August, depending on what sort of a

winter we've had. When it has been mild—like this year—they begin
to shed earlier. A shedder is soft, but if he's full length we keep him
and hold him in the car until his shell grows again."

Once more they raced head on into the waves, stopped, drifted
down upon another buoy, kept off to gaff it, and ran before the
wind while Desire pulled in and unloaded the pots.

Many were empty and some were badly damaged, with broken
bows or cracked sills and rungs, several having the funnel eyes,
through which lobsters entered the trap, half-torn from the heads.

"The sea treats 'em rough," she commented. "I have to spend half
my time mending my traps. I lose quite a few, too,—guy-line frays
off or the warps break, and sometimes a trap will catch in the rocks
and refuse to come up for keeps. But it's a fairly good business. If
the lobsters go back on us we take to trawling or fall back on ground
and hand lines. I can carry six tubs of trawls right in this boat. We
get seventy-five cents a quintal—that's a hundred and twelve pounds
—for hake, and seventy-two cents a quintal for cod. We pack 'em
in hogsheads—drums, we call them—holding eight quintals apiece
and ship to Boston and New York. It's all right in summer; great
fun in fact—as you can see."

"Great!" echoed Mr. Dingle, beginning to feel like a hardy
mariner. He was really enjoying himself a little, although now and
again a particularly big surge would make him catch his breath. The
sun by this time was well up, the wind had gone down, and the
sea, deep blue and sparkling, was covered with boats. He felt
reasonably confident that if any accident happened someone would
come to their rescue. He started to hum:

> *"All's well on the land;*
> *All's well on the sea!"*

Was it? Surely it was—on the sea! Even if this girl were not a
suitable mate for a boy of Robert's wealth and social opportunities,
she would be a splendid wife for anybody who had to make his
way in the world. If Robert were beginning now at the bottom
instead of the top! There really wasn't such a terrible difference
between the lobster business and any other, except that it took a lot
more skill and courage. For an instant his Napoleonic mind dallied
with the idea of a gigantic lobster trust.

"What are you thinking about?" he yelled to the lank figure in
the bow.

"I was just wondering whether or not a lobster was a fish," answered Mr. Tutt.

The bait kegs were empty, the bottom of the launch full of writhing crustaceans, when Desire, having pulled her one hundred and twenty-sixth trap, headed the launch shoreward. Running with the wind, it was hot, and they took off their oilskins.

"Certainly a fine-looking girl," admitted Mr. Dingle. "Put her in a ball gown and she—— No, by thunder, I'd rather keep her in a sweater!"

Confronted with her frank and disarming smile, he felt decidedly ashamed of himself. Really, he'd never seen a prettier girl—of that type.

"I was also thinking over what you said yesterday about Nordics," mumbled Mr. Tutt as he bent over in the cockpit to light a stogy.

At the entrance of the cove, Desire steered the launch alongside a huge floating car into which she tossed her catch of forty-three.

"The smack will be by here Friday," she said; then, shading her eyes, she added, looking toward the beach, "I see the 'Arrow' is afloat again."

A young man who had been awaiting them on the wharf arose at their approach. His face wore an expression of amusement.

"Hello, Diz! Hello, Dad! Hello, Mr. Tutt! Where have you been?"

"Oh, just for a little sail after lobsters," replied the elder Dingle airily. "What are you doing here, Robert?"

"I got nervous when you didn't turn up last evening, so this morning I hired a launch myself and came to look for you."

The constraint between father and son had disappeared. In fact there was no constraint apparent upon the part of anyone as they all walked back together to the house.

Mrs. Zucker was standing on the porch.

"Breakfast ready!" she called. "Come right in and sit down!"

Mr. Dingle, who up to that time had not thought of food, ate ravenously of cereal, hot rolls, bacon, griddle-cakes and coffee. He was not only content; he was positively happy, the final factor in his absolute satisfaction being the gayly colored package of Dingle's Korn Pops that stood in the middle of the table.

"Well," said Mr. Tutt, as he joined his client for a postprandial smoke upon the piazza, "how shall we go about this business? Will you speak to the girl or shall I?"

Desire and Robert had wandered off toward the grove.

"How do you mean?" demanded Mr. Dingle vaguely.

"You haven't forgot the purpose of your visit, have you?"

Mr. Dingle fidgeted. "Naturally—not!" he said. "But I don't want to be too hasty. When it comes to matters of this sort I don't believe in too much interference with other people's lives."

They looked at each other and grinned. "Absolutely, Mr. Dingle?"

"Positively, Mr. Tutt!"

"In that case I might as well beat it back to New York," said the lawyer. "How soon before you start for Bar Harbor?"

"I think I'll spend the day here with Robert," replied his client. "The 'Arrow' can run you up to Bangor in time to catch the afternoon express. Incidentally, how much do I owe you?"

Mr. Tutt pondered for a moment.

"One hundred dollars," he said finally.

"A hundred dollars! Nonsense! That's not enough! Besides, you had your expenses."

"My fee is one hundred dollars—or nothing," replied the old lawyer. "I've always wanted to see Mt. Desert, and anyhow, I've had a swell time."

Mr. Dingle peeled a bill from the roll in his pocket.

"Well, there you are!" he protested. "But you make me feel pretty cheap."

"That's what I set out to do," muttered Mr. Tutt to himself as he went into the house. Presently he returned carrying Great-gran'ther Leicester's family Bible.

"You might stick your nose in that," he suggested—"after I'm gone!"

Desire and Robert waved at him from the promontory as he shot out of the harbor, and Mr. Tutt blew them a kiss. Two hours and a half later he shook hands with Captain Hull on the steamboat landing at Bangor.

"Here's the hundred dollars I promised you," he said. "You certainly did your part of it. But how on earth did you know just where to run the 'Arrow' aground?"

"Oh, that was easy," replied that worthy sea-dog. "I was born on Mud Island, although I ain't been thar since I was a boy."

Mr. Tutt stopped halfway up the gang-plank.

"And I forgot to pay you for that package of Korn Pops," he remarked. "How much did it cost?"

"Oh, that's all right," said Captain Hull.

SAVING HIS FACE

The Honorable Amos T. Wiltbank was a regular fellow. This was shown by the fact that he did not call himself A. Todhunter Wiltbank, which he had a legal right to do. He knew better. Neither did he wear a tall silk hat or burnsides, nor sport a gold-headed cane. On the contrary, he covered his bald spot with a green fedora, uncovered his neck with a turnover collar, and sported a pair of antlers on his lapel. He was no gilded lily, no old-fashioned millionaire, but an up-to-date, Lambs-Club and sheriff's-jury guy who owned an interest in the Giants, and sometimes threw the ball into the arena at the opening game. A live one!

That was what made the situation so intolerable for those about him. For he had all the window-dressings of geniality, with the disposition of Caligula. He was a special motor policeman; had a pass inside the fire lines and could always get seats right down in front centre. He also had a box at the Polo Grounds, and on Saturday afternoons in the spring a short foul into it might easily knock the blocks off a number of persons high up in the city government who like as not would be sitting there. In a word or two, he was a heavy political and business swell, and what he said went. He was a widower.

The Honorable Amos T.'s office was on the very top—the thirty-seventh floor—of the office building in which the law firm of Tutt & Tutt were tenants—considerably lower down. He dwelt on an Olympus of Kurdistan rugs, smoked oak, mother-of-pearl push buttons, and best-quality green-grained imitation Spanish leather; they, amid the grime and dust of the New York Criminal Reports, *Abbott's Practice and Forms*, and the smoke of old Ephraim Tutt's poisonous stogies—all the difference, in fact, between the parlor floor and the kitchen, and in much the same way, the higher the colder.

But Tutt & Tutt were nothing in the life of Amos T., whose own lawyers were the great combination politico-legal firm of Vanderpoel, Callahan & Levitsky. Occasionally Amos T. would come up in the elevator with Mr. Tutt, but he did not know him. Contrariwise Mr. Tutt, who knew everything, knew Amos T., but did not like him. The cause of their difference lay in the imponderable trifle that one day, when Amos T. in getting out had tried to push in front of an old lady, Mr. Tutt had held him back. Later that morning, Amos T. had fired two office boys and a salesman, and had made his stenographer cry. Yes, he had a mean streak, but he was It.

Many stories below where the magnate sat in grandeur, on the same floor with Tutt & Tutt, and adjacent to their suite, was situated the modest real-estate office of Mr. Moses Icklebaum, who dealt in lands, tenements, hereditaments, messuages, rents, and insurance of all kinds. It consisted of but a single room with two desks, at one of which, when he was there, he sat, and at the other a certain Miss Margaret Haggerty, aged twenty-two, his assistant. As often happens, Moses was the figurehead, but Maggie was the brains.

The sign on the door read:

MOSES ICKLEBAUM
REAL ESTATE AND INSURANCE
M. HAGGERTY, NOTARY

It should have read:

MARGARET HAGGERTY
REAL ESTATE AND INSURANCE
M. ICKLEBAUM

The Honorable Amos T. had never heard of either of them,— yet Maggie Haggerty, with the inconspicuous aid of Mr. Ephraim Tutt, was the cause of a revolution in the magnate's character, the making of a man.

Far up among the hills of Dutchess County, Amos T. Wiltbank had built for himself a great estate. With his usual business acumen he had gone there ahead of everybody else, had bought up several thousand acres and, having utilized what portion of them he wanted for his lawns, gardens, farms, and game preserves, had sold off the remainder to such as would pay for it. Among the latter had been Ezra Carter, a young farmer, who had purchased fifty acres together with the house and barn standing thereon. Those transactions were in the days of Mrs. Wiltbank, and of course, as a matter of the simplest business precaution, all the land Amos T. had originally purchased he had taken over in his wife's name. Thus nominally Carter bought his farm from Mrs. Wiltbank, who was in turn to deed it to Carter's young wife.

The disposal of what was to him but a few acres of useless land was a negligible affair to the magnate. To Carter, on the other hand, it was a matter of the deepest moment, for it meant a livelihood, a home for his family, a future. The fifty acres cost him the savings of nine years. But the deal once put through, the magnate suffered the unsigned deed to lie upon his desk for days. The local real-estate dealer dictated a polite note to Mr. Wiltbank, who tossed it aside; Carter wrote, asking the great man kindly to have his wife sign the deed, but Wiltbank was too busy overseeing the building of his kennels to take the trouble to remember about it.

Then one morning the farmer appeared with his money in his hand and the proprietor called his wife over, showed her where to write her name, and signed his own as witness. Carter counted out the purchase price in soiled and crumpled bills, Wiltbank stuffed them in his pocket, and the deed was done—or, rather, delivered. The young farmer brought his wife to the farm; a child was born, a boy; and just as he had got the place in shape to make an honest living, Carter died.

This was all ancient history and only remotely connected—as a back-drop, so to speak—with the little one-act comedy of which we write. And then Mrs. Wiltbank died; and Wiltbank himself gave up his country place in favor of a sort of second blooming in the city.

Mrs. Carter struggled on, trying to run the farm, found herself not strong enough to do so, and offered it for sale. In due time a purchaser appeared, but, when the day came to pass title, it was discovered that Carter had never had the original deed to his wife recorded, and the county clerk now refused to do so, on the ground that Mrs. Wiltbank, the grantor, had not acknowledged it before a commissioner of deeds. Of course the buyer would not pay over his money until his grantor's title was clear on the records. There was only one thing to do, according to the clerk, and that was for Mrs. Carter, the grantee in the first deed, to secure from Mr. Wiltbank, who had signed as an attesting witness, an affidavit—as provided by statute in such cases—to the effect that he had been present when his wife signed the deed, and saw her execute it.

Now this may seem to the reader a very simple matter: all the woman had to do, he will say, was to hop on a train, find the Honor-

able Amos T. Wiltbank and get him to put his name at the bottom
of a paper. But that is the mockery of the law. What it requires
may be the merest trifle—a "yes" or "no," the scratch of a pen,
the delivery of a sheet of paper, the lifting of a hand. Yet the pro-
curing of that "yes" or "no," that mark, that signature or that oath
may involve difficulties rendered well-nigh insuperable by the ignorance, the poverty, or other fortuitous circumstances surrounding
the person obliged to secure it.

It would have been one thing for the Honorable Amos T. Wiltbank to shroud himself in his furs and to motor at sixty miles an
hour to New York, call up his lawyer on the telephone, and procure
an affidavit on any subject, executed by almost anybody, from the
mayor himself up or down, in half an hour; it was quite another for
Mrs. Carter to lock her house and barn, arrange for transportation
for herself and baby seven miles to the railroad station, and, once in
New York, to secure an audience with the great man and induce
him to give her the paper that she needed to make her record title
to the farm complete. She had been in the city only twice in her
life, she possessed but a few dollars, she knew nothing of law or
lawyers, and her only guide was a slip of paper given her by the local
Dutchess County real-estate agent, with the name and address of
Moses Icklebaum upon it.

Now let us take our stand on the sidewalk in front of a Broadway
office building and watch our characters one by one as they emerge
from the Subway and pass inside the revolving doors to play their
parts. First Moses Icklebaum, thin, bald, nervous, hurrying along
with a bundle of fire-insurance policies in his hand; then old Lawyer
Tutt, in his stove-pipe hat, carrying his ivory-headed cane, pausing
to scratch a match and light a long rat-tailed stogy before entering;
then the crisp, brisk Miss Minerva Wiggin, Mr. Tutt's chief clerk
and confidential assistant, or, as he often called her, his legal conscience, in tailor-made suit of gray, her leather brief-case under her
arm; next the Honorable Amos T. Wiltbank, ulstered and begoggled,
emerging from his automobile, puffing a cigar, authoritative, regal.

Let us trail along with them. Behold the starter touch his cap as
the great man stalks by! See him speed an elevator on its way, that
the god may shoot up to Olympus, unsullied by contact with mere
common mortals! "Right through to the thirty-seventh—Jim!" he
says. Behold the pomp with which Amos enters his office and greets
his creatures, the air with which the urbane clerk relieves him of his

fur coat in the antechamber of his business suite, and the anxious celerity with which Miss Madden, his social secretary, indicates the relative importance of his mail. Note the atmosphere of sanctity that pervades the cubicle in which he sits, and the hush that has fallen upon the office. What is greater than greatness? There is but one Amos Todhunter Wiltbank—and this is it!

> *"My name is Ozymandias—king of kings!*
> *Look on my works, ye mighty, and despair!"*

Maggie Haggerty was late coming in from Flushing that morning. There had been a block on the B. R. T. and she had had to get out and walk. She did not really mind, for this had the advantage of giving her the opportunity of a moment's banter with Officer Dennis O'Leary on the corner. Some day, she knew quite well, she was going to marry Dennis—when he got to be a captain, maybe—but she had no idea of making it too easy for him. That would be fatal, later on. So almost always she held him at arm's length.

"Your easy day, is it, Maggie?" said he, holding up the traffic to let the wisp of a colleen cross the street under his arm. "Sure, you look prettier than ever! If it wasn't right in the middle of Broadway, I'd be tempted to steal a kiss."

Maggie dug into his heavily padded ribs with a fairy elbow.

"Hold your tongue, you big booby!" she laughed. "I thought you were set to catch thieves, not to be one. You—steal a kiss! Don't make me laugh!"

He half-lifted her to the curb.

"For ten cents I'd do it this minute!" he grinned as he released her.

Maggie made as if to cuff him and darted across the sidewalk, but on the steps she paused and called back at him: "Why not drop in at twelve o'clock when you go off duty?"

He nodded assent, grinning over his shoulder as he waved the traffic onward. He was a big man, was Dennis O'Leary—six feet four of muscle, bone and sinew—one not to be trifled with when resolved. So fine a figure of a cop, indeed, that the Honorable Amos T. Wiltbank regularly once a month gave him a box of Havana cigars, thus supposing that he would gain immunity from arrest if he violated the traffic laws. Oh, vanity! What is a box of cigars compared to the love of a maid?

We freely admit that the Honorable Todhunter was about the limit. Whether he sat sternly at his smoked-oak desk in his green-grained cordovan-leather armchair or strode thoughtfully up and down the Kurdistan rug with a cigar between his teeth, his subordinates eyed him furtively, as they might the lion at the zoo, ready to jump out of their skins at his gentlest roar; and the sanctum in which he sat was guarded by a series of antechambers full of wild beasts.

Actually to reach and see the Honorable Todhunter was an achievement akin to climbing the Matterhorn. Royalty was nothing to him. A cat may look at a king, but a common human animal couldn't get even a look at A. T. W. No insurance or book-agent, no bill-collector, missionary, or bond-broker could get over the threshold of the outer office—the first-line trenches. For a lynx-eyed intelligence-officer sat at an advance observation post, and the minute an enemy appeared let him have it point-blank:

"Whom do you wish to see? Have you an appointment? No? Mr. Wiltbank never sees anybody except by appointment. I'm sorry, but I cannot interrupt him. He is in an important conference. . . . Yes, you had better write him a letter."

Even if successfully past the O. P.—by appointment—you were only tangled in the wire, as it were. You were grudgingly allowed to take a seat in the outer anteroom—Room 1—where you were told that Mr. Wiltbank would be free to see you in a few minutes. Here various suspicious persons, sauntering casually in, gave you the once-over to make sure you did not have homicidal mania or an infectious disease, or a subpœna, injunction, or capias hidden up your sleeve. The thing the Honorable Amos T. most abhorred in this life was a subpœna. The mere sight of one would turn him green. Once they got you on the stand in one of these infernal investigations or John Doe proceedings, they could tear the very innards out of you! They were so beastly unfair.

Amos T. held that it was nobody's business whether he was an interlocking director, had a pooling agreement with other companies, had contributed to the campaign funds of both parties, or had promised somebody's wife's cousin's nephew a job if his concern got a government contract. He regarded this prying into a man's private affairs as undemocratic, unconstitutional, and contrary to the very principles of liberty upon which our government was founded.

And no one had ever got to him yet. No one had ever slapped a subpœna on him. No one had ever made him hold up his right hand before a mahogany horseshoe draped with up-State Legislators and quaver "I do" in answer to a complicated adjuration to tell the whole truth and not merely a part thereof. And no one ever would! So after you had been combed in Room 1—you were shoved along to Room 2—and the door was locked behind you; then, in course, to Room 3; and at last you were face to face with—no, not Mr. Wiltbank, but with Mr. Baer, his business secretary.

Mr. Baer was almost as much of a swell as his master. Nobody had ever subpœnaed him, either. He was the last trench, the Cerberus, the high priest or muckamuck, or whatever, who passed you in through the temple door to the shrine where A. T. W. sat smoking his cigar. You see how impossible it was to catch the great man. Besides, he had a secret exit which he could use if necessary. The process-servers had given him up years ago.

On the beautiful spring morning when our story opens, the Honorable Amos Todhunter Wiltbank was sitting in his office on the thirty-seventh floor of the building, with his feet on six hundred dollars' worth of fumed oak, with a fifty-five-cent cigar in his mouth, while twenty-seven stories below him Mr. Ephraim Tutt reclined in the same position before an ancient rickety affair knocked down in a Liberty Street auction room for $3.70 and smoking a Wheeling stogy costing $.009 by the thousand. But the higher you are the bigger the bump.

"Mr. Tutt!" remarked Miss Minerva Wiggin, appearing in the doorway.

"Yes, my dear!" returned the old lawyer, smiling at her through the blue smoke of his stogy.

"You are always ready to help people."

"Yes, my dear."

"Well, I wish you'd help my friend Miss Haggerty. She's the notary across the hall, you know—with Moses Icklebaum."

"Where is she?"

"In the outer office. She's got a poor, helpless woman with her. The trouble isn't with the law—it's just the tremendous difficulty under which the poor and insignificant inevitably labor when they have to approach the rich and powerful; just getting to them, you understand. She——"

"Send her in!" cried Mr. Tutt, his congress shoes describing a perfect arc as they descended toward the floor. "Send her in!" And he sprang up.

"Here they are!" remarked Miss Wiggin, producing the visitors from behind her. "You know Mr. Tutt, Maggie. And this is Mrs. Carter, from Valley Fair."

Mr. Tutt shook hands with each ceremoniously and drew up a couple of chairs.

"Now," said he, returning to his desk, "what can I do for you— or Mrs. Carter?"

Miss Haggerty's freckles were almost submerged in the dull red that suffused her face. She was a wiry, nervous little thing not quite five feet in height.

"I'm just hopping mad!" she informed him. "Here's poor Mrs. Carter—her husband's only been dead a few months—come all the way down from Dutchess County with her baby, to straighten out the deed to her farm, and she can't get within a mile of the man who could fix it for her in half a minute."

"Who is he?"

"Amos T. Wiltbank."

"Oh!" exclaimed Mr. Tutt with interest. "You mean friend Todhunter?"

"Exactly."

The lawyer turned to Mrs. Carter. "Why do you wish to see this man?"

Mrs. Carter shifted the baby to her other arm.

"You see, sir—" she began. "Oh, do keep quiet, Ezra! Mr. Wiltbank's wife sold us the farm and signed the deed, but she didn't acknowledge it, and so the county clerk won't record it."

"Why not have her acknowledge it now?" he asked.

"She's dead," replied Mrs. Carter simply. "But Mr. Wiltbank saw her sign it, and put his own name on as a witness; and everything will be all right, if only he will make an affidavit that he did. But I can't reach him."

Mr. Tutt's long face tightened.

"Why didn't you write him about it?"

"I did, but he never answered."

"It makes me furious!" interjected Maggie Haggerty. "Mrs. Carter's all alone with her baby,—nowhere to stay here—has to get back to look after her cow and chickens,—and is unable to communicate with this man, who is right in this very building! First she goes up there and they won't let her cross the threshold; and then I go up and they shoo me out like a tramp!"

"Did you explain what you wished to see Mr. Wiltbank about?" asked Mr. Tutt.

"Why, of course! But they didn't half-listen! They're so smooth and oily you can't get anywhere. They wouldn't even say whether he was in or not. And I had the affidavit all ready too. It would have been no trouble at all for them to take it in, or for him to sign it. But they pretended they didn't know where he was, or when he would be in, or how I could see him; acted almost as if they had never heard of such a man, although his name is on the door in great big letters; treated me like a book-agent!"

Mr. Tutt caressed his lantern jaw.

"As I understand it, all you want of Wiltbank is that he shall make affidavit that he saw his wife, now deceased, sign the deed, as grantor, of the land she sold to Mrs. Carter, she not having acknowledged her signature before any notary or commissioner of deeds at the time."

"That's it precisely," nodded Miss Haggerty. "The statute provides that such an affidavit by the subscribing witness shall be equivalent to an acknowledgement of execution by the maker of the instrument."

"Let's see your affidavit," suggested Mr. Tutt, and the notary handed it to him.

STATE OF NEW YORK ⎱
COUNTY OF NEW YORK ⎰ *ss:*

On the twenty-seventh day of April, nineteen hundred and twenty-seven, before me came Amos T. Wiltbank, the subscribing witness to the foregoing instrument, with whom I am personally acquainted, who, being by me duly sworn, did depose and say that he resides in New York City; that he knew Sarah M. Wiltbank to be the individual described in, and who executed, the foregoing instrument; that he, the said subscribing witness, was present and saw Sarah M. Wiltbank execute the same, and that he, said witness, at the time subscribed his name as witness thereto.

"Quite all right," approved Mr. Tutt. "If you ever need a job, call in here."

"But how is Mrs. Carter going to make Mr. Wiltbank sign and swear to this affidavit?" demanded Miss Haggerty. "I know he's in his office, from the way they all acted. Besides, the starter told me that, although Wiltbank went up this morning, he hadn't seen him come down—and that he usually has his lunch served in his office on a tray. You can get within forty feet of him, and yet he's as far away as if he were in China."

Mr. Tutt was fingering the telephone-book. "Give me West 9991," said he, lifting the receiver.

"Office of Amos T. Wiltbank," answered a silvery female voice.

"I want Mr. Wiltbank, please."

"Who is calling?"

"Ephraim Tutt, attorney at law."

"Do you know Mr. Wiltbank?"

Mr. Tutt ground his teeth. "Yes, yes!" he retorted. "Certainly I do!"

"Well, does he know you?" chuckled the telephone.

The old lawyer shook his fist toward the picture of Lord Eldon on the wall in front of him.

"He's heard of me, I guess."

There was a provoking laugh at the other end. "Kindly tell me what you wish to speak to him about?"

"I want to speak to him about a legal paper."

"Oh—a legal paper?"

"Yes. An affidavit I want him to sign."

"Mr. Wiltbank doesn't sign affidavits."

"Well, he'll sign this one!" roared Mr. Tutt. "Will you kindly tell him this is a very important matter and that a grave injustice——"

"Mr. Wiltbank is out of town," remarked the voice conclusively.

"When is he coming back?"

"We don't know. You'd better write him a letter."

Mr. Tutt suddenly sat bolt upright, turned to Maggie Haggerty, and placed the end of his forefinger upon the point of his nose.

"You say he's in his office?"

"I'm sure of it!"

"Did you ever hear of Section 305?"

"No; what is it?" demanded Miss Haggerty excitedly. "Should I have?"

Mr. Tutt did not reply to this counter-question.

"I'll give him one more chance!" he muttered. "One more chance."

Five minutes later a curious group emerged from the elevator and approached the outer office of the great Mr. Wiltbank. First came Mr. Tutt, lean, rackety, sardonic, in his shabby frock-coat and baggy breeches, his wrists protruding from frayed round cuffs adorned with huge onyx buttons, holding an old-fashioned stove-pipe hat. Just behind him followed Mrs. Carter, her baby in her arms, shabby but neat, her face pale against her threadbare mourning. Then Maggie Haggerty, hopping along like a small angry bird, ready to fly at the first head that might appear.

The middle-aged guardian arose, in his careful cut-away and equally careful manner, at their approach.

"Is Mr. Wiltbank in?" demanded Mr. Tutt.

"Who wishes to see him?" inquired Mr. Hosmer, the intelligence officer.

"Please tell him Mr. Ephraim Tutt, representing Mrs. Ezra Carter, of Valley Fair. I wish to get Mr. Wiltbank to sign an affidavit of his wife's execution of a deed, as grantor of some land sold to this lady here."

Mr. Hosmer looked faintly amused.

"Have you an appointment?"

"I have not. My client has come all the way down to the city to see Mr. Wiltbank, and she must return home to-day. If he does not sign this paper for her, her journey will have been fruitless, her time and money thrown away. Merely as a matter of justice——"

Something in Mr. Tutt's manner impressed Mr. Hosmer.

"Wait a moment," said he. "I will see if something cannot be done. William! Take my place at the door."

A stout youth arose from a neighboring desk and usurped the place of Mr. Hosmer, who disappeared toward the rear of the office. The fact was that he had heard of Mr. Tutt, and it was the second time Mrs. Carter had been there that morning! Perhaps Mr. Wiltbank might be persuaded——

"Better not go in there!" warned Mr. Baer. "The boss is on the rampage. He'll bite your head off!"

But the captain of the guard pushed by him and knocked respectfully.

"Well?" came from within.

He entered. The Honorable Amos T. Wiltbank raised a plethoric countenance.

"Well?" he snorted.

"If you please, sir," began Mr. Hosmer timidly, "there's a woman here from up your way in the country. Her attorney is with her, too—Mr. Tutt—a very well-known lawyer. They want you to sign an affidavit——"

The Honorable Todhunter's massive face seemed suddenly to swell.

"What do you mean," he demanded, "interrupting me in the

middle of my work this way? You know my orders! I see nobody without an appointment! Nobody! Tell these people to go and talk to Mr. Vanderpoel. If it's anything demanding my attention, he can write to me."

Mr. Hosmer hesitated.

"Excuse me, sir," he began again. "Might it not be better for you to make an exception for once? This Mr. Tutt can be very disagreeable——"

"So can I!" yelled the apoplectic Todhunter, lumbering to his feet. "Tell him I'm the most disagreeable man in New York. Tell him to go to Vanderpoel, and, if he doesn't want to do that, tell him to go to hell!"

"Take this!" directed Mr. Tutt to Miss Sondheim, his stenographer. "And knock it out on your machine now—before you go out to lunch:

"The People of the State of New York to Amos T. Wiltbank, greeting:

"I command you, that all and singular business and excuses being laid aside, you appear and attend before me, Margaret Haggerty, a notary public, duly qualified and appointed under the laws of the State of New York, in Room 11,012 of the building known as 61 Broadway, Borough of Manhattan, New York City, forthwith, on this the 29th day of April, to testify under oath before me concerning the execution of a deed, in which Sarah M. Wiltbank appears as grantor and Emily P. Carter as grantee, and to the execution of which you were a subscribing witness. And for failure to so attend and testify you shall forfeit to said Emily P. Carter one hundred dollars and shall be committed to the Prison of the City of New York, there to remain without bail and without the liberties of the jail until you answer under oath as required by the law.

"Margaret Haggerty, notary public in New York County.

"Ephraim Tutt, attorney for Margaret Haggerty, 61 Broadway, New York City."

"What is all that?" asked Maggie in amazement. "I can't issue a subpœna!"

"You can do a lot more than that, my child!" he replied. "You can commit this bulldozing ruffian to jail!"

"Little me?" she gasped. "It can't be. I never heard of such a thing."

"Very few lawyers have. Or, if so, they've forgotten it. It's the law, though," he informed her. "That is, it is how the statute reads. It's worth trying out, anyhow. Listen, I'll read it to you. It's Section 305 of the Real Property Law:

> "Real Property Law, Section 305, compelling witnesses to testify.
> "On the application of a grantee in a conveyance, his heir or personal representative, or a person claiming under either of them, verified by the oath of the applicant, stating that a witness to a conveyance, residing in the county where the application is made, refused to appear and testify concerning its execution, and that such conveyance cannot be proved without his testimony, any officer authorized to take, within the state, acknowledgment or proof of conveyance of real property may issue a subpœna, requiring such witness to attend and testify before him concerning the execution of the conveyance. A person who, on being duly served with such a subpœna, without reasonable cause refuses or neglects to attend or refuses to answer under oath concerning the execution of such conveyance, forfeits to the person injured one hundred dollars, and may also be committed to prison by the officer who issued the subpœna, there to remain without bail and without the liberties of the jail until he answers under oath as required by this section.

"Now I propose to teach this mannerless brute what he is clearly too selfish or ignorant to realize, that the mere fact that he is a human being entails a certain recognition upon his part of the existence of other people."

"Hear! Hear!" cried Miss Wiggin. "I have always hated that man!"

"If," continued the lawyer grimly, "our friend Todhunter refuses to do that which the law requires of him, even if he be ignorant of his duty, we will take advantage of that same ignorance and stick him in jail—for a while anyhow!"

"Do you really mean—" stammered Maggie.

"Mean? Of course I mean!" shouted Mr. Tutt. "Take this, too:

> "City and County of New York, ss: In the matter of the committal of Amos T. Wiltbank for a criminal contempt.
> "On this 29th day of April, 1927, at about the hour of noon, the above-named Amos T. Wiltbank having been duly subpœnaed by me the undersigned to appear, attend, and testify as a witness

before me concerning the execution of a certain deed to which he was a subscribing witness, between Sarah M. Wiltbank, grantor, and Emily P. Carter, grantee, and the said Amos T. Wiltbank having without reasonable cause, refused, and neglected to so attend, appear, and testify with respect thereto, now therefore it is ordered and adjudged that the said Amos T. Wiltbank forfeit to the said Emily P. Carter the sum of one hundred dollars and be forthwith committed to the City Prison of the City of New York, there to remain without bail and without the liberties of the jail until he answers under oath as required by Section 305 of the Real Property Law of the State of New York.

"MARGARET HAGGERTY, notary public in New York County."

"Lord love you!" exclaimed Maggie. "Who ever would mind that?"

"Amos T. Wiltbank," answered Mr. Tutt grimly. "Or I'll know why! Do you know a friendly cop?"

"Do I *know* one!" ejaculated Her Honor.

"Then produce him," returned Mr. Tutt.

Officer Dennis O'Leary had just been relieved from post and was about to attend, in accordance with the previous command of his superior officer, at the office of Moses Icklebaum, when Maggie, hatless, met him at the curb.

"Do you love me, Dennis?" she demanded.

"Do I—" he began, astounded.

"Then prove it! Or I'll never speak to you again—or marry you —or anything!"

"Give me the chance!" he ejaculated. "What is it?"

"I want you to make an arrest—maybe!"

Dennis' kindly face expanded into a receptive grin. "If that's all —lead me to him!" he swaggered.

"Oh, I knew you would!" she panted.

"Who is it?" he asked curiously.

"Amos T. Wiltbank!" she shot at him.

O'Leary's jaw dropped and he stared at her blankly. "For the love of Mike!" he gasped.

"No, Denny dear," she responded archly, "for love of me!"

Ten minutes thereafter Mr. Baer, who happened to have gone into the outer office, saw the young policeman emerge from the elevator. Denny's monthly visits had rendered him a familiar figure, and the secretary had made a point of cultivating a sort of intimacy. You never knew when you would need a cop.

"Hello," he greeted him cordially. "Want to see the boss?"

"Sure," replied the officer. "Is he in?"

Baer nodded and motioned toward the communication trench.

"I guess it'll be all right for you to go in there. You know the way. Miss Madden, just tell Mr. Wiltbank that Officer O'Leary is here and wants to speak with him a minute."

The Honorable Amos T. was in the act of taking a fresh box of cigars from the bottom drawer of his desk when Denny appeared at the doorway.

"Well," exclaimed Mr. Wiltbank with an affectation of delight at seeing his visitor, "how are you, old man? What can I do for you? Have a box of cigars?"

"Guess I'll pass 'em up this time, gov'nor," said Denny.

There was something in his tone that bothered Amos T., who in his entire experience had never before known a cop to refuse anything. "What do you want, then?" he demanded.

"I've got a paper for you to sign, gov'nor," he answered quietly.

Instantly the Honorable Todhunter was on his feet.

"Look here!" he said. "You ought to know better than to intrude on me like this without permission! You should have stated your business in the outer office. I never see anybody without an appointment. Please go out and confer with Mr. Baer."

"This ain't got nothin' to do with Mr. Baer," explained Denny. "This here is a subpœna——"

At that, the world went bad for Amos Todhunter. Blackness descended. Devils shrieked.

"I don't care what it is!" he cried. "Get out of here!"

"Listen, Mr. Wiltbank," urged Dennis in a vain endeavor to pacify him. "You sold some land to a man named Carter——"

"Go and see my lawyer!" shouted Todhunter. "I know nothing whatever about it. I didn't sell any land to him. I never sold any land to anybody in my life."

"Well, your wife—" began Dennis.

"Get out of my office," repeated Todhunter, "or I'll send for the pol——"

His voice died away. Obviously, they were already there.

"First I'm goin' to serve you with this subpœna!" announced the cop.

"I won't take it!" yelled A. T. W. "Keep away from me!"

Dennis began to get angry.

"Yes, you will!" he growled. "You'll take that and a lot more, before I get through with you."

Then he put his hand in the middle of the fumed-oak writing

table and leaped over it—he had taken a prize in the hurdles at the police games down at Belmont Park—and slapped the horrid thing on Todhunter's chest just above the solar plexus.

"Take it!" he ordered.

Todhunter took it.

"Read it!" he commanded.

"I can't without my glasses!" expostulated Todhunter. "What is it?"

"It's a subpœna ordering you to testify about a deed."

"Who issued it?"

"Miss Haggerty."

"Who's Miss Haggerty?"

"She's the finest little woman——"

"I mean," interrupted Todhunter, getting hold of himself, "what is she? How can she issue a subpœna?"

"She's a notary public."

Todhunter bit off the end of a cigar, lit it, and laughed.

"A notary can't issue a subpœna!"

Denny eyed him belligerently.

"Well, she has!" he announced.

"But I don't have to obey it," retorted Todhunter. "Who sent you here?"

"None of your business!" replied the cop. "A subpœna is a subpœna!"

"It's of no validity unless issued by a proper officer—a judge," answered Todhunter, now, as he supposed, on firm ground. "You'll get yourself in trouble if you lend yourself to such tricks. I know the commissioner and I'll see you get sent out among the goats."

The Honorable Amos T. felt a hand hard as iron grab the linen adjacent to his Adam's apple and yank him to his feet.

"You come with me!" roared O'Leary. "You'll see who's the goat!"

Todhunter, choking, tried to free himself. His sacred person was unused to violence.

"Let go of me!" he stuttered. "There's obviously some mistake!"

But Denny did not relax his hold.

"You're going with me—now—like this! Come along!" he directed.

Todhunter half-swooned. Go through an alley of smirking, sneering clerks like that—in front of Baer, Wadhams, Miss Madden, the elevator boys! If he did he could never hold up his head again.

"Wait a minute!" he gagged. "I'll go with you—that is, I'll go as far as the elevator, anyway. You're a nice fellow, you are! I don't know what this is all about, but can't I fix it with you somehow? How would a twenty-dollar bill look?"

"A thousand-dollar bill would look so small I couldn't see it!" snorted Denny. "Cut that out, Mr. Wiltbank! There's nothin' doin'. You come outside and I'll give you plenty of time to make up your mind what you'll do. But that's all."

"All right!" snarled Todhunter. "You take back that subpœna and forget you ever served it, or I'll have your job! I'll break you—understand?"

For reply Dennis propelled his prisoner vigorously toward the door.

"Easy!" whined A. T. W. "I'm going!"

"You bet you are!" retorted O'Leary.

They passed through the shrouded sanctuary known as Room 3, the more blatant ostentation of Room 2, the austere elegance of Room 1, and into the large outer office, where it seemed to Todhunter as if no less than fifty pairs of derisive eyes were focused upon him.

In the middle of the room, in full view of all the clerks, accountants, bookkeepers, stenographers, attendants, and office boys, stood a tall, lean, ramshackly, wizened old cuss, who looked something like a lamp-post wrapped in a frock coat, and whom the miserable magnate suspected he had seen somewhere before. Beside this gaunt Nemesis was a small, but furious, female.

"I have subpœnaed you," she announced in a high, firm voice, "to appear before me and testify regarding the execution of a deed to which you were a subscribing witness. Are you coming?"

Todhunter could hear the hush descending upon the office. The babble of voices, the rattle and ring of typewriters ceased. No jaws moved. It was as if a forest, swaying in the wind, had suddenly become motionless.

"My good woman," began Todhunter nervously, "this sort of thing is quite unpardonable. I do not recall the matter to which you refer. But whatever assistance I might have been to you is now out of the question. I shall decline to help you in any way."

A curious smile played elusively over Mr. Tutt's gaunt face, but he swiftly repressed it.

"All right," he muttered *sotto voce* to the little pepper-pot beside him. "Go to it."

"Then," exclaimed Maggie dramatically, "I fine you one hundred dollars and commit you to the City Prison, without jail privileges, until you are prepared to testify. Of-fi-cer"—her voice shook almost imperceptibly—"of-fi-cer! Arrest that man and take him to the Tombs!"

Utter silence, as in the curvature of space, followed. It was broken by a brazen laugh from A. T. W.

"What nonsense!" he remarked. "You must be crazy! You couldn't send a dog to jail!"

"She can send you!" smiled the tall old man who towered above him.

"Who in hell are *you?*" snapped the Honorable Todhunter.

"I suppose I am known by the same name everywhere," answered Mr. Tutt benignly. "Let it suffice that I am the young lady's attorney. I advise you that she has full authority to send you to prison. Here is the necessary commitment, signed by her, and this officer is ready to execute it. Would you like to convey any messages to your friends before you start? To send for a toothbrush or anything?"

The Honorable Todhunter's face sank like a blazing sun into the purple horizon of his neck. To be insulted thus in the presence of his clerks; baited and jeered at! Suffocating with repressed fury he turned to Miss Madden.

"Call up Mr. Vanderpoel," he directed her.

A moment later she handed him the instrument.

"That you, Vanderpoel? Yes, A. T. W. Listen. Can a notary commit a person to jail simply because that person refuses to be questioned about a real-estate transaction?"

"Notary—send—a person—to jail!" ejaculated Mr. Vanderpoel. "Of course not! Who ever heard of such a thing? Nobody except a judge can send anybody to jail."

"Well, there's a notary trying to send me," answered Todhunter.

"You? You! That's a good one!" laughed the learned Vanderpoel. "Tell him to go to the devil."

The Honorable Amos T. Wiltbank hung up the receiver.

"My lawyer instructs me to tell you to go to the devil!" he informed Miss Haggerty.

"Very well! Arrest him, of-fi-cer!" she directed.

At that Officer Dennis O'Leary brought his hand down with a bang upon the magnate's shoulder, gripped him roughly by the collar and dragged him toward the elevator. A gasp of astonishment and horror escaped from half a hundred throats. The great A. T. W. treated like that—so rough!

"Help!" cried the magnate. "Look here——"

"Under the law," said Mr. Tutt calmly, "you may be sent to prison. I will show you the statute, if you care to read it. I confess it is rather obsolete, but it will serve. It is Section 305 of the Real Property Law. But you may still escape the humiliation of going to jail by acceding to the young lady's demands and signing the necessary affidavit—which I hold in my hand."

The Honorable Amos T. Wiltbank hesitated. Should he now yield he could never again be the same to his employees. He would be an exploded balloon, a shattered idol, a busted phenomenon. But if he didn't——

"Come along, you!" snarled Dennis, jerking him ignominiously.

Tears of baffled rage and humiliation smarted in the great man's eyes. The cop's knuckles dug painfully into the cords of his neck. His collar hurt him.

"Come on!"

What difference did it make whether this outrageous performance was legal or illegal? Here was an officer who was prepared to yank him into the elevator and, if need be, club him to a pulp and drag him by the heels down Broadway to the Tombs. Even if he didn't beat, club, and mangle him, he would bruise and maltreat him by word and deed, conduct him along by the arm in the presence of a jeering crowd, who would follow, snarling, at his heels. It was not so much the idea of jail—even without the usual courtesies—as the puncturing of his pride, the writhing humiliation, the awful irony that he, the great A. T. W.—a man who had had cigarettes named after him—should be— Oh, it was inconceivable! And think of the newspapers!

The shadow of the descending elevator flashed across the ground-glass and the door slid open.

The magnate went suddenly weak in the knees. He was beaten; he knew it! For the first time in his life his bluff had been called— and by a woman! He wavered, he caved!

"Goin' down?" intoned the elevator man.

"I think not," answered the Honorable Amos T. Wiltbank sheepishly.

CONTEMPT OF COURT

"Well, honor is the subject of my story."—JULIUS CÆSAR, ACT I, SC. 2.

"What has become of Katie—the second waitress?" asked Miss Althea Beekman of Dawkins, her housekeeper, as she sat at her satinwood desk after breakfast. "I didn't see her either last night or this morning."

Dawkins, who was a mid-Victorian, flushed.

"I really had to let the girl go, ma'am!" she explained with an outraged air. "I hardly know how to tell you—such a thing in this house! I couldn't possibly have her round. I was afraid she might corrupt the other girls, ma'am—and they are such a self-respecting lot—almost quite ladylike, ma'am. So I simply paid her and told her to take herself off."

Miss Beekman looked pained.

"You shouldn't have turned her out into the street like that, Dawkins!" she expostulated. "Where has she gone?"

Dawkins gazed at her large feet in embarrassment.

"I don't know, ma'am," she admitted. "I didn't suppose you'd want her here, so I sent her away. It was quite inconvenient, too—with the servant problem what it is. But I'm hoping to get another this afternoon from Miss Healey's."

Miss Beekman was genuinely annoyed.

"I am seriously displeased with you, Dawkins! Of course, I am shocked at any girl in my household misbehaving herself, but—I—wouldn't want her to be sent away—under such circumstances. It would be quite heartless. Yes, I am very much disturbed!"

"I'm sorry, ma'am. But I was only thinking of the other girls."

"Well, it's too late to do anything about it now. But I'm sorry, Dawkins; very sorry, indeed. We have responsibilities toward these people! However—this is Thursday, isn't it?—we'll have veal for lunch as usual—and she was so pretty!" she added inconsequently.

"H'm. That was the trouble!" sniffed the housekeeper. "We're

258

well rid of her. You'd think a girl would have some consideration
for her employer—if nothing else. In a sense she is a guest in the
house and should behave herself as such!"

"Yes, that is quite true!" agreed her employer. "Still—yes, Brown
Betty is very well for dessert. That will do, Dawkins."

Behind the curtain of this casual conversation had been enacted
a melodrama as intensely vital and elemental as any of Shakespeare's
tragedies, for, the day Dawkins had fired Katie O'Connell—"for
reasons," as she said—and told her to go back where she came from
or anywhere she liked, for that matter, so long as she got out of
her sight, Katie's brother Shane in the back room of McManus' gin
palace gave Red McGurk—for the same "reasons"—a certain option
and, the latter having scornfully declined to avail himself of it, had
then and there put a bullet through his neck. But this, naturally,
Miss Beekman did not know.

As may have been already surmised, Miss Althea was a gracious,
gentle and tender-hearted lady, who never would have knowingly
done a wrong to anybody and who did not believe that, simply
because God had been pleased to call her into a state of life at least
three stories higher than her kitchen, she was thereby relieved from
her duty toward those who occupied it.

Nevertheless, from the altitude of those three stories she viewed
them as essentially different from herself, for she came of what is
known as "a long line of ancestors." Since, however, Katie O'Connell
and Althea Beekman were practically contemporaries, it is somewhat
difficult to understand how one of them could have had a succession
of ancestors that was any longer than that of the other. Indeed,
Miss Beekman's friend, Professor Abelard Samothrace, of Columbia
University, probably would have admitted that just as the two had
lived in the same house—albeit at different levels—on Fifth Avenue,
so their forebears at some prehistoric period had, likely as not, occupied the same cave and had in company waded on frosty mornings
the ice-skimmed swamps of "Mittel Europa" in pursuit of the cave
bear, the mastodon and the woolly rhinoceros, and for afternoon
relaxation had made up twosomes for hunting wives, with stone
clubs, instead of mashies, in their hairy prehensile hands.

It would seem, therefore, that—whatever of tradition might
have originated in the epoch in question—the same glimmerings of
sportsmanship, of personal pride, of tribal duty or of conscience
ought to have been the common heritage of them both. For it was
assuredly true that while Miss Katie's historic ancestors had been

Celtiberians, clad on occasion only in a thin coating of blue paint, Miss Althea's had dwelt in the dank marshes of the Elbe and had been unmistakably Teutonic, though this curse had been largely removed by racial intermarriage during subsequent thousands of years. Indeed, it may well have been that in the dimmer past some Beekman serf on bended knee had handed a gilded harp to some King O'Connell on his throne. If the O'Connells were foreigners the Beekmans, from the point of view of the aboriginal American, were no less so simply because they had preceded them by a couple of hundred years.

Tradition is not a matter of centuries but of ages. If Katie inherited some of hers from the peat bogs adjacent to Tara's Halls in that remote period when there were still snakes in Ireland, Miss Althea had vicariously acquired others from the fur-clad barbarians described by Tacitus who spent their leisure time in drinking, gambling or splitting each other's skulls with stone mallets. But all this entirely escaped Miss Althea, who suffered from the erroneous impression that because she was a Beekman and lived in a stone mansion facing Central Park she differed fundamentally, not only from the O'Connells, but from the Smiths, the Pasquales, the Ivanovitches and the Ginsbergs, all of whom really come of very old families. Upon this supposed difference she prided herself.

Because she was, in fact, mistaken and because the O'Connells shared with the Beekmans and the Ginsbergs a tradition reaching back to a period when revenge was justice, and custom of kinsfolk the only law, Shane O'Connell had sought out Red McGurk and had sent him unshriven to his God. The only reason why this everyday Bowery occurrence excited any particular attention was, not that Shane was an O'Connell, but that McGurk was the son of a political boss of much influence and himself one of the leaders of a notorious cohort of young ruffians who when necessary could be relied upon to stuff a ballot box or otherwise to influence public opinion. As Red was a mighty man in Gideon, so his taking off was an event of moment, and he was "waked" with an elegance unsurpassed in the annals of Cherry Hill.

"An' if ye don't put the son-of-a — who kilt me b'y in th' chair, ye name's mud—see?" the elder McGurk had informed District Attorney Peckham the next morning. "I've told the cops who done it. Now you do the rest—understand?"

Peckham understood very well. No one seeing the expression on McGurk's purple countenance could have failed to do so.

"We'll get him! Don't you worry!" Peckham had assured the desolated father with a manner subtly suggesting both the profoundest sympathy and the prophetic glories of a juridical revenge in which the name of McGurk would be upon every lip and the picture of the deceased, his family, and the home in which they dwelt would be featured on the front page of every journal. "We'll get him, all right!"

"See to it that ye do!" commented his visitor meaningly.

Therefore, though no one had seen him commit the crime, word was passed along the line to pick up Shane O'Connell for the murder of Red McGurk. It mattered not there was no evidence except the report of a muttered threat or two and the lie passed openly the week before.

Everybody knew that Shane had done it, and why; though no one could tell how he knew it. And because everybody knew, it became a political necessity for Peckham to put him under arrest with a great fanfare of trumpets and a grandiose announcement of the celerity with which the current would be turned through his body.

The only fly in the ointment was the fact that O'Connell had walked into the district attorney's office as soon as the rumor reached him and quietly submitted to being arrested, saying merely: "I heard you wanted me. Well, here I am!"

But though they badgered him for hours, lured him by every pretext to confess, put a stool pigeon in the same cell with him, and resorted to every trick, device and expedient known to the prosecutor's office to trap him into some sort of an admission, they got nothing for their pains. It was just one of those cases where the evidence simply wasn't forthcoming. And yet Peckham was aware that, unless he convicted O'Connell, his name would indeed be mud —or worse. This story, however, is concerned less with the family honor of the O'Connells than with that of the Beekmans.

Miss Althea was the last surviving member of her branch of the family. Though she would probably have regarded it as slightly vulgar to have been referred to as "one hundred per cent American" she was so nearly so—except for a reminiscent affection for "the late dear Queen"—that the phrase in her case would have been substantially correct. Her mother had been the daughter of a distinguished Revolutionary statesman who had been a signer of the Declaration of Independence, an ambassador and justice of the Supreme Court as well; her father a celebrated newspaper editor.

She had been born in Gramercy Park near what is now The

Players' Club, and the old colonial house with its white trimmings and ornamental ironwork had been the scene of many a modest gayety at a time when Emerson, Lowell, and George William Curtis were viewed less as citizens than as high priests of Culture, sharing equally in sanctity with the goddess thereof. She could remember the many veterans of the Civil War who dined at her father's decorous mahogany and talked of the preservation of the Constitution and those other institutions to found which it is generally assumed the first settlers landed on the Atlantic seaboard and self-sacrificingly accepted real estate from the wily native in return for whisky and glass beads. She was fifty-one years of age, a Colonial Dame, a Daughter of the American Revolution, a member of the board of directors of several charitable institutions, and she was worth a couple of million dollars in railroad securities. On Sundays she always attended the church in Stuyvesant Square frequented by her family, and as late as 1907 did so in the famous Beekman C-spring victoria, driven by an aged negro coachman.

But besides being full of rectitude and good works—which of themselves so often fail of attraction—Miss Althea was possessed of a face so charming even in its faded prettiness that one wondered how it was possible that she could successfully have withstood the suitors who must have crowded about her. Her house on Fifth Avenue was full of old engravings of American patriots, and the library inherited from her editorial parent was replete with volumes upon subjects which would have filled a Bolshevik with disgust. Briefly, if ever Trotzky had become Commissary of the Soviet of Manhattan, Miss Althea and those like her would have been the first candidates for a drumhead court-martial.

She prided herself equally upon her adherence to religious principle and the Acts of Congress. For the law, merely as law, she had the profoundest veneration, viewing the heterogeneous statutes passed from time to time by desultory legislators much as if they had in some mysterious way been handed down from Mount Sinai along with the Ten Commandments.

For any violator of the law she had the uttermost abhorrence, and the only weakness in her ethics arose out of her failure to discriminate between relative importances, for she undoubtedly regarded a violation of the Volstead Act as being quite as reprehensible as grand larceny or the bearing of false witness. To her every judge must be a learned, wise and honorable man because he stood for the enforcement of the law of the land, and she never questioned whether or not that law was wise or otherwise, which latter often—it must be confessed—it was not.

In a word, while there was nothing progressive about Miss Althea, she was one of those delightful, cultivated, loyal and enthusiastic female citizens who are rightfully regarded as vertebræ in the backbone of the country. It was characteristic of her that carefully folded inside the will drawn for her by her family solicitor was a slip of paper addressed to her heirs and next of kin requesting that at her funeral the national anthem should be played and that her coffin should be draped with the American flag.

But there was a somewhat curious, if not uncommon, inconsistency in Miss Beekman's attitude toward lawbreakers in that, once they were in prison, they instantly became objects of her gentlest solicitude. Thus she was a frequent visitor at the Tombs, where she brought spiritual, and more often, it must be frankly admitted, bodily comfort to those of the inmates who were recommended by the district attorney and prison authorities as worthy of her attention; and Prosecutor Peckham, being not unmindful of the possible political advantage that might accrue from being on friendly terms with so well-known a member of the distinguished family of Beekman, lost no opportunity to ingratiate himself with her and gave orders to his subordinates to make her path as easy as possible. Thus quite naturally she had heard of Tutt & Tutt, and had a casual acquaintance with the senior partner himself.

"That O'Connell is a regular clam—won't tell me anything at all!" remarked Mr. Tutt severely, hanging his hat on the office tree with one hand while he felt for a match in his waistcoat pocket with the other, upon the afternoon of the day that Miss Beekman had had the conversation with Dawkins with which this story opens.

"National temperament," answered Bonnie Doon, producing the desired match. "It's just like an Irishman to refuse point-blank to talk to the lawyer who has been assigned to defend him. He's probably afraid he'll make some admission from which you will infer he's guilty. No Irishman ever yet admitted that he was guilty of anything!"

"I've never met a defendant of any other nationality who would, either," replied Mr. Tutt. "Even so, this chap O'Connell is a puzzle to me. 'Go ahead and defend me,' said he to-day, 'but don't ask me to talk about the case, because I won't.' I give it up. He wouldn't even tell me where he was on the day of the murder."

Bonnie grunted dubiously.

"There may be a very good reason for that!" he retorted. "If what rumor says is true, he simply hunted for McGurk until he found him and put a lead pellet back of his ear."

"And also, if what rumor says is true," supplemented Tutt, who entered at this moment, "a good job it was, too. McGurk was a treacherous, dirty blackguard, the leader of a gang of criminals, even if he was, as they all agree, a handsome rascal who had every woman in the district on tenterhooks. Any girl in this case?"

Bonnie shrugged.

"They claim so; only there's nothing definite. The O'Connells are well spoken of."

"If there was, that would explain why he wouldn't talk," commented Mr. Tutt. "That's the devil of it. You can't put in a defense under the unwritten law without besmirching the very reputation you are trying to protect."

The senior partner of Tutt & Tutt wheeled his swivel-chair to the window and, crossing his congress shoes upon the sill, gazed contemplatively down upon the shipping.

"Unwritten law!" sarcastically exclaimed Tutt from the doorway. "There ain't no such animal in these parts!"

"You're quite wrong!" retorted his elder partner. "Most of our law—ninety-nine per cent of it, in fact—is unwritten. For every statute in print there are a hundred that have no tangible existence, based on our sense of decency, of duty and of honor."

"Don't you agree with that, Tutt?" demanded Bonnie. "Every man's conscience is his own private unwritten law."

Tutt looked skeptical.

"Did you say every man had a conscience?" he inquired.

"In matters of conscience—which, I take it, is the same thing as one's sense of honor—one has got to be one's own judge," declared Miss Wiggin.

"The simplest way," announced Tutt, "is to take the position that the law should always be obeyed and that the most honorable man is he who respects it the most."

"The safest and also the most cowardly!" retorted Miss Wiggin. "Supposing the law required you to do something which you personally regarded not only as morally wrong but detestable, would you do it?"

"It wouldn't!" protested Tutt with a grimace. "The law is the perfection of reason. As our highest duty is to the state, it is a mere juggling with words, in my humble opinion, to speak of honor as distinguished from law or the obligation of one's oath in a court of justice. I bet I can find plenty of authorities to that effect in the library!"

"Of course you can," countered Miss Wiggin. "You can find an authority on any side of any proposition you want to look for. That's why one's own sense of honor is so much more reliable than the law. What is the law, anyhow? It's what some judge says is the law—until he's reversed. Do you suppose I'd surrender my own private ideas of honor to a casual ruling from a judge who very likely hadn't the remotest idea of what I think is honorable?"

"You'll be jailed for contempt before you get through!" Tutt warned her.

"The fact of the matter is," concluded Mr. Tutt, "that honor and law haven't anything to do with one another. The courts have constantly pointed that out from the earliest days, though judges like, when they can, to make the two seem one and the same. Chief Baron Bowes, I remember, said in some case in 1743, 'The court can't determine what is honor.' No, no; the two are different, and that difference will always make trouble. Isn't it nearly tea time?"

Miss Beekman was just stepping off the elevator on the first floor of the Tombs the next afternoon on one of her weekly visits when she came face to face with Mr. Tutt.

She greeted him cordially, for she had taken rather a fancy to the shabby old man, drawn to him, in spite of her natural aversion to all members of the criminal bar, by the gentle refinement of his weather-beaten face. "I hope you have had a successful day."

"Unfortunately, I have not," he answered. "My only client refuses to speak to me! Perhaps you could get something out of him for me."

"Oh, they all talk to me readily enough!" she replied. "I fancy they know I'm harmless. What is his name?"

"Shane O'Connell."

"What is his offense?"

"He is charged with murder."

"Oh!"

Miss Althea recoiled. Her charitable impulses did not extend to defendants charged with homicide. There was too much notoriety connected with them, for one thing; there was nothing she hated so much as notoriety.

"Seriously," he went on with earnestness, "I wish you'd have a word with him. It's pretty hard to have to defend a man and not to know a thing about his side of the case. It's almost your duty, don't you think?"

Miss Althea hesitated, and was lost.

"Very well," she answered reluctantly, "I'll see what I can do. Perhaps he needs some medicine or letter paper or something. I'll get an order from the warden and go right back and see him."

Twenty minutes later Shane O'Connell sullenly faced Miss Beekman across the deal table of the counsel room. A ray of late sunshine fell through the high grating of the heavily barred window upon a face quite different from those which Miss Althea was accustomed to encounter in these surroundings, for it showed no touch of depravity or evil habits, and confinement had not yet deprived its cheeks of their rugged mantle of crimson or its eyes of their bold gleam.

He was little more than a boy, this murderer, as handsome a lad as ever swaggered out of County Kerry.

"An' what may it be that leads you to send for such as me, Miss Beekman?" he inquired.

She felt suddenly unnerved, startled and rather shocked at his use of her name. Where could he have discovered it? From the keeper, probably, she decided. All her usual composure, her quiet self-possession, her aloof and slightly condescending sweetness—had deserted her.

"I thought," she stammered—"I might—possibly—be of help to you."

"'Tis too late to make up for the harm ye've done!" His coal-black eyes reached into her heart.

"I!" she gasped. "I—do harm! What do you mean?"

"Did not my sister Katie work for ye?" he demanded. "Did you see after her or watch her comings and goings, as she saw after you—she a mere lass of sixteen? Arrah! No!"

With a sensation of horror Miss Althea realized that at last she was in a murder case in spite of herself! This lad, the brother of Katie, the waitress whom she had discharged! How curious! And how unfortunate! His charge was preposterous; nevertheless a faint blush stole to her cheek and she looked away.

"How ridiculous!" she managed to say. "It was no part of my obligation to look after her! How could I?"

His hawk's eyes watched her every tremor.

"Did ye not lock her out the night of the ball when she went wid McGurk?"

"I—how absurd!"

Suddenly she faltered. An indistinct accusing recollection turned her faint,—of the housekeeper having told her that one of the girls insisted on going to a dance on an evening not hers by arrangement, and how she had given orders that the house should be closed as usual at ten o'clock for the night. If the girl couldn't abide by the rules of the Beekman *ménage* she could sleep somewhere else. What of it? Supposing she had done so? She could not be held responsible for remote, unreasonable and discreditable consequences!

And then by chance Shane O'Connell made use of a phrase that indirectly saved his life, a phrase curiously like the one used on a former occasion by Dawkins to Miss Althea:

"Katie was a member of your household; ye might have had a bit of thought for her!" he asserted bitterly.

Dawkins had said: "You'd think a girl would have some consideration for her employer, if nothing else. In a sense she is a guest in the house and should behave herself as such."

There was no sense in it! There was no parallel, no analogy. There was no obligation to treat the girl as a guest, even though the girl should have acted like one. Miss Beekman knew it. And yet there was—something! Didn't she owe some sort of duty at any rate toward those in her employment,—to those who slept under her roof?

" 'Twould have been better to have been kind to her then, than to be kind to me now!"

The proud Miss Althea Beekman, the dignified descendant of a long line of ancestors, turned red. Heretofore serenely confident of her own personal virtue and her own artificial standards of democracy, she now found herself humiliated and chagrined before this rough young criminal.

"You are right!" she confessed, her eyes smarting with sudden tears. "My position is quite illogical. But of course I had no idea! Please, please let me try to help you, if I can,—and Katie, too, if it isn't too late."

Shane O'Connell experienced contrition. After all, it was not seemly that he should be dictating to a lady. And he could never abide seeing a woman—particularly a pretty woman—cry.

"Forgive me, madam!" he begged, lowering his head.

"You were quite justified in all you said!" she assured him. "Please tell me everything that has happened. I have influence with the district attorney and—in other places. No doubt I can be of assistance to you. Of course, you can absolutely trust me!"

Shane O'Connell, looking into her honest gray eyes, knew that he could trust her. Slowly—brokenly—tensely, he told her how he had killed Red McGurk, and why.

The corridors were full of shadows when Althea Beekman put her hands on Shane O'Connell's shoulders and bade him good night. Though she abominated his crime and loathed him for having committed it, she felt in some way partially responsible, and she also perceived that, by the code of the O'Connells, Shane had done what he believed to be right. He had taken the law into his own hands and he was ready to pay the necessary penalty. He would have done the same thing all over again. To this extent at least he had her respect.

She found Mr. Tutt waiting for her on the bench by the warden's office.

"Well?" he asked.

"I haven't very good news for you," she answered. "He's confessed to me—told me everything—why he shot him and where he bought the pistol. It's a sad case! He's a brave boy, though! But what can you do with people who believe themselves justified in doing things like that?"

She did not notice Detective Eddie Conroy, of the D. A.'s office, standing behind an adjacent pillar, ostentatiously lighting a cigar; nor see his smile as he slowly walked away.

"Talk about luck!" exulted O'Brien, the yellow dog of the district attorney's office, an hour later to his chief. "What do you think, boss? Eddie Conroy heard Miss Beekman telling old man Tutt over in the Tombs that O'Connell had confessed to her! Say, how's that? Some evidence—what?"

"What good will that do us?" asked Peckham, glancing up with a scowl from his desk. "She won't testify for us."

"But she'll have to testify if we call her, won't she?" suggested his assistant.

The district attorney drummed on the polished surface before him.

"We—ell, I suppose so," he admitted. "But you can't just subpœna a woman like that without any warning and put her on the stand and make her testify. It would be too rough!"

"It's the only way to do it!" retorted O'Brien with a sly grin. "If she knew in advance that we were thinking of calling her, she'd beat it out of town."

"That's true," agreed his chief. "That's as far as she'd go, too, in defying the law. But I don't much like it. Those Beekmans have a lot of influence, and, if she got sore, she could make us a heap of trouble! Besides, it's sort of a scaly trick making her give up on him like that."

O'Brien raised his brows.

"Scaly trick! He's a murderer, isn't he? And he'll get off if we don't call her. It's a matter of duty, as I see it."

"All the same, my son, your suggestion has a rotten smell to it. We may have to do it—I don't say we won't—but it's risky business!" replied Peckham dubiously.

"It's a good deal less risky than not doing it, so far as your candidacy next autumn is concerned!" retorted his assistant. "We won't let her suspect what we're goin' to do; and the last minute I'll call her to the stand and cinch the case! She won't even know who called her! Perhaps I can arrange with Judge Babson to call her on some other point and then to pretend to sort of stumble onto the fact of the confession and examine her himself. That would let us out. I can smear it over, somehow."

"You'd better," commented Peckham, "unless you want a howl from the papers! It would make quite a story, if Miss Althea Beekman got on the rampage. She could have your scalp, my boy, if she wanted it!"

"And McGurk could have yours!" O'Brien reminded him with the impudence born of knowledge.

The prosecution of Shane O'Connell, which otherwise might have slowly languished and, languishing, died, took on new life owing to the evidence thus innocently delivered into the hands of the district attorney; in fact it became a *cause célèbre*. The essential elements to convict were now all there,—the *corpus delicti*, evidence of threats on the part of the defendant, of motive, of opportunity, and—his confession. The law which provides that the statement of an accused "is not sufficient to warrant his conviction without additional proof that the crime charged has been committed" would be abundantly satisfied, though without his confession there would have been no proof whatever that the crime charged had been committed by him.

Thus, without her knowing it, Miss Beekman was an essential witness and, in fact, the pivot upon which the entire case turned.

The day of the great sporting event came. With it arrived in full panoply the McGurks, their relatives and followers. All Cherry Hill seemed to have packed itself into Part I of the Supreme Court. There was an atmosphere somehow suggestive of the races or a prize fight. But it was a sporting event which savored of a sure thing,—really more like a hanging. They were there to make holiday over the law's revenge for the killing of the darling of the Pearl Button Kids.

Peckham personally assured McGurk that everything was copper-fastened.

"He's halfway up the river already!" he said jocularly.

And McGurk, swelling with importance and emotion, pulled a couple of cigars from his pocket and the two smoked the pipe of peace.

But the reader is not particularly concerned with the progress of the trial. It is enough to say that a jury with undershot jaws, who had proved by previous experience their indifference to capital punishment and to all human sympathy, were finally selected and that the witnesses were duly called, and testified to the usual facts, while the Pearl Button Kids and the rest, spitting surreptitiously beneath the benches, eagerly drank in every word. There was nothing for Mr. Tutt to do; nothing for him to deny. The case built itself up, brick by brick. And Shane O'Connell sat there unemotionally, hardly listening. There was nothing in the evidence to reflect in any way upon the honor of the O'Connells in general or in particular. He had done that which that honor demanded and he was ready to pay the penalty,—if the law could get him. He assumed that it would get him. So did the Tutts.

But when, toward the end of the third day, nothing had yet been brought forward to connect him with the crime, Tutt leaned over and whispered to Mr. Tutt, "D'ye know, I'm beginning to have a hunch there isn't any case!"

Mr. Tutt made an imperceptible gesture of assent.

"Looks that way," he answered out of the corner of his mouth. "Probably they'll spring the connecting evidence at the end and give us the *coup de grâce*."

At that moment a police witness was released from the stand

and O'Brien stepped to the bench and whispered something to the judge, who glanced at the clock and nodded. It was twenty minutes of four, and the jury were already getting restless, for the trial had developed into a humdrum, cut-and-dried affair.

Miss Beekman sitting far back in the rear of the court room suddenly heard O'Brien call her name, and a quiver of apprehension passed through her body. She had never testified in any legal proceeding, and the idea of getting up before such a crowd of people and answering questions filled her with dismay. It was so public! Still, if it was going to help O'Connell——

"Althea Beekman," bellowed Captain Phelan, "to the witness chair!"

Althea Beekman! The gentle lady felt as if she had been rudely stripped of all her protective clothing. Althea! Did not the law do her the courtesy of calling her even "Miss"? Nerving herself to the performance of her duty she falteringly made her way between the crowded benches, past the reporters' table, and round back of the jury box.

The judge, apparently a pleasant-faced, rather elderly man, bowed gravely to her, indicated where she should sit and administered the oath to her himself, subtly dwelling upon the phrase "the whole truth," and raising his eyes heavenward as he solemnly pronounced the words "so help you God!"

"I do!" declared Miss Beekman primly but decidedly.

Behind her upon the court-room wall towered in its flowing draperies the majestic figure of the Goddess of the Law, blindfolded and holding aloft the scales of justice. Beside her sat, in the silken robes of his sacred office, a judge who cleverly administered that law to advance his own interests and those of his political associates. In front of her, treacherously smiling, stood the cynical, bullet-headed O'Brien. At a great distance Mr. Tutt leaned on his elbows at a table beside Shane O'Connell. To them she directed her gaze and faintly smiled.

"Miss Beekman," began O'Brien as courteously as he knew how, "you reside, do you not, on Fifth Avenue, in this city and county?"

"I do," she answered with resolution.

"Your family have always lived in New York, have they not?"

"Since 1630," she replied deprecatingly and with more confidence.

"You are prominent in various philanthropic, religious and civic activities?"

"Not prominent; interested," she corrected him.

"And you make a practice of visiting prisoners in the Tombs?" She hesitated. What could this be leading to?

"Occasionally," she admitted.

"Do you know this defendant, Shane O'Connell?"

"Yes."

"Did you see him on the twenty-third day of last month?"

"I think so,—if that was the day."

"What day do you refer to?"

"The day I had the talk with him."

"Oh, you had a talk with him?"

"Yes."

"Where did you have that talk with him?"

"In the counsel room of the Tombs."

O'Brien paused. Even his miserable soul revolted at what he was about to do.

"What did he say?" he asked, nervously looking away.

Something in his hangdog look warned Miss Beekman that she was being betrayed, but before she could answer, Mr. Tutt was on his feet.

"One moment!" he cried. "May I ask a preliminary question?"

The court signified acquiescence.

"Was that conversation which you had with the defendant a confidential one?"

"I object to the question!" snapped O'Brien. "The law recognizes no confidential communications as privileged except those made to a priest, a physician or an attorney. The witness is none of these. The question is immaterial and irrelevant."

"That is the law," announced the judge, "but, under all the circumstances, I will permit the witness to answer."

Miss Beekman paused.

"Why," she began, "of course it was confidential, Mr. Tutt. O'Connell wouldn't have told me anything, if he had supposed for one moment I was going to repeat what he said. Besides, I suggested that I might be able to help him. Yes, certainly, our talk was confidential."

"I am sorry," gloated O'Brien, "but I shall have to ask you what it was."

"That is not a question," said Mr. Tutt calmly.

"What did the defendant say to you in the counsel room of the Tombs on the twenty-third of last month?" cautiously revised O'Brien.

"I object!" thundered Mr. Tutt, his form towering until seemingly it matched that of the blind goddess in height. "I object to the answer as requiring a breach of confidence which the law could not tolerate."

Judge Babson turned politely to Miss Beekman.

"I regret very much that I shall be obliged to ask you to state what the defendant said to you. You will recall that you yourself volunteered the information that you had had the talk in question. Otherwise"—he coughed and put up his hand—"we might possibly never have learned of it. A defendant cannot deprive the people of the right to prove what he may have divulged respecting his offense merely by claiming that it was in confidence. Public policy could never allow that. It may be unpleasant for you to answer the question but I must ask you to do so."

"But," she protested, "you certainly cannot expect me to betray a confidence! I asked O'Connell to tell me what he had done so that I could help him,—and he trusted me!"

"But you are not responsible for the law! He took his chance!" admonished the judge.

Slowly Miss Althea's indignation rose as she perceived the dastardly trick which O'Brien had played upon her. Already she suspected that the judge was only masquerading in the clothing of a gentleman. With a white face she turned to Mr. Tutt.

"Does the law require me to answer, Mr. Tutt?" she inquired.

"Do not ask questions—answer them," ordered Babson brusquely, feeling the change in her manner. "You are a witness for the people,—not for the defendant."

"I am not a witness against O'Connell!" she declared. "This man"—indicating O'Brien scornfully—"has in some way found out that I— Oh, surely the law doesn't demand anything so base as that!"

There was silence. The wheels of justice hung on a dead centre.

"Answer the question," remarked His Honor tartly.

All Miss Beekman's long line of ancestors turned in their graves. In her Beekman blood the chief justice, the ambassador, the great editor, the signer of the Declaration of Independence, stirred, awoke, rubbed their eyes and sternly reared themselves. And that blood,—blue though it was, instead of scarlet like the O'Connells'—boiled in her veins and burned through the delicate tissue of her cheeks.

"My conscience will not permit me to betray a confidence!" she cried angrily.

"I direct you to answer!" ordered the judge.

"I object to the court's threatening the witness!" interjected Mr. Tutt. "I wish it to appear upon the record that the manner of the court is most unjudicial and damaging to the defendant."

"Take your seat, sir!" barked Babson, his features swelling with anger. "Your language is contemptuous!"

The jury were leaning forward intently. Trained militiamen of the gibbet, they nevertheless admired this little woman's fearlessness and the old lawyer's pugnacity. On the rear wall the yellow face of the old self-regulating clock, that had gayly ticked so many men into the electric chair, leered shamelessly across at the blind goddess.

"Answer the question, madam! If, as you claim, you are a patriotic citizen of this commonwealth, having due respect for its institutions and for the statutes, you will not set up your own ideas of what the law ought to be in defiance of the law as it stands. I order you to answer! If you do not, I shall be obliged to take steps to compel you to do so."

In the dead silence that followed, the stones in the edifice of Miss Beekman's inherited complacency, with each beat of the clock, fell one by one to the ground until it was entirely demolished. Vainly she struggled to test her conscience by her loyalty to her country's laws. But the task was beyond her.

Tightly compressing her lips she sat silent in the chair, while the delighted reporters scribbled furious messages to their city editors that Miss Althea Beekman, one of the Four Hundred, was defying Judge Babson, and to rush up a camera man right off in a taxi, and to look her up in the morgue for a front-page story. O'Brien glanced uneasily at Babson. Possible defiance on the part of this usually unassuming lady had not entered into his calculations. The judge took a new tack.

"You probably do not fully understand the situation in which you are placed," he explained. "You are not responsible for the law. Neither are you responsible in any way for the consequences to this defendant, whatever they may be. The matter is entirely out of your hands. You are compelled to do as the court orders. As a law-abiding citizen you have no choice in the matter."

Miss Althea's modest intellect reeled, but she stood her ground, the ghost of the Signer at her elbow.

"I am sorry," she replied, "but my own self-respect will not allow me to answer."

"In that case," declared Babson, playing his trump card, "it will be my unpleasant duty to commit you for contempt."

There was a bustle of excitement about the reporters' table. Here was a story!

"Very well," answered Miss Beekman proudly. "Do as you see fit, and as your own duty and conscience demand."

The judge could not conceal his annoyance. The last thing in the world that he wished to do was to send Miss Althea to jail. But, having threatened her, he must carry out his threat or forever lose face.

"I will give the witness until to-morrow morning at half after ten o'clock to make up her mind what she will do," he announced after a hurried conference with O'Brien. "Adjourn court!"

Miss Beekman did not go to bed at all that night. Until a late hour she conferred in the secrecy of her Fifth Avenue library with her gray-haired solicitor, who, in some mysterious way, merely over the telephone, managed to induce the newspapers to omit any reference in their morning editions to his client's contemptuous conduct.

"There's no way out of it, my dear," he said finally as he took his leave—he was her father's cousin and very fond of her—"this judge has the power to send you to jail if he wants to—and dares to! It's an even chance whether he will dare to or not. It depends on whether he prefers to stand well with the McGurks or with the general public. Of course I respect your attitude, but really I think you are a little quixotic. Points of honor are too ephemeral to be debated in courts of justice. To do so would be to open the door to all kinds of abuses. Dishonest witnesses would constantly avail themselves of the opportunity to avoid giving evidence."

"Dishonest witnesses would probably lie in the first place!" she declared.

"True! I quite overlooked that!" he replied. "But to-day the question isn't open. It is settled, whether we like it or not. No pledge of privacy, no oath of secrecy, can avail against demand in a court of justice. Even confessions obtained by fraud are admissible—though we might wish otherwise."

"Nothing you have said seems to me to alter the situation."

"Very well," he replied. "I guess that settles it. Knowing you and the Beekman breed! There's one thing I must say," he added as he stood in the doorway after bidding her good night—"that old fellow Tutt has behaved pretty well, leaving you entirely alone this way. I always had an idea he was a sort of shyster. Most attorneys of that class would have been sitting on your doorstep all the evening trying to persuade you to stick to your resolution not to give their client away, and to do the square thing. But he's done nothing of the sort. Rather decent on the whole!"

"Perhaps he recognizes a woman of honor when he sees one!" she retorted.

"Honor!" he muttered as he closed the door. "What crimes are sometimes committed in thy name!"

But on the steps he stopped and looked back affectionately at the library window.

"After all, Althea's a good sport!" he remarked to himself.

At or about the same moment a quite dissimilar conference was being held between Judge Babson and Assistant District Attorney O'Brien in the café of the Passamaquoddy Club.

"She'll cave!" declared O'Brien, draining his glass. "Holy Mike! No woman like her is going to stay in jail! Besides, if you don't commit her everybody will say that you were scared to,—yielded to influence. You're in the right, and it will be a big card for you to show that you aren't afraid of anybody!"

Babson pulled nervously on his cigar.

"Maybe that's so," he said, "but I don't much fancy an appellate court sustaining me on the law and at the same time roasting hell out of me as a man!"

"Oh, they won't do that!" protested O'Brien. "How could they? All they're interested in is the law!"

"I've known those fellows to do queer things sometimes," answered the learned judge. "And the Beekmans are pretty powerful people."

"Well, so are the McGurks!" warned O'Brien.

"Now, Miss Beekman," said Judge Babson most genially the next morning, after that lady had taken her seat in the witness chair and the jury had answered to their names, "I hope you feel differently to-day about giving your testimony. Don't you think that after all it would be more fitting if you answered the question?"

Miss Althea firmly compressed her lips.

"At least let me read you some of the law on the subject," continued His Honor patiently. "Originally many people, like yourself, had the mistaken idea that what they called their honor should be allowed to intervene between them and their duty. And even the courts sometimes so held. But that was long ago—in the sixteenth and seventeenth centuries. To-day the law wisely recognizes no such thing. Let me read you what Baron Hotham said, in Hill's Trial in 1777, respecting the testimony of a witness who very properly told the court what the accused had said to him. It is very clearly put:

" 'The defendant certainly thought him his friend, and he'—the defendant—'therefore did disclose all this to him. Gentlemen, one has only to say further that, if this point of honor was to be so sacred as that a man who comes by knowledge of this sort from an offender was not to be at liberty to disclose it, the most atrocious criminals would every day escape punishment; and therefore it is that the wisdom of the law knows nothing of that point of honor.' "

Miss Beekman listened politely.

"I am sorry," she replied with dignity. "I shall not change my mind. I refuse to answer the question, and—and you can do whatever you like with me."

"Do you understand that you are in contempt of this court? Do you intend to show contempt for this court?" he demanded wrathfully.

"I do," answered Miss Althea. "I have contempt for this court."

A titter danced along the benches and some fool in the back of the room clapped his hands.

Judge Babson's face grew hard and his eyes narrowed to steel points.

"The witness stands committed for contempt," he announced bitingly. "I direct that she be confined in the city prison for thirty days and pay a fine of two hundred and fifty dollars. Madam, you will go with the officer."

Miss Althea rose, while the ghost of the Signer encircled her with his arm.

Mr. Tutt was already upon his feet. He knew that the ghost of the Signer was there.

"May I ask the court if the witness, having been committed for the contemptuous conduct of which she is obviously guilty, may remain in your chambers until adjournment, in order that she may arrange her private affairs?"

"I will grant her that privilege," agreed Judge Babson with internal relief. "The request is reasonable. Captain Phelan, you may take the witness into my robing-room and keep her there for the present."

With her small head erect, her narrow shoulders thrown back, and with a resolute step Miss Althea passed behind the jury box and disappeared.

The twelve looked at one another dubiously. Both Babson and O'Brien seemed nervous and undecided.

"Well, call your next witness," remarked the judge finally.

"But I haven't any more witnesses!" growled O'Brien. "And you know it almighty well, you idiot!" he muttered under his breath.

"If that is the people's case, I move for the defendant's immediate discharge," cried Mr. Tutt, jumping to his feet. "There is no evidence connecting him with the crime."

McGurk, furious, sprang toward the bar.

"See here! Wait a minute! Hold on, Judge! I can get a hundred witnesses——"

"Sit down!" shouted one of the officers, thrusting him back. "Keep quiet!"

Babson looked at O'Brien and elevated his eyebrows. Then, as O'Brien gave a shrug, the judge turned to the expectant jury and said in apologetic tones:

"Gentlemen of the jury, where the people have failed to prove the defendant's guilt beyond a reasonable doubt, it is the duty of the court to direct a verdict. In this case, though by inference the testimony points strongly toward the prisoner, there is no direct proof against him and I am accordingly constrained—much as I regret it—to instruct you to return a verdict of not guilty."

In the confusion which followed the rendition of the verdict a messenger entered breathlessly and, forcing his way through the crowd, delivered a folded paper to Mr. Tutt, who immediately rose and handed it to the clerk; and that official, having hurriedly perused it and pursed his lips in surprise, passed it over the top of the bench to the judge.

"What's this?" demanded Babson. "Don't bother me now with trifles!"

"But it's a writ of habeas corpus, Your Honor, signed by Judge Winthrop, requiring the warden to produce Miss Beekman in Part I of the Supreme Court, and returnable forthwith," whispered Mr. McGuire in an awe-stricken voice. "I can't disregard that, you know!"

"What!" cried Babson. "How on earth could he have issued a writ in this space of time? The thing's impossible!"

"If Your Honor please," urbanely explained Mr. Tutt, "since—having known Miss Beekman's father—I anticipated that the witness would pursue the course of conduct which, in fact, she has, I prepared the necessary papers early this morning and, as soon as you ordered her into custody, my partner, who was waiting in Judge Winthrop's chambers, presented them to His Honor, secured his signature and brought the writ here in a taxicab."

Nobody seemed to be any longer interested in O'Connell. The reporters had left their places and pushed their way into the inclosure before the dais. In the rear of the room O'Brien was vainly engaged in trying to placate the Pearl Button Kids, who were loudly swearing vengeance upon both him and Peckham. It was a scene as nearly turbulent as the old yellow clock had ever witnessed. Even the court officers abandoned any effort to maintain order and joined the excited group about Mr. Tutt before the bench.

"Does Your Honor desire that this matter be argued before the Supreme Court?" enquired Mr. Tutt suavely. "If so, I will ask that the prisoner be paroled in my custody. Judge Winthrop is waiting."

Babson had turned pale. Facing a dozen newspapermen, pencil in hand, he quailed. To hell with "face." Why, if he went on any longer with the farce, the papers would roast the life out of him. With an apology for a smile that was, in fact, a ghastly grin, he addressed himself to the waiting group of jurymen, lawyers and reporters.

"Of course, gentlemen," he said, "I never had any real intention of dealing harshly with Miss Beekman. Undoubtedly she acted quite honestly and according to her best lights. She is a very estimable member of society. It will be unnecessary, Mr. Tutt, for you to argue the writ before Judge Winthrop. The relator, Althea Beekman, is discharged."

IN WITNESS WHEREOF

I

"What I want is a lawyer who can deliver the goods; I don't care what it costs. Can I talk business with you?"

The grim-visaged woman sitting opposite Mr. Ephraim Tutt looked across the desk at him significantly.

"I don't know why not," replied the lawyer affably. "Business is what I'm looking for; what every lawyer is after, I guess!"

"Well"—she hesitated, striving to penetrate the sphinxlike mask of his wizened old face, which had defied lawyers and judges and poker players alike for half a century—"you drew Cabel's will, and you're the executor named in it. I know that much, because he's told me so. Now, it's this way: Cabel wants to make some changes in that will of his, but, besides being old and feeble, he's crotchety and cantankerous and suspicious of almost everybody. But he'll listen to you. You're his executor and the proper one to do it anyway."

"Well," hazarded Mr. Tutt blandly, "as I said before—why not?"

"So naturally I've come to you. Besides, I've heard quite a lot about your firm; and I guess you and I can get along pretty well together."

"I'm sure we can," smiled the attorney. "I always strive to please."

"What's more, I'll see that your fee is promptly paid—with maybe a little besides!" she concluded meaningly.

Mr. Tutt searched her face.

"Am I to understand then that you—and not Mr. Baldwin—are my client?" he inquired pointedly.

Mrs. Alfreda Baldwin smiled to herself. She wasn't going to let the old fox catch her—put her in a position where maybe she would have to pay his bill.

"Not at all!" she retorted. "It is my husband who wants his will changed. He's your client—not me. All I say is that you don't need to worry about getting paid. Anyhow I don't see what difference it makes which of us is your client."

Mr. Tutt fumbled in a long box upon his desk and selected a cigar resembling in shape and general appearance what a coiffeur would refer to as "a rat."

"Do you mind if I smoke?" he inquired ceremoniously. "Answering your question—it might make a lot of difference which of two persons happened to be one's client."

"How do you mean?" she demanded. "Of course I don't mind if you smoke."

Mr. Tutt carefully ignited the attenuated stogy which he had excavated from its stratified brethren.

"A lawyer has to be faithful to his retainer—even if sometimes he doesn't get it," he announced, exhaling a poisonous cloud of greenish-gray smoke. "It is the duty of the attorney to be loyal to the interests of the person who employs him and to carry out his wishes to the best of his ability, just as it is the duty of the client to compensate him for his services. Now, if those interests conflict with those of any other person——"

"Oh, I understand all that!" she interrupted. "That doesn't enter into it here. Mr. Baldwin is your client. I am only his agent—his messenger, if you choose. He will pay your bill. But, as it happens, our interests and wishes are identical."

Mr. Tutt nodded behind his smoke screen.

"That's all right, then!"

She returned his glance fixedly. He had not put anything over on her and he had, she opined, absorbed her hint about the "little besides" and all the rest of it.

"I don't want to have Mr. Baldwin disturbed any more than is absolutely necessary," she continued. "We both thought that I could tell you what he wanted to do with his money and that you could draw up a codicil here in your office and bring it up to the house for him to sign. That's the simplest, easiest way, isn't it? A codicil?"

"Quite so!" agreed Mr. Tutt. "I can easily do that if you really know what changes he wants to make in the disposition of his property. But there's no use preparing a codicil and having it engrossed only to find you've got to do it all over again."

"You won't have to do that in this case. I know—that is, Mr. Baldwin knows—exactly what he wants to do. I've been over it with him most carefully. It's all written down right here."

She produced from a black bead bag several sheets of folded note-paper covered closely with handwriting. Mr. Tutt drew toward him a yellow pad, regretfully laid down his stogy and took up a pencil. Mrs. Baldwin put on a pair of heavy spectacles, which intensified her already hawkish appearance, and settled back in her chair.

"First, he wants to bequeath outright ten thousand dollars each to the Museum of Art, the Museum of Natural History, the Children's Aid Society, the Charity Organization Society, St. Luke's Hospital, and Columbia University."

"That makes sixty thousand dollars," commented Mr. Tutt, jotting down their names. "What next?"

"Then he wants to leave thirty thousand dollars to Alvin H. Spearman, of Englewood, New Jersey."

"Who is he?" asked the lawyer, his pencil poised.

"An old friend of his," she answered. "And thirty thousand dollars to his wife, Rowena Howell Spearman."

"That makes another sixty thousand dollars," said Mr. Tutt.

"Twenty thousand each to Alfred Spearman, the son of Alvin Spearman; Esther S. Bowman, of Trenton; Anna S. Rawson, of Scranton; and Josephine S. Briggs, of New York City."

"Now you've got two hundred and forty thousand."

Mrs. Baldwin eyed him a trifle suspiciously.

"What's that?" she snapped.

"In personal legacies, I mean," he explained quickly. "He's disposed of two hundred and forty thousand in all."

Mrs. Baldwin checked off something on the sheet of note-paper in her lap.

"Then he wants to leave ten thousand each to the following: Almina Bostwick, of Jersey City; Georgina H. Hibbard, of Flatbush, Long Island; Isabel F. Hawkins, of Flushing, Long Island; Mary P. Daly, of Riverdale, New York; Edith L. Mills, of Yonkers, New York; and Althea W. Rose, of Ringwood, New Jersey."

"Sixty more," scored Mr. Tutt. "Makes three hundred thousand dollars. Then what?"

"Twenty-five thousand to the Nurses' Benefit Club."

"What's that?"

"A charitable corporation," she answered shortly. "Then fifteen thousand each to his physicians, Doctor Samuel Woodman and Doctor Richard Aspinall."

"I have it," said the lawyer.

"Then there are a few smaller legacies: Five thousand dollars to Bridget Mulcahy, the cook; five thousand to Patrick Moynahan, the butler; five thousand to Pierre Larue, the valet; and five thousand to Agnes Roony, the parlor maid. He believes in being liberal with servants."

"So I see!" observed Mr. Tutt. "And with the medical profession as well!"

"Oh, he's very fond of both Doctor Woodman and Doctor

Aspinall!" she assured him. "They have been lifelong friends!"

"Anything more?"

"Only his legacy to me—two hundred and fifty thousand—and, of course, I'm also to be the residuary legatee," said Mrs. Baldwin, folding up her notes. "You'll continue as executor. How soon can you have the codicil ready?"

"By to-morrow afternoon," he replied. "It's quite simple."

"Then bring it up to-morrow evening so that Mr. Baldwin can sign it," she directed. "About nine o'clock, say?"

"As you like," he agreed. "If that will be more convenient for your husband than to have him come here."

"Oh, he couldn't possibly come here!" she asserted. "He's sick in bed!"

Mrs. Baldwin arose and pulled down her black jacket, which had a tendency to ride upward upon her ample figure; and Mr. Tutt arose also. There was something about her which inspired in him more than dislike—he could not say exactly what, whether it was the beetling nose, the compressed lips, the expansive, tightly corseted bosom, the flabby brown skin beneath her chin, which merged into the pendulous cheeks—like an old mastiff, he decided. A full-rigger! How could any man in his senses have married her? And the thought quite naturally suggested that perhaps the man hadn't been.

II

"Where did you get little Eva?" chirped Tutt, peering at his partner over his goggles through the door after the lady's departure. "I was quite worried at first over leaving you alone with her!"

Mr. Tutt's long wrinkled face wreathed itself in an expansive grin. "Isn't she terrible!" he ejaculated.

"Some crocodile!" asserted the lesser Tutt. "I can see now what the fellow meant when he said that the female of the species is more deadly than the male! What kind friend passed her on to us?"

"Nobody—she came herself," replied the senior partner. "I think she must like my looks!"

"B-r-r-h!" shivered Tutt, shielding his face with his hands. "I hope she won't take a fancy to me!"

"You're safe!" laughed his partner. "Mrs. Georgie Allison has rendered you immune to the attractions of the opposite sex for all time."

"Who told you about that?" queried Tutt rather peevishly.

"Never mind! Never mind!" returned the old lawyer airily. "You can't keep all your little peccadilloes concealed from the public eye."

"I know! Miss Wiggin must have double-crossed me!" growled Tutt. "Well, reverting to the subject we were discussing, what was the Lady Gorgon's name?"

"Mrs. Cabel Baldwin."

"Wife of the old fellow that married his trained nurse?"

Mr. Tutt gave a fervid start of surprise.

"What!" he ejaculated. "Really?"

"Don't you recall the case? 'Nurse Spearman'—and all that? It was in the papers," Tutt reminded him. "He got out of bed when he had the pneumonia or something and beat it over to Jersey and married her before a J. P. without even telling his own daughter. That was about three years ago. He was seventy-two; she was forty-seven. He'd be over seventy-five now, and she'd be fifty."

"She would! She is!" assented Mr. Tutt. "Or stronger!"

"There was a grand row about it!" said Tutt. "But nobody could do anything. The Constitution guarantees to every man the inalienable right to marry his trained nurse. But she was such an old chisel-face that it seemed as though she must have chloroformed him first. She'd been married before, too; twice, I mean!"

"So that's it!" remarked Mr. Tutt. "Did you say there was a daughter?"

"I have an idea there was, but if I remember correctly she was away at college or somewhere. I don't recall all the details. But look out for nursie! What did she want?"

"To have us draw a codicil to her husband's will."

"Oho!" piped Tutt. "And does little birdie get the big fat worm?"

"She gets half of it; the other half of the worm goes to various individuals and charities."

"That's funny!" commented the junior Tutt, pursing his lips. "If she was after the kale why should she let anybody else have a rake-off?"

Mr. Tutt took a turn up and down his office, then he amputated another stogy, lit the remains, leaned back in his swivel chair, crossed his congress boots upon his desk and folded his hands behind his head.

"Simply because that's the artistic way to do it," said he. "Don't you remember the Blodgett case? Blodgett was ninety-one and dead at the top; he'd had senile dementia for fifteen years. A woman got hold of him—only that time it was a young one—and induced him to make a will in her favor. All she had to do was to take him out to concerts and ride him round the park in a victoria. Well, when he died it was discovered that he'd left her the greater part of his fortune—a couple of millions; but—and here was the clever part of it—he'd apparently divided another million between Harvard, Yale, and Princeton, with the result that, although the heirs at law and next of kin contested the probate, they found the three most influential universities in the country lined up against them, with all their counsel, naturally including the leaders of the bar, alongside Little Bright Eyes—who succeeded in probating the will, got her two millions and bought a foreign prince and a château on Lake Geneva with them."

"Pretty good!" nodded Tutt. "And is that the game our old battle-axe is trying to pull?"

"Here's the horoscope. Read it for yourself," answered Mr. Tutt, pushing the yellow pad toward his partner with his toe. "You'll note that the very first thing she did was to square a few of our more select public institutions—like the Museum of Art and St. Luke's Hospital."

"Holy crickets!" mused Tutt. "I wonder if she could be the same girl—tired of living on Lake Geneva with her prince—and looking for further adventures!"

"No," declared his partner. "You couldn't give this one away with a bonus of two million dollars."

"Aha! What's this?" suddenly cried Tutt, scanning the prospectus of Mr. Baldwin's proposed benefactions. "Here's another little joker! Twenty thousand dollars to the domestics and thirty to the doctors! She's got all the witnesses signed, sealed and delivered! He could be a raving maniac and there'd be nobody to prove it. No doctor—that is, no 'bug doctor'—is going to admit that any patient of his can have senile dementia who has sense enough to leave him fifteen thousand dollars! We ought to take Alfreda into partnership!"

"But you haven't covered it all yet!" said Mr. Tutt. "I'll wager that if we looked into it we'd find she's not only given herself a quarter of a million and the residuary but in order to prevent any possible slip-up she's salted a quarter million around where she can get hold of it afterward if she misses out on her own legacy. She's left her father and mother thirty thousand each, and the four little Spearmans eighty more; to say nothing of half a dozen of her intimate female friends and a nursing society of which she probably controls the board of directors."

"Rather a speedy client!" affirmed Tutt.

Mr. Tutt shook his head.

"She's not our client."

"Who is, then?"

"Her husband."

"It's all the same thing," affirmed the lesser Tutt. "You can soak her a thousand or fifteen hundred just for drawing a codicil like that! And think of the fight we'll have on our hands when the old boy dies! Makes no difference to us which way the cat jumps. If she gets him to execute your codicil we'll have to defend it against the heirs on the ground of mental incapacity; and if he won't execute it she'll have us attacking all his prior wills in her behalf on the same ground. Coming and going! Both ends against the mid. It'll take six months in court—after we finally get there! Why, it's worth thirty thousand dollars to us!"

"Do you really think so, now?" murmured his partner. "Thirty thousand dollars is a lot of money—a powerful lot of money!"

The morality—or rather the immorality—of lawyers has been the subject of jest since the days when the bare fact that a man could read and write rendered him immune to punishment for crime. "Benefit of clergy" was felt to be a joke; and so was the law. The pun that made "lawyer" and "liar" indistinguishable dates doubtless from considerably before the days of Falstaff. Not only, as Bumble said, was the law "a ass, a idiot," but lawyers were natural-born pettifoggers, crooks, thieves, tricksters, and rascals. An honest lawyer? There was no such animal!

We have no desire at the present writing to enter into a general defense of the conduct of our brethren of the bar, but merely take occasion to point out that in many instances the lawyer is really no more deserving of censure than the layman the product of whose skill is subsequently used by another for an unlawful or immoral purpose. Shall no more whips be manufactured because some ruffians use them upon their wives? Or chisels, lest burglars avail themselves of them in their unholy business? Shall the cobbler cease from cobbling for fear that some one may hurl his shoe after a blushing bride? Tut-tut! There is nothing under the sun that cannot be made subject to the devil's ingenuity. We have even heard of two murders committed within a single month by means of oyster shells. Yet, shall we be forbidden oysters?

The reader has already grasped our analogue. Shall there be no cakes and ale because a custard pie can be used as an instrument of assault? And, similarly, because a will, deed, bond or other paper writing may, perhaps, be used eventually to perpetrate a fraud, is that any reason why an innocent attorney should not draw it up? He may suspect that old Hardscrabble intends to cheat the Widow Perkins, or that the rifles for which he has drawn the bill of sale to Mr. Jones are intended for Mr. Villa; but the very law by which the attorney earns his livelihood requires him to give the benefit of the doubt to an accused and presume him innocent until the contrary is proved. Why, then, should he not give that same doubt to old Hardscrabble, to Mr. Jones—and to himself?

Thus, shall a lawyer refuse to draw a will because his client might— if he were made the subject of prolonged study by a faculty of alien-ists—be shown to be without testamentary capacity? Shall he take the bread out of his children's mouths because the fruit of his professional labors may, in the hands of another, be used to work an injustice? Must every attorney maintain a hospital, an observation ward in connection with his office? Nay! Such a thought is nonsense! It is no part of a lawyer's business to act as a spy upon his client or anticipate and expose his contemplated iniquities.

Had Tutt & Tutt refused to draw the codicil to Mr. Baldwin's will Alfreda would simply have given the job to some other firm. They knew well that a will is like any article of merchandise purveyed in market overt; for instance—a bologna. If the buyer is planning to administer the bologna to an infant of tender years—or days—it may, it is true, thereby become an instrument of infanticide; and in like case if a will or a codicil is about to be offered for signature to an imbecile it may become a link in a chain of fraud; but why gratuitously visit upon either the will or the bologna a foul suspicion which may in fact be entirely unwarranted?

Let us admit at once—whether or not the reader be convinced by this tosh, which we contend is as sound as most legal argument and equally edifying—let us admit freely, frankly, and without reserve that it did not occur to Tutt or even to Mr. Tutt to decline to draw the codicil proposed by Mrs. Baldwin. It was a perfectly good legal job for anybody. It would take Mr. Tutt, with a stereotyped office form before him, twenty minutes—no more, probably—to dictate it to Miss Sondheim, who would thereupon pound it out on the typewriter; then Mr. Tutt would correct and possibly revise it; and Scraggs, the inebriated scrivener in the wire cage in the outer office, would have a perfect time writing it all out in a beautiful Spencerian hand on glossy imitation parchment; after which Miss Wiggin, the

chief clerk, Willie, the office boy, and Miss Sondheim would deck
it out like a new born babe in dainty blue ribbons, tie a beautiful
red seal around its neck, roll it up tenderly in tissue-paper and put
it to sleep in the top drawer of a desk until it was time for somebody
to unwrap it, spread it out upon the counterpane of the death chamber and, pointing to the final paragraph, beginning with the fateful
words "In witness whereof," place the pen in the shaking hand of
the testator and say: "Well, Mr. Baldwin, you understand, of course,
that this is your will? Yes, I said, 'Your will.' Will. W-i-l-l—WILL!
Yes! Sign here!"

And Tutt & Tutt would thereupon receive in due course from
the executors a check for a thousand dollars, of which about nine
hundred and ninety-three would be net. Why should Mr. Tutt have
refused this choice tidbit of humdrum practice—particularly as
will-drawing was one of the best things that he did? Can he properly
be censured for so doing?

Yet, quite naturally, what might be called the internal evidence of
possible fraud contained in the codicil itself excited his interest. Certainly every step had been taken to render the instrument, if executed,
impregnable to attack. However, there was no particular reason why
it should be assumed that the scheme had not emanated from the mind
of the old gentleman himself. Many a testator provides his legatees
with a doughty legal champion by leaving a fat legacy to some
eleemosynary institution which will lose it if the will is denied probate. But in this instance, it is true, there were other indications that
Mrs. Baldwin was engaged in feathering her nest in an expert manner
and safely anchoring said nest against the assaults of outraged heirs
and next of kin.

Now, Mr. Tutt practised law largely for the fun of it, for he really
didn't need the money, and he scented in the visit of Mrs. Alfreda
Baldwin a plot almost as exciting as a detective story. And that was
why he sent for Mr. Bonnie Doon, that wise and finished specimen
of young-gentleman-about-town, who made himself generally useful
to Tutt & Tutt, and instructed him to ascertain by whatever means
were at his disposal all he could about the past career of Mrs. Cabel
Baldwin, née Alfreda Spearman, daughter of Alvin Spearman, Es-
quire, of Englewood, New Jersey.

III

"Tell Oscar I want him here at nine o'clock without the car," said
Mrs. Baldwin from her desk in the library to the girl sitting listlessly
by the centre table with her hands in her lap. "Don't send the message,

either. Speak to him yourself. And tell the other servants they can have the evening out."

The girl arose silently. She was languid, pale, harassed, with dark circles under her eyes, but she bore herself with dignity.

"Why don't you answer when you're spoken to?" snapped the older woman. "One would think you—and not I—was the mistress of this house!"

"I haven't any such delusion," answered the girl tonelessly. "I will take your message. You know very well I'd not stay here another day except for my father."

"You know well enough where your bread is buttered!" shot back her stepmother with a sneer. "You are dependent upon me for everything you have in this world. And you had better mind your p's and q's."

"Shall I tell Oscar what you want him for?" asked the girl.

"Ha!" replied the other. "You want to find out, do you? Well, it's none of your business!"

The girl shrugged her shoulders and walked slowly toward the door.

"And then come back here!" ordered Mrs. Baldwin. "I don't want you hanging round your father. He can't stand your whining and crying!"

The girl controlled herself with difficulty, and once in the privacy of the hall outside the library burst into tears. She had been living under the same strain ever since the previous spring upon her graduation from college, where her father had sent her at the death of her mother four years before that. She had gone away from home leaving him a melancholy but apparently well old man. A year later she had received a sudden telegram from him announcing his marriage in Jersey City to an unknown woman who, it turned out, had been acting as his nurse during a sudden attack of pneumonia.

She had been crushed not only by her father's forgetfulness of her mother in so short a time but also by the notoriety that had followed the old man's escapade and the state of mental and physical deterioration in which she found him on her return. From being a handsome, vigorous, upstanding old gentleman he had shrivelled away into a bent, tottering, querulous invalid afraid of his own shadow; at times, when they were alone, responding to her caresses with something of his former affection, but in general furtive, suspicious, cowering before this strange, ugly woman who had in some sinister way secured mastery over him—fearful in her presence to call his soul his own. There seemed to be something hypnotic about the ex-nurse's influence, for the mere sound of her voice was enough to set his shrunken old limbs trembling. And if when she was downstairs she heard him up and moving about in his room she had only to call up through the well, and he would obediently clamber back into bed again.

So Lydia Baldwin found herself half servant, half prisoner in her father's house. She would, as she had said, have fled out into the world and earned her own living had it not been for the possibility that she might be of some service to him. She saw her father getting weaker and weaker, but was not allowed to minister to him save under the direction and supervision of her jailer. Everybody employed in the establishment—in fact everybody who came there—was on her stepmother's pay-roll. Even the doctors were persons of the latter's own choosing, with whom she had had some mysterious association in the past. Surrounded by spies, without money, Lydia Baldwin was treated as a hostage, all her movements watched and reported upon.

At rare intervals her father would awake as from a nightmare and, once a month, perhaps, would have a day when he seemed almost like himself again and would even make feeble jokes about his condition. These exceptional phases occurred without premonition and were immediately followed by states of depression in which he believed his end to be near and during which he insisted upon the constant presence of his wife, upon whom he then seemed utterly dependent. At such times Lydia suffered torture, since she could not even render her father the solace of her affection. Then, and only then, was she really tempted to accept Henry Holborn's offer of marriage and escape from the domestic hell in which she lived. For, although Henry was only twenty-five—she was twenty-three—he was earning a good salary in an architect's office, and his abilities were recognized as such as to entitle him to view the future with confidence. That she would remain penniless Lydia had no doubt. Her stepmother would never permit her father to leave her anything; and although he had once told her shortly after her mother's death that she would one day be a rich woman, since his second marriage he had never referred to the subject.

IV

It was precisely nine o'clock when Mr. Tutt mounted the front stoop of the Baldwin mansion and rang the bell. Mrs. Baldwin opened the door herself.

"Good evening," she said affably, extending a muscular hand, with a smile as convincing as that of a hyena. "Glad you're so prompt!"

Over her shoulder the old lawyer could see the drooping figure of a young girl standing disconsolately at the head of the stairs leading to the next floor. As he took off his coat and hat she turned away and retreated into the shadow.

"Lydia, come down here!" called up Mrs. Baldwin. "I don't want you bothering your father. Come and meet Mr. Tutt!"

The girl obediently emerged once more and, resting her hand upon the rail of the staircase, came wearily down. Descending thus, with the half light falling upon her pale face against the background of shadow, she reminded him of a Burne-Jones figure standing at evening beside some lily-covered pool. Mr. Tutt's parched old soul yearned to her like a withered tree whose leaves thirst for a cool breeze after a sultry day.

"Hurry up!" ordered Mrs. Baldwin. "Don't keep us waiting all the evening."

The girl lifted her chin proudly and as she did so caught the tender gleam in the old man's eyes. There was no mistaking that look of pity, almost of affection with which he was regarding her. She smiled faintly.

"This is my stepdaughter, Lydia," said Mrs. Baldwin.

Mr. Tutt moved a step forward, and took the girl's hand and bent over it as she stood upon the stairs above him. Then, still holding it in his, he led her down the remaining steps. Something—we do not know what it is that leaps from heart to heart on such occasions—passed between them. Neither spoke. Yet each said to the other, "I am your friend!"

"I want you to sit here in the front parlor, Lydia," said Mrs. Baldwin, "and when I call to you, send up Oscar to your father's bedroom. If anybody should ring the front-door bell, you answer it. The servants are out."

"Very well," answered Lydia coldly.

"Now," continued Mrs. Baldwin, "if you are all ready we'll go up-stairs." She lowered her voice to a whisper, so that Lydia, who had gone into the drawing-room, might not hear. "Have you got the codicil all ready?"

Mr. Tutt nodded and followed her up to the next landing. The woman turned the knob of the door nearest the head of the stairs and pushed it open with a suggestion of stealth. Certain people cannot move without giving the impression of trying to stalk some prey. Usually it is a man trying to stalk a woman. This time it was a woman trying to stalk a man.

In a large high-ceiled room, dimly lighted by only a green-shaded reading-lamp, an old man lay propped up in bed. The face was gaunt, the eyes lustreless, the mouth drooping. Both arms were extended across the sheet in front of him, motionless and parallel.

"Here is somebody to see you, Grandpa!" said Mrs. Baldwin as if she were speaking to a child who must be at one and the same time cajoled and warned to be good.

The old man in the bed licked his lips and a hardly perceptible quiver passed over his features.

"This is the lawyer," announced his wife. "Mr. Tutt. You know him."

A puzzled look—of recollection, almost of recognition—flickered in the senile eyes, followed by one of dread fused with cunning.

"Yes," he replied thickly in a half whisper, "I know him."

"He has drawn up the codicil for you to sign." She might as well have added the words "like a good little boy."

Mr. Baldwin made no reply. He appeared for the moment to have forgotten that they were there.

"Cabel!" said Mrs. Baldwin in a metallic tone, stepping toward the bed. "Cabel—pay attention!"

The old man shrank back as if he had been slapped in the face.

"I'm listening," he protested feebly, blinking.

"Sit down, won't you?" directed the wife. "He's a little dopey to-night. But he's all right. You take that chair by the bed."

Mr. Tutt did as he was told. What was the truth behind this rather grisly tableau? What was the old man's real condition? Was he of sound and disposing mind and memory?

Mrs. Baldwin stepped to the foot of the bed, facing her husband.

"Now, Cabel, listen to me!" she repeated, articulating with meticulous distinctness. "You're going to make a codicil to your will—understand?"

The old man peered craftily at her out of the shadowy caverns of his eyes.

"My will," he muttered slyly. "I've made my will."

"But you're going to make a codicil to it. You want to!" she said, focusing her eyes upon him. "Grandpa wants to make a codicil to his will—all nice and fresh!"

"A codicil," mumbled Mr. Baldwin, as if to himself. "Yes—yes! That's so. I want a codicil. Where is it?"

"The lawyer has it—right there!" she said. "Here is the pen. Put the paper there in front of him."

"But I must read it over to him first," declared Mr. Tutt. "I must be sure it contains his wishes."

"It isn't necessary!" she answered quickly. "I've been all over it with him a dozen times. You see how hard it is to get him to concentrate! I was a week finding out what he wanted. The sooner it is done the better!"

"But it is necessary that I should read it to him!" protested the lawyer. "It would be most irregular if I did not! Mr. Baldwin, I am about to read over to you the provisions of the codicil which I have drawn according to what I understand to be your wishes. Will you kindly give me your attention?"

Mr. Baldwin turned and stared vacantly at Mr. Tutt.

"I've made my will," he repeated.

"This is a codicil."

"Oh, yes. A codicil."

Mr. Baldwin nodded once or twice as if now entirely conversant with what was going on.

"Shall I read it to you?" inquired Mr. Tutt a little impatiently.

"Yes—read it to me," said Mr. Baldwin.

Mr. Tutt held the carefully engrossed document beneath the lamp and began:

" 'In the name of God, amen! I, Cabel Baldwin, being of sound mind and memory, do hereby make, publish and declare this as and for a codicil to my last will and testament——' "

Suddenly the old gentleman began to whimper.

"I want my milk!" he whined. "I want my hot milk! Where is it?"

Mrs. Baldwin uttered an exclamation of annoyance.

"Can't you wait a minute?" she cried angrily. "It will only take a moment."

"I want my milk! I can't do anything without my milk!" he moaned pettishly.

"Well, well! I'll get it for you!" she exclaimed. "I'll be right back."

She was gone about five minutes, at the end of which she returned with a glass of warm milk, which she put to the old gentleman's lips.

"Have you read him the will?" she asked out of the corner of her mouth.

"No," answered Mr. Tutt. "I waited for you to come back. 'In the name of God, amen! I, Cabel Baldwin, being of sound mind and memory, do hereby make, publish and declare this as and for a codicil to my last will and testament, which I otherwise confirm in all respects not inconsistent herewith:

" 'First: I give and bequeath out of my personal estate ten thousand dollars each to the Metropolitan Museum of Art——' "

Slowly, carefully, Mr. Tutt proceeded to read through the document. It was impossible to tell whether Mr. Baldwin heard him or not.

"Do you understand what I have been reading to you?" asked Mr. Tutt at the end of the performance.

"Yes; it is a codicil to my will," assented Mr. Baldwin. "The codicil you have drawn for me to sign."

"Now," said the wife eagerly, "I will have the chauffeur come up and we can witness it." She hurried to the door. "Lydia! Send up Oscar!"

Almost immediately there was a sound of footsteps, and a man in livery entered.

"This is the other witness," explained Mrs. Baldwin to Mr. Tutt. "Oscar Boynton, our chauffeur."

Mr. Tutt arose and spread open the last page of the instrument upon the bedclothes in the old man's lap.

"This is the codicil to his last will and testament, which Mr. Baldwin desires you to witness," he stated. "He will sign first, and after him Mrs. Baldwin and yourself. You must both sign in his presence and in the presence of each other. Mr. Baldwin, do you understand this to be a codicil to your will? And do you wish these witnesses to attest it by signing their names?"

"Yes—yes," murmured the old man in the bed.

"Then," said Mr. Tutt, "write your name in the blank space at the foot of the paragraph beginning 'In witness whereof.' "

He held out the fountain pen supplied by the wife. But Mr. Baldwin did not seem to see it.

Mr. Tutt placed it gently in the fragile blue-veined right hand.

"Here!" he directed. "Below the words 'In witness whereof.' "

Mr. Baldwin's fingers closed over the pen. He appeared to be making an heroic effort to bring his mind to bear upon what was expected of him. Helplessly, like a child, he looked from the pen to Mr. Tutt and back again.

"Write!" ordered his wife icily.

"Write!" repeated the old man. "Yes, write!"

Dropping his chin toward the paper, he pressed down the pen and painfully began tracing the word "Cab——"

Mrs. Baldwin watched him hungrily. The strain was too much for her.

"Here!" she cried, going round beside him and, taking the trembling fingers firmly in her own. "I'll help you!" And she guided the pen along the paper until below the inscription "In witness whereof" appeared in straggling characters the signature of Cabel Baldwin.

Mr. Tutt blotted the name and removed the codicil to a table, where Mrs. Baldwin and Boynton each signed it as a witness. Then he folded it and placed it again in the envelope from which he had removed it. Mr. Baldwin had fallen back on his pillow and closed his eyes, exhausted.

"What shall I do with the codicil?" asked Mr. Tutt. "Put it in my safe?"

"No," returned Mrs. Baldwin tartly. "You can leave it here. I'll attend to it."

V

Contrary to his wife's expectations, Mr. Baldwin did not die for a long time, but when at last he did, on that same day Lydia Baldwin left the house forever, and within the week after her father's funeral was married to Henry Holborn before a justice of the peace. It was on the afternoon of Lydia's marriage that the Widow Baldwin appeared at the offices of Tutt & Tutt and asked for the senior partner. He received her in silence, standing.

"Well," she greeted him, looking more vulturelike than ever in her weeds, "I guess it's time to start probating the will and codicil. Is there anything particular I have to do?"

Mr. Tutt did not invite her to sit down. Coldly he replied: "Mrs. Baldwin, I cannot undertake any business for you."

"What's the matter?" she demanded acidly. "Isn't my money as good as anybody else's?"

He shook his shaggy head.

"No," he returned shortly, "it isn't. A lawyer has some choice in the matter of clients, and I want no business of yours."

"That's pretty good!" she cried, flushing. "You were ready enough to act as my attorney the last time I called on you and asked you to draw the codicil. What's the matter? Are you scared of anything? Don't go back on me now!" she begged, changing her attack. "You can charge me what you like!"

"You may recall," answered Mr. Tutt sternly, "that on that occasion I specifically inquired for whom I was acting, and that you

replied categorically that I represented your husband and not you.
I drew a codicil and superintended its execution by my client at his
request. I was paid for it. That ended the matter. I shall, of course,
proceed at once to offer for probate the will in my possession, in
which I am named as executor. In so doing I represent your husband's
estate and not you. If you are legally entitled to anything, you will
get it in due course."

She stared at him, open-mouthed.

"Get anything! Why, I get a couple of millions!"

"Do you?" tossed off Mr. Tutt coolly.

"You drew the codicil yourself! Unless you fooled me by substi-
tuting another paper!"

The old lawyer grunted savagely.

"Be assured, I did not."

"What's the hitch, then?"

"If you want to know, Mrs. Baldwin, that I will have nothing to do
with you."

Mrs. Baldwin seemed to swell until her dimensions threatened to
prevent her exit.

"Well, I never!" she exploded. "I never heard of such treatment!"
She paused, swallowed and lost color. "If you've tricked me—put
anything over—I'll——" She dropped her shoulders limply, turning
momentarily sick with apprehension. "Is there——" she gasped.

"Simply to relieve your anxiety," said Mr. Tutt coldly, "I will say
that the codicil executed—or partly executed—in your husband's bed-
chamber isn't worth the paper it is written on."

"Nonsense!" she cried, losing all control of herself. "I know what's
the matter! You've got cold feet! You're afraid to go on with it!
You're scared they'll show Cabel had senile dementia or something—
wasn't legally fit to make a codicil. Well, you might as well stick! Be
as well hung for a sheep as a lamb. It would look fine, wouldn't it, for
Ephraim Tutt to admit in court that he allowed a senile old man to
execute a codicil when he didn't know what he was doing? Why, it
would ruin you forever! All right, coward! There are plenty of
lawyers who've got courage as well as brains. Some day when I've
got millions in the bank you'll wish you had your share!"

Mr. Tutt gave a low chuckle. Reaching over to the cigar-box he
selected the usual stogy and lighted it with deliberation.

"I remember you don't mind smoking," he remarked reminiscently,
"or I shouldn't venture." Then as he exhaled a voluminous cloud of
sulphurous vapor he added: "As I was saying, that document will

never be probated. The only instrument of your husband's that is of any value is the one I drew six months after you married him, in which he leaves practically everything to his daughter, Lydia."

VI

When Surrogate Sampson entered the great courtroom of the Hall of Records at half after ten the following Friday morning, he found it more than ordinarily crowded. Indeed, it seemed to him as if he had never before seen so many noted counsel sitting together in the leather armchairs at the long mahogany table whose marvellous patina had been polished by generations of distinguished legal elbows. The surrogate liked to see his court filled with the leaders of the bar, for it gave him a sense of importance and stirred his pride.

"Good morning, Mr. Philbrick!" he murmured genially as he bestowed his gown on the judicial chair. "Ah, Mr. Goodwin! And Mr. Lowenthal! What is the occasion of this illustrious gathering?"

Mr. Philbrick, Mr. Lowenthal, and the rest of the constellation of juridical luminaries simpered and bowed in unison, and Surrogate Sampson, who did not expect any answer to his interrogation, since it had been purely hortatory, blew his nose with one hand, picked up the calendar with the other and cleared his throat.

"Matter of Baldwin?" he called out briskly.

Simultaneously the company of the elect before him arose and with military precision presented arms. So did several other rows immediately behind them; a cohort of office boys, clerks, assistants, and junior counsel, carrying bags, books, parcels, and bundles of papers, closed in behind in a compact body.

"Er—if Your Honor please!" began Mr. Philbrick, in his capacity of chief of staff, in an ingratiating voice, "this is the contested probate of the codicil to the last will and testament, offered coincidently, of the late Cabel Baldwin, a distinguished resident of this city, under which he gives a large percentage of his property to various public institutions, of which I represent one."

"Who appears in opposition?" inquired the surrogate over his spectacles. "I may as well get this straight from the beginning. There are so many of you!"

For a moment there was no response; then out from behind the jury box sauntered Mr. Ephraim Tutt.

"I appear for Mrs. Henry Holborn, who was Lydia Baldwin," said he quietly, "the daughter and only child of the deceased, the sole heir and next of kin, who is also the chief beneficiary under the will."

"Ah, Mr. Tutt," commented Surrogate Sampson, "I suppose you have duly filed your objections?"

"I certainly have!" answered the lawyer, and there was something ominous in his manner. "I drew the original will for Mr. Baldwin and am the executor named in it. I have offered it for probate—and so far as I know, there is no objection to it. Indeed, there can't very well be any, since unless the will stands the codicil which these distinguished gentlemen are offering—and to which I object—falls too."

"Quite so!" nodded the judge. "Let me see the will."

Immediately a clerk handed a paper to Mr. Philbrick, who in turn passed it to an officer, who gave it to an attendant, who duly delivered it to His Honor, while the throng round the table parted to allow Mr. Tutt to approach the dais.

"Well," remarked His Honor curtly, after glancing through it, "the will seems simple enough. The testator revokes all previous wills and after a provision in lieu of dower to his wife devises a large quantity of realty described specifically by metes and bounds to his only daughter, Lydia, whom he thereafter makes the residuary legatee of all his property, both real and personal. He names you as executor. The usual affidavits are before me, made by the attesting witnesses. Is there any reason, gentlemen, why I should not receive this will for probate?"

He looked along the table. Obviously in the nature of things there could be no opposition, for the reception of the codicil depended upon the acceptance of the will.

"I'll receive it for probate, then," announced the surrogate. "Now we come to the codicil. Who offers it?"

"I do," answered Mr. Philbrick, "at the request of the chief beneficiary and sole residuary legatee, the widow."

"Is she in court?"

Mr. Philbrick waved toward a figure behind him.

"Yes, Your Honor."

"Please step forward, madam. Perhaps it will be more comfortable if you sit here beside me in the witness chair." He bowed courteously.

Mrs. Baldwin, aggressive as ever in her habiliments of mourning, yet with a worried look superimposed upon the usual malevolence of her features, now drawn into the semblance of grief, took the seat indicated.

"Are you the widow of Cabel Baldwin, deceased?"

"Yes, I am," she replied aggressively.

"You offer for probate a codicil to his will?"

"Yes, I do."

"Let me see it, please."

Mr. Philbrick promptly handed up the document.

"H'm!" exclaimed His Honor. "This is a rather lengthy instrument. I'll not bother to go through it now." And he leaned back and began polishing his glasses, in anticipation of an interesting morning. "What are the grounds of your objections to my admitting it to probate, Mr. Tutt?"

"Simply that the proposed paper is not sufficiently attested under our statutes," stated the lawyer solemnly.

The surrogate turned to the last page of the codicil, which lay on the desk before him.

"There seem to be two witnesses," he remarked, "—all the law requires."

"But one of them is the lady beside you, who under this codicil is made chief beneficiary and sole residuary legatee. As an interested party she cannot qualify—unless, to be sure, she is prepared to waive her legacy, which amounts to a quarter of a million dollars, besides the residue amounting to over a million," declared Mr. Tutt quietly.

Mrs. Baldwin had grown white. Defiantly she watched the surrogate as he now perused the codicil in its entirety.

"That seems to be so," he said with a puzzled air. "Mr. Tutt's point is perfectly well taken. There are only two witnesses to this propounded codicil, and one of those witnesses is undoubtedly an interested party; in fact could hardly be more interested. Madam, do you understand the situation? Under the law you can't qualify as a witness to prove the codicil unless you renounce your legacy; and if you don't qualify I shall have to reject the codicil, having only one witness, as insufficiently attested. Extraordinary!" he added to himself.

There was a murmur of interest throughout the rows and a closer crowding together of the group of counsel before the dais. Mrs. Baldwin sucked in her cheeks.

Mr. Philbrick smiled conciliatingly in the direction of the bench.

"That is, of course, true," said he. "But we—that is, Mrs. Baldwin has arranged, after consulting with counsel, to waive her legacy and qualify as a witness."

"Is that correct, madam?" queried the surrogate, peering at her over his spectacles. "Are you willing to forfeit your legacy of two hundred and fifty thousand dollars, as well as your residuary interest, under this codicil if I admit it to probate?"

"If that's the law I guess I've got to!" she snapped viciously. "But I've been tricked—hoodwinked! All the same, the rest will get their money!"

The surrogate gazed bewilderedly at the cluster of attorneys. Then he turned to Mr. Tutt.

"Under these circumstances is there any reason why I should not admit the codicil after the witness has signed a written waiver and given her testimony? That meets your objection, doesn't it? Have you anything further?"

"Only that it would be an act of supererogation—productive of no result whatever—as far as this lady's benefit is concerned," replied the lawyer, and the courtroom became as quiet as a country church-yard at midnight. "Two years ago, at the request of Mr. Baldwin, I drew the will which you have just admitted to probate and in which, as you have observed, after a provision for his widow in lieu of dower, he left all his property to his only daughter, my present client. She is here. Please stand up, Mrs. Holborn."

There was a rustle to the right on the lower seat of the jury box as Lydia arose, pale as a ghost in her black dress. With her stood up a tall young man, as if to protect her from the stares of the spectators. The woman in the witness chair shot in their direction a single venomous shaft.

"Thank you," went on Mr. Tutt. "That will do. If Your Honor will refer to the instrument you will see that in it Mr. Baldwin describes himself as 'of the city of Fall River, in the State of Massachusetts.' That was his permanent legal residence, his domicile. He had been in business there all his life, had lived, voted, and paid his personal taxes there. He was merely taking a vacation and spending the winter in New York City when his wife died."

"He was previously married to another lady?" asked the surrogate.

"Oh, yes; for fifteen years," said Mr. Tutt. "Now all his property —both real and personal—with the exception of a comparatively trifling sum in a Fifth Avenue bank where he kept a checking account —is situated in Massachusetts, the place of his domicile. And his estate consists almost entirely of various parcels of land and office buildings in Fall River, which he specifically bequeathed to his daughter, Lydia, in the will drawn by me, which has three witnesses as required by Massachusetts law. The schedules, which I have prepared, show that his personal estate amounts to less than fifteen thousand dollars."

There was a buzz of consternation from the lawyers about Mr. Philbrick, whose owl-like countenance wore an expression of dismay and wrath.

"Now," continued Mr. Tutt amiably, "even if this good lady with the laudable object of sacrificing the quarter million and her interest in the residuary which this codicil purports to give her—in order that these charitable institutions, represented by my friend Philbrick and his associates, and her manifold relatives and friends named in the codicil as legatees, may secure what is given them —even if, I say, she renounces her legacy and qualifies as a witness, and, in consequence, Your Honor is enabled to admit the codicil to probate, there will be nothing out of which to pay the legacies given under it, for"—and he could not help a chuckle—"the testator has expressly directed in each instance that the legacy shall be paid out of his personal estate—and there isn't any!"

A wave of astonishment swept across the benches.

"But," began Mr. Philbrick pompously, "they—the realty is more than sufficient to pay them all; and under the principles governing equitable conversion——"

"Oh, no!" contradicted the surrogate briskly. "Even if the codicil is probated it will not affect the real estate devised to the daughter under the will."

The woman in the witness chair swayed.

"I've been robbed—cheated!" she cried savagely, gritting her teeth.

"Please be quiet, madam," rebuked the surrogate. "We must have no scenes here."

"Anyhow," she declared, glaring at him, "as widow I'll take my third under the Massachusetts law! I'll get that much anyway!"

"That is for the courts of Massachusetts to decide!" returned the surrogate with asperity.

"That question won't bother them much," interjected Mr. Tutt carelessly. "For the woman sitting in that chair beside Your Honor is not the legal widow of Cabel Baldwin. She has a husband living— a railroad brakeman from whom she has never been legally divorced. I have here affidavits showing that he was never served in the divorce proceedings brought by her and upon which she must rely to establish the validity of her subsequent marriages. I say 'marriages,' for this is not her only matrimonial experience. She was wedded to two others of her patients who subsequently died; and, I may add, she inherited property from both."

The ex-nurse had half started from her seat. Mr. Philbrick had turned a bright pink.

"If this is so——" he began faintly.

"It's a lie!" cried the woman in a shrill voice. "An absolute lie! I am Cabel Baldwin's widow—and I'll prove it! I don't care what that old crook says!"

"Be quiet, madam!" shouted the surrogate angrily, banging with his gavel. "I will adjourn this matter for one week." Then he paused as he gathered the papers together. "One more question, gentlemen," said he with an expression of curiosity. "I should like to know who drew the codicil that is here offered for probate."

"I did," affirmed Mr. Tutt boldly.

There was a hiatus during which the only noise audible was the hysterical intake of the relict Baldwin upon the witness chair.

"You did!" exclaimed the surrogate. "And you now appear in opposition to it—contest the legality of your own work? That is a most astounding proceeding!"

"Exactly," answered Mr. Tutt, entirely unmoved. "I drew the codicil which this woman is now seeking to probate, and I superintended its execution."

"Knowing that she could take nothing under it?" persisted the judge.

"Knowing that she wouldn't get one red cent!"

Surrogate Sampson leaned back and removed his spectacles with amazement.

"Did you do this with the approval and consent of the testator?" he demanded.

Mr. Tutt smiled inscrutably.

"What passed between my client and myself at the time he executed this codicil," he replied, picking up his stovepipe hat, "is a privileged communication made in the course of my professional employment, which the law does not permit me to reveal!"

YOU'RE ANOTHER!

"We have strict statutes, and most biting laws."—MEASURE FOR MEASURE, ACT I, SC. 4

"I am further of opinion that it would be better for us to have [no laws] at all than to have them in so prodigious numbers as we have."—MONTAIGNE. OF EXPERIENCE, CHAPTER XVIII

Mrs. Pierpont Pumpelly, lawful spouse of Vice President Pumpelly, of Cuban Crucible, erstwhile of Athens, Ohio, was fully conscious that even if she wasn't the smartest thing on Fifth Avenue, her snappy little car was. It was, as she said, a "perfec' beejew!" The two robes of silver fox alone had cost eighty-five hundred dollars, but that was nothing; Mrs. Pumpelly—in her stockings—cost Pierpont at least ten times that every year. But he could afford it with Cruce at 791. So, having moved from Athens to the metropolis, they had a glorious time. Out home the Pierpont had been simply a P. and no questions asked as to what it stood for; P. Pumpelly. But whatever its past the P. had now blossomed definitely into Pierpont.

Though the said Pierpont produced the wherewithal, it was his wife, Edna, who attended to the disbursing of it. She loved her husband, but regarded him socially as somewhat of a liability, and Society was now, as she informed everybody, her "meal yure."

She had eaten her way straight through the meal—opera box, pew at St. Simeon Stylites, Crystal Room, musicales, Carusals, hospital entertainments, Malted Milk for Freezing France, Inns for Indigent Italians, Biscuits for Bereft Belgians, dinner parties, lunch parties, supper parties, the whole thing; and a lot of the right people had come, too.

The fly in the ointment of her social happiness—and unfortunately it happened to be an extremely gaudy butterfly indeed—was her next-door neighbor, Mrs. Rutherford Wells, who obstinately refused to recognize her existence.

At home, in Athens, Edna would have resorted to the simple expedient of sending over the hired girl to borrow something. But here there was nothing doing. Mrs. Rutherford had probably never seen her own chef and Mrs. Pumpelly was afraid of hers. Besides, even Edna recognized the lamentable fact that it was up to Mrs. Wells to call first, which she didn't. Once when the ladies had emerged simultaneously from their domiciles Mrs. Pumpelly had smiling waddled forward a few steps with an ingratiating bow, but Mrs. Wells had looked over her head and hadn't seen her.

Thereupon the iron had entered into Mrs. Pumpelly's soul and her life had become wormwood and gall, ashes in her mouth and all the rest of it. She proposed to get even with the cat at the very first chance, but somehow the chance never seemed to come. She hated to be living on the same street with that kind of nasty person. And who was this Wells woman? Her husband never did a thing except play croquet or something at a club! He probably was a drunkard—and a roo-ay. Mrs. Pumpelly soon convinced herself that Mrs. Wells also must be a very undesirable, if not hopelessly immoral lady. Anyhow, she made up her mind that she would certainly take nothing further from her. Even if Mrs. Wells should have a change of heart and see fit to call, she just wouldn't return it! So when she rolled up in the diminutive car and found Mrs. Wells' lumbering limousine blocking the doorway she was simply furious.

"Make that man move along!" she directed, and Jules honked and honked, but the limousine did not budge.

Then Mrs. Pumpelly gave way to a fit of indignation that would have done her proud even in Athens, Ohio. Fire-breathing, she descended from her car and, approaching the limousine, told the imperturbable chauffeur that even if he did work for Mrs. Rutherford Wells, Mrs. Rutherford Wells was no better than anybody else, and that gave him no right to block up the whole street. She spoke loudly, emphatically, angrily, and right in the middle of it the chauffeur, who had not deigned to look in her direction, slyly pressed the electric button of his horn and caused it to emit a low scornful grunt. Then a footman opened the door of the Wells mansion and Mrs. Rutherford Wells herself came down the steps, and Mrs. Pumpelly told her to her face exactly what she thought of her and ordered her to move her car along so her own could get in front of the vestibule.

Mrs. Wells ignored her. Deliberately—and as if there were no such person as Mrs. Pumpelly upon the sidewalk—she stepped into her motor and, the chauffeur having adjusted the robe, she remarked in a casual, almost indifferent manner that nevertheless made Mrs. Pum-

pelly squirm, "Go to Mr. Hepplewhite's, William. Pay no attention
to that woman. If she makes any further disturbance call a policeman."

And the limousine rolled away with a sneer at Mrs. Pumpelly from
the exhaust. More than one king has been dethroned for far less
cause!

"You telephone Mr. Edgerton," she almost shrieked at Simmons,
the butler, "that he should come right up here as fast as he can. I've
got to see him at once!"

"Very good, madam," answered Simmons obsequiously.

And without more ado, in less than forty minutes, the distinguished Mr. Wilfred Edgerton, of Edgerton & Edgerton, attorneys
for Cuban Crucible and hence alert to obey the behests of the wives
of the officers thereof, had deposited his tall silk hat on the marble
Renaissance table in the front hall and was entering Mrs. Pumpelly's
Louis Quinze drawing-room with the air of a Sir Walter Raleigh
approaching his Queen Elizabeth.

"Sit down, Mr. Edgerton!" directed the lady impressively. "No,
you'll find that other chair more comfortable; the one you're in's
got a hump in the seat. As I was saying to the butler before you came,
I've been insulted and I propose to teach that woman she can't make
small of me no matter what it costs—and Pierpont says you're no
slouch of a charger at that."

"My dear madam!" stammered the embarrassed attorney. "Of
course, there are lawyers and lawyers. But if you wish the best I feel
sure my firm charges no more than others of equal standing. In any
event you can be assured of our devotion to your interests. Now
what, may I ask, are the circumstances of the case?"

"Mr. Edgerton," she began, "I just want you should listen carefully to what I have to say. This woman next door to me here
has——"

At this point, as paper is precious and the lady voluble, we will
drop the curtain upon the first act of our legal comedy.

"I suppose we'll have to do it for her!" growled Mr. Wilfred
Edgerton to his brother on his return to their office. "She's a crazy
idiot and I'm very much afraid we'll all get involved in a good deal
of undesirable publicity. Still, she's the wife of the vice president
of our best paying client!"

"What does she want us to do?" asked Mr. Winfred, the other
Edgerton. "We can't afford to be made ridiculous—for anybody."

This was quite true since dignity was Edgerton & Edgerton's long suit, they being the variety of Wall Street lawyers who are said to sleep in their tall hats and cutaways.

"If you can imagine it," replied his brother irritably, "she insists on our having Mrs. Wells arrested for obstructing the street in front of her house. She asked me if it wasn't against the law, and I took a chance and told her it was. Then she wanted to start for the police court at once, but as I'd never been in one I said we'd have to prepare the papers; I didn't know what papers."

"But we can't arrest Mrs. Wells!" expostulated Mr. Winfred Edgerton. "She's socially one of our most prominent people. I dined with her only last week!"

"That's why Mrs. Pumpelly wants to have her arrested, I fancy!" replied Mr. Wilfred gloomily. "Mrs. Wells has given her the cold shoulder. It's no use; I tried to argue the old girl out of it, but I couldn't. She knows what she wants and she jolly well intends to have it."

"I wish you joy of her!" mournfully rejoined the younger Edgerton. "But it's your funeral. I can't help you. I never got anybody arrested and I haven't the least idea how to go about it."

"Neither have I," admitted his brother. "Luckily my practice has not been of that sort. However, it can't be a difficult matter. The main thing is to know exactly what we are trying to arrest Mrs. Wells for."

"Why don't we retain Tutt & Tutt to do it for us?" suggested Winfred. "Criminal attorneys are used to all that sort of rotten business."

"Oh, it wouldn't do to let Pumpelly suspect we couldn't handle it ourselves. Besides, the lady wants distinguished counsel to represent her. No, for once we've got to lay dignity aside. I think I'll send Maddox up to the Criminal Courts Building and have him find out just what to do."

It may seem remarkable that neither of the members of a high-class law firm in New York City should ever have been in a police court, but such a situation is by no means infrequent. The county or small-town attorney knows his business from the ground up. He starts with assault and battery, petty larceny and collection cases and gradually works his way up, so to speak, to murder and corporate reorganizations. But in Wall Street the young student whose ambition is to appear before the Supreme Court of the United States in some constitutional matter as soon as possible is apt to spend his early years in brief writing and then become a specialist in real estate, corporation, admiralty or probate law and perhaps never see the inside of a trial court at all, much less a police court, which, to the poor and ignorant, at any rate, is the most important court of any of them, since it is here that the citizen must go to enforce his everyday rights.

Mr. Wilfred Edgerton suspected that a magistrate's court was a dirty sort of hole, full of brawling shyster lawyers, and he didn't want to know any more about such places than he could help. Theoretically he was aware that on a proper complaint sworn to by a person supposing himself or herself criminally aggrieved the judge would issue a warrant to an officer, who would execute it on the person of the criminal and hale him or her to jail. The idea of Mrs. Wells being dragged shrieking down Fifth Avenue or being carted away from her house in a Black Maria filled him with dismay.

Yet that was what Mrs. Pumpelly proposed to have done, and unfortunately he had to do exactly what Mrs. Pumpelly said; quickly too.

"Maddox," he called to a timid youth in a green eye-shade sitting in lonely grandeur in the spacious library, "just run up to the—er—magistrate's court on Blank Street and ascertain the proper procedure for punishing a person for obstructing the highway. If you find an appropriate statute or ordinance you may lay an information against Mrs. Rutherford Wells for violating it this afternoon in front of the residence next to hers; and see that the proper process issues in the regular way."

To hear him one would have thought he did things like that daily before breakfast—such is the effect of legal jargon.

"Yes, sir," answered Maddox respectfully, making a note. "Do you wish to have the warrant held or executed?"

Mr. Wilfred Edgerton bit his mustache doubtfully.

"We-ell," he answered at length, perceiving that he stood upon the brink of a legal Rubicon, "you may do whatever seems advisable under all the circumstances."

In his nervous condition he did not recall what, had he stopped calmly to consider the matter, he must have known very well—namely, that no warrant could possible issue unless Mrs. Pumpelly, as complainant, signed and swore to the information herself.

"Very well, sir," answered Maddox, in the same tone and manner that he would have used had he been a second footman at Mrs. Pumpelly's.

Thereafter both Edgertons, but particularly Wilfred, passed a miserable hour. They realized that they had started something and they had no idea of where, how or when what they had started would stop. Indeed they had terrifying visions of Mrs. Wells being beaten into insensibility, if not into a pulp, by a cohort of brutal police officers, and of their being held personally responsible. But before anything of that sort actually happened Maddox returned.

"Well," inquired Wilfred with an assumption of nonchalance, "what did you find out?"

"The magistrate said that we would have to apply at the court in the district where the offense occurred and that Mrs. Pumpelly would have to appear there in person. Obstructing a highway is a violation of Section Two of Article Two of the Police Department Regulations for Street Traffic, which reads: 'A vehicle waiting at the curb shall promptly give way to a vehicle arriving to take up or set down passengers.' It is not usual to issue a warrant in such cases, but a summons merely."

"Ah!" sighed both Edgertons in great relief.

"Upon which the defendant must appear in default of fine or imprisonment," continued Maddox.

The two lawyers looked at one another inquiringly.

"Did they treat you—er—with politeness?" asked Wilfred curiously.

"Oh, well enough," answered the clerk. "I can't say it's a place I hanker to have much to do with. It's not like an afternoon tea party. But it's all right. Do you wish me to do anything further?"

"Yes!" replied Wilfred with emphasis. "I do. I wish you would go right up to Mrs. Pumpelly's house, conduct that lady to the nearest police court and have her swear out the summons for Mrs. Wells herself. I'll telephone her that you are coming."

Which was a wise conclusion, in view of the fact that Edna Pumpelly, née Haskins, was much better equipped by nature to take care of Mr. Wilfred Edgerton in the hectic environs of a police court than he was qualified to take care of her. And so it was that just as Mrs. Rutherford Wells was about to sit down to tea with several fashionable friends her butler entered, bearing upon a salver a printed paper, which he presented to her, in manner and form the following:

CITY MAGISTRATE'S COURT, CITY OF NEW YORK
In the name of the people of the State of New York
To "Jane" Wells, the name "Jane" being fictitious:

You are hereby summoned to appear before the ———— District Magistrate's Court, Borough of Manhattan, City of New York, on the eighth day of May, 1920, at ten o'clock in the forenoon, to answer the charge made against you by Edna Pumpelly for violation of Section Two, Article Two of the Traffic Regulations providing that a vehicle waiting at the curb shall promptly give way to a vehicle arriving to take up or set down passengers, and upon your failure to appear at the time and place herein mentioned you are liable to a fine of not exceeding fifty dollars or to imprisonment of not exceeding ten days or both.

Dated 6th day of May, 1920.

JAMES CUDDAHEY, Police Officer,
Police Precinct ————,
New York City.

Attest: JOHN J. JONES,
Chief City Magistrate.

"Heavens!" cried Mrs. Wells as she read this formidable document. "What a horrible woman! What shall I do?"

Mr. John De Puyster Hepplewhite, one of the nicest men in New York, who had himself once had a somewhat interesting experience in the criminal courts in connection with the arrest of a tramp who had gone to sleep in a pink silk bed in the Hepplewhite mansion on Fifth Avenue, smiled deprecatingly, set down his Dresden-china cup and dabbed his mustache decorously with a filigree napkin.

"Dear lady," he remarked with conviction, "in such distressing circumstances I have no hesitation whatever in advising you to consult Mr. Ephraim Tutt."

"I have been thinking over what you said the other day regarding the relationship of crime to progress, Mr. Tutt, and I'm rather of the opinion that it's rot," announced Tutt as he strolled across from his own office to that of his senior partner for a cup of tea at practically the very moment when Mr. Hepplewhite was advising Mrs. Wells. "In the vernacular—bunk."

"What did he say?" asked Miss Wiggin, rinsing out with hot water Tutt's special blue-china cup, in the bottom of which had accumulated some reddish-brown dust from Mason & Welsby's *Admiralty and Divorce Reports* upon the adjacent shelf.

"He made the point," answered Tutt, helping himself to a piece of toast, "that crime was—if I may be permitted to use the figure—part of the onward urge of humanity toward a new and perhaps better social order; a natural impulse to rebel against existing abuses; and he made the claim that though an unsuccessful revolutionary was of course regarded as a criminal, on the other hand, if successful he at once became a patriot, a hero, a statesman or a saint."

"A very dangerous general doctrine, I should say," remarked Miss Wiggin. "I should think it all depended on what sort of laws he was rebelling against. I don't see how a murderer could ever be regarded as assisting in the onward urge toward sweetness and light, exactly."

"Wouldn't it depend somewhat on whom you were murdering?" inquired Mr. Tutt, finally succeeding in his attempt to make a damp stogy continue in a state of combustion. "If you murdered a tyrant wouldn't you be contributing toward progress?"

"No," retorted Miss Wiggin, "you wouldn't; and you know it. In certain cases where the laws are manifestly unjust, antiquated or perhaps do not really represent the moral sense of the community their violation may occasionally call attention to their absurdity, like the famous blue laws of Connecticut, for example; but as the laws as a whole do crystallize the general opinion of what is right and desirable in matters of conduct a movement toward progress would be exhibited not by breaking laws but by making laws."

"But," argued Mr. Tutt, abandoning his stogy, "isn't the making of a new law the same thing as changing an old law? And isn't changing a law essentially the same thing as breaking it?"

"It isn't," replied Miss Wiggin tartly. "For the obvious and simple reason that the legislators who change the laws have the right to do so, while the man who breaks them has not."

"All the same," admitted Tutt, slightly wavering, "I see what Mr. Tutt means."

"Oh, I see what he means!" sniffed Miss Wiggin. "I was only combating what he said!"

"But the making of laws does not demonstrate progress," perversely insisted Mr. Tutt. "The more statutes you pass the more it indicates that you need 'em. An ideal community would have no laws at all."

"There's a thought!" interjected Tutt. "And there wouldn't be any lawyers either!"

"As King Hal said: 'The first thing we do, let's kill all the lawyers,'" commented Mr. Tutt.

"Awful vision!" ejaculated Miss Wiggin. "Luckily for us, that day has not yet dawned. However, Mr. Tutt's argument is blatantly fallacious. Of course, the making of new laws indicates an impulse toward social betterment—and therefore toward progress."

"It seems to me," ventured Tutt, "that this conversation is more than usually theoretical—not to say specious! The fact of the matter is that the law is a part of our civilization and the state of the law marks the stage of our development—more or less."

Mr. Tutt smiled sardonically.

"You have enunciated two great truths," said he. "First, that it is a 'part'; and second, 'more or less.' The law is a very small part of our protection against what is harmful to us. It is only one of our sanctions of conduct, and a very crude one at that. Did you ever stop to think that compared with religion the efficacy of the law was almost *nil?* The law deals with conduct, but only at a certain point. We are apt to find fault with it because it makes what appear to us to be arbitrary and unreasonable distinctions. That in large measure is because law is only supplementary."

"How do you mean—supplementary?" queried Tutt.

"Why," answered his partner, "as James C. Carter pointed out, ninety-nine per cent of all law is unwritten. What keeps most people straight is not criminal statutes but their own sense of decency, conscience or whatever you may choose to call it. Doubtless you recall the famous saying of Diogenes Laertius: 'There is a written and an unwritten law. The one by which we regulate our constitutions in our cities is the written law; that which arises from custom is the unwritten law.' I see that, of course you do! As I was saying only the other day, infractions of good taste and of manners, civil wrongs, sins, crimes—are in essence one and the same, differing only in degree. Thus the man who goes out to dinner without a collar violates the laws of social usage; if he takes all his clothes off and walks the streets he commits a crime. In a measure it simply depends on how many clothes he has on what grade of offense he commits. From that point of view the man who is not a gentleman is in a sense a criminal. But the law can't make a man a gentleman."

"I should say not!" murmured Miss Wiggin.

"Well," continued Mr. Tutt, "we have various ways of dealing with these outlaws. The man who violates our ideas of good taste or good manners is sent to Coventry; the man who does you a wrong is mulcted in damages; the sinner is held under the town pump and ridden out of town on a rail, or the church takes a hand and threatens him with the hereafter; but if he crosses a certain line we arrest him and lock him up—either from public spirit or for our own private ends."

"Hear! Hear!" cried Tutt admiringly.

"Fundamentally there is only an arbitrary distinction between wrongs, sins and crimes. The meanest and most detestable of men, beside whom an honest burglar is a sympathetic human being, may yet never violate a criminal statute."

"That's so!" said Tutt. "Take Badger, for instance."

"How often we defend cases," ruminated his partner, "where the complainant is just as bad as the prisoner at the bar—if not worse."

"And of course," added Tutt, "you must admit there are a lot of criminals who are criminals from perfectly good motives. Take the man, for instance, who thrashes a bystander who insults his wife —the man's wife, I mean, naturally."

"Only in those cases where we elect to take the law into our own hands we ought to be willing to accept the consequences like gentle-men and sportsmen," commented the senior partner.

"This is all very interesting, no doubt," remarked Miss Wiggin, "but as a matter of general information I should like to know why the criminal law doesn't punish the sinners—as well as the criminals."

"I guess one reason," replied Tutt, "is that people don't wish to be kept from sinning."

"Thou hast spoken!" agreed Mr. Tutt. "And another reason is that the criminal law was not originally devised for the purpose of eradi-cating sin—which, after all, is the state into which it is said man was born—but was only intended to prevent certain kinds of physical violence and lawlessness—murder, highway robbery, assault, and so on. The church was supposed to take care of sin, and there was an elaborate system of ecclesiastical courts. In point of fact, though there is a great deal of misconception on the subject, the criminal law does not deal with sin as sin at all, or even with wrongs merely as wrongs. It has a precise and limited purpose—namely, to prevent certain kinds of acts and to compel the performance of other acts.

"The state relies on the good taste and sense of decency, duty and justice of the individual citizen to keep him in order most of the time. It doesn't, or anyhow it shouldn't, attempt to deal with trifling peccadillos; it generally couldn't. It merely says that if a man's conscience and idea of fair play aren't enough to make him behave himself, why, then, when he gets too obstreperous we'll lock him up. And different generations have had entirely different ideas about what was too obstreperous to be overlooked. In the early days the law only punished bloodshed and violence. Later on, its scope was increased, until thousands of acts and omissions are now made criminal by statute. But that explains why the fact that something is a sin doesn't necessarily mean that it is a crime. The law is artificial and not founded on any general attempt to prohibit what is unethical, but simply to prevent what is immediately dangerous to life, limb and property."

"Which, after all, is a good thing—for it leaves us free to do as we choose so long as we don't harm anybody else," said Miss Wiggin.

"Yet," her employer continued, "unfortunately—or perhaps fortunately from our professional point of view—our lawmakers from time to time get rather hysterical and pass such a multiplicity of statutes that nobody knows whether he is committing crime or not."

"In this enlightened state," interposed Tutt, "it's a crime to advertise as a divorce lawyer; to attach a corpse for payment of debt; to board a train while it is in motion; to plant oysters without permission; or without authority wear the badge of the Patrons of Husbandry."

"Really, one would have to be a student to avoid becoming a criminal," commented Miss Wiggin.

Mr. Tutt rose and, looking along one of the shelves, took down a volume which he opened at a point marked by a burned match thrust between the leaves.

"My old friend Joseph H. Choate," he remarked, "in his memorial of his partner, Charles H. Southmayde, who was generally regarded as one of the greatest lawyers of our own or any other generation, says, 'The ever-growing list of misdemeanors, created by statute, disturbed him, and he even employed counsel to watch for such statutes introduced into the legislature—mantraps, as he called them—lest he might, without knowing it, commit offenses which might involve the penalty of imprisonment.' "

"We certainly riot in the printed word," said Miss Wiggin. "Do you know that last year alone to interpret all those statutes and decide the respective rights of our citizens the Supreme Court of this state wrote five thousand eight hundred pages of opinion?"

"Good Lord!" ejaculated Tutt. "Is that really so?"

"Of course it is!" she answered.

"But who reads the stuff?" demanded the junior partner. "I don't!"

"The real lawyers," replied Miss Wiggin innocently.

"The judges who write them probably read them," declared Mr. Tutt. "And the defeated litigants; the successful ones merely the final paragraphs."

"But coming back to crime for a moment," said Miss Wiggin, pouring herself out a second cup of tea; "I had almost forgotten that the criminal law was originally intended only to keep down violence. That explains a lot of things. I confess to being one of those who unconsciously assumed that the law is a sort of official Mrs. Grundy."

"Not at all! Not at all!" corrected Mr. Tutt. "The law makes no pretense of being an arbiter of morals. Even where justice is concerned it expects the mere sentiment of the community to be capable of dealing with trifling offenses. The laws of etiquette and manners, devised for 'the purpose of keeping fools at a distance,' are reasonably adapted to enforcing the dictates of good taste and to dealing with minor offenses against our ideas of propriety."

"I wonder," hazarded Miss Wiggin thoughtfully, "if there isn't some sociological law about crimes, like the law of diminishing returns in physics?"

"The law of what?"

"Why, the law that the greater the force or effort applied to anything," she explained a little vaguely, "the greater the resistance becomes, until the effort doesn't accomplish anything; increased speed in a warship, for instance."

"What's that got to do with crime?"

"Why, the more statutes you pass and more new crimes you create the harder it becomes to enforce obedience to them, until finally you can't enforce them at all."

"That is rather a profound analogy," observed Mr. Tutt. "It might well repay study."

"Miss Wiggin has no corner on analogies," chirped Tutt. "Passing statutes creating new crimes is like printing paper money without anything back of it; in the one case there isn't really any more money than there was before and in the other there isn't really any more crime either."

"Only it makes more business for us."

"I've got another idea," continued Tutt airily, "and that is that crime is a good thing. Not because it means progress or any bunk like that, but because unless you had a certain amount of crime, and also criminal lawyers to attack the law, the state would never find out the weaknesses in its statutes. Therefore the more crime there

is the more the protective power of the state is built up, just as the
fever engendered by vaccine renders the human body immune from
smallpox! Eh, what?"

"I never heard such nonsense!" exclaimed Miss Wiggin. "Do let
me give you some more tea! Eh, what?"

But at that moment Willie announced that Mr. Rutherford Wells
was calling to see Mr. Tutt and tea was hastily adjourned. Half an
hour later the old lawyer rang for Bonnie Doon.

"Bonnie," he said, "one of our clients has been complained against
by her next-door neighbor, a got-rich-quick lady, for obstructing
the street with her motor. It's obviously a case of social envy, hatred
and malice. Just take a run up there in the morning, give Mrs. Pierpont Pumpelly and her premises the once-over and let me know of
any violations you happen to observe. I don't care how technical
they are, either."

"All right, Mr. Tutt," answered Bonnie. "I get you. Isn't there a
new ordinance governing the filling of garbage cans?"

"I think there is," nodded Mr. Tutt. "And meantime I think I'll
drop over and see Judge O'Hare."

"I'll settle her hash for her, the hussy!" declared Mrs. Pumpelly
to her husband at dinner the following evening. "I'll teach her to
insult decent people and violate the law. Just because her husband
belongs to a swell club she thinks she can do as she likes! But I'll
show her! Wait till I get her in court to-morrow!"

"Well, of course, Edna, I'll stand back of you and all that," Pierpont assured her. "No, thank you, Simmons, I don't wish any more
'voly vong.' But I'd hate to see you get all messed up in a police
court!"

"Me—messed up!" she exclaimed haughtily. "I guess I can take
care of myself most anywheres—good and plenty!"

"Of course you can, dearie!" he protested in a soothing tone. "But
these shyster lawyers who hang around those places—you 'member
Jim O'Leary out home to Athens? Well, they don't know a lady
when they see one, and they wouldn't care if they did; and they'll
try and pry into your past life——"

"I haven't got any past life, and you know it too, Pierpont Pumpelly!" she retorted hotly. "I'm a respectable, law-abidin' woman, I
am. I never broke a law in all my days——"

"Excuse me, madam," interposed Simmons, with whom the second footman had just held a whispered conference behind the screen, "but James informs me that there is a police hofficer awaiting to see you in the front 'all."

"To see me?" ejaculated Mrs. Pumpelly.

"Yes, madam."

"I suppose it's about to-morrow. Tell him to call round about nine o'clock in the morning."

" 'E says 'e must see you to-night, ma'am," annotated James excitedly. "And 'e acted most hobnoxious to me!"

"Oh, he acted obnoxious, did he?" remarked Mrs. Pumpelly airily. "What was he obnoxious about?"

" 'E 'as a paper 'e says 'e wants to serve on you personal," answered James in agitation. " 'E says if you will hallow 'm to step into the dining-room 'e won't take a minute."

"Perhaps we'd better let him come in," mildly suggested Pierpont. "It's always best to keep on good terms with the police."

"But I haven't broken any law," repeated Mrs. Pumpelly blankly.

"Maybe you have without knowin' it," commented her husband.

"Why, Pierpont Pumpelly, you know I never did such a thing!" she retorted.

"Well, let's have him in, anyway," he argued. "I can't digest my food with him sitting out there in the hall."

Mrs. Pumpelly took control of the situation.

"Have the man in, Simmons!" she directed grandly.

And thereupon entered Officer Patrick Roony. Politely Officer Roony removed his cap, politely he unbuttoned several yards of blue overcoat and fumbled in the caverns beneath. Eventually he brought forth a square sheet of paper—it had a certain familiarity of aspect for Mrs. Pumpelly—and handed it to her.

"Sorry to disturb you, ma'am," he apologized, "but I was instructed to make sure and serve you personal."

"That's all right! That's all right!" said Pierpont with an effort at bonhomie. "The—er—butler will give you a highball if you say so."

"Oh, boy, lead me to it!" murmured Roony in the most approved manner of East Fourteenth Street. "Which way?"

"Come with me!" intoned Simmons with the exalted gesture of an archbishop conducting an ecclesiastical ceremonial.

"What does it say?" asked her husband hurriedly as the butler led the cop to it.

"Sh-h!" warned Mrs. Pumpelly. "James, kindly retire!"

James retired, and the lady examined the paper by the tempered light of the shaded candles surrounding what was left of the "voly vong."

"Who ever heard of such a thing?" she cried. "Just listen here, Pierpont!"

"CITY MAGISTRATE'S COURT, CITY OF NEW YORK
"In the name of the people of the State of New York"
"To 'Maggie' Pumpelly, the name 'Maggie' being fictitious:
"You are hereby summoned to appear before the ———— District Magistrate's Court, Borough of Manhattan, City of New York, on the tenth day of May, 1920, at ten o'clock in the forenoon, to answer to the charge made against you by William Mulcahy for violation of Section One, Article Two, of the Police Traffic Regulations in that on May 7, 1920, you permitted a vehicle owned or controlled by you to stop with its left side to the curb on a street other than a one-way traffic street; and also for violation of Section Seventeen, Article Two of Chapter Twenty-four of the Code of Ordinances of the City of New York in that on the date aforesaid, being the owner of a vehicle subject to Subdivision One of said section and riding therein, you caused or permitted the same to proceed at a rate of speed greater than four miles an hour in turning corner of intersection highways, to wit, Park Avenue and Seventy-third Street; and upon your failure to appear at the time and place herein mentioned you are liable to a fine of not exceeding fifty dollars or to imprisonment of not exceeding ten days or both.

"Dated 7th day of May, 1920.
"PATRICK ROONY, Police Officer,
"Police Precinct ————,
"New York City.

"Attest: JOHN J. JONES,
"Chief City Magistrate."

"Well, I never!" she exploded. "What rubbish! Four miles an hour! And 'Maggie'—as if everybody didn't know my name was Edna!"

"The whole thing looks a bit phony to me!" muttered Pierpont, worried over the possibility of having wasted a slug of the real thing on an unreal police officer. "Perhaps that feller wasn't a cop at all!"

"And who's William Mul-kay-hay?" she continued. "I don't know any such person! You better call up Mr. Edgerton right away and see what the law is."

"I hope he knows!" countered Mr. Pumpelly. "Four miles an hour —that's a joke! A baby carriage goes faster than four miles an hour. You wouldn't arrest a baby!"

"Well, call him up!" directed Mrs. Pumpelly. "Tell him he should come right round over here."

The summons from his client interrupted Mr. Edgerton in the middle of an expensive dinner at his club and he left it in no good humor. He didn't like being ordered round like a servant the way Mrs. Pumpelly was ordering him. It wasn't dignified. Moreover, a lawyer out of his office was like a snail out of its shell—at a distinct disadvantage. You couldn't just make an excuse to step into the next office for a moment and ask somebody what the law was. The Edgertons always kept somebody in an adjoining office who knew the law —many lawyers do.

On the Pumpelly stoop the attorney found standing an evil-looking and very shabby person holding a paper in his hand, but he ignored him until the grilled iron *cinquecento* door swung open, revealing James, the retiring second man.

Then, before he could enter, the shabby person pushed past him and asked in a loud, vulgar tone: "Does Edna Pumpelly live here?"

James stiffened in the approved style of erect vertebrata.

"This is Madame Pierpont Pumpelly's residence," he replied with hauteur.

"Madam or no madam, just slip this to her," said the shabby one. "Happy days!"

Mr. Wilfred Edgerton beneath the medieval tapestry of the Pumpelly marble hall glanced at the dirty sheet in James's hand and, though unfamiliar with the form of the document, perceived it to be a summons issued on the application of one Henry J. Goldsmith and returnable next day, for violating Section Two Hundred and Fifteen of Article Twelve of Chapter Twenty of the Municipal Ordinances for keeping and maintaining a certain bird, to wit, a cockatoo, which by its noise did disturb the quiet and repose of a certain person in the vicinity to the detriment of the health of such person, to wit, Henry J. Goldsmith, aforesaid, and upon her failure to appear, and so on.

Wilfred had some sort of vague idea of a law about keeping birds, but he couldn't exactly recall what it was. There was something incongruous about Mrs. Pierpont Pumpelly keeping a cockatoo. What did anybody want of a cockatoo? He concluded that it must be an ancestral hereditament from Athens, Ohio. Nervously he ascended the stairs to what Edna called the saloon.

"So you've come at last!" cried she. "Well, what have you got to say to this? Is it against the law to go round a corner at more than four miles an hour?"

Now, whereas Mr. Wilfred Edgerton could have told Mrs. Pumpelly the "rule in Shelly's case" or explained the doctrine of *cy pres,* he had never read the building code or the health ordinances or the traffic regulations, and in the present instance the latter were to the point while the former were not. Thus he was confronted with the disagreeable alternative of admitting his ignorance or bluffing it through. He chose the latter, unwisely.

"Of course not! Utter nonsense!" replied he blithely. "The lawful rate of speed is at least fifteen miles an hour."

"Excuse me, madam," said James, appearing once more in the doorway. "A man has just left this—er—paper at the area doorway."

Mrs. Pumpelly snatched it out of his hand.

"Well, of all things!" she gasped.

"To 'Bridget' Pumpelly," it began, "said first name 'Bridget' being fictitious:

"You are hereby summoned to appear . . . for violating Section Two Hundred and Forty-eight of Article Twelve of Chapter Twenty of the Health Ordinances in that you did upon the seventh day of May, 1920, fail to keep a certain tin receptacle used for swill or garbage, in shape and form a barrel, within the building occupied and owned by you until proper time for its removal and failed to securely bundle, tie up and pack the newspapers and other light refuse and rubbish contained therein, and, further, that you caused and permitted certain tin receptacles, in the shape and form of barrels, containing such swill or garbage, to be filled to a greater height with such swill or garbage than a line within such receptacle four inches from the top thereof."

"Now what do you know about that?" remarked the vice president of Cuban Crucible to the senior partner of Edgerton & Edgerton.

"I don't know anything about it!" answered the elegant Wilfred miserably. "I don't know the law of garbage, and there's no use pretending that I do. You'd better get a garbage lawyer."

"I thought all lawyers were supposed to know the law!" sniffed Mrs. Pumpelly. "What's that you got in your hand?"

"It's another summons, for keeping a bird," answered the attorney.

"A bird? You don't suppose it's Moses?" she exclaimed indignantly.

"The name of the bird isn't mentioned," said Wilfred. "But very likely it is Moses if Moses belongs to you."

"But I've had Moses ever since I was a little girl!" she protested. "And no one ever complained of him before."

"Beg pardon, madam," interposed Simmons, parting the Flemish arras, upon which was depicted the sinking of the Spanish Armada. "Officer Roony is back again with two more papers. 'E says it isn't necessary for him to see you again, as once is enough, but 'e was wondering whether being as it was rather chilly——"

"Lead him to it!" hastily directed Pierpont, who was beginning to get a certain amount of enjoyment out of the situation. "But tell him he needn't call again."

"Give 'em here!" snapped Mrs. Pumpelly, grasping the documents. "This is a little too much! 'Lulu' this time. Fictitious as usual. Who's Julius Aberthaw? He says I caused a certain rug to be shaken in such place and manner that certain particles of dust passed therefrom into the public street or highway, to wit, East Seventy-third Street, contrary to Section Two Hundred and Fifty-three of Article Twelve of Chapter Twenty of the Municipal Ordinances. Huh!"

"What's the other one?" inquired her husband with a show of sympathy.

"For violating Section Fifteen of Article Two of Chapter Twenty, in that on May 7, 1920, I permitted a certain unmuzzled dog, to wit, a Pekingese brown spaniel dog, to be on a public highway, to wit, East Seventy-third Street in the City of New York. But that was Randolph!"

"Was Randolph muzzled?" inquired Mr. Edgerton maliciously.

"Of course not! He only weighs two pounds and a quarter!" protested Mrs. Pumpelly.

"He can bite all right, just the same!" interpolated Pierpont.

"But what shall I do?" wailed Mrs. Pumpelly, now thoroughly upset.

"Guess you'll have to take your medicine, same's other violators of the law," commented her husband.

"I never heard of such ridiculous laws!"

"Ignorance of the law excuses no one!" murmured Wilfred.

"It don't excuse a lawyer!" she snorted. "I have an idea you don't know much more about the law—this kind of law, anyway—than I do. I bet it is against the law to go round a corner at more than four miles! Do you want to bet me?"

"No, I don't!" snapped Edgerton. "What you want is a police-court lawyer—if you're goin' in for this sort of thing."

"My Lord! What's this now, Simmons?" she raved as the butler deprecatingly made his appearance again with another paper.

"I think, madam," he answered soothingly, "that it's a summons for allowing the house man to use the hose on the sidewalk after eight A. M. Roony just brought it."

"H'm!" remarked Mr. Pumpelly. "Don't lead him to it again."

"But I wouldn't have disturbed you if it hadn't been for a young gentleman who 'as called with another one regardin' the window boxes."

"What about window boxes?" moaned Mrs. Pumpelly.

" 'E says," explained Simmons, " 'e 'as a summons for you regardin' the window boxes, but that if you'd care to speak to him perhaps the matter might be adjusted——"

"Let's see the summons!" exclaimed Wilfred, coming to life.

" 'To Edna Pumpelly,' " he read.

"They're gettin' more polite," she commented ironically.

" 'For violating Section Two Hundred and Fifty of Article Eighteen of Chapter Twenty-three in that you did place, keep and maintain upon a certain window sill of the premises now being occupied by you in the City of New York a window box for the cultivation or retention of flowers, shrubs, vines or other articles or things without the same being firmly protected by iron railings——' "

"Heavens," ejaculated Mr. Pumpelly, "there'll be somebody here in a minute complaining that I don't use the right length of shaving stick."

"I understand," remarked Mr. Edgerton, "that in a certain Western state they regulate the length of bed sheets!"

"What's that for?" asked Edna with sudden interest.

"About seeing this feller?" hurriedly continued Mr. Pumpelly. "Seems to me they've rather got you, Edna!"

"But what's the use seein' him?" she asked. "I'm summoned, ain't I?"

"Why not see the man?" advised Mr. Edgerton, gladly seizing this possibility of a diversion. "It cannot do any harm."

"What is his name?"

"Mr. Bonright Doon," answered Simmons encouragingly. "And he is a very pleasant-spoken young man."

"Very well," yielded Mrs. Pumpelly.

Two minutes later, "Mr. Doon!" announced Simmons.

Though the friends of Tutt & Tutt have made the acquaintance of Bonnie Doon only casually, they yet have seen enough of him to realize that he is an up-and-coming sort of young person with an elastic conscience and an ingratiating smile. Indeed the Pumpellys were rather taken with his breezy "Well, here we all are again!" manner as well as impressed by the fact that he was arrayed in immaculate evening costume.

"I represent Mr. Ephraim Tutt, who has been retained by your neighbor, Mrs. Rutherford Wells, in connection with the summons which you caused to be issued against her yesterday," he announced pleasantly by way of introduction. "Mrs. Wells, you see, was a little annoyed by being referred to in the papers as Jane when her proper name is Beatrix. Besides, she felt that the offense charged against her was—so to speak—rather trifling. However—be that as it may— she and her friends in the block are not inclined to be severe with you if you are disposed to let the matter drop."

"Inclined to be severe with me!" ejaculated Mrs. Pumpelly, bristling.

"Edna!" cautioned her husband. "Mr. Doon is not responsible."

"Exactly. I find after a somewhat casual investigation that you have been consistently violating a large number of city ordinances— keeping parrots, beating rugs, allowing unmuzzled dogs at large, overfilling your garbage cans, disregarding the speed laws and traffic regulations, using improperly secured window boxes——"

"Anything else?" inquired Pierpont jocularly. "Don't mind us."

Bonnie carelessly removed from the pocket of his dress coat a sheaf of papers.

"One for neglecting to have your chauffeur display his metal badge on the outside of his coat—Section Ninety-four of Article Eight of Chapter Fourteen.

"One for allowing your drop awnings to extend more than six feet from the house line—Section Forty-two of Article Five of Chapter Twenty-two.

"One for failing to keep your curbstone at a proper level—Section One Hundred and Sixty-four of Article Fourteen of Chapter Twenty-three.

"One for maintaining an ornamental projection on your house —a statue, I believe, of the Goddess Venus—to project more than five feet beyond the building line—Section One Hundred and Eighty-one of Article Fifteen of Chapter Twenty-three.

"One for having your area gate open outwardly instead of inwardly—Section One Hundred and Sixty-four of Article Fourteen of Chapter Twenty-three.

"And one for failing to affix to the fanlight or door the street number of your house—Section One Hundred and Ten of Article Ten of Chapter Twenty-three.

"I dare say there are others."

"I'd trust you to find 'em!" agreed Mr. Pumpelly. "Now what's your proposition? What does it cost?"

"It doesn't cost anything at all! Drop your proceedings and we'll drop ours," answered Bonnie genially.

"What do you say, Edgerton?" said Pumpelly, turning to the disgruntled Wilfred and for the first time in years assuming charge of his own domestic affairs.

"I should say that it was an excellent compromise!" answered the lawyer soulfully. "There's something in the Bible, isn't there, about pulling the mote out of your own eye before attempting to remove the beam from anybody's else?"

"I believe there is," assented Bonnie politely. " 'You're another' certainly isn't a statutory legal plea, but as a practical defense——"

"Tit for tat!" said Mr. Edgerton playfully. "Ha, ha! Ha!"

"Ha, ha! Ha!" mocked Mrs. Pumpelly, her nose high in air. "A lot of good you did me!"

"By the way, young man," asked Mr. Pumpelly, "whom do you say you represent?"

"Tutt & Tutt," cooed Bonnie, instantly flashing one of the firm's cards.

"Thanks," said Pumpelly, putting it carefully into his pocket. "I may need you sometime—perhaps even sooner. Now, if by any chance you'd care for a highball——"

"Lead me right to it!" sighed Bonnie ecstatically.

"Me, too!" echoed Wilfred, to the great astonishment of those assembled.

MR. TUTT STAGES A RODEO

If old man Tutt had not been so hell-bent the evening before on fishing that last pool he and his guest, Mr. Bonright Doon, would have caught the New York express instead of having to flag the local, sit up until midnight in a smoker filled with lumbermen, and wait over all next day in Sterlington.

Moreover, they would have arrived in that famous old New England city decently dressed, instead of looking like a couple of roughnecks. Both had plenty of good clothes in their bags—Bonnie was always a snappy dresser—but they had clambered aboard The Whooper, rods in hand, just as they were; and now, as they stood on the sidewalk outside the station the next morning, unwashed and unkempt, with three weeks of stubble on their chins, in flannel shirts, soiled khaki trousers, weather-beaten felt hats and moccasin boots, surrounded by a hodgepodge of rod cases and gunny sacks, not even their best friends would have recognized them, and it was not surprising that the negro porter should have been staggered at the size of his tip.

"What's the best hotel in Sterlington now, George?" asked Mr. Tutt. "I haven't been here for some years."

"De Palace Gardens, boss," answered George instantly. "Hit's a swell joint! Yassah! Bes' dere is in town!"

"All right! We'll go to it. Call a taxi."

The cab pulled alongside and they piled in with their paraphernalia.

"Where to?"

"Palace Gardens," answered Mr. Tutt.

The driver stared at the two scarecrows on the back seat.

"Where'd you say?" he repeated, with a rising inflection of incredulity.

"I said 'Palace Gardens'—and step on it!" retorted the old lawyer.

The fellow had a nerve! But what did it matter? A few minutes more and they would be enjoying the hospitality of one of the best hostelries in New England.

"I know one thing!" he declared. "I may be a poor fly fisherman, I may be tired and hungry and not have slept a wink since I boarded that infernal train, but within fifteen minutes I'm going to

324

be wallowing in a nice hot bath in a porcelain tub, and inside of another ten I'll be tucking away a Duxbury clam chowder, a porterhouse steak smothered in onions, fried potatoes, pork and beans, fishballs, apple pie, coffee, and——"

"A nip of malt extract?" concluded Mr. Doon.

"Precisely! Unless some idiot has smashed the bottle!" Mr. Tutt leaned back stiffly against a gunny sack. "Wasn't it Samuel Johnson," he ruminated, "who said, 'There is nothing which has yet been contrived by man by which so much happiness is produced as by a good tavern or inn'?"

"I guess so—unless it was Will Rogers," replied Bonnie, glancing up the wide, elm-shaded streets. "This is a kind of nice old burg."

"Sterlington? I'll say it is! A fine old Yankee town, famous for its sturdy independence, its patriotism, its historic past. Home of bed-rock Americanism! There's no foolishness about the folks who live here, Bonnie, my boy. What was good enough for their forefathers is good enough for them."

"How about the talkies? I just noticed Kidnaped on Her Wedding Night and Flaming Kisses advertised over there opposite what looked to me like a Baptist church. I missed 'em both in New York."

"Oh, well, the movies!" conceded the old lawyer. "A place can't remain precisely the same forever. Nevertheless, it stands for the real values of life—solid comfort as contrasted with display."

"Yeah?" inquired his henchman, as the taxi turned a corner and stopped before an imposing Renaissance structure opposite a park, wherein a fountain played amid a series of carefully laid-out flower beds so arranged as to spell the words "Palace Gardens."

Granite steps led upward to an ornate doorway, beneath a stone escutcheon showing a lion rampant, a few crowns and what, at first glance, looked like a fistful of billiard balls. Beside a pillar loitered a *concierge* in the full-dress uniform and gold-laced kepi of a British field marshal. A row of scarlet-and-yellow taxis lined the curb. Obviously it was, as George had said, a "swell joint," utterly foreign to Mr. Tutt's recollections.

The driver leaned over.

"This here's your Palace Gardens. Those babies'll soak you fifty cents for a cup of coffee. Take a tip and try the Hancock House."

Mr. Tutt, endeavoring to disengage his legs from his rod cases and gunny sacks, ignored him.

The field marshal—he was a fat field marshal whose military collar gave him more than his quota of chins—descended in the stately fashion of those who exist by virtue of pride and circumstance.

"Pull along there, taxi!" he ordered, indicating a point an inch or two farther on, then opened the door with a flourish. When, however, he caught sight of the travellers within, his expression of benevolence changed to one of outraged bewilderment.

Mr. Tutt was too weary to be interested in the reactions of the field marshal, who was disdainfully assisting Mr. Doon to remove the mess amid which he was ensconced.

"Come on, Bonnie!" he said, paying off the driver. "Now for bath, breakfast and bed! . . . Bring in the luggage, general!"

M. Pierre Henri, the manager of the Palace Gardens, had just finished his morning tour of inspection of the hotel kitchens and stepped behind the reception desk to arrange the details of a luncheon to be given next day in the Romanoff Room, when he saw some one coming up the steps, and automatically thumped the bell sacred to "arrivals" and "departures."

"Fr-ront!" he called.

Two bellhops garbed like West Point cadets lunged forward; M. Pierre, rubbing his hands together, assumed an expression of beatific welcome, while the room clerk swung the registration card expectantly around to the proper angle. Then a look of displeasure —almost of disgust—gathered about the manager's nose, and his little mustaches stiffened like a pointer's tail when he scents a bird.

A strange and disreputable-looking old man had entered the foyer, accompanied by an even more disreputable-looking companion. Both were unshaven, disheveled. Behind them staggered the two West Point cadets under a heavy load of miscellaneous dunnage in which rubber boots and mud-stained canvas sacks prominently figured.

"Good morning," said Mr. Tutt pleasantly. "My friend and I would each like a room and bath."

Now, though M. Pierre was short, sallow and narrow-shouldered, with a sleek, round head like an umbrella's, and wore white canvas spats over his pointed patent-leather shoes, he could on occasion make himself look quite formidable. He now assumed his most haughty and supercilious aspect.

"I am sor-ry," he replied with a markedly Gallic enunciation, "but I have not got two unoccupied rooms at present."

Mr. Tutt glanced about the empty foyer.

"If you haven't two rooms, we can get along with one," he answered.

"Everything is taken," reiterated the manager coldly. "Tomorrow, perhaps."

Unfortunately for M. Pierre, at that very instant a stout, pink-faced man in plus-fours entered, followed by a bellhop carrying a heavy golf bag and a pigskin suitcase. The golfer was one of those cheerful, breezy golfers, radiating cleanliness, leisure, wealth, and he did not even so much as look at Mr. Tutt.

"I want a small suite," he announced brusquely, shoving past him. "One facing the park."

It was an awkward moment, but M. Pierre did not flinch. This was the kind of customer he wanted.

"Good morning," he replied, handing the new guest a pen. "Your suite is reserved and being held for you."

"Some service!" answered the golfer. "How could you know I was coming, when I didn't know it myself?"

"We received a telegram reserving a suite and have been holding it," said M. Pierre quickly. "Fr-ront!"

"But quite evidently not for this gentleman," interrupted Mr. Tutt. "We applied first. If any rooms are given up, we should have first call."

"You asked for rooms—not a suite," countered M. Pierre. "Fr-ront! Take Mr."—he looked at the registration—"Mr. Osgood's luggage to A1."

The golfer grinned at Mr. Tutt.

"Sorry, brother! No doubt they'll let you use the washroom!"

The old lawyer did his best to control himself. Arrogance was the quality he most detested—and these two were the highest exponents of it. Should he shake off the dust from his feet and seek hospitality elsewhere?

"You heard what I said?" continued M. Pierre. "We have no rooms. I suggest that you go to some other hotel where they can offer you the sort of accommodations you are obviously used to."

Mr. Tutt's lips trembled. He took a step forward. Eye to eye, he returned M. Pierre's stare. By this time a small crowd of patrons, waiters, bellhops and other employees, who sensed that something unusual was in progress, had collected about them.

"Are you the manager of the Palace Gardens?" asked the old lawyer.

"I am."

"And is this a regularly licensed inn and hotel?"

"It is."

"You know, do you not, that in this country, at least, the regulations of inns is a matter regarded as concerning public health and morals and is within the police power of the state?"

"Perfectly."

"And you are perhaps also aware that an innkeeper, as one carrying on a public employment, is obliged to receive all travellers who properly apply to be admitted, provided he has room and they can pay his reasonable charges?"

"I have already told you that we have no room," retorted M. Pierre icily.

"That is a question of fact, to be determined later perhaps." Mr. Tutt pulled out a water-logged wad of bills. "I now demand that you give me a room and I hereby tender you the price—whatever it may be in reason. How much do you want?"

M. Pierre began to be very much annoyed. He did not enjoy either having his conduct challenged or being interrogated so sharply in the presence of other guests.

"We are under no obligation to receive tramps!" he sneered. Then turning to the bellhops: "Take this luggage out and put it on the sidewalk. If it isn't removed within ten minutes, call the nearest policeman."

Bonnie had edged forward.

"Shall I knock his block off?" he whispered.

Mr. Tutt shook his head.

"No, leave him to me!"

"Now then, get a move on!" ordered M. Pierre, confident of his solidity with the local constabulary.

But Mr. Tutt did not budge.

On the contrary, he pulled out his old-fashioned cigar case, extracted a stogy and lit it with provoking deliberation.

"Exactly as you like, my friend," he remarked. "But bear this in mind: An innkeeper unjustifiably refusing to receive a traveller who applies for lodging is liable not only to a civil penalty but to the revocation of his license."

"I do not need any information from you, sir!" replied the manager.

"Once more—and for the last time—I ask for lodging and offer to pay for it in advance," continued Mr. Tutt.

"And once more I refuse!" snapped M. Pierre, forgetting his supposed nationality in his excitement. "Get the hell out of here!"

"That is the most objectionable apology for a human being I have met in recent years!" declared the old man as, having betaken themselves to the Hancock House, he and Bonnie sat after breakfast looking out of the window. "By jumping Jehoshaphat, I'd like to swangdangle him!"

"Can't you?" inquired Mr. Doon hopefully. "He wouldn't be the first! I hate to take anything lying down from one of those frog eaters!"

"He's no Frenchman!" returned his employer. "He's just an imitation."

"I thought, from the questions you asked him, you intended to try to break his license. You're not going to let him get away with it, are you?"

"That was only a bluff on my part. Of course, everything I said was technically true, but if we made a test case of it we'd be kept dangling around here for weeks. Besides, we couldn't prove that they had any unoccupied rooms. They'd swear us out of court. It's the first time in my rather long life that I've been kicked out of a hotel. But I'm afraid we're licked."

"Give the word and I'll go back and clean out the place," urged his henchman.

"No! No! The train for New York doesn't leave until 9:30 this evening. Give me time to study the situation."

Mr. Tutt, with his blood still boiling at the treatment they had received, unscrambled his long legs, got up and wandered about the room, scrutinizing the walls and furniture. Beside the door hung an oak-framed placard in small type headed: RULES AND REGULATIONS FOR INNKEEPERS. He studied it with his head cocked on one side.

"Bonnie," he said suddenly, "I'm going out for a while. Suppose we meet here at lunchtime for a council of war?"

"All right," agreed Mr. Doon. "And don't forget, Mr. Tutt, that, as General Sherman said, 'War is hell.'"

To savor properly what occurred thereafter in the ancient city of Sterlington, and particularly at the Palace Gardens, it should be borne in mind that, just as there is one glory of the stars, another of the sun, and still another of the moon, and that one star differeth from another in glory, there is a vital difference between a genuine luxury hotel and the counterfeit thereof. The Palace Gardens was an imitation of the most blatant variety. Obviously, no reason in the world exists why Sterlington or any other city should not have a hostelry of the ultra-modern type, if it needs and wants it; but until the coming of the Palace Gardens it had never occurred either to the inhabitants themselves or to the motoring strangers who paused within its gates, that the old Hancock House wasn't good enough for anybody.

On the contrary, the idea that Sterlington needed a luxury hotel —or what passed for a luxury hotel—had been conceived by a fertile-brained young man in Wall Street, who had thereupon organized a corporation, bought the site, arranged for a first and second mortgage, erected the building, furnished it, unloaded the stock at a handsome profit, and then stepped out, leaving the rest to Sterlington and M. Pierre.

It was as fundamentally simple an idea as that every town of a certain size should support a specified number of movie houses. But there was this difference: The movies filled an already existing need; but the need for crooners, French cooking and a nonchalant disregard for money in paying for such entertainment in a somnolent New England city required to be artificially stimulated. This M. Pierre Henri had successfully accomplished by rendering it possible for the more lively burghers of Sterlington to enjoy *caneton à la Palisse, poulet de bonne femme* and *crêpes Suzette* without adventuring into the dangerous purlieus of the Sodom of New York or the Gomorrah of Boston, thus satisfying their craving for a vicarious primrose dalliance upon the Great White Ways of sin, and enabling them to spend what would otherwise have gone for railroad fare in rollicking at the Palace Gardens, which, in consequence, he sought to make just a little more Parisian than anything on Park Avenue.

Outwardly it was the real thing—quite as swank, only more so. The blocks of ice containing the fresh beluga, the fields of snow surrounding the pale terra-cotta cocktails of tomato juice, the hot rolls, smoking inside the rubber-tired wagon, were identical with what you would find on the Rue de la Paix. The bellhops were as sprayed with buttons and the porters as bedecked with cordons and medals as in the Place Vendôme; only the waiters were mostly Greeks and Lithuanians, and the chambermaids came from the lesser suburbs instead of from gay Paree. In a word, the Palace Gardens was a firstclass fake, like M. Pierre himself.

Now, at any good American hotel, the guest is treated with an attention and a courtesy that he rarely finds elsewhere in his native land or, for that matter, in any other. He "is always right." He is made to feel that he and his patronage are desired—as indeed they are. M. Pierre, on the contrary, pursued an antipodal method in order to separate the suckers of Sterlington from their money, seeking to create an atmosphere of supercilious superiority, of insolent smartness, by which to impress the boobs, not that they were "always right," but, so far as possible, "always wrong," and that they were enjoying only on sufferance the privilege of paying several times over the worth of what they got.

It is obvious that in order to maintain a high standard of exclusiveness, Mr. Pierre had perforce to exercise a certain amount of selection. He could not receive all comers indiscriminately. He must be quick to detect the undesirables—whether threadbare or resplendent in the contemporary equivalent of diamonds and chinchilla. Upon his acuteness in this respect much of his success depended, for a vulgar, noisy, or sufficiently shabby patron might contaminate the air of quiet and expensive elegance which had been so studiously created. Hence M. Pierre must, of necessity, be able, at a moment's notice, to switch from suavity to coldness—even to bluster and intimidation. And in this he had the support of no less authority than Holy Writ. For doth not the Bible speak with approval of the host who cast into outer darkness the guest who came without a wedding garment?

At any rate, because M. Pierre was M. Pierre and, perhaps, because Sterlington had a distinctly bucolic environment, he had managed—at least until Mr. Tutt came along—to get away with it. He had been born in Cedar Rapids under the humble moniker of Peter Henry, but six years in Paris had given him his waxed mustaches, an abdominal flexibility of great value in kowtowing to wealthy dowagers, and a French accent that could fool not only any travelling salesman but most college professors. His experience with the travelling public abroad had taught him exactly when to be polite, when subservient, when to bully, and when and how to shame a reluctant applicant for lodgings into taking a parlor, bedroom and bath instead of a three-dollar single. Suave, glib, dapper and debonair, this extraordinary metamorphosis of an American was a psychological artist who could call a bluff as well as anybody, and scent a dead beat long before that unfortunate had reached the lobby.

A dashing sort of Merry Widow fellow was M. Pierre! An up-and-coming fellow, who had cleverly added a flavor of cosmo-politanism to an atmosphere otherwise too conservative to attract the younger element, by introducing a daily *thé dansant*—cover charge two dollars—presided over by Chocolate Charlie and his Pleasure Babies.

This unique combination of red-hot jazz against a Puritan back-ground had been a huge success. The Palace Gardens had become the fashionable center of Sterlington, and M. Pierre himself had achieved a notable popularity in the youthful smart set, which re-garded his insouciant personality and French accent as both fascinat-ing and distinguished. He was, in fact, quite a figure on the Bannock-y-byrn golf course as well as at the rude cocktail parties of the baser sort, where his presence was felt to impart a *haut ton* and gave the girls a chance to air their French:

"*Alo! Alo! Est-ce vous, M. Pierre? Comment allez-vous? . . . Bon! Je suis tout à fait bien aussi.*"

He had, indeed, so far established himself that he had begun to consider seriously the desirability of proposing marriage to Miss Annabelle Higgins, the only daughter and heiress of old Cy Higgins, the proprietor of the Woodside Dairy, where he purchased the Grade C milk subsequently served at the Palace Gardens as "clotted Devonshire."

Annabelle was a lusty, efflorescent blonde who packed a nasty wallop with both mid-iron and tennis racket and, had it been neces-sary or desirable, would have been quite capable of taking M. Pierre over her knee and administering what was what; but, naturally, no such idea entered her maidenly, if vigorous, mind. On the contrary, she thought him just too cute, and each and every afternoon, prop-erly chaperoned by Mrs. Rufus Hicks, a matron only three years younger than herself, she spent the hours from five to seven in the Palace Gardens tearoom, swaying for the greater part of the time in the arms of M. Pierre to the amorous croonings of Chocolate Charlie and the Pleasure Babies.

Somehow we seem to be spending a lot of time on M. Pierre Henri, but, after all, if this story has any moral, he is it.

It was five o'clock of that same afternoon, the hour of the daily *thé dansant* at the hotel, and the foyer was crowded with guests waiting at the crimson rope until the head waiter should find them places. Prominent among those present were Miss Annabelle Higgins and her friend Mrs. Hicks, who were already seated at a special table carefully reserved by M. Pierre. It was hot and all the doors and windows were open to take advantage of the cool air from the park outside, where the manager was indulging in a stroll until the dancing should get sufficiently under way so that his attentions to Annabelle would not be conspicuous. He had decided that he could not do better than to propose to her that same afternoon. No use losing time. Within half an hour he would be holding a quarter of a million dollars in his arms. Not so bad! If he had stayed in Cedar Rapids he might still be sweeping out his Uncle Elmer's feed-and-grain store. Musing thus upon the roseate future, M. Pierre lit another cigarette and continued to saunter among the blue and yellow flower beds that spelled "Palace Gardens."

It was at just this moment, a new room clerk having relieved the one who had been on duty in the morning, that a benign, white-haired, elderly man in a frock coat and tall hat made his way to the desk and asked for a room. His luggage, he explained, would be along later. It is improbable that, even had M. Pierre himself been there, he would have identified Mr. Tutt as the disreputable-looking person who had made a similar application eight hours before. Hence the clerk unhesitatingly invited the old gentleman to register, assigned him a room and handed him the key. But the new arrival did not follow the bellhop. Instead he lighted a villainous-looking, rat-tailed cigar.

"And now," said he quietly, "will you kindly look after my cattle?"

The clerk gaped at him.

"I beg your pardon?"

"I said," repeated the old lawyer, "will you please care for my cattle—in other words, put them under cover and give them proper feed?"

But the clerk still seemed at a loss to understand what Mr. Tutt was talking about.

"Cattle?" he returned vaguely. "Did you say 'cattle,' sir?"

"Yes, cattle—C-A-T-T-L-E. My cattle are outside and I want them provided with stable room, hay and provender."

The clerk smiled amiably.

"Very good, sir! Meantime, I suppose, you'd like to see your room."

Mr. Tutt did not move.

"I am quite serious," he said. "I have half a hundred head of cattle with me and, naturally, they must be properly looked out for."

And then it was that the clerk observed for the first time that the social leaders and motor guests in the tearoom had left their tables and were gathered about the windows staring into the street. Above the syncopated wails and yawpings of the Pleasure Babies rose an overtone of bovine snorts and gruntings, accompanied by a strange clatter. The room clerk suffered a constriction of the epiglottis. It was true then, by heck! What should he do? Where was M. Pierre?

That elegantly bumptious gentleman, having finished his stroll among the spring flowers and formulated his proposal to Miss Higgins, was on the point of leaving the park and returning to the tearoom, when a curious and unfamiliar sound reached his ears and an unwonted sight met his eyes. Down the ordinarily placid street upon which stood the Palace Gardens was coming a herd of steers, running hither and thither and bellowing loudly, followed by two drovers with long whips in their hands. For a moment he was rather interested than otherwise. Where could they be going? He had never seen any cattle there before. And then he uttered an ejaculation of annoyance. The drovers had stopped the herd directly in front of the Palace Gardens, and the undisciplined animals—forty or fifty of them at least—were wandering about everywhere, entangling themselves among the standing taxicabs and even climbing up the steps. He hoped they wouldn't dirty everything up. They *were* dirtying everything up! This was not going to do at all. The Palace Gardens could not be turned into a cowyard!

"Here, you!" he shouted to the nearest drover. "Why don't you go along?"

But the drover, a husky yokel in overalls, high boots and wide-brimmed straw hat, vouchsafed no reply. The steers filled the entire pavement in front of the entrance to the Palace Gardens, completely tying up the traffic and preventing either access to or egress from the hotel. Things were getting messier and messier every moment. They must be driven away! But how? There was no policeman to be seen and, had there been one, there was small reason to suppose that he would know how to handle a careering mob of steers apparently bent on climbing up and looking in the windows. Already one of the brutes had caught its hoof in the grillwork of the iron fence and was clamoring for help, while another—a horrible-looking creature with great white patches about the eyes—had capered up the steps and was standing directly before the door.

M. Pierre perceived that, should this unseemly incident receive publicity, the Palace Gardens might become the laughingstock of the town. Duty called. Pulling his Panama hat down over his ears, the manager lowered his head and, hugging the line of taxicabs for protection, darted for the steps. But between him and the door stood the steer with the white eyes! M. Pierre hesitated. He had never even so much as milked a cow. All horns, short or long, looked equally vicious to him. He reconnoitered cautiously. By a brave dash, he might win past the bull—or whatever it was—to the entrance. But he would be tempting fate.

M. Pierre regarded the steer, and the steer regarded M. Pierre. It is doubtful which gave more pleasure to the other. The steer was quite an ordinary steer, with the manners and customs common to yearlings; it had never visited Sterlington, it had never seen the Palace Gardens—or any other gardens, for that matter—and, what is more important, it had never beheld anything in the least like M. Pierre. Hence, being of an inquiring and playful disposition, it stretched out its neck, tapped with one hoof upon the granite slab whereon it stood, executed a few steps of the fox trot, and uttered a sharp, deprecatory snort. To M. Pierre, the snort sounded more terrible than the roar of a man-eating lion or the warwhoop of a savage. He was no toreador.

"Go along!" he quavered. "Get off the steps!"

But the steer, momentarily excited by the yodelings of the Pleasure Babies coming from the windows of the tearoom, showed no intention of obeying. Instead it frisked its tail, drew back its lips in a playful grin, bucked, and gave a good-humored hook in the general direction of M. Pierre, who, convinced that he was about to be impaled, turned and, without casting so much as a look to see whether or not he was, in fact, pursued, ignominiously plunged over the rail to the grass plot beneath and fled along the geranium beds. It was certainly most undignified, and to Miss Higgins—who, from her table in the bow window just above, had an unimpeded view of the entire performance—it put M. Pierre in a new and highly unfavorable light. As she watched him zigzagging from side to side in his efforts to dodge the imaginary animal behind him, saw him fall flat in the middle of a recently watered bed of yellow pansies and, clambering to his knees, dash for safety to the service entrance, her former admiration turned to contempt. It was not lessened by his general appearance as, panting, with hands, trousers and waistcoat covered with mud, he entered the foyer from the rear.

"What are those animals doing in front of the hotel?" he demanded of the room clerk whom he had left in charge. "Why don't you have 'em removed?"

His subordinate pointed at Mr. Tutt.

"This old guy says we've got to put 'em up!"

"Put what up?"

"All these cows and—and things!"

"Nonsense!" sputtered M. Pierre.

"Not at all!" interposed Mr. Tutt. "I am a guest of your hotel, these are my cattle, and I insist that you provide stable room and provender for them."

"You're crazy!" gasped the manager.

"That is the law."

What reply M. Pierre might have made is problematical, had a new element not been unexpectedly injected into the situation. The steer, instead of remaining upon the steps outside, decided to come in. It may have heard Mr. Tutt's remarks about the hotel's obligation to provide hay and provender for hungry animals; it may have been lured by the appetizing odors from the tearoom; it may have taken the Palace Gardens for a palatial barn, or it may have mistaken the moaning of Chocolate Charlie's saxophone for the wistful call of some lonely heifer yearning for companionship; but whatever the reason—and so far as those present were concerned, the reason was wholly immaterial—it followed the gleam of adventure, and thrusting forward an inquiring pair of horns, trotted through the undefended doorway like a bull entering an arena. The crowd in the foyer scattered up the stairs, down the adjacent corridors and into the grill, leaving Mr. Tutt and M. Pierre standing there alone. The field marshal and his supporting platoon of bellhops had long since taken refuge among the *chevaux-de-frise* of taxicabs.

For a second or two the steer paused, nosing a cigarette butt, then, perhaps recognizing the manager as the object of former attentions, elongated its neck and moved toward him. The white patches about its eyes gave it the ghastly look of a demon that had assumed an earthly form for its foul purposes. M. Pierre did not doubt that those purposes concerned himself. Uttering a cry of terror, he dashed toward the tearoom, followed in a more leisurely fashion by the steer. Chocolate Charlie, in the middle of a wandering *obbligato*, turned pale and, with the whites of his eyes rivalling in size those of the ghostly visitor, congealed into immobility with a dying fall in B flat. The Pleasure Babies dropped their instruments and leaped from the platform, while guests, waiters, bellhops and dishwashers, without regard to age, color, sex or previous condition, fought their way into the pantry. Miss Annabelle Higgins, from her vantage point in the window, regarded the rout with disgust—particularly that of M. Pierre. Not for nothing had she been brought up on a farm.

"Lily-livered little greaser," she muttered to Mrs. Hicks. "I always thought he was a washout."

Then calmly picking her way among the overturned tables and approaching the steer, which was now engaged in munching cream puffs, she took it by the horns and twisted its head toward the door.

"Co' boss!" she said, slapping it smartly upon the buttocks. "G'lang!"

Rather astonishingly, and without an instant's hesitation, the steer trotted obediently from the tearoom, across the foyer, past where Mr. Tutt was standing, capered out of the doorway and down the steps.

It was at this, the usual, juncture—that is to say, after almost everything had happened—that the police, represented by a traffic cop, arrived. Already the drovers and taxi drivers had restored something like order upon the pavement outside. A few steers had escaped and were still wandering among the flower beds that spelled "Palace Gardens," but the majority of the herd, weary after a twenty-mile trek, had unprotestingly allowed themselves to be corralled upon one side of the street, where a cautious traffic had been resumed. The crowd had overcome its panic, the field marshal and bellhops had courageously returned, and the entire clientele of the hotel, including the guests of the *thé dansant*, now gathered about Mr. Tutt, M. Pierre and the representative of the law.

"What's this all about?" loudly demanded the traffic cop. "Who's responsible for the rodeo?"

M. Pierre indicated Mr. Tutt.

"This man brought a herd of cows here and says I've got to put them up!" he stated, with all the outraged dignity which, in his dishevelled state, he could command.

"That is correct," calmly stated Mr. Tutt. "As a guest of his hotel, I insist that he take care of my cattle."

"What are you talking about?" exclaimed the cop. "How the devil can he take care of a lot of steers?"

"That is not my concern, but his," answered the old man. "The law requires that an innkeeper shall provide stable room, hay and provender for the horses and cattle of his guests."

"That's the first I ever heard of it!" retorted the officer. "We'll see what the magistrate has to say. Anyhow, you've violated the local ordinance prohibiting the driving of cattle through the streets without a license."

"Not at all," replied the old lawyer, taking out his wallet. "Here is my license, permitting me to drive my cattle through the streets to the slaughter-house. You will observe that it doesn't say how, or through what streets, I shall drive them there."

The traffic cop examined the paper carefully.

"That's right too!" he assented less confidently. "But it don't give you no right to block traffic or keep your cattle standing here in the roadway all night. You're committing a public nuisance."

"The nuisance is not of my making. As a stranger in the city, I naturally have no place to put up my cattle. That is the responsibility of the management of the hotel where I lodge," declared Mr. Tutt, looking at M. Pierre, who suddenly experienced a curious and unpleasant feeling that sometime, somewhere, he had encountered this eccentric old gentleman before.

The cop, having recovered from the shock of the permit, made a pass at resuming his authority. It lacked conviction, however.

"Aw, what are you giving us?" he grunted irresolutely. "Get them steers along to the slaughter-house or I'll have to arrest you."

"You will do so at your peril."

"What's to prevent me?"

"The law."

"That's a good one! Come on, now. Get your cattle off the street!" He took a step forward.

"One moment, officer. As you seem to be so skeptical about the law—although it is your duty to know it—I will read it to you."

Mr. Tutt opened a book which he had been unobtrusively holding under his arm.

"Chapter 140, Section 5, of the Revised Statutes of the state, reads: 'Every innholder and every common victualer shall at all times be provided with suitable food for strangers and travellers. Every innholder shall also have upon his premises suitable rooms with bed and bedding for the lodging of his guests, and' "—Mr. Tutt raised his voice so that all could hear—" 'if the licensing authorities so require, be provided with stable room, hay, and provender for their horses and cattle.

" 'Section 6. An innholder's or common victualer's license shall not be granted unless at the time of making application thereof the applicant has upon his premises the necessary implements and facilities for cooking, preparing and serving food for strangers and travellers, and if he is an applicant for an innholder's license, also has the rooms, bed and bedding and the stable room and provender for horses and cattle required by law.

" 'Section 7. An innholder who, upon request, refuses to receive and make suitable provision for a stranger or traveller, and also for his horses and cattle, when he may under the provisions of this chapter be legally required to do so, shall be punished by a fine of not more than fifty dollars.

" 'Section 8. An innholder who violates Section 7, or an innholder who violates Section 8, shall forfeit his license.' "

Mr. Tutt closed with a bang the book from which he had been reading.

"The sections I have last read—by assessing a penalty—make the violation of the statute a criminal offense. . . . Officer, I demand this man's arrest!"

M. Pierre Henri almost jumped out of his white-canvas spats.

"Well, I'll be damned!" gasped the cop. "Is that really the law?"

"It is!" Mr. Tutt informed him sternly. "You can read it for yourself. This man is guilty of a crime. It is your duty to take him into custody."

"Pouf!" protested M. Pierre unconvincingly. "That's just a silly old law that doesn't mean anything!"

This ill-advised reflection upon the source of the officer's authority gave the latter his opportunity. Up to that moment his determination had merely wabbled. Now his allegiance shifted. This white-haired old geezer was evidently somebody of importance. Anyhow, the law was the law.

"That's right," he declared firmly. "It is my sworn duty to make an arrest upon the complaint of any citizen whenever the law has been violated. Monseer Onree, are you going to take care of this gentleman's cattle or not?"

M. Pierre stared hopelessly at his former friend, the cop.

"But how can I take care of them?"

"Damn if I know! That's up to you!"

"Pardon the suggestion," intervened Mr. Tutt, "but what you call your 'park' was originally a pasture in front of a former tavern, and doubtless was used for this precise purpose. I should be satisfied with that. Why not put my cattle there?"

"And ruin our flower beds! Impossible!" M. Pierre was almost crying.

The crowd jeered. For some reason it seemed to enjoy the discomfiture of M. Pierre.

"I am not interested in your flower beds," replied Mr. Tutt. "And I am less concerned with the housing of my cattle than with your treatment of me as one of the travelling public. Hotels are not run solely for the profit of the management. When my friend and I applied here this morning for rooms, we happened to have just come back from a fishing trip. We had on our old clothes, to be sure, but you rudely, insultingly, and in open violation of your duties as an innkeeper, refused to receive us, although you supplied accommodations to a traveller who came after us. We were too shabby—not good enough for your smart hotel! Well, my friend, you've got to be taught that what you call the Palace Gardens has the same obligation to receive the wayfarer and look after his needs as if it were just an old-fashioned country inn, which, from a legal point of view, it still is.

"Sterlington is the metropolis of what is still essentially a rural community. These very streets were originally paths made by cattle as they were driven, or wandered, down to the pond to drink. This elaborate imitation of the palace of some French king, with its Caenstone trimmings and painted ceilings, stands on the site of what was once the old Washington Tavern and, later on, the Lincoln House. The patrons were hard-working, substantial people, most of whom drove from a distance to transact their business, spent the night and returned home. When you built the Palace Gardens, I find that you took over the old Lincoln House license, which requires it to supply stable rooms, hay and provender for the horses and cattle of its guests.

"Well, son, you can call your dump—and yourself—what you please, you can serve your patrons on mutton hash and call it '*ris de veau noisette*,' you can try and fool the boys and girls into thinking that they are being devilish on Montmartre or at Monte Carlo, but you can't change the fundamental character of an American community by introducing a foreign-language bill of fare and a bunch of Greeks disguised as French waiters. Neither can you bulldoze and insult honest wayfarers without paying the penalty. All I want is my rights—and I propose to have them."

M. Pierre crumpled. Who could this terrible old man be! He could not put up his cattle; neither could he afford to be arrested.

The Palace Gardens would be ruined! Annabelle would never consent to be his wife! M. Pierre pursued the only course left open to him. He grovelled abjectly.

"I beg your pardon, sir," he apologized. "I am very sorry for what occurred this morning. You're quite right. You were treated abominably. I hope you will overlook my rudeness. If there's anything I can do——"

Mr. Tutt had no desire to push his revenge beyond due limits. He softened.

"All right, son!" he said. "I will relieve you from the duty of taking care of my cattle upon one condition."

"Name it!" fervently ejaculated the manager.

"It is that you will assign my friend and me a certain suite—A1—overlooking the park. Just now it's occupied by a gentleman who plays golf. You can put him elsewhere, for you gave him the rooms over my head, and I am entitled to them."

"That's fair enough!" agreed the cop. "Better accept his terms before he changes his mind!"

"I certainly do!" replied M. Pierre in relief. "And you shan't be charged a single cent."

"I shall pay for whatever I have," returned Mr. Tutt. "My wants are few and easily supplied."

The circle of patrons opened to give the old man access to the door.

"All right, Bonnie!" he called to one of the drovers. "You can come in! . . . And, Johnson, drive those steers to the slaughter-house. Everything's all right!"

An hour later, Mr. Tutt and Bonnie Doon sat smoking at the window of the parlor of A1, looking down upon the park. Some of the flower beds looked a little ragged, but otherwise they had suffered no great damage. The words "Palace Gardens" were still fairly legible. Everything was quiet. The herd of steers had disappeared and the British field marshal was playing a hose over the pavement in front of the hotel. From the grill below arose the happy murmur of jazz. Chocolate Charlie and his Pleasure Babies had returned.

Presently the electric doorbell buzzed.

"Come in!" called Bonnie.

Outside stood a fat chef, immaculate in white, a menu in his hand.

"*Bon soir, m'sieu'*," he smiled. "Ze management wish to know if zey cannot offer you sometin' special for dinner? It will be entirely on ze house. You can order anyt'in' you want."

He held out the *carte du jour* to Mr. Tutt.

"We have some ver' good *consommé printempts*—pompano Miami —*caneton à la Palisse.* How you like first some fresh caviar? I make you some nice little pancakes, eh? *à la Russe?*" He waited expectant.

Mr. Tutt waved aside the bill of fare.

"No thanks, Bill," he replied. "It's very kind of you, but you can cut out the school of languages. We know exactly what we want."

"Yes, saire."

"We want a Duxbury chowder made of soft clams, a big, juicy porterhouse steak smothered in onions, fried sweet potatoes, pork and beans, fishballs, apple pie, ice cream and coffee."

"Okeh, boss!" answered Bill. "You're tellin' me!"

Mr. Tutt crossed his long legs and rested his congress shoes comfortably upon the window sill of the Palace Gardens. "Did you give Johnson his fifty bucks?" he asked.

"Sure," answered Bonnie. "I paid him in advance. . . . Well, we got into the best hotel after all."

Mr. Tutt let a stream of gray smoke trickle through his nostrils.

" 'Shall I not take mine ease in mine inn'?" he inquired contentedly.

HIS HONOR, THE JUDGE

"There are two kinds of lawyers,—one who knows the law, the other who knows the judge."—JOSEPH H. CHOATE

Judge Rufus Bunbury caught sight of a ramshackly figure scuttling through the crowd like a land crab toward the door of the General Sessions, and rapped with his gavel.

"Come back here, Mr. Tutt!" he ordered good-naturedly. "I'm going to assign you as counsel to the defense."

It was just what Mr. Tutt had feared, for he knew that the prosecutor had it in for him and that this would be a swell chance for O'Brien to hang another scalp on his belt. His attempted getaway having been frustrated, he straightened up and faced the bench.

"Your Honor, I am an old man, stricken in years and bowed down with the sorrows of the world. I beg that you will not add to my already grievous burdens."

"This defendant is entitled to the best counsel the State can offer. I am paying you a compliment."

"One I could easily do without," muttered the lawyer.

He had read about the case in the papers. Joe Cotillo, alias Joe the Barber, had been a powerful and sinister character on the Italian East Side, mixed up in every sort of racket. The defendant, James Gavin, one of his underlings, had been previously convicted and sentenced to prison for having policy slips in his possession. A year later, two nights after his discharge, he had gone to the Barber's hangout, shot him, and been arrested as he fled from the apartment. The case was dead open and shut. No wonder Gavin couldn't get a lawyer to defend him. He hardly glanced at his new client as he took his place beside him at the bar.

"We plead not guilty," he told the clerk. Then to the prisoner, "My assistant, Mr. Doon, will be over to see you shortly in the Tombs."

"Next!" The dejected file of prisoners inched along as James Gavin was led away.

Judge Bunbury watched him curiously, struck by the fact that a murderer so rarely looked the part. It was hard for him to imagine this young fellow, with his gaunt, frightened face, killing any one. Certainly he was a queer type to be mixed up in the numbers racket.

The Honorable Rufus, on the other hand, looked exactly like a judge. He was fifty-one years old, portly, with a clean-shaven, rather flabby face, pale blue eyes and an impressive dome streaked with thin gray hair and dotted with liver spots. His elevation to the bench had been largely due to his appearance, since in a world of roughnecks he was considered good political window dressing. As a result of this biological accident, he had drawn a salary of twenty-five thousand dollars per annum for the last fourteen years,—a total of three hundred and fifty thousand dollars in return for sitting in court five hours a day, five days in the week, for nine months of the year. This was the reason why, at his last college reunion, he had been voted the most successful man in his class. "Three cheers for good old Rufus!"

He was a kindly, well-intentioned man, devoted to his wife and children—three boys and two little girls—all of whom adored him, and most of his salary went into sending the three older ones to school and college and making a comfortable home for the others. He liked to think of himself as impartial and courageous, but since he was dependent upon the district attorney for all important cases, he was apt to rule in the latter's favor on doubtful points, endeavoring to even things up after conviction by "tempering justice with mercy." Occasionally he was a little troubled as to what justice was. Certainly the law was by no means always just, nor the district attorney either, but although he often would have liked to take things into his own hands and tell them both to go hang, he never was quite brave enough to do so.

Judge Bunbury knew that he was not an admirable person, but, being a pragmatist, whenever his conscience reared its head he pushed it gently down. He had been contented and happy in his sinecure for more than thirteen years when he suddenly realized that, unless he was re-elected the next November, his life of comfort would come to an abrupt end. The mere thought of no longer being on the bench threw him into a cold sweat. What on earth would happen to him? He had laid nothing by and it was doubtful if he could earn a living. He often thought, when humiliated by O'Brien's arrogance, Once I'm re-elected, I'll show that legal ape where he gets off.

Now, as James Gavin disappeared behind the little door leading to the Tombs, The Ape gave him a confidential nod.

"That baby is halfway to the hot squat already," he remarked with a gummy grin.

Judge Bunbury smiled faintly in response.

"Please, sir, are you the lawyer who's going to defend my husband?"

The woman who accosted Mr. Tutt in the courthouse corridor had the same haunted look as the prisoner, the dry, lusterless complexion due to undernourishment. A scrawny child clung to her dress.

"If you're Mrs. Gavin, I am."

"Well, he's not guilty! He's one of the best men who ever lived!"

Mr. Tutt was still angry over what Bunbury and O'Brien had put over on him.

"Is that why he went into the policy racket?" he countered.

The woman winced. "No, it wasn't!" she retorted fiercely. "He got drawn into it. He couldn't bear to see Gracie and me go hungry, so, when Mr. Cotillo offered him a job, he jumped at it. He didn't know—" Her voice faded out and she leaned weakly against the adjacent pillar.

Mr. Tutt's heart melted. What if her husband had killed Cotillo?

"Let's go across the street and get a bite of lunch," he said gently. "One can't prepare a case on an empty stomach."

Mother and child wolfed the food. Crime obviously had not paid, so far as the Gavins were concerned. The woman's story was that, her husband having lost his job as a bookkeeper, they had gone on relief until Cotillo had offered to employ him as a messenger. He did not suspect that he was, in fact, a runner for the numbers. When he had found it out and given notice that he wanted to quit, the cops had suddenly jumped on his neck and charged him with carrying policy slips. He realized that Cotillo had turned him in to get him out of the way, and had threatened to get even, but he couldn't prove anything, and when, having no defense, Cotillo's lawyer had agreed that, if he'd take the rap, The Boss would look out for the family while he was away and find him an honest job afterward, he had pleaded guilty.

So far, it was sufficiently plausible, but her explanation of her husband's connection with the homicide was less satisfactory, being nothing more than a vehement denial that he could possibly have done such a thing. He had never owned a pistol. Surely any good lawyer could make the jury see that it must be all a mistake on the part of the police. Mr. Tutt, promising to do his best, gave her ten dollars and sent her home. No wonder O'Brien had wished the case on him.

He found Bonnie Doon gloomily awaiting him at the office. "A nice juicy lemon they've handed us! Gavin is as guilty as hell!" declared his henchman. "The evidence is ironclad. Cotillo's office was in a three-room corner flat that used to belong to a doctor, on the ground floor of a small apartment house. You can go in either through the foyer or by a private entrance on the side street. That's the one Cotillo used mostly. Gavin's story is that, not wanting to embarrass the boss, he waits until about midnight and goes in the side door, which opens into a sort of vestibule. He is just about to press the office bell when he hears a shot inside. Naturally, he's scared stiff. He don't know what's happened, and don't want to. So he beats it out the way he came and runs straight into the cops. He claims the guy that did it must have got away through the other door, that leads into the foyer."

"In that case, wouldn't the doorman have seen him?"

"You'd certainly think so. But Gavin says the negro was upstairs with the elevator."

Mr. Tutt sent the wastebasket spinning across the room. "Jumping Jehoshaphat! They can prove motive, threats, actual presence at the scene of the crime! They've got everything!"

"Everything except the gun. That hasn't been turned up as yet."

Mr. Tutt sat up with a jerk. "What's that? They haven't found the gun? Why didn't you tell me that before? We've got to find it!"

"Oh, yeah?" sarcastically inquired Mr. Doon. "I suppose all we've got to do is to put an ad in the papers: 'Will party who murdered Joe the Barber kindly return weapon used and receive ten dollars reward? No questions asked.'"

As Mr. Tutt had expected, People vs. Gavin was rushed to the top of the calendar. To convict the murderer of a big shot like Cotillo was almost as good as convicting the racketeer himself. With the autumn elections in sight, Assistant District Attorney O'Brien had no intention of allowing public attention to subside. A few nights later, while sitting in his library pondering what possible defense he could put in, the old man was called to the telephone.

"Don't ask my name," said a quiet voice, "but I have just left the bedside of a dying man who is anxious to give you information which will exonerate your client. There is no time to be lost. Some one will call for you immediately and take you to him. Ask no questions, go alone, and may God be with you!" There was a click at the other end. Less than two minutes later the area bell rang. Grabbing his overcoat and stovepipe hat, Mr. Tutt hurried downstairs. A taxi was drawn up to the curb, and beside it stood a man in a heavy ulster, a soft cap over his eyes.

"Get in and keep your mouth shut!" he directed, shoving a hard object against the old man's hip. The cab twisted and turned through unfamiliar streets, until at the end of ten minutes it stopped and the man in the cap cautiously opened the door.

"Four flights up in the rear. I'll be waiting for you," he said.

Mr. Tutt was in a cluttered courtyard surrounded by shabby tenement houses. He was not given to considering his personal safety, but as he dragged himself up the narrow stairs into what seemed an eternity of obscurity, he realized that in such a rabbit warren almost any crime could be committed with impunity. A yellow crack showed under the door in the rear, and in answer to his knock, a gruff voice bade him enter. A couple of toughs lolled in a small kitchen where, at a table, a slatternly woman was sobbing with her head in her hands.

One of the men nodded toward the adjoining room. On a rumpled bed lay a figure, the head swathed in bloody bandages. The man's eyes were already glazed, and as much of his face as could be seen was bathed in sweat. Mr. Tutt knew that he was in the presence of death.

"Did you send for me?"

The eyes tried to focus on him. "Are you Gavin's mouthpiece?" came from the bed in a whisper.

"I am assigned to defend him."

"Then listen, counselor. My name's Capper—Jake Capper. I'm one of the Cotillo mob. I'm handin' in my checks. I want to square myself. I don't want no guy to get the hot squat for what I done. I shot Joe the Barber."

He stopped, panting.

"This Gavin had nuthin' to do with it. He's just a sucker. Cotillo shortchanged me, and that night I went to his office to talk him out of it. He poked his gun at me, and I grabbed it and shot him. Then I beat it out through the main entrance. Gavin must have come in the other way. The cops got the wrong guy."

"What did you do with the gun?"

"The elevator was upstairs when I ran out front, and I chucked it over the top of the grille into the shaft."

"Will you swear to all this?"

"Sure!"

"Then try not to die before I can write it out," prayed the old man. Taking out his notebook, he copied the statement in pencil, read it over to Capper, administered the oath, and assisted him to sign his name.

"You can die now with a clear conscience," he said. "This will save the life of an innocent man."

But would it? Once again in his library, he began to wonder. If the revolver was not where Capper said it was, his confession would fail of corroboration. Although it was nearly midnight, he telephoned for another taxi and drove to the Cotillo apartment house. The Negro elevator boy was just going off duty for the night, but, at the sight of the bill in Mr. Tutt's hand, readily agreed to take him to the cellar. There, in the bottom of the elevator pit, almost submerged in a black, oily mass of debris, protruded the muzzle of the missing gun.

"I have interesting news for you, Mr. O'Brien," said Mr. Tutt as he laid the revolver on the assistant district attorney's desk next morning. "Here's what you have been looking for—People's Exhibit A."

O'Brien examined it suspiciously. He distrusted all Greeks bearing gifts.

"What's the big idea? Are you goin' to plead guilty?"

"On the contrary, my client has been completely exonerated. The true murderer has confessed." Triumphantly, the old man recounted his experiences of the night before, while O'Brien read over the confession. "I assume that, of course, under the circumstances you will consent to the dismissal of the indictment."

"Then you've got another guess coming!" retorted O'Brien, who, although bothered, had no idea of being cheated out of a *cause célèbre*. "How do you know who the guy you saw was? The whole thing may have been a plant."

Mr. Tutt was staggered by his callous attitude. "But the statement is absolutely corroborated by my finding the weapon where he said he had thrown it!"

"Gavin could have put it there himself, couldn't he? He could have run out into the lobby, chucked the gun into the shaft, gone back into the office and made his getaway by the side door. Even if your story is true——"

Mr. Tutt's fist crunched the rim of his stovepipe hat. "Do you dare to question——"

"I've only got your word for it."

"Only my word! I am an officer of the court!"

"So is every attorney," sneered O'Brien. "Why, I've sent a dozen to Sing Sing myself! Anyhow, your testimony is pure hearsay. No court could admit it. That was settled long ago in State *versus* Greenberg, Eighty-five New York Seventy-five. This case is going to be tried according to the established rules of evidence. Excuse me, I'm busy."

Mr. Tutt realized, with a shock, that what O'Brien said was true. Capper's confession, being hearsay, was technically inadmissible as evidence and would undoubtedly be excluded upon the district attorney's objection. Yet that a prosecutor, aware that another had confessed to the crime, would allow an accused to go to trial without investigating and weighing the evidence would have been inconceivable had he not known O'Brien so well.

He walked back to his office with his blood boiling. What poppycock the law was. People acted on hearsay every day of their lives, and Capper's statement would have been received in any Continental court as a matter of course. Even in America there were exceptions to the doctrine—although this was not one of them. Here the rule vaguely was that hearsay could be allowed in certain instances when the surrounding circumstances were "such as to guarantee its trustworthiness." Thus the statement of the victim in a murder case, made in expectation of impending and almost immediate death, that the accused had been guilty of an attack upon him, might be testified to in court by a third party. On the other hand, the declaration of a dying man, made under precisely similar circumstances, that he himself was guilty and that the accused had nothing to do with it, could not be received. The law was utterly illogical and inconsistent. If Gavin had been charged with the murder of Capper, and Capper, believing himself about to die, had told Mr. Tutt that Gavin had shot him, he could so testify, but when Capper said that Gavin did not shoot Cotillo, for the excellent reason that Capper had done it himself, his testimony must be excluded.

The law was perfectly plain. And it gave O'Brien and Bunbury, that precious pair, a complete alibi. What could he do about it? After fifty years at the bar, he ought to be able to find some way out of his predicament. The pledge taken by an attorney, on his admission to

the bar, that he will faithfully uphold the Constitution and the laws
is as sacred to him as the Hippocratic oath is to the physician. Mr.
Tutt had never consciously violated it—that is, hardly ever. At any
rate, when skating on thin legal ice, he always comforted himself
with the argument that if a law was unfair he was justified in doing
his best to change it.

As he sat in his Twenty-third Street library smoking stogy after
stogy on the evening before the trial, he was, frankly, less bothered
over the ethical aspect of whatever course he might elect than by the
probable result. Only a technical objection raised by a perverse and
unscrupulous official prevented his telling what he knew. At a pinch,
he could defy the court and blurt the whole thing out for the benefit
of the jury, over O'Brien's objections. If he did so, Bunbury would
undoubtedly sentence him to jail for contempt and charge Gavin
straight into the electric chair. On the other hand, the jury might
revolt and acquit on the strength of his testimony thus illegally given.
But it would be dangerous. He would hold it in reserve only as a last
resort.

He poured himself out a glass of Burgundy, lit another stogy and
paced thoughtfully up and down before the sea-coal fire.

O'Brien, of course, was hopeless, but how about Bunbury? Except
for being an old jelly-back, the judge seemed a pretty decent sort. He
probably had a heart—and perhaps even a conscience, if you could
reach it. Certainly what O'Brien proposed to do outraged all decency.
Yet Bunbury would be coming up for renomination, and hence even
more anxious than usual to keep solid with the machine.

But was Bunbury going to be renominated? If he wasn't he'd
have nothing to be afraid of, and would be open to an appeal to his
better nature.

Mr. Tutt stopped short in his perambulations and grabbed up the
telephone.

"What's the low-down on Bunbury's renomination?" he asked
Bonnie Doon.

"There's always some one around who'd like to have twenty-five
thousand a year," answered his handy-man. "I heard a rumor—nothing more—that they don't think he's got enough guts and that it may
go to young McBride, of the Twenty-third District."

"Know any of the judiciary committee?"

"Sure. Tom Sweeney, the chairman, is a particular friend of mine."

"Good!" cried the old man. "I want you to run down Sweeney

tonight—even if you have to drag him out of bed—and find out exactly how Bunbury stands."

Then he clapped on his stovepipe hat, tucked a lawbook under his arm and took a taxi to the judge's house.

Mrs. Bunbury was upstairs putting the younger children to bed, and her husband, having put on his dressing gown and slippers, had just lit a cigar and settled down comfortably over a mystery story when the doorbell rang. Since it was not answered promptly and his library was only a few feet away, he went to the door himself.

"Good evening, Judge," said Mr. Tutt. "I hope you'll pardon this intrusion upon your privacy. I want to speak to you about that Cotillo case."

"Why, certainly; come right in," answered Bunbury, leading the way into his library. "Sit down. Have a cigar? You mean People *versus* Gavin? It's set for tomorrow morning, isn't it?"

"Exactly. I know this is a little unusual, but there seemed to be no other way out of it."

Bunbury took a noncommittal puff on his cigar. Mr. Tutt had never ventured to speak to him privately about any case, but plenty of other lawyers had done so, and the district attorney made a regular practice of it. Anyhow, he rather looked forward to a chin with the old boy.

"I have entire faith in your sense of propriety, Mr. Tutt. You are an officer of the court. Does your client wish to plead guilty to a lower degree of homicide?"

"Far from it! I have conclusive proof of his innocence."

Then with all the artistry at his command, Mr. Tutt told Bunbury the entire story.

"Have you explained this to the district attorney?" inquired His Honor.

"I went to him at once and gave him the revolver, but he refuses to allow me to testify as to Capper's confession, on the ground that it is hearsay."

The sudden tightening of Bunbury's lips encouraged him to go on.

"The trouble is that technically O'Brien's position is correct. But the law is hopelessly out of date, illogical and unjust. Imagine, if you can, judge, your own son on trial for murder, and the judge refusing to allow testimony that another person had confessed his guilt! In fact, it's utterly preposterous! You were doubtless familiar with what Professor Wigmore says about it in the latest edition of his famous work on Evidence." He opened the volume which he had brought. "Section 1477 reads: 'It is therefore not too late to retrace our steps and to discard this barbarous doctrine of law, which would refuse to let an innocent accused vindicate himself even by producing to the tribunal a perfectly authenticated written confession made on the very gallows by the true culprit now beyond the reach of justice. Those who watched in 1899 with self-righteous indignation the course of proceedings in Captain Dreyfus' trial, should remember that, if that trial had occurred in our own courts, the spectacle would have been no less shameful if we, following our supposed precedents, had refused to admit what the French court never for a moment hesitated to admit—the authenticated confession of the escaped Major Esterhazy avowing himself the guilty author of the treason there charged.' "

Bunbury had allowed the cigar in his hand to go out. "Bless my soul!" he ejaculated. "I never imagined— What do you think I should do?"

Mr. Tutt got up and warmed his coattails before the fireplace. "Judge Bunbury," he said earnestly, "you know, as well as I do, that what is law is not always justice. You can, if you see fit, and possibly without unfavorable criticism, rule out this evidence. If so, I shall not prophesy as to what my course will be. On the other hand, you can play the part of a courageous public officer by refusing to be bound by a hidebound technicality when a human life is at stake. As our great Chief Justice, John Marshall, said, in Hoffman *versus* Porter, 'I do not think that law ought to be separated from justice, where it is at most doubtful.' Here it is more than doubtful. This is an opportunity to show yourself a great and independent judge—one that perhaps will send your name echoing down the ages. It is not only the just but the right thing for you to do, and a thing which your conscience must approve."

All that was best in Judge Bunbury responded to the old man's appeal. Of course Mr. Tutt was right; the law was absurd; O'Brien was a filthy crook; and what a chance to get even with him for what he had endured at his hands all these years. He'd do it!

He was on the point of saying so when he heard his wife coming down the stairs. He hesitated. What would be the effect on her and on the children, if he acted as his heart and sense of justice dictated? It would undoubtedly cost him his renomination. He would lose his twenty-five thousand a year, his comfortable home. The boys would have to leave college and hunt for jobs. He'd be lucky to get anything to do himself. He could imagine people pointing him out and saying, "That's old Bunbury. He used to be a judge of the General Sessions, but he's never amounted to anything since." Mr. Tutt had read it all in his face.

Mrs. Bunbury entered, a pretty, faded woman, and her husband stood up ceremoniously to greet her. How well he remembered when they were so hard up that, besides taking care of the babies, she had done all the housework. Could he ask her to go back to that?

"Come in, my dear," he said gallantly. "I want you to meet Mr. Tutt. . . . Oh, no! You're not interrupting. We've just been having a little chat on legal matters. Nothing important."

"Is anything the matter, Rufus?" asked his wife anxiously in the early hours as she listened to the tossing and groaning on the adjacent bed.

"No, darling, nothing! I just can't seem to get to sleep," the judge had answered while his conscience and his self-interest struggled in a death grip. "I'll pop off all right now, I guess."

But he didn't pop off and it wasn't all right. The only right thing was to do what Mr. Tutt urged, but if he did, he could kiss his judgeship good-by. Otherwise, of course he'd be renominated and re-elected. They never would have brought the Cotillo case into his court and given him such a build-up in the papers, unless they intended to run him again. He was sworn to uphold the law, and the law was State *versus* Greenberg, Eighty-five New York Seventy-five! If he let in Capper's confession he'd be violating his oath, wouldn't he? No! That was a quibble, and he knew it. It wasn't a question of what he let in or kept out. It was whether he should insist that the district attorney do the decent thing.

Worn to a frazzle, he went to his chambers to find the assistant district attorney already there.

O'Brien greeted him, "Everything's all set. There's only one little thing. Old Tutt may try to run in a third-party confession and, of course, you'll have to keep it out."

Bunbury's hand trembled as he reached for a glass of water. "Don't you think that perhaps you're making a mistake?" he asked uneasily.

O'Brien thought he recognized the symptoms. The old fuddy-duddy was losing his nerve.

"If there's any mistake, it won't be on my part!" he said icily, and Bunbury knew exactly what he meant.

"Order in the court! His Honor, the Judge of the General Sessions. All rise."

The Honorable Rufus, a dignified figure in his robes of black silk, after hesitating for an instant to secure the proper effect, swept in, ascended the bench, bowed and sat down. He had never seen his court so jammed with reporters and cameramen. A few privileged spectators were even ensconced on the steps of the dais. It was a field day. The high spot of his career. He felt his old thrill at being a judge. He couldn't give it up. Every one had to compromise a little. Not that he was compromising; he was just following the law.

"People *versus* Gavin. Both sides ready. Proceed."

It took O'Brien only a little more than an hour to put in his case.

"I will now call my last witness—Ephraim Tutt," he announced, for the old man was needed to identify the revolver.

Jury and spectators alike leaned forward as Mr. Tutt walked to the chair and took the oath.

"You do solemnly swear that in the case of the People *versus* Gavin you will tell the truth, the whole truth, and nothing but the truth, so help you God?" intoned the clerk.

"I do!"

O'Brien handed him the gun. "Where did you find this revolver?"

"In the elevator shaft adjoining Cotillo's flat."

"That is all," said O'Brien. "No more questions."

Mr. Tutt did not budge. "There will be more questions," he said, "and I shall put them."

O'Brien gave Bunbury the alert. Now was the time to crack down on the old bozo. Mr. Tutt took Capper's confession from his pocket.

"What led you to look in the elevator shaft?" he asked himself.

"I object!" interrupted O'Brien. "It is irrelevant, incompetent and immaterial why he looked there."

"I have just taken an oath to tell the whole truth," said the old lawyer. "Is it possible that the law will stultify itself by refusing to let me do so?" He fixed his eyes appealingly on the judge. Would he do the right thing? Probably not.

Bunbury looked away. He'd rather have old Tutt's good opinion than any one else's he knew. It did seem damnably unfair to exclude the solemn confession of another than the defendant that he alone was guilty. He wanted—oh, he so wanted to do the courageous thing! But, how could he give up twenty-five thousand dollars a year when the law was actually on his side? Think of all the good he could do in fourteen more years. He'd jolly well show them where they got off then. He wavered, teetering like a walker on a tightrope. What should he do?

O'Brien sensed something wrong. Could the blundering ass be going sour? He stepped sideways toward the bench.

"Sustain my objection," he muttered out of the corner of his mouth. "Shut out every bit of that stuff."

It was almost the last straw. The blood surged up over the judge's dome and through his hair. For the fraction of a second, Bunbury was on the point of telling O'Brien to go straight to hell where he belonged. But he managed to control himself. Anyhow, he could at least assert his dignity as judge.

"Mr. District Attorney—" he began severely, then noticed his attendant standing with a telegram in his hand. "Excuse me a moment," he said, grateful for even a slight respite. He slit the envelope and unfolded the sheet within.

> HON. RUFUS BUNBURY
> CRIMINAL COURTS BUILDING
> CONFIDENTIAL STOP THE COMMITTEE IN CHARGE OF JUDICIAL NOMINA-
> TIONS AT ITS MEETING LAST NIGHT UNANIMOUSLY SELECTED HUGH T
> MCBRIDE AS THE ORGANIZATION CANDIDATE FOR THE VACANCY ON THE
> GENERAL SESSIONS BENCH TO BE CREATED BY THE END OF YOUR TERM
> STOP THERE WAS A FULL ATTENDANCE STOP MCBRIDE WAS SPONSORED
> BY PETER HARRIGAN LEADER OF THE TWENTY-THIRD DISTRICT STOP THE
> COMMITTEE AGREED TO MAKE NO ANNOUNCEMENT UNTIL THE ENTIRE
> SLATE HAD BEEN MADE UP STOP THE ABOVE CAN BE EASILY VERIFIED
> BY INQUIRING OF HON T J SWEENEY ASSISTANT DISTRICT ATTORNEY
> O'BRIEN OR ANY MEMBER OF THE COMMITTEE
>
> A FRIEND

Judge Bunbury felt as if he had been dealt a heavy blow in the stomach. He knew only too well that it was true. They had passed him over. O'Brien had deliberately brought the Cotillo case before him, knowing what they were going to do. Well, O'Brien could do nothing to him now. He was his own master—free at last. What was the famous saying? "All is lost save honor." The ghastliness of his disappointment gave place to a strange sense akin to ecstasy as he thrust the telegram in his pocket and turned benignly toward the witness chair.

"What is it you wish to prove, Mr. Tutt?"

O'Brien leaped forward, his hand raised in protest. "Don't answer that question!" he shouted.

"Take your seat, Mr. District Attorney!" rapped Bunbury. "I am the sole judge of what is proper here. . . . What do you wish to prove?"

"That the defendant is innocent and that another person is guilty by his own confession. I took this man's dying declaration myself and reduced it to affidavit form. That is how I knew where to look for the revolver. I offer the statement in evidence."

"I object to it on the ground that it is pure hearsay, and absolutely inadmissible under State *versus* Greenberg!" barked O'Brien.

Bunbury had no suspicion that revenge could be so sweet. "I will hear Mr. Tutt's testimony. If, in my opinion, it proves incompetent, I will order it stricken out," he said.

So Mr. Tutt detailed the entire story of how he had been called to the bedside of the dying Capper, received his confession and discovered the revolver.

"In conclusion, I wish to add that I at once took the gun to Mr. O'Brien and told him exactly what I have just testified to."

"Is that true, Mr. O'Brien?" frowned Bunbury.

"In general. I told him that his story could not be received in evidence."

His Honor eyed him contemptuously. "Gentlemen of the jury," he said, "the fundamental purpose of our legal system is to do justice. When technicalities defeat that end, they should be disregarded. It is true that under the antique decision cited by the district attorney, I could lawfully exclude Mr. Tutt's testimony; but when, as here, a man's life is at stake, I should be less than human if, simply out of common fairness, I did not allow you to consider it. When a judge is faced with a rule of law that seems to be unjust and unreasonable, he ought to be man enough to say so. I do not care what higher courts may say or what the effect may be upon my future career, but I shall admit the declaration in evidence, in the hope that hereafter the legislature will make such testimony technically admissible."

He bowed to Mr. Tutt.

"You may step down, sir. . . . I shall not take the case from the jury," he added, "since I do not care to usurp their functions. I wish, however, to state publicly that even if courts may feel themselves bound to consider only such evidence as conforms to the strict rules, there is no such obligation on the part of the district attorney. He is an investigating as well as a prosecuting officer, and it is his duty to weigh everything that may have the slightest bearing on the defendant's innocence or guilt. I am surprised and shocked that he did not see fit to do so in this case. . . . Are both sides willing to submit?"

O'Brien had turned as white as his jaundiced cheeks would permit. He could have murdered Bunbury then and there.

"I object to the court's outrageous reflections upon the conduct of the district attorney as well as His Honor's refusal to obey the law which he is sworn to uphold. After such an exhibition, I wash my hands of the case." He grabbed up his papers and stalked out.

The foreman looked inquiringly along the rows of jurors. "I don't think we need to retire, Your Honor. Our minds seem to be pretty well made up."

"The defendant will rise. . . . Gentlemen of the jury, do you find the defendant guilty or not guilty?"

"Not guilty!" answered the foreman.

There was a stampede of cameramen and reporters toward the rail as Mrs. Gavin threw herself into her husband's arms.

"Hold it!" "Once more, please!"

The Honorable Rufus gathered his robes around him and retired to his chambers. No one, in that confusion, was paying any attention to him, but he felt like a new man. After all, it was really the high spot in his career.

That night Mr. Tutt received a summons to St. Louis which kept him there for several weeks. Meantime he wired Bonnie Doon to turn over to the Gavins the five-hundred-dollar fee allowed him by the State and to ship them west to start life over again.

The reply read:

GAVINS GRATEFUL FOR DOUGH STOP JUST IN CASE YOU HAVE MISSED THE BIG HULLABALOO IN NEW YORK PAPERS OVER COTILLO CASE YOU OUGHT TO KNOW THAT IT HAS BEEN ENTHUSIASTICALLY ACCLAIMED AS A TRIUMPH OF JUSTICE STOP O'BRIEN HAS LOST HIS JOB AND BUNBURY IS SUCH A POPULAR HERO THAT THE BOYS HAVE DUMPED MCBRIDE OVERBOARD AND ARE GOING TO RUN BUNBURY AGAIN   A FRIEND